Chronicles of the Future Foretold

Book 1:

The Girl who Rode the Unihorn

Compiled and edited by
Professor Harold Harishandra Higginsbottom, AA, AS, ASS, BA, BS,
MA, MS, PhD, MFA, MLitt, BFD, POS

Channeled, Translated, and Transcribed
By

mìcheal dubh

mìcheal dubh

Published by

Seanchaidh

Illustrations by
Tuigse NicFhuadain

DEDICATION

The Seven-Generation ethic is based on the ancient foundational principle of the people of the Wayp that the decisions made today should be considered in light of their effects on people seven generations from now – or seven centuries, or seven millennia (keeping in mind that "seven" should probably be understood metaphorically rather than literally).

In the hope that those seven ages hence will find that we have left them a green and flourishing planet,

this book is dedicated to G.T.
who inspires warriors
in the protection of our
Mother
Earth.

mìcheal dubh

TRIGGER WARNING

Those who are personally offended by criticism of corporate greed,

who deny the prospect of environmental devastation,

or who are driven into a rage at any suggestion that human beings

do not have a right to unbridled domination over the planet,

read on.

You are about to be triggered.

Disclaimer

None of the incidences depicted in this work are intended to replicate any actual events that have happened or are happening. Nor do any of the characters appearing in this book intentionally resemble persons living or dead; nor corporations, companies, enterprises, businesses; nor plots, plans, or schemes to defraud, steal, or exploit; nor actions undertaken by any of the named or undesignated entities that have devastated, degraded, desolated, despoiled, decimated, or otherwise harmed the natural resources of our Mother Earth, since those actors and actions have not existed or taken place.

Yet.

But they will if you don't do something about it.

Nota bene: No animals were harmed in the writing of this book.

mìcheal dubh

In the year 9595
I'm kinda wonderin' if man is gonna be alive
He's taken everything this old earth can give
And he ain't put back nothing.
Whoa, whoa.
Attributed to ForeTime artist ZagerandEvans.
Fragment retrieved from *Leabhar an Leaghaidh Mhòir*
— The Book of the Great Melting[1]

---

[1] *Leabhar an Leaghaidh Mhòir* — The Book of the Great Melting, a
compendium of stories, histories, poetry, songs, moral lessons,
and proverbs collected from *Tìr fo na Tuinn* - the land under
waves — circa the time of the Great Melting. The original version
is now lost.

1. The girl in the forest

Far a bheil do ghràdh, 's ann sin a bhios tu a' tathaich.
Where your love is, that's where you will often be.
Leabhar an Leaghaidh Mhòir —
The Book of the Great Melting

Wiktionary: Foreword

Professor Harold Harishandra Higginsbottom (editor)

In the YEAR OF GAWD[2] 9595 ATM,[3] I, Professor Harishandra Higginsbottom, am recording in this *Wiktionary* and the accompanying Chronicles some of the events, the incidences, their causes, and their effects, across the planet from the time of the Great Melt[4] to the present, including the various adaptations to the changes that have been wrought over the past millennia, for anyone who reads this should know that the world has not always been as it is now. The earth was once green and fertile (as strange and unnatural as that may seem to the casual reader), the only known such refuge in our solar system, and while conceding the limitations of humanoids' feeble attempts to penetrate the abyss of space between our planet and galaxies light years distant, our world remains the only known sanctuary for life in the universe.

I have been tasked -- or perhaps, more accurately, I have tasked myself -- with compiling and editing a series of documents consisting of random reports on the research of a secretive team of informational "spelunkers," as they fancifully call themselves. Why I was selected, I can only guess: I have wide and scattered interests, though by no means am I an expert in anything. I am a nonentity — as I have no reputation, I have nothing to lose from putting my name on such a project. Indeed, I was the last name on this list; no one else would participate in such a cockroach-brained scheme. I am gullible enough to believe anything anybody tells me (which might open the possibility that this is all some massive practical joke, the purpose of which, however, escapes me).

Or, some combination of these.

---

[2] GAWD (sometimes, Gawd) -- Global Agency for Wealth Development
[3] ATM -- After the Melt
[4] Great Melt (or, Great Melting) – the phenomenon that occurred coincident with the heating of the planet, which entailed the melting of all formerly frozen ice caps and the freeing of formerly inaccessible land masses to gowp exploration and exploitation.

According to my contact and informant, the consortium believes that it has penetrated and tapped into what they call the Darchives,[5] the memory banks, so to speak, of the cosmic neuralnet which comprises the consciousness that forms the universe. This place is actually a *nonplace* as it exists everywhere and nowhere. Although even here, language misleads us with the use of the term "exists" because in the universal mind, neither time nor place as we know it *exists* per se, as we understand the word; or to phrase it differently, place exists as a figment of the neuralnet's dreaming, and all time is simultaneous, where there is no past nor present nor future, no "then" nor "yet to be," only an eternal *now* where the record of everything that is, that was, and that will be, is "remembered".

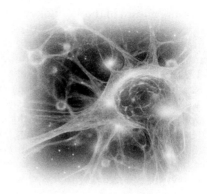

I have been informed that this consortium has hacked into a network of supercomputers around the world. From this network the researchers have been able to extract small bits of computer time — sometimes only seconds, milliseconds, microseconds, nanoseconds, picoseconds, femtoseconds, attoseconds, or even nano-attosceconds -- and that when linked and in sync, the network has an EFLOPS[6] capacity of more than 1,000,000 (which, being completely scientifically and computer illiterate, I have to take on trust as being *a lot*).

This patchwork of computers — government, military, corporate — has heretofore been undisclosed, a secrecy that was necessitated by the fact that the owners and operators of the various linked computers are ignorant of the project. So, in essence, the consortium has "stolen" computer time and resources from more important and vital applications such as governments' calculating and manipulating citizens' opinions, militaries' devising operation plans for the next war, corporations' projecting and molding consumer preferences, or financial institutions' forecasting the next fraction of a percent rise or fall in the prices of

---

[5] Darchives -- the dark archives – contained within the neuralnet; the "memory" of the cosmic mind, the source of all being and the repository of all knowledge.

[6] EFLOPS - computing performance in the exaFLOPS (EFLOPS) range. An EFLOPS is one quintillion (10^{18}) FLOPS (one million TFLOPS). A FLOPS *FLoating point Operations Per Second*.

stocks, bonds, index or commodity futures, investment options, or tranche derivatives. In light of the very real possibility of objections to diversion from prioritized usage, secrecy was paramount for the success of this data mining. If the owners of the computer systems were not ignorant of this unauthorized use, they would doubtlessly not permit such — to their eyes — frivolous usage of valuable computer time.

Though depending on who reads this document, the clandestine nature of the spelunkers' diversion of informational resources may now be defunct. (Although admittedly, the likelihood of anyone in this day and age actually "reading" is an extremely small but nonzero probability.)

The neuronal net pioneers are at a loss to explain the source of their collected data as it falls outside of everything else that they know, except to analogize it as a "cosmic mind" in which all that transpires is remembered (or, should I say, "remembered"). These entries in the record of non-time and non-space are scattered and random; they have been collected and passed to me for sorting and collating (though the term "entry" is only a metaphor, as there has been no entity detected which is *entering* data). Over time, I hope to be able to grow, nurture, and correlate these unrelated and fragmentary data bits (if taken individually) into a substantial, collective body of knowledge. Or, if not substantial, at least coherent. And if not coherent, at least comprehensible in parts.

Again, my informant used an analogy to explain the state of the memory embedded in what might be tentatively postulated as an infinite mind: The *memory*, the *thinking*, or the *dreaming* (words are inadequate to express) of the universal mind is like fragments of data on a computer "hard drive" (the primitive physical object on which the ancients used to encode information), which gowp[7] miners occasionally find in their underwater excavations as they stumble upon and bore through ruins left from before the Great Melt. On these artifacts are inscribed cyphers in the form of 0's and 1's that have been interpreted as parts of words, or whole words, or at most, individual lines of ancient, sacred codex, although (as they admit), the scientists have no way of telling whether their reconstruction of the data bits are really comprehensible, intentional messages, and if they are, whether the code has been correctly interpreted and translated. That said, there is currently some dispute as to how the phenomenon uncovered by my informants should be understood.

Possibilities include (but are not limited to) the bullet points below:

---

[7] GOWP - General-purpose organically derived waste and propellant

4

- As Izuna-Biggs (9502 ATM) argued, the "information" is actually just random assortments of unconnected bits of meaningless data -- in other words, unrelated, meaningless binary bits, just *noise* — that have been forced into intelligibility by the ever pattern-seeking human brain, the same process by which people claim to see the face of the Profit on a tortilla, or the shape of the Monstrato[8] Corps logo in the clouds.
- The findings constitute a hoax, perpetrated either by the supposed self-identified (or, *not* identified) spelunkers themselves, who have rigorously maintained their anonymity, or by some individual or individuals who planted the information to titillate and excite the imaginations of the scientists (not necessarily these in particular, but any who embarked upon such a quest), and eventually hornswoggle an ever-gullible, credulous public. In other words, a highly obscure prank dependent upon a convergence of factors: the linked supercomputers, the scientists conducting such research, their finding the information and deciphering it, all of which was by no means certain to occur, nor to occur in synchrony.
- The cosmic-brain spelunkers (who wish, for already-stated reasons, to remain anonymous) purport to believe the transcriptions are recognizable as some meaningful communication – a language, although in many cases of a form that is still undecipherable. Regardless, the fragmentary bits of information are in one way or another "true." Accounts from a time and place outside time and place (which a Bayesian probability analysis would indicate is least likely).

As well, I can't be certain how long these archives that I have transcribed will last. For the moment, my records are secreted in various hiding places in the neuronal net, where at least for now, they are secured from the discovery and scrutiny of the Monstrato Corps authorities.[9]

---

[8] Monstrato Corps – (in full, MMMMonstrato Corps, but most often shortened) -- Multi-Pelago Manufacturing, Marketing, and Merchandising Undertaking, Un-Limited Amalgamated Hegemonic Corps. The ruling corporate body over the Pelagoes and any other area, resource, asset, or property to which it laid claim.

[9] I believe the ancients used to call this practice "squirreling away," named after the tiny mammalian creatures that existed in antediluvian times and which used to hide their gatherings — mostly "nuts" that fell from "trees" -- in all sorts of

[Here, the fragment breaks off.]

~~

---

unlikely places for them to eat during "winter," a formerly cold period of the
year before the climate regularized to a consistent temperature of about .15
degrees AIPM.*
*Footnote to footnote: AIPM: Autonominous Ignition Point of Methane. People
     in ancient times used widely varying scales to measure things rather than
     referring to constants. For instance the same temperature the
     autonomous ignition point of methane could be referred to variously, 999
     f., 537 c, or 810k. Distances were measured in widely varying scales such
     as inches, miles, kilometers, meters, parsecs, light years, fathoms, knots,
     cubits, hands, a megalithic yard, an English yard, a bloit, a sheepey, a
     Sirius-meter, a parsec, a double-decker meter, and innumerably more, too
     many to mention, permutations of the concept of subdividing or
     demarcation of space.
Time likewise was measured in units as diverse as seconds, minutes, hours,
     days, years, centuries, dog years, God years, seasons, jiffies, secs (not the
     same as and much longer than seconds, as often attested in the literature
     by someone who's been asked to wait "just a sec"), solar months, lunar
     months, and Scaramouchis.
All of which illustrates the confusion the ancients inflicted upon themselves,
     which some historians point to as one of the causes for the constant and
     unending conflict in the ancient world. There were so many names for
     things that no one could agree on what a thing was called, even as simple
     a thing as the distance between here and there, or how hot it was on a
     particular day. Hence, the wisdom of the ancients after the Melt (ATM)
     who established and mandated the One Universal Grammar (OUG).

Silent scream

Tha an saoghal a' crochadh air a' Mhàthair.
The whole world depends on the Mother.
Proverb from *Leabhar an Leaghaidh Mhòir* —
The Book of the Great Melting

Ròna of the Spreckled Cheeks[10] tapped her heels against the flanks of the giant *aon-adharcach* - the one-horned, the unihorn she called Faithful, or in the language of the Children of the Mother -- *Dìleas*.

The animal stood taller at the shoulder than a man (and so towered over the girl when she stood next to him) and was of a more solid build than the horses that ran wild in the Wayp (though in some ways, resembling those), and was covered with a matted fur coat, suitable for its snowy habitat, and was crowned with a single horn that jutted out from his forehead, a thick, formidable weapon.

Although the unihorns were usually fiercely independent and resisted taming or domestication of any kind, some years before, Ròna had found the colt at the edge of a meadow, still barely able to stand on its tottering legs, beside the bear-wolf ravaged body of what she could only suppose had been his mother, and had brought him home to her father's croft – or small farm. There she had raised him as her own. (Her practice of adopting stray and wounded animals was a predilection her parents had not always approved of, but as they had not been able to squelch it, they had come to tolerate it.) Thus, the creature had imprinted the girl as his mother, sister, comrade, friend, from its very earliest days.

---

[10] Ròna -- or more precisely, *Ròna Gruaidh-bhreac ni Màiri ni Iseabail ni Raonaid ni Sìne ni Sìle ni Magaidh ni Mòr ni Ùna* – Ròna of the Spreckled Cheeks, daughter of Mary, daughter of Isabel, daughter of Rachel, ... and so on and so forth till the exhaustion of the iterations of more than 300 generations (or so) of foremothers since the ship they called *An Long-dìon* – the Refuge – had brought the original settlers from *an seann tìr* – the old land – at the time of the Great Melt.

From where she had paused at the edge of the forest, mounted on her huge animal companion and perched in her saddle (really little more than a stiffened blanket woven from mammoth wool), Ròna surveyed the field before her.

She was a slender young woman, of less than medium height and with a compact frame. Besides the shock of deep dark red hair that flowed to her shoulders, a color they called *ruadh* in the FT[11] -- a color term used only in reference to hair or fur, never to inanimate objects -- the most striking feature about her was the startling intensity of her eyes, whose focus had been accentuated from her long practice of aiming down the shaft of an arrow, and whose green gaze was as sharp as the razor tips of the long projectiles she carried in her quiver.

Her plaid – the tartan-patterned light blanket draped over her shoulders and belted kilt-like around her waist – was hung with flakes of crystalline frost, which had accumulated over the night she'd been patrolling on the lookout against poachers -- those who'd cut the trees or kill the creatures of the forest or fish from the lake, all sacred to the Mother.

Besides minding the family's herd, Ròna had the informal responsibility (that is, not officially conferred, but widely acknowledged[12]) of caring for and protecting the forest and the fields and the waters and all their inhabitants around the village of Balnabane.[13] She'd taken on this role several years before while still a child, when she'd come upon her brother Seumas uprooting a fir sapling. The act – or even the idea -- of desecrating the Mother's body enraged her, inflamed her child's heart, and shook her scrawny frame. Though her brother was much larger than she was, she attacked him with the ferocity of a wild cat protecting its cubs; she picked up a stick and chased him away, and after replanting the little tree, she'd camped out in front of it, refusing to come home, despite the entreaties of her parents. She guarded it, cared for it, watered it until it looked like it could live on its own again. It was from this that she acquired the *far-ainm* -- or nickname -- of the Little Sister of the Forest -- *Piùthrag na Coille* in the FT.

She rode her unihorn mount lightly, directing him with a tap of her knee or thigh, or a pat of her left hand. In her right hand, she carried a bow that was curved like the horns of a *tarbh-allaidh* – a wild bull -- whose rack joined together in the likeness of a cap in the

---

[11] FT = a polysemic acronym: Forbidden Tongue / Forbidden Thought

[12] As a matter of fact, there were no "official" positions amongst the people of the Wayp. One 'moved into' a role by inclination or tendency, or assumed it by practice or informal agreement amongst the People.

[13] Balnabane -- A transliteration from the FT, *Baile na Beinne*, or "village of the mountain."

center and curved down and finally up to the ends.

The tall grasses wafted back and forth before her in the breeze. Bees half the size of her hand murmured above the wild flowers -- tall clumps of violet rhododendrons, purple heather blossoms, scatterings of white daisies, and a blanket of bright yellow primroses, a scene interspaced with a dappling of blue bells and tall stalks of thistle -- *cluaran* in the FT --each stalk capped with a delicately variegated white and purple crown.

Butterflies whose wings spanned from her fingers to her wrist – known in the FT as *dealan na bàn-dè*, or "lightning of the Goddess" – skipped across the tops of the assorted grasses and herbs.

Beyond that, in the near distance, a copse of firs and pines introduced the forest that graduated into a grove of redwoods thousands of years old.

She listened. The wind susurrated in the upper branches of the trees – conifers and pines with their needles, aspens with their parchment-white mottled barks, and oaks with their broad, fingered leaves. Under the whispering of the wind and the rustling of the leaves, she heard a murmuring drone rising up from the branches and the trunks, and from beneath that, a whispering from the under-carpet of mycelium, the synapses of fungi, that connected all. She eavesdropped as if on a conversation in another room that was low, distant, muffled (if *conversation* was the right word).

She braced herself with her knees pinching the unihorn's flanks and perched herself upright on Dìleas' back. She took a deep breath and let out a high-pitched call. This note quickly took on a melodic quality in the form of a song of some unhappy, far-off occurrence - something that had happened long before she was born — but its words of sorrow, loss, and pain that once was and perhaps would be again echoed in her heart the same way the sound of her voice echoed from the high hills between which the small valley was nestled.

She swung off Dìleas' back onto a tree stump. There she stood and broke into another song, one that was happier – a quick-paced tune that celebrated the man whom the original singer had loved: a song that *Clann na Màthar* – the Children of the Mother – had brought with them from the *Tìr fo na Tuinn* – the land under the waves -- when they fled the Great Melt. The lyrics were humorous and the tune lively. The song was not to be taken totally seriously in its celebration of the Fair Donald's "great bonnet," which on his head was higher than the roof joist. (Evidently, this Donald was a tall fellow.) She loved the song – it made her spirit laugh, and when she sang it, her voice rose high to penetrate the distance between her and the giant beasts she was summoning home.

In the distance, she heard an answering trumpet of the woolly mammoths of her father's herd, first one and then another, and at the edge of the clearing, she saw the shaking of the trees that presaged the coming of the parade. First there was a distant, gentle waving of the upper branches, an occasional collection of trumpeting as the herd made its way through the forest, and as the massive beasts pushed more closely through the brush, the sound of foliage bending, cracking, and breaking grew louder, and the trees nearer swayed dramatically, and finally the first mammoth breached the wall of the forest across from her.

When Ròna saw the massive cow mammoth who was the leader and protector of the herd, she called out, "*A Bheathaig Mhòir, a ghràidh*! — Big Bertha, my love!"

With a raised trunk and a trumpeting bellow, the mother mammoth charged forward. The others in the herd, startled into action by their leader's sudden movement, not knowing whether its impetus was attack or flight, stampeded behind, advancing across the field in a cloud of dust, dirt, and flying grass.

A bevy of startled quail, following a long, low warning whistle from the covey leader, rose in frightened flight from their nestling place in the meadow of knee-high foliage.

Dìleas planted his feet solidly and lowered his snout to aim the one-horn at the charging behemoth in the event of a collision, but otherwise he made no sign that he was disturbed by the charge. He was accustomed to the ways of the mammoths and knew that for all their intimidating size and bluster, they were timid creatures.

Ròna fixed her bow crosswise over her shoulder and stood quietly and still on the stump as the beasts pounded and shook the earth in their charge forward, and just as quickly as Big Bertha had started, just a few woman-lengths from the girl, the mammoth stopped suddenly with a four-footed landing – much like a bull-leaper's dismount – and rooted itself in the ground on its column-thick legs, coming to a halt close enough to Ròna that the girl could feel its hot breath on her face and arms.

Ròna stroked Bertha's trunk, which was much thicker than her own slender arm, and swung herself atop Dìleas. Tapping the unihorn's flanks with her heels, the girl turned her mount, and saying softly, "*Trobhadaibh!* -- Come on! – *A h-uile duine!* – Everybody!" she started the herd of mammoths the way back to the pasture where the animals stayed the night.

This assemblage traversed through the *coille* – the forest. The trees were spaced widely. The mammoths themselves, having acted over the ages as caretakers and maintainers of the forest by their ambling bulks, had kept the lanes wide and clear, free of entangling branches, and flourishing with yummy browsable undergrowth for the smaller denizens of the woodland.

Ròna heard an inaudible shriek, though it wasn't really through *hearing*, per se, that it came to her, for it was a silent scream that was passed from tree to tree, from the tallest redwoods to the slender white-barked birches. She saw the tops of the trees shake stormily. The  unsounded screeching of the trees shot a galvanizing jolt through her body. The tall redwoods trumpeted noiselessly like gathering mammoths calling everyone together. The oaks bellowed mutely like one-horns, angry and threatening, while the slender birches cried out voicelessly in distress like blind mouths screaming for help.

These wordless shrieks pinioned Ròna with sharp stabs through her frame.

She caught her breath and jumped down from her mount. In succession, she put her ear to the rough bark of a mother yew tree, placed her hand flat on the ground, dug her fingers into the soil, and listened to the fibrous synapses of the intertwined roots and the fungal mycelium. The import of what she heard shuddered through her body from the intricate network she had tapped into.

In a skip and a bound, with a grabbing of and a gripping on Dìleas's shaggy coat, she vaulted atop the unihorn.

She reached back over her shoulder and unslung her curved bow. The weapon readied in her right hand, she let out a wild shriek – the shriek of hawk about to swoop from its aerie perch down on a *coineanach mòr* – a giant rabbit about the size of medium-sized *madadh-ruadh* – a red fox. Only, Ròna was filled with a rage unlike that of some predator on a routine errand to collect breakfast for the nest, but that of a fearsome mother eagle protecting her brood from a thief that would steal her hatchlings.

All blood left the center part of her body and flooded to her arms and chest and legs. Leaning forward, with a tap of her heels to urge Dìleas forward, she gave a sharp command – "*Air adhart!* -- Forward! *Ruith*! -- Run! -- *Ruaig e*! -- Chase it down!" and the massive quadruped broke into a charge.

~~

Sanctuary

'S craobh an sealladh a bu bhòidhche leam a chunnaic mi a-riamh.
The most beautiful sight I ever saw was a tree.
Proverb from *Leabhar an Leaghaidh Mhòir* —
The Book of the Great Melting

It wasn't that far until behind a thick copse of maples and over a ridge, Ròna came on a couple of local men standing at the base of the thick-trunked, broad-branched oak tree – of all the denizens of the forest, most sacred to the Mother.

There stood *Bhaltair Beag* -- Little Walter -- who lived in a cabin by the shore of the lake and supported himself by cutting peat and gathering fallen firewood, which he then sold as fuel around the community. Walter was a wizened little man, white-haired and cringey, who eyed whomever he met as if they might hit him.

He was holding an axe, but when he spotted Ròna charging up – or to be more exact, when he first heard her, and turning, saw her – as if hoping not to be seen holding the tree mangler, he quickly tossed it into the underbrush with a low, underhanded, motion.

"*An aire!* – Watch out!" Walter warned in a hushed voice -- not a whisper, not quite a shout, intended to be heard by his companion but not by Ròna herself. "*'S i a' Phiùthrag!* -- It's the little Sister!"

Not that Walter's caution had really been needed because Dìleas's crashing through the underbrush and the overhanging branches was warning enough.

Walter's companion, Duncan Macpherson, or as he was known, *Donnchadh na Misge* – Duncan of the Drinks – froze with his hand on the rope that looped down from the overhead canopy of foliage. He was a big straggly- haired, sloppy fellow, an enthusiastic *bòdhran* drummer at any *cèilidh* up and down the mountain range that constituted the Wayp, such so that he was always welcome and was always sure to be gifted with his fill of food and *teatha na Màthar* – tea of the Mother -- and to be sent on his way in the morning with a few coins in his pocket, and as he was generally quite handy with small tasks, he otherwise earned a meagre living hiring himself out for occasional odd jobs to anyone else who needed an extra set of hands.

With hardly a break in her unihorn's gait, Ròna charged into the middle of the two, bowling them over like grasses before a mammoth rush. She pivoted her mount to face the men, who were scrambling to their feet. "What're you doing!" she demanded.

"Nothing?" Little Walter said.

"Just looking ..." Duncan added.

"What're you looking at?"

"Just stuff."

Silence.

Then as a non sequitur, Little Walter offered: "The squirrels are gathering nuts early."

"I've noticed that," Ròna observed coldly.

Duncan, still frozen in his wave, added, "I saw a mammoth with an extra thick layer of wool."

Ròna nodded at the observation.

Little Walter broke the silence: "Big Walter[14] did something funny the other day," he said, referring to his son.

"Did he, now?"

"Something you might relate to: He found a baby fox lost in the forest and brought it home, and he's been feeding it. They seem to have taken to each other."

"He's always been a bit of a *buaireadair* – troublemaker. It's good to hear he's got a gentle side."

Silence as thick as overcooked porridge.

Presently, Ròna added: "But that's not *funny*."

"No, I guess not," Walter conceded with a shrug. "Just what he should do."

Ròna turned to Duncan who was still frozen in his wave. "*A Dhonnchaidh* – Duncan – The trout are thick up at the north end of the loch. You going fishing?"

"Still working on my boat," Duncan answered. Trying to appear as if his frozen posture were a natural position to be stuck in, he made as if to lean into the rope. "Have to put a new keel on it."

---

[14] Big Walter -- *Bhaltair Mòr* -- was Little Walter's young son. Naturally, the child was presently smaller than his father, but he could hardly be called "Little Walter," too, as that would be confusing, and "Little Little Walter" would be awkward and inelegant, so in a spirit of irony, and perhaps in anticipation that one day he would grow to be larger than his father, he came to be known as "Big Walter" even though at the present time he was smaller. If that makes any sense.

"Come over to my dad's house," Ròna invited. "Talk to him. He'll help you with that."

"Thanks, maybe I will."

Silence again.

The arrow was notched, half-cocked, and ready to shoot. Ròna pointed with the tip of the arrowhead at the axe handle that protruded from the underbrush. "What's that?" she asked, as if she had just noticed it.

"What?" Little Walter asked innocently enough but fooling no one.

"That thing you chucked under the bush."

"Nothing ..." Little Walter repeated in a childlike manner, as in, *nothing to see here* – but at the same time taking a step to occlude Ròna's line of sight.

"Whole lot of 'nothing' going on."

"Oh, that!" he exclaimed as if surprised to just now notice it. "I guess it's an axe!"

"What're you doing with an axe? You know you're not allowed to chop any trees in the Mother's forest."

After a moment of deep reflection: "Chopping fire wood from fallen trees."

"There's not a fallen tree around here."

"There could be. No harm in looking."

A noise overhead: A blue jay – with its broad wings folded back to resemble a bright blue overcoat, and its black crest sweeping back like the rudder of a ship (resembling a fashion popular amongst younger teenagers in the village and surrounding area) squawked and chittered and scolded as if calling out *Liar! Liar! Liar!* while it flapped its wings vigorously.

Ròna looked up. "*Dè tha dragh ort, a charaid?*" she asked. "What's bothering you, friend?"

Duncan looked away quickly from the disturbance as if he were afraid that he was about to be told on.

Ròna shot a question at him. "What's that in your hand?"

"What?"

"That," she said, pointing her arrow at the rope.

"Oh!" as if he had just at that moment noticed what it was that was coiled in his hand. "A rope!" he announced surprised. As though it were a snake he'd just discovered, he released the strand and snatched his hand away.

At Duncan's slackening of his grip on the line, it whipped away from him and up. As the tension in the rope went slack, there was a rustling in the branches, a clattering, a muffled shout, and a stream of cursing overhead.

Turning away from the noise up in the tree as if he'd not heard anything, Walter tried his best not to look.

Duncan jerked his gaze upwards, as if he had just now come across the man dangling high overhead in the branches of the tree and had paused to stare up in curiosity.

The man at the other end of the rope yelped in protest as his support line suddenly went slack, and he dropped a good woman-length, and the monkey of Ròna's wrath came into full view: a stooped, broad-backed man with the posture of a forest ape who was swinging uneasily from the ropes that had secured him high in the branches of the towering oak whose branches arched high and spread wide and whose roots stretched out far beneath all the other trees, and whose all-encompassing span had sheltered and nurtured the entire forest going back to the time of the Great Melt itself.

Ròna's heart pounded. Her eyes lanced darts of fury. Her face tightened in angry concentration. Her eyes narrowed to slits that saw only one thing: This monkey-man who was now swinging from the branches with the jagged-toothed saw that he'd used to hack away at the tree's limbs.

A deranged murderer!

It became apparent to Ròna as she urged Dìleas forward that the monkey-man was too high up in the tree to reach although even as high up as he was, she recognized him: Robert Morunx, who had come to the Wayp requesting sanctuary several years before. On account of his being a half-speesh[15] – the son of one of the people of the Wayp and a Zziippp – he'd applied for asylum based on the claim of having been a victim of specism in the DownBlow. The Mothers had allowed him to settle on a small plot of land near *Coille na Màthar* – the grove of the Mother.

He was a short, broad-shouldered man with a balding patch on his forehead, and he walked with a stoop such that his arms seemed to dangle forward towards the ground, a trait that had earned him the *far-ainm* – the nickname – of *Rob a' Mhuncaidh* – or Rob the Monkey, a resemblance accentuated by his continuously sneaking surreptitious glances to his side and behind him, as if casting about for something to snatch and run away with. And like a troublesome, mischievous monkey he was thought to resemble, he'd been nothing but a disturbance ever since his arrival, his motto seeming to be *Get one over on them before they could even think of bamboozling you.*

In a moment, Ròna decided if she couldn't reach her target, she

---

[15] Half-speesh – a species epithet, pejoratively and dehumanizingly referring to someone who was the product of a Zziippp and Anboarnh parentage.

could bring it down to her. As Dìleas did a clomping prance, she arched up, and in a single motion, she lifted the bow, drew back the arrow, and fired a shaft.

The arrow flew directly and exactly and severed the rope that was looped over the branch above the *muncaidh's*[16] head and secured him mid-air. As the line went loose, the man dropped suddenly in what must have been a stomach-lurching plunge, breaking through a couple branches along the way.

"Hey!" he shouted reflexively, startled, unaware of what had happened. Using a DownBlow expletive, he called out, "What the ratfuck're you doing!?!"

No sooner had he yelled than Little Walter and Duncan responded with a cacophony of shouted warnings, half of these in the FT.

"She's cutting the line!"

"*Thig a-nuas!* -- Get down!"

And several others that were unintelligible.

But before the *muncaidh*-man in the tree could process any of that, Ròna had swung Dìleas around and was circling for another angle. Again, she loosed a bolt; this one cut through another support-rope. Morunx fell another length as if through a hole in a floor, bouncing at the extent of the tie before dropping again.

By this time, Morunx had figured out what was happening. He'd spied Ròna as the cause of his predicament and shouted to her in Simspeek,[17] "Stop that!"

But even if Ròna had had any inclination to heed the *muncaidh's* demand, she had already drawn and aimed and released her next arrow. Just as with the previous shots, this dart cut through another tie line with a whizzing sound.

Morunx felt that support give away -- the one that had held him

---

[16] Muncaidh – Metamorphosed Untypically Neuronal -physiological Contagion Affected In-utero Devolved Humanoid (though some experts favor Mutant Ungendered (by) N- Contagion Anomaly Initiating Deviant Humanoid): Mutated humanoid sub-species, thought to have been reverted to ancient ancestral hominid form through exposure to Z-virus during gestation in utero of human mother. Sometimes, muncaidh-man or muncaidh-woman, etc. A cognate with the FT word for "monkey" – *muncaidh.*

[17] Simspeek / SIMSPPIWEEEEC – (Written and pronounced "Simspeek.") Simplified Interpersonal Messaging Speech Parlance (for) Phonic (and) Inscribed/Written Expression (and) Exchange (of) Efficient Effective Communication. The only authorized and official language in the Monstrato corporate domains (notwithstanding the existence of such non-standard varieties such as TokTok -- the patois of the Zziipps – and the outlawed FT of the Wayps, and other such extra-territorial languages).

upright -- and he flipped *tòn os cionn* – ass-over-head -- and plummeted three woman-lengths towards the ground with a sickening, heart-stopping plunge. In the process of the fall, he lost grip on the saw, and it clattered down the length of the tree ahead of him, only itself to come to a halt and swing at the end of its securing line.

Morunx let out a scream – non-worded, or a garbling of words that sounded more like an animal's shrieking -- and just as he came to a bone jerking, joint separating stop and a bounce at the end of the tether, Ròna sliced through the last support line.

With a satisfied outrush of breath, the girl watched the tree mangler plunge from the middle branches of the desecrated Mother of Trees towards the ground.

It was paradoxically fortunate for Morunx that the man hit nearly every branch on the way down, each tree limb delivering a stunning blow as if in reprimand for his assault, each thud accompanied by an incoherent shout or groan or moan, but each impact also slowing the velocity of his fall, bringing the plummet to intermittent pauses, slowing his descent, although just for a moment reversing the direction of the rebound before plunging again.

Finally, he bounced off the last thick branch and dropped two lengths to the ground, only to have his descent stopped by a joint-separating jolt, as the last length of rope reached its limit. His foot tangled in the snare of the rope, he dangled upside down, pendulating back and forth.

"What're you doing!?!" he wailed, more rhetorically than anything else as it was perfectly obvious what Ròna had just done.

His swinging at the end of the rope banged him into the tree trunk, and upon that impact, he cursed a blasphemy from the DownBlow: "Damn the Profit!"

Then swinging out away from tree, he shouted an order with all the ferocity a ridiculously upside-down man could muster: "Let me go!"

Although it was sure that no one would obey.

Slyly and a bit maliciously complying with his demand, Ròna responded with, "*Ma tha thu ga iarraidh* ... If that's what you want," and with a deft stroke, she cut the rope securing him to the last branch, and the man swung clear, slammed into the trunk one last time, and plummeted the last span to the ground where he landed with a thud and -- as the air was forcibly compressed out of his lungs -- an *ooff.*

A mass of bruises, scrapes, and cuts, and plastered with needles, nettles, bits of bark and leaves that he'd accumulated during the course of his drop, Morunx took a long moment to recover enough to even start groaning. At the base of the tree, he lay in a crumpled heap, his nearly inaudible moaning being the only sign that he was still alive – like that of a little boy just thrown from a mammoth calf and splayed across the ground – grew in volume and intensity until finally his groans intermixed with curses, which were first generalized and not directed anywhere or at anyone in particular, but soon became fixed – as soon as his head and his vision cleared – on Ròna, seated on her unihorn mount above him.

"You ... you ..." He was groping for the vilest, most insulting, dirtiest imprecation: "You *giant vagina!*" he shouted. "You did that!"

"Yes," Ròna agreed, "I did," an admission that brought a hint of a *fiamh-gàire* – a smug smirk of pride – creeping into the corner of her lips and eyes, a smile not unalloyed with the amusement that always came to her when she contemplated how the Downblowers thought the word that signified the source of all life was an insult.

She vaulted off Dìleas's back and strode to the crumpled man who lay as if a squashed bug at the base of the broad oak trunk.

"I'll have you arrested!" he threatened from his back.

Ignoring his threat, she asked, "What were you doing up there?"

Well aware that it was permitted to prune deadwood from the forest, Morunx temporized. "Trimming the hair of the Mother."

Ròna lifted her chin in acknowledgement. A slow nod, one that purposely gave her time to consider his justification.

She glanced at his two assistants – *Biorachan Beag* and *Biorachan Mòr*, as she thought of them – Little Pointy Head and Big Pointy Head.

They mirrored each other with noncommittal shrugs and

spread hands.

Contemplating what to do, Ròna scrutinized him long and hard (well, not objectively "long" per se, but to Robert Morunx, it seemed like an excruciatingly interminable length of time): *Would it be worth it to arrest him and haul him in front of the Council of the Sisters?*

Sensing her indecision – and taking it as his get-out-of-jail-free card -- Morunx gathered himself into a less uncomfortable position.

Looking up at the tree, Ròna assayed the damage. Fortunately for Morunx, it might be supposed that he'd not had much of a chance to inflict much maiming. She weighed the possibility that his claim of just pruning deadwood would carry weight with the Sisters. Or at least justify giving him the benefit of the doubt.

"Well?" he asked with a smirk, sensing that he might snake out of this predicament. "Can I go?"

He stood and brushed off himself the accumulated foliage, twigs, bits of leaves, brush, and other nondescript vegetative debris that he'd accumulated in the course of his descent.

Ròna hesitated in her answer. Reflecting on the question, she cast a glance down. Her vision fell on a small form on the ground.

She stooped and picked up the body of the murder victim and thrust the tiny corpse of the vibrantly electric-blue butterfly – *dealan na bain-dè* in the FT, literally the lightning of the goddess -- at Morunx and demanded, "What's this?"

"Nothing," which he contradicted by adding, "I don't know."

"Did you do this?"

"Not that I know of," which he apparently feared might not be a sufficient enough denial, so he followed that with, "What if I did?"

But his equivocation was enough to spark her decision.

She pulled the rope tight. "*Tiugainn.* – Let's go."

"What!" Morunx yelped in indignant surprise. "You can't!"

"I can and I will," she said, snatching up the bit of rope that dangled from the branches, and using it and that which still remained tied around Morunx's waist, with a deft whipping and circling motion, Ròna whipped the trailing length of the former guide and support line around the man whom she was making her prisoner. In a moment, she quickly cinched him, calf-tying being something she'd learned many years ago working her father's mammoth ranch.

"What for?!" Morunx protested – as much against the ropes that now bound him as against her words.

"Desecration of the Sanctuary."

"It's just open land!"

"It's the Mother's forest."

"Nothing but a bunch of stupid *trees*!" The complaint of a child declaring that being denied what he wanted was unfair.

Without answering Morunx, Ròna called out to the other men, who had been standing frozen by the spectacle. "You! I know who you are. Don't be slinking off like stinkcats in the underbrush! You're coming with me."

"*Càite? -- Where?*"

"*Cha d' rinn sinn dad! -- We didn't do anything.*"

"He said he had approval."

"*Tha fios agaibh nas fheàrr! -- You know better than that!*" she snapped back, although Ròna would not have liked to admit it, this last claim was probably true. She knew the muncaidh-man well and knew him capable of any deceit to get his way.

"You don't have any reason ..." Morunx muttered feebly in protest. He spoke in Simspeek since despite the length of time he'd lived in the Wayp, he had never bothered to acquire more than a passing acquaintance with *Teanga Clann na Màthar* -- the Tongue of the Children of the Mother.

"We'll hear what the Sisters say about that," Ròna retorted without pausing.

"I was just trying to make a profit," Morunx complained. "What's wrong with that!?!" Before she could answer, as if she were going to attempt an explanation, he wailed, "They'll send me back!"

"You're lucky. If I had my way, I'd give you the short road to the DownBlow," she said, alluding to the edge of the cliff that plummeted several thousand woman-lengths to the Land of Smudge.

Morunx again changed his tone, pleading, "It's my right ..."

The unvoiced thought glimmered across Ròna's mind: *Was the man really that stupid?* But she'd had enough of this shit – a mammoth pile of mammoth shit, as it were -- and if she heard him, much less heeded him, the girl gave no sign, for his complaint was drowned out by her shout: "*Thusa! A Mhic a' Phearsain! -- You!* MacPherson" she called out. "*Cuidich mi -- Help me,*" she commanded in a tone and with an authority that could not be challenged.

With that, she gave a click of her tongue against her teeth, and Dìleas left off browsing amongst the high ferns – tasty treats indeed! – and ambled over. Ròna gripped his shaggy mane at about head level, and using that hold as a lever, she swung herself back into her mount.

"*Thoir an ròpa dhomh. -- Give me the rope,*" she ordered.

MacPherson hurried to hand her the free end of the rope that bound the muncaidh-man, and she secured the line around the unihorn's thick neck and shoulders.

"Let me go! Untie me! Better not ..."

But his protest was cut short by Ròna's bark: "*Dùin do chlab*! -- Shut your snout!" There was something about the young woman's tone -- the sharpness and fierceness of it that would not suffer disobedience and implied dire significances should she be ignored or disobeyed -- that stopped Duncan's and Walter's ears to the imprecations, unconvincing threats, and feeble attempts at orders of the hog-tied lump of humanity now tethered to Ròna's mount.

Even Morunx himself quickly moderated his demands into pleadings and weak entreaties: "Please ... I won't do it again ... begging you ..."

"*Thalla*! -- Away!" Ròna commanded the unihorn. She set off, glancing back periodically to keep an eye on the three men arrayed behind her ambling steed: the most important being the hog-tied miscreant, the defiler of the temple of the Mother, the desecrator of the holiest of sanctuaries, now alternately groaning and swearing and pleading as he was dragged along – or at best, when he could manage it, lugged in a stumbling gait; and of lesser concern, the other two men whom she knew and who should have known better (but they'd be dealt with later).

And so tugging, half dragging, frequently yanking to his knees the entangled one, Ròna led the straggly caravan towards *Taigh nam Peathraichean* -- the House of the Sisters.

~~

2. *Wisdom in madness*

'S ann gu tric a bhios gliocas ann anns an caothach
It's often that there is wisdom in madness.
Leabhar an Leaghaidh Mhòir —
The Book of the Great Melting

Wiktionary: The Great Melt and the Creation of the Merican Pelago

Professor Harold Harishandra Higginsbottom (editor)

What is now known by the synecdoche of the "Great Melt" was actually a confluence of environmental events which certainly included— as its name indicates — the melting of the glaciers and ice caps of the world but entailed so much more environmental devastation than that simple appellation indicates.

The Merican Pelagoes:

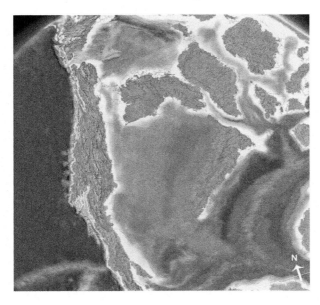

As difficult as it might be for modern readers to give credence to the historical fact, water once existed in abundance – in both a free-flowing and frozen state throughout the world. Our present world was formed in the period during the Great Melt following the thawing and deliquescing of the water locked in glacial ice. The Merican Pelagoes emerged from what had previously been known as the North American continental landmass.

Perhaps, the reader will more greatly appreciate the impact of the change that came over the earth by reading the words of the historian Raghnaid Carson Abeni Bose[18] writing in the aftermath of the Great Melt from the point of view of those who were alive during the BM era.

> *We didn't note when the earth cracked, leaving a patchwork pattern like so many dried brick tiles, and when on buildings and cars a fine white dust settled, as if a perpetual sugar sprinkling. We hardly paid attention when the fertilizer leached into the groundwater (what little was left), and what wells that could still be drilled were rendered as toxic as cyanide from the leaching of poisons from our grubbing in the dirt for the last drop of gowp or speck of copper, silicon, and other toxic or rare-earth minerals we deemed vital to life; and the sludge run-off from the meat-producing and processing factories poisoned what little water was left in the rivers and aquifers; and the soil burned from the heat above and from within by the acids, bases, oxidants, vesicants, phosphates, heavy metals, and other miscellaneous poisons, caustics, chemicals, and salts.*
>
> *Because most of us had never ventured out from the edges of our manicured lawns nor looked farther for water than the nearest tap or plastic bottle, no one regarded the rivers nor heeded the waters that were once crystalline when they turned a yellow-brown or putrid green. Deprived of oxygen because of the fertilizer run off, fish floated belly up to the surface of the waters, and the shores of the dried-up lakes and seas grew shin deep with the black muck of rotting fish and water vegetation. Everywhere, the wildlife that drank from those waters grew sick and died, and the waters flowed (when they did flow -- more often than not, they lay stagnant and moribund) around the carcasses of dogs, cats, cows, badgers, possums, weasels, deer, coyotes, and every other creature still in existence, both domestic and wild. Grasses died by the river banks. Copses of trees -- maple, elm, oak, beech, and every other kind that had once dotted the shores, luxuriating in the nutrients that the waters had spread along the banks, sagged weakly, and when their*

---

[18] Bose, R.C.A. (2525). *Silent Scream*. Beech Island, Eastern Merica Pelago: Random Hachetted MacShyster Penguins Publishing.

*branches dipped into the water that remained, they were
burnt brown, and they, too, gradually died.*

*When the Mississippi dribbled to a mere trickle and then
to a 3,000-mile sickly ribbon of muddy brown sewage, we
merely shrugged our shoulders and paved it over, and so the
Mighty Mississippi Freeway, half a mile wide in some spots,
was born. Where once barges and great transport ships had
plied their ways up and down the currents of the once-broad
river, now, freight trucks, cargo trucks, semi-trucks, and
smaller delivery vans hauled the wealth of the continent.
Public and private transport vehicles conveyed people north
and south through the eastern middle of what had once been
the American Continent.*

*We hadn't heeded when the agro-industrial farming
corporations growing corn, wheat, soy, palm oil, rapeseed, as
well as wood-providing forests and bamboo groves to burn
as biofuel drilled deeper and deeper into the aquifers that
had once filled the entire substrata under the surface -- first
5,000 feet, and then 10,000, and then 20,000 feet -- until the
surface of the lands above the now empty underground seas
collapsed, and the rising oceans rushed in, creating the
Grand Sea Canyon between what is now East Merican Pelago
and West Merican Pelago.*

After the Great Melt, and afterwards, the Submerging, when it
was realized that only some few regions on the planet still
harbored supplies of water, the Inter-Pelago International Senate
(IPIS) held that historical habitation of lands was purely random
and arbitrary, and that it was unjust that small and weak
indigenous populations should be able to claim remaining water
resources and thus obstruct access to the gowp deposits under
them, for those resources rightly belonged to all the people of the
world, as represented by designated corporate bodies, and that any
attempt to prevent access, expropriation, or exploitation by the
assigned corporation would constitute illegitimate appropriation –
in a word, theft.

The Senators elected by the voting corporations to the IPIS
decided that the Monstrato Corps was justified in undertaking –
indeed was forced to launch -- a preemptive seizure of one of the
last remaining sources of water in the world and the reserves of
untapped gowp that water covered in the territories around the
mountain lake of Wayp.

~~

Scared shitless

(actually, really, literally)

Is mios' an t-eagal na cogadh.
Fear is worse than fighting.
Proverb from *Leabhar an Leaghaidh Mhòir* —
The Book of the Great Melting

In the northern Merican Pelago half a world away from Ròna and the Wayp, over the massive MMMMM[19] stadium that stretched from here to there (*there* being near the horizon where lines of perspective narrowed to a pinpoint), flew the Monstrato flag, the symbol of all that was wholly the corporation's: a gowp-wyrm, its pulpy head attached to a long neck that darted in and out of the protective shell that encased its back, which was itself capped with two small fins that looked like wings on the top side of the helmet-like cowl. The wyrm was depicted with its eight tentacles entwined around and gripping the girders of a gowp derrick rising out of a frothing sea of churning, boiling black gowp.

The stadium was crammed with diverse mixture of Natborn Zziipppaeis,[20] humanoid ex-vitro Anboarnhs, even some emancipated aiReps, and half-speesh Unclassifieds. Some of the organics wore atmopuro masks[21] dangling from their faces loosely,

---

[19] MMMMM - Mixed Maximum Martial Melee Match, also known simply as Melee Match, or Melee, or *mmmmm*.

[20] Zziipppaei – Zzyzx Zymotic In-uterine Infected Partial Person Presenting Abnormalities Externally and Intellectually. That is, a person (though this designation is subject to disputation), "naturally" born and because of that, infected with the ZZyzx virus, which caused almost universal congenital abnormalities and defects. Often shortened (pejoratively, as an epithet) to Zziip or Zziiphead. It is a matter of linguistic controversy whether the plural adds an "s" as in standard Simspeak, or whether the plural form is unmodified from the singular. (See Muncaidh, Natborn)

[21] atmopuro or atmopuro *mask* – atmosphere purifying mask, filters out harmful gasses and impurities from the ambient atmosphere, including toxin amounts of oxygen, and creates individualized mini-atmospheres suitable for breathing.

as the air in the dome had supposedly been pressurized and filtered so it was breathable, and some still wore their face masks sealed out of habit or not trusting to the purity of the atmosphere, while the more affluent amongst these, having been fitted surgically with permapura implants, had dispensed with such accessories, but whatever their station or preference, almost as one, the crowd either cheered at the prospect of the penalty or booed, according to their respective team affiliation.

From the heights of the farthest reaches of the Crucifixion Bowl, the figures on the distant Melee Match field below were but little cockroach-dots scurrying around, however large they loomed on the overhead screoins[22] that showed in glorious detail each hit, each blow, each stab, each mutilation, each loss of limb, and each decapitation that took place during the course of the game that was being waged for the entertainment, the delectation, and the elucidation of the fans in the stands and in the screoin-cast audience, alike.

Under the stadium dome, the cheers, the hoots, the whoops, the howls, and the hollering; the stomping, the banging and pounding of sonorous drums and clangy metal cymbals; the warring braying of vuvuzelas and the ear-shattering blasts of air horns drowned out any and all other sounds until a synthesized voice boomed loud enough to be heard above the cacophony: "Let us stand, for the Pledge of Achievance." And with that, the crowd hushed to a low, indistinct rumble like thunder rolling in the distance as they lifted on high their glowing digital wallets and chanted (not quite in synchrony, but sort of) the words of the pledge:

> *I pledge achievance to the swag of the United Incorporated*
> *Pelago[23]. And to the Profit for which it stands, one*
> *corporation under GAWD, indivisible, with profitability for*
> *just us all.*

At the drop of the last words of the pledge, the clamor burst forth again and all but drowned out the voice of Fred Finkel, the one-armed broadcast announcer (a former all-pro himself), attempting a play-by-play to the handheld screoins of those trying to follow the

---

[22] screoin -- Scanning Remote Environs Optic INstrument

[23] Pelago, plural, Pelagoes – the disconnected chains of islands in the Western Hemisphere that stretch in north-south chains from the Bluridg Atoll and the Palation Isles in the east to the Seera Islands in the west, from which they are separated by the Grand Canyon Cesspool and drainage sump.

action but were too far away from the field to actually see anything (much less, hear anything).

"If you're just now joining us, welcome to the Electoral Combat Bowl, everyone ... those in the stadium and all those at home watching us on your home screoins. Up here in the owners' boxes, we're joined by the Game Master of all InterWeb entertainment and screoin show host, Magnus Mugwump, The Mayor of Larmo, Whyming Cays – up in the far north islands -- who is here with us to welcome the two team owners contesting for the indisputable leadership of the United Pelagoes.

Mayor Mugwump appeared on the screoin, looking like an overfed ferret with the perpetual scowl of somebody who suspected you of double-scooping your gowp-wyrm chip in the dip bowl, but now doing his best to imitate a smile.

"The Mayor is doing us the honor of inaugurating the Ticking Bomb of the Super Rigamarole that will decide the winner of the Electoral Combat Bowl Presidential Championship."

"Oh, yes," another voice chimed in, adding to the tweedledumb-and-tweedledumber, back-and-forth refrain. "We've seen many exciting *mmmmm* matches in the run-up to today's contest. And I'm sure our losing team-owners are just as eager as we are to see the outcome of today's competition."

The screoin audience was treated to a quick panning glimpse of the row of severed heads on spikes that ringed the stadium, each suspended in life-sustaining animation and exhibiting various moods of anger, distress, tearful wailing, and somber resignation.

The image was replaced by another as the Finkel continued, "Introducing our first owner-contestant -- Fellatio Hibiscus, the ever-popular host of the long-running game show *How Low Will You Go!*"

Flashed on the screoin was the image of the flamboyant game-show host: a lacquered-skinned, pear-shaped, hermaphroditic Fellatio Hibiscus with a head of hair like hay tossed in stiff cross currents of wind and wearing a spangled low-cut evening gown, a diamond-encrusted necklace with an emerald pendant the size of a baby's fist around their neck, and a boa over their shoulders woven from the tentacles of young gowp-wyrms.

Fellatio Hibiscus lifted their jaw and exposed a neck like that of a desserliz[24] about to lick a flying cockroach out of the air and

---

[24] Desserliz - a venomous desert lizard that lived in the barren wastelands outside the domed cities, scuttering between the toxic sea and the barren gowp-permeated sands

waved a hand in a bored and self-satisfied benediction to the imagined crowd represented by the cameras.

This image was replaced by one flashed on the screen of a pudgy, grandmotherly woman waving cheerily to the crowd. "And our other owner-contestant: Goowhiggie Clawntrip!" the announcer boomed. "Outgoing Vice President of the Pelagoes!"

The crowd booed. The vuvuzelas and the air-horns resounded in disapproval. Evidently, Clawntrip was far from being a favorite.

"In our pre-game show, we broadcast retrospectives on each candidate's career. It was truly inspiring to see the different paths each one has taken to get to this spot, the final match-up of the Electoral Combat."

The screoin displayed a montage of Fellatio Hibiscus' stellar business career, capped off by his legendary (and perhaps, apocryphal) leveling of the last tree as a boy in the DownBlow (before the sex non-assignment surgery that transitioned them to bigendered). The screoin displayed a younger version of Hibiscus (already pear-shaped and dressed in a cute floral-print summer dress). The (then) boy was poised in the midst of a small stand of felled trees (a bit of irony in the choice of the words "stand" and "felled" -- but we'll let it go).

A man's voice was heard coming from off-screoin angrily demanding, "Who cut down <u>my</u> forest!?!" The older version of the boyish Hibiscus looked remarkably like the man the boy would have become (if they hadn't transitioned, that is).

"Male parental-unit, I cannot tell a lie," the boy piped. "I did with my little chainsaw."

The elder Hibiscus looked about him sternly and declared, "Good boy! Those damn things were a nuisance anyway! Always getting in the way of my view of the beautiful sandscape!"

The view on the screoin cut quickly to a landscape of orangish desert, topped by an orange, sandy mist.

The crowd in the stadium erupted in cheers.

Next the screoin displayed "Grandma" Goowhiggie Clawntrip's feeding of the poor, unfortunate (and oftentimes misfigured) natborn children, a controversial policy that her political opponents charged constituted illicit compassion trafficking, which no doubt lost her many votes in the run-up to today's Electoral Combat Bowl© finals. As a picture of Goowhiggie walking among an encampment ward of crippled, flapper-armed, three legged, two-headed, and no-limbed, ZZyzx-virus infected children, a rumble of booing swelled from the crowd, making it readily apparent who the crowd's favorite was.

(Hint: not *her*.)

Fred Finkel enthused, "Oh, it's exciting times! Everything is on the line, including -- I know I don't have to add," he added with a chuckle at his own cleverness, "the neck of the owner of the losing team! Whose head will end up as the Melee Match ball for next term's Electoral Combat Bowl death match? How exciting! As they say ... LET THE HEADS ROLL!" This last was delivered with great enthusiasm and verve.

In a more settled tone, the announcer continued. "Let's rejoin the action that has already started on the field ..." where great cheers were going up with each act of mayhem, along with a

collective ooohhs, aahhs, sympathetic groans, and moans, not to omit shrieks of laughter and general exclamations of delight.

The Port Denver Ratkillers had advanced the ball -- which was the encased and preserved head of the previous election cycle's losing candidate encased in a pliable but rupture-proof gowpaleen to prevent it from bursting in the rough handling of the game -- to the 10 arl[25] line. The head blinked its eyes in response to the kick and pleaded, "That was hard! Take it easy, fellas!"

The opposing teams pushed back and forth, neither offense nor defense gaining the upper hand. The deafening blast of the penalty siren honked. Captured on the screoin was the fault: One of the defenders had stabbed a receiver in the back outside the blood zone. This infraction called for a free shot at the goal for the offending team.

"Well done!" Finkel proclaimed over the din. (Not that anyone heard, or if they did hear, paid attention, which fact had never intruded upon the announcer's perception, for he perceived himself to be the center of the action merely because of his garrulous jabbering on the figurative sidelines.)

The Port Denver Ratkillers -- their uniforms blood-red and gowp-streaked kilts -- were lined up facing the goal. The score had

---

[25] Arl - average rat length. As this was determined from the height of the "average" rat, which stood about as tall as the knee of a Zziipppaei , for consistency, the "official," "standard," arl was established as 3.1415926535 8979323846 2643383279 5028841971 6939937510 5820974944 5923078164 0628620899 8628034825 3421170679 times the "average," "standard," "official" height of the rat.

the Everest Wyrms -- their one-pieces the color of brackish sea water (offset with black streaks of patriotic gowp) -- ahead by a point (points being calculated by a complicated algorithm that factored hits, maimings, deaths, and actual goals), and the time was down to a few ticks of the clock (though according to the rules, the game could be paused in the middle of a play, skirmish, fight, or deathblow). The Ratkillers were fighting for their lives ... well, not actually *their* lives (players being too valuable a property to destroy), but those of their coach, team captain, and owner. This being the championship, the final spectacle of the game was to be the execution of the losing team's leadership, whose heads would be preserved in a gowpaleen-sphere for the next season's championship.

But with the penalty, the game was thrown into sudden-death overtime. Literally. A player selected from each squad would face off in a fight to the death.

In the lock-up room, the slaiv[26] warriors prepared for overtime. They huddled around the coach. "Bospela, who fight?" one of the Zziippps asked.

On the wide-stretched overhead screoins was projected a close-up, ground shot of the Ratkiller team huddle. The superimposed image of the Fred Finkel (who was actually in the farther reaches of the stadium many miles away) knelt in the middle of the players. He intoned in a hushed voice as if he feared disturbing their deliberations, "The game plan is a little unclear here. They seem to be arguing. Not boding well for a cohesive strategy in this do-or-die moment. What an exciting game! Here we arrive at the moment we've all been waiting for! The culmination of the Melee Match: Every Anboarnh and Zziippp for himself, because there's no "we" in Melee Ball, no 'uspela' as the Zziippps would say in **me**-lee ball." (Laying special emphasis on the syllable.) "Not us-lee ball. Just '**me**,' not 'us.'"

The camera intruded on the team deliberations, and caught the coach, Monstrato Corps Focwaod[27] Buttwater-Bates (Priamus Thorben Beezow Doo-Doo Zipitty-Bop-Bop Buttwater-Bates, that is, of the genetic line of the West Virginia Isles Buttwaters) in consultation.

Buttwater-Bates was a thin, pale Anboarnh of medium height. One could speculate that he'd possibly been manufactured at a discount gestation factory, as his head featured oversized ears, and his mouth twisted around oddly and irregularly configured teeth, which individually and collectively proved unequal to the task of

---

[26] SLAIV – Situation: Lifelong Assignment, Involuntary or Voluntary
[27] Focwaod = Facilitator of Corporate Work And Other Doings

containing sprays of sputum upon the enunciation of certain plosive sounds, especially words which began with *p, b,* and *sp*.

Looking around the scrum, Buttwater-Bates attempted to decide who was to fight the crucial, match-determining one-on-one. His gaze settled on his chief-assistant and the team-mascot – a medium-sized Zziippp by the naim[28] of 7q9cgynsqnBilWee (who went by the understandably shortened name of BilWee).

"What do you speculum might be the most suspicious match-up?" Buttwater asked.

Despite having to back up half a step to dodge the incoming barrage of spittle, BilWee was overwhelmed that his opinion had been sought. He eagerly tilted his head in the direction of the lean foreigner who had produced so many points during the season, made so many kills (literally, in the case of Melee Match). "Coo-win," he gushed (full and correct enunciation being difficult for the Zziippps).

Cuilean stood non-committally in the midst of the huddle. His fighting kilt was smeared with blood – both red from the splattering of teammates' final throes, and green from the wounds he had inflicted on his Zziipppaei gladiator opponents. His head and face were capped with a cowl, a living hood, formed by a tentacle sea-wyrm that constituted his control leash[29] -- called that, but in some sense, more a helmet than a leash as the shell of the wyrm encased his head and the top part of his face, leaving only narrow eye-slits to see out of. Clamped securely on his head, it arched up from his eyes, swept over the top of his skull, ran down the back of the head to the nape of his neck, was anchored at the base of his skull by the fangs of the gowp-wyrm, and was secured by pulsing tentacles around his throat.

Peeking out beneath the hood was a shock of hair – *ruadh,* or chestnut red; then on the other side, another lock of hair – *dubh,* or black; and draped over the man's forehead, a strand – *bàn,* or blond.

---

[28] NAIM - case-sensitive Numeric Alphic Identifying Mark for short-lived and disposable Zziipppaeis. The "naim" is encoded in a microchip and then embedded into the folds of the Zziipppaei's pericardium when their generation has been registered, as well as being tattooed across their forehead.

[29] leash - Livestock Evasion Avoidance Shackling Harness -- a bio-engineered, micro-chip-implanted sea-wyrm, the body of which snakes around the neck, and its fangs imbedded in the brain stem of the recipient. This bio-machine monitors movement and facilitates control of the actions and thoughts of the wearer through a remote monitoring device, which controls the infusion of the serpent's venom, which has also been bio-engineered to induce various moods, emotions, and thought patterns. Attempts to remove the leash could result in the injection of lethal dose of toxin.

"Why Coo-win!" complained another Zziippp Melee Matcher, zUP (short for xuBHWzWRMwQ3dzUP, his full naim). Even though the Zziippps on the team were as massive as the bear-wolves that Cuilean sometimes dreamed of, his voice, typical of Zziipppaeis, piped high and shrill like a squeaky wheel. "Mepela winim Coo-win!" came the repeated protest from zUP.

Buttwater-Bates considered the protest. "zUP opines that the choice of Cuilean is a mis-satisfactory elocution of our resourcefulnesses."

"Yeah!" zUP squealed. "Sma-hed idea!" The Zziipppaei marked as zUP purposely shouldered Cuilean, pushing him back a half step. "Lookit! Mepela more strong himpela," zUP squeaked.

Ignoring the other Zziipppaeis, BilWee asked Cuilean in his truncated TokTok what he thought of his chances: "Kan Yupela killim Slaiya die?"

Cuilean made as if to answer but with the first sound out of his lips – "'S urrainn – I can ..." a not-quite completely formed response, but even though he hadn't completed the expression, because he'd even started to speak in the FT, as a penalty, his wyrm control leash jolted him with a white-hot warning blast to the base of his skull, a blow that hit him as if an opponent on the field had clobbered him with an electric mace set to full charge.

He blinked back the tears and shook his head to clear the blinding, burning light that had exploded in it. The restraining tentacles of the wyrm tightened around his neck, constricting his breathing.

Slithery to the touch, the tentacles of the wyrm-leash wriggled against his adjustment and gripped his throat all the more tightly. Cuilean reflexively pulled more firmly. The wyrm released its toothhold for a moment from the nape of Cuilean's neck and darted its head forward. It hissed, displaying two needle-sharp teeth in threat, and dug its fangs back into the base of his skull.

Cuilean shivered from the injection of a warning toxin and ceased his attempt to adjust the collar, rasping instead pained wheezes of breath.

"Mepela no savay wha yupela tok," BilWee pressed on, oblivious to what had just transpired. "But mepela tink yupela tok yesa.'"

"You came pretty contagiousness to Frotch talk, there," Buttwater-Bates taunted. "Not acquiesced," he warned. "But I confer. Get ready."

Cuilean narrowed his eyes, shuddered, and directed his gaze at Buttwater-Bates. This time, he held his tongue, not trusting it, except to mutter, "Yes, sir, Focwaod, sir," and dipped his head tightly.

They all knew what that meant. When Cuilean got the nod, he both wanted it and feared it. In this, he wasn't that much different than any of the other slaiv Melee Match  players. Winning meant more perks, perhaps even eventually, freedom – whatever that word meant within the bounds of the DownBlow.

Whereas losing meant being "retired" to the farm, as the euphemism went.

His mouth was as parched and arid as the landscape outside the stadium. In fact, it felt like he'd taken a whole gulp of hot ground dust – replete with sand, salt, gowp, arsenic, and whatever stray metals had been mixed into or filtered down onto it. He was afraid the heaving of his chest was visible, although he tried to control his panting so his distress wasn't as obvious as he felt. His face grew ashen as if he'd just gone for a dunk in the briny, mildly radioactive, definitely flaming Grand Inland Catchbasin.

Fear immobilized him so that he could barely stumble to the toilet, where he dropped himself like a sack of gowp slabs just a moment before everything in his bowels evacuated with the force of a strip-mining hose washing down a mountain to get at the minute traces of precious metals lodged in it (it seemed to him).

The flow burnt as it gushed out. His teammates could all smell the high-sickly-sweet, foul odor of acidic excrement as he sat riveted to the toilet bowl evacuating his bowels, his insides running as if melted into gooey, stinky, sea sludge, causing his teammates to mock that Cuilean was taking a "trip to the beach."

35

But Cuilean was beyond caring what the others could smell. He shivered from cold even though the temperature of the field's surface had been hot enough to scald a person's feet, and the temperature inside the lock-up was not that much cooler. His eyes focused in the middle distance as if he were blind, or as if he could see through the walls.

Riveted to the toilet bowl, he squatted head down, concentrating deeply, meditating profoundly. The pipes gurgled as they received his offering, which, following the "Law of Seven Profits" from *The Book of the Profit* – "Seven Times re-used before it is diffused and has to be refused" – twisted and curled straight down to the cafeteria (typically situated directly under the lavatory) so the nutrients could be extracted and the refuse recycled.

"Yupela fraid?" zUP asked.

"*Gu dearbh* – naturally," Cuilean snapped, not looking up, the FT exclamation escaping him in this time of extremity even though it was forbidden – perhaps, *because* it was a time of extremity. He winced from the jolt from the leash for his transgression. "Anybody with any sense would be afraid."

"Mepela no fraid," the Zziippp boasted.

"That's exactly what I said," Cuilean muttered and lowered his head again -- down nearly between his knees, preparing for the last discharge. He took a deep breath, and slowly, as he contemplated the fight he was about to engage, his mouth twisted into a snarl, his eyes protruded, his nostrils flared.

"Yupela say mepela sma-hed?" zUP challenged.

Cuilean exaggerated sucking on his teeth. "Yupela no sma-head."

The Zziippp nodded in satisfaction over having forced Cuilean to back down.

Or so he thought, for Cuilean let the Zziippp savor his supposed moral victory for just the swish of a rat's tail before he added with a challenging grin, "Yupela *sma*-sma-head."

The Zziippp didn't have time to answer the double jibe before Cuilean was jolted from the toilet to his feet by a shock from the leash.

Buttwater-Bates stood in front of him, his hand on the handheld control-screoin. He knew the signs. Cuilean was ready. "Now!" he commanded and again jabbed the control button on the handheld.

Cuilean winced, straightened his kilt, spat out a blood-infused stream, and wiped his mouth with the one dry spot left on his sleeve. Roughly, he pushed past Buttwater-Bates, whose body offered no resistance but rather wafted away like *canach* – cotton grass -- in a light breeze. Cuilean cut his way through the massed bunch of his teammates (who had gathered to amuse themselves with the spectacle his "preparation") and sprinted down the long dark tunnel to the arena and the fighting cage.

~~

In the gowp-dark

Cothrom na Féinne
The opportunity of heroes: a fair fight.
Proverb from *Leabhar an Leaghaidh Mhòir* —
The Book of the Great Melting

The gates of the fight cage swung open, and the contestants entered – Slaiya with a definitive, ominous plod, and Cuilean in a rush to the center of the ring. Both ways of moving communicated a determination to get the fight over with. Slaiya's demonstrated the confidence of hundreds of such fights that all had had but one outcome, and Cuilean's quick onrush was driven by a fear so consuming and that could have but one resolution – a quick attack and the immediate killing of that which made him afraid ... or his own death.

When Cuilean emerged into the blinding light, he squinted to see his opponent who had just entered the fighting circle -- a Zziipppaei gladiator who went by the shortened naim of Slaiya (full corporate designation, DKFJeIOLSLAiyA, but called, for obvious reasons, the shortened version), a grizzled Melee Match veteran of 1,500 games, seven-time All-Pro Killer (set to retire after this one – if she won -- that is, *really* retire, not *be retired* to the FARM[30] -- there was a difference).

Slaiya was a giantess who typically fought half-naked – that is, nude from the waist up -- her team's colors tattooed across her leathery skin. Belted around her waist was one of her many championship belts (themselves crafted from the tanned skin of vanquished opponents).

She was massive by even Zziipppaei standards. Her weight was supported on short, tree-trunk legs, and her arms hung monkey-like to her lower thighs. She towered a full head-and-shoulders over most of her opponents (all of whom appeared puny by comparison) and was so heavily scarred that it looked more like she was covered with the wrinkled bark of a tree trunk than any

---

[30] FARM — Final Allocation to Repurposing Manufactory

human or humanoid skin.

Her squat skull lacked, as that of most Zziipppaeis did, any semblance of a forehead, the top of the crown sloping abruptly to her eyebrows, the effect of which was accentuated by it having been shaved bare to display the many scars she proudly wore. Slaiya's face was scarred beyond recognition as a *face*, appearing more like a battered aptrac[31] tread rock guard, made even more grotesque by the eye dangling from its socket which had been gouged out earlier in the game and which was now barely held in place by the gowp-caked bandage cantilevered across her skull and face, which was itself riven by cavernous mutilations left by past injuries, including the scowl permanently etched there by one of the many wounds she had survived in her 13 seasons in the Melee Match arena – a career length which testified to her prowess as the average career of most Melee Matchers extended to little more than two years before they were "retired" to the FARM.

The pair of combatants was let into the cage, the floor of which was covered in a slippery coating of sludgy gowp that rose to a man's ankle (or to the Zziippp's instep) – just enough to add an element of slip-and-slide difficulty to the contest.

The announcer shouted over his mic as loudly as if he had to project his voice without assistance across the world. "These champions will decide the outcome of the Corporate Electoral Combat Bowl." To which he added the self-congratulatory aside: "Isn't it wonderful how democracy works!"

He continued, "On one side of the Ring of Death, representing the tropical Isle of Everest and the defending Melee Match champion -- the Zziipppaei Melee Match warrior we all know and love, for whom little introduction is needed: Slaiya from Himalaya! The Slaiv[32] that puts 'em in the Grave! The Master of Disaster! The Mistress of Darkness! The Rainer of Painer!" And repeating in a long, drawn-out yowl that covered his mic and the area within an arl radius of his mouth with saliva, spittle, snot, and chunks of his most recent meal of sautéed wyrm and raratatouille[33]: "SLAIYYY-YAAA!"

"And opposite her, the challenger – for his first-time

---

[31] APTRAC -- Armored Personnel TRAnsport Conveyance. More often than not, written simply in lower case as "aptrac."

[32] Slaiv - Situation: Lifelong Assignment, Involuntary or Voluntary

[33] *Raratatouille* being thought redundant, although there were those such as linguist Nimh Chimsky who held that the original form was actually "rat atouille" – *atouille* being an ancient dish of various ingredients, and the "rat" being a prefix narrowing and specifying what kind of *atouille* was being referred to. However, as *ratatouille* became associated with the general type of dish, speakers affixed the modifying rat- (or ra-) to designate this particular ingredient.

appearance in the Electoral Combat Bowl ..." And dropping his tone ominously for the digression, he added, "and maybe his last if Slaiya continues her winning streak: The *Mayhem from Waypland*[34]. *The Killer from the Land of Chiller! The Fighter from the Higher! The Mortifier from Portafire!*"[35] -- "CUUU-LANNN!!!"

In the fighting arena, Cuilean and Slaiya readied for the shooting of the departing one that would begin the match. Just moments before the referee would shoot the start, Slaiya stepped close, leaned in, and covering her mic so her words – possibly her last – would not be picked up, said in her squeaky, high-pitched voice -- her larynx not having descended, which was typical of her kind -- "Coo-win ... Strayt play, gudpela?" (Though it wasn't clear what exactly that might mean in this context – *straight play*, that is -- from which only one of them would emerge alive, if either.) In saying this, Slaiya gave Cuilean the Zziipppaei salute -- an open palm sliding from the top of her skull and down her

---

[34] Wayp – The mountainous territory at the Southern Pole of the planet that rose in elevation when the massive ice-sheets that had been weighing the southernmost continent down melted. *Etymology*, derived from proto-Simspeek "Way Up." In this enunciation – *Wayp-lan* -- the speaker is creating a wordplay variation for the effect of rhythm and rhyme.

[35] Portafire -- the sea-level port city that was ringed by the South Fire Ocean, many thousand lengths below The Wayp – so not really where Cuilean was from, but it *rhymed,* so ...

steeply-sloping forehead to extend in the air like a skier off a gowp-sludge jump.

Far away, the announcer, along with everyone else in the stadium and around the world strained to hear. He exhaled in exasperation. "Can't make out exactly what's being said, but the two opponents are no doubt trash talking each other, trying to demoralize each other. Wish we could hear. Wish they'd let us in on the fun!"

Puny opposite the massive Slaiya, Cuilean nodded in agreement. *"Cothrom na Fèinne, a charaid,* -- Fair play, friend." He was now so hyped on the leash injections of steroids, adrenalin, testosterone, amphetamine, and methylphenidate, that he hardly noticed the penalty jolt for using the phrase from his days in the Wayp that popped out of his mouth before his mind could process and block it.

Slaiya tilted her head quizzically like a cartoon rat might in a screointoon: "Huh? Frotch TokTok?"

"I don't know, it just came to me." And indeed, the words had erupted from his lips as if from a handheld on autoplay -- a phrase that had resonance for him in a way that words of the Simspeek would not, though he could not have told what they meant. *A fighting chance for heroes,* a phrase that echoed out of the proverbs he'd heard many years before: words that had emerged out of the misty past before the Great Melt, words that spoke of mutual respect between opponents, which, though he could not have elucidated the idea at the time, were relevant to his situation here. After all, he had much more in common with this poor ratfucked ratfucker mutant Zziipppaei slaiv opposite him — in spite of her monstrous appearance and size — than any of the wispy petri-bred Anboarnh corporate executives that even now were throwing down bets of millions of gowp-creds over their PetrAles[c] on which Melee Matcher would die and which would live.

The two champions faced off at the edges of the inner circle. The head-ball was placed between them by the referee, who immediately turned and hurriedly slushed through the muck of the fighting pit towards the exit-gate, which was slammed shut with a clang.

Immediately afterwards, the metal fencing around the fighting cage flashed and sparked with thousands of jolts of electricity.

"That's it now, folks!" the Finkel shouted. "They're in there until only one walks out!"

"Come on, guys," the head in the ball, pled. "Let's be a little careful now."

Without looking down, still eying the Zziippp gladiator opposite him with wariness, Cuilean noted, "I don't remember you ever being careful."

"Well, now it's different."

"Yeah, because it's *you*."

The conversation was cut short as the referee shot the starter – a Zziippp gladiator from the previous year's losing team -- who fell with a dramatic and crowd-pleasing plop. The lights went out, and the stadium, including the fight cage, lurched into pitch blackness. But just before that moment of stygian darkness, the audience – and the combatants – had gotten a quick glimpse of the various armaments mounted on the fencing -- daggers, swords, spears, clubs, spiked maces, halyards, axes, two-handed swords, broadswords, rapiers, sabers, brass knuckles, switchblades, whips, pitchforks, tridents, scythes – anything and everything someone harboring gory mayhem and bloody murder in their heart might wish for in their Listmus[36] stocking.

For the audience, it was a moment of stomach-fluttering, genital-tickling anticipation. For the contestants, it was the last opportunity they'd have to map the location of their weapon of choice – or chance.

In the stands, the spectators quickly slipped on or fumbled with their night-vision goggles (whichever the case might be, depending on their familiarity with or their preparation for the proceedings), and on screoins all over the world, the images shifted to eerie infra-red, and the two combatants circled each other and the head-ball like two specters in a ghost world.

Slaiya lumbered forward, while Cuilean, with his tentacled cowl, stood absolutely still and listened for the heavy, sloshing footfalls. Then he quietly swept -- first with one foot and then with the other -- the area in front of him for the ball.

Locating the head-ball with a soft toe-touch, Cuilean nudged it aside just as the Zziipppaei lunged for where she remembered it being. Cuilean, feeling the push of the air propelled by the monstrous body coming for him, ducked beneath the giant's outstretched arms.

He righted himself at the cage fence and groped along the surface for a weapon, any weapon.

Feeling ... feeling ... finding nothing.

There were so many of them before.

Where were they now?

---

[36] Listmus -- annual Wholly Day of the Profit, for which Anboarnh and Zziipppaei pupae make lists of all their "must-haves," which they hope to receive as gifts.

In the stands, the audience gasped, gulped, and tittered, as the weapons shifted places, moved out of reach, sometimes just before Cuilean was about to lay his hand on one.

But he had only a moment before he felt Slaiya's hot breath on the back of his neck and had to dodge away.

"Ooohh! So close!" the announcer sympathized (though not really, there being a tone of thrill at the prospect of havoc – at least, of havoc being wreaked upon someone *else* – and a bit of disappointment at having missed it).

Slaiya, being the wily veteran that she was, knew too well not to depend on finding the illusionary, elusive fighting implements. It was by her size, her strength, and her ferocity that she had won 13 straight Electoral Combat Bowls, and it was on those qualities that she now depended.

That and her preternatural ability to smell fear. She sniffed the air and charged towards the place where the stench of Cuilean's dread was the thickest. Cuilean dodged out of the way of the attack, but Slaiya quickly maneuvered and reached out her giant paws within a finger's length of him.

Whatever it was that the head in the sphere was going to say was lost as Slaiya lumbered at the ball, moving with a definiteness that indicated neither doubt that she'd reach it nor fear that she would be opposed, much less impeded, but having mapped its location in his memory, Cuilean neatly side-kicked it away.

As the sphere bounced just out of Slaiya's grip, the head let out a series of groans. "Ouh ... ouh ... OUH!" the head yelped. "That was hard!" Which was amplified throughout the stadium and which in turn were met with a resounding outburst of the crowd's shared laughter.

Slaiya cast about for the head-ball but managed to grip only empty air. The gowpaleen-encased face grinned tauntingly at the clumsy Zziipppaei. "Ya move like ya got three left feet and a fargleslag of ratshit in your shorts!" the encased head mocked.

The fans in the stands hooted in appreciation of this running commentary.

Deftly, Cuilean dashed ahead of the Zziippp, dove for the ball, caught it up and rolled out of Slaiya's reach.

Following the sound, Slaiya plodded directly at Cuilean, but the kilted melee matcher dodged her again, this time skipping to the side and keeping just out of reach, but the quick lateral movement threw Cuilean off balance, and he brushed the electrified cage boundary, and a thousand sparks went up, illuminating the ring for a moment.

Slaiya, who'd been groping in the other direction, pivoted, and grasping the opportunity to locate with certainty Cuilean's position, charged with a terrifying shriek. But before she could reach her prey, darkness again enshrouded the ring.

Cuilean swerved just a rat's body-length out of the way. Slaiya chased, Cuilean scooted just ahead, and so for two circuits of the melee cage match it went: Slaiya chasing, Cuilean running away; Slaiya reaching out to grapple Cuilean and crush him in her powerful grip, and Cuilean keeping just one finger length out of reach.

"He's running away!" Finkel exclaimed. "That's not the way to fight! You're going the wrong way there, Fighter from the Higher!" And adding encouragement for Cuilean's opponent, he chimed, "He's over there, Playa from Himalaya!" (Of no real help, of course, as where was *there* in a bitch black fight arena? But it added to the color commentary.)

The fans in the stands and watching on screoins around the world were delighted, appalled. They hooted derisively and cheered enthusiastically, depending upon their team affiliations or their penchant for seeing others shed blood or otherwise be maimed themselves.

Slaiya maneuvered Cuilean into the corner, and it looked as if finally, the massive champ would get her mitts on the much smaller challenger, but as she lunged, Cuilean dove forward and slid on the gowp slip between her legs, and the Zziippp fell headlong into the electrified cage.

Slaiya was crucified on the fence and sent up shrieks of rage and pain as a thousand electrified flares shot up from the chain-link like a stratospheric auroric display over the Southern Ocean.

Which light show gave Cuilean a chance to scan the ring, and there on the opposite wall, he saw what he'd been looking for: a weapon he knew full well, one he had grown up with, a *claidheamh mòr* – a man-length, two-handed sword.

If only the sword would stay there long enough for him to reach it and didn't evanesce like everything else he'd tried for!

He dashed, and just as the fire show died, Cuilean dove for it and grasped for it, but the image of the weapon flickered before fading completely. He curled in mid-air and rolled to his feet empty handed.

~~

Whop me with your best shot

An uair a bhuaileas tu an Rìgh, buail gu math e.
When you strike the King, strike him well.
Proverb from *Leabhar an Leaghaidh Mhòir* —
The Book of the Great Melting

Cuilean stood perfectly still, perfectly quiet, not even the sound of a breath coming from him as he listened instead to his opponent's heavy breathing – the gasping and panting and huffing and puffing – and the equally clumsy footfalls of her slow-footed advance. Although he couldn't see in the darkened fight-cage, the noise proceeding from his opponent was as good as a sound picture.

From Cuilean, in contrast, there were no footfalls. No sound of feet hitting the floor or sloshing through the muck that formed the fighting mat. Just a careful sliding, a delicate touching, a tentative inching forward, as if stalking a deer in the forests of the Wayp.

The audience hushed with the sense that there was now a completely different game afoot.

Slaiya sniffed the air but the scent she inhaled was diffuse, having been wafted away by the air circulation and recycling systems. She turned in a circle, waving her arms about, groping in the lightless fighting ring.

As Cuilean crept toward her.

Then just as Cuilean had slipped within reach of striking, the massive Zziippp and reigning champion of the Melee field swiveled around, lunged forward, struck out blindly in the darkness, and by luck and guess delivered a crushing blow to the side of Cuilean's head. (The hulking Zziippp could move faster than it looked like she should be able to.)

At the strike, Cuilean experienced a flash of brilliant, blinding light (or would-be blinding light, if it were visible), which was to be expected as the flying roundhouse whomp was delivered with the Zziippp's full weight behind it, but what was surprising -- (in that he had had his leash jarred loose before and had experienced nothing more than a lightning-white searing flash at the back of his

45

skull) – was that now his sight – or what came to him as a sight – was filled with a flood of green and blue.

The wyrm released its tentacled grip on Cuilean's neck, flashed its fangs and hissed its objection at Slaiya to being assaulted. Then again, it bit deeply into the spinal nerve at the base of Cuilean's skull. The man staggered under the double assault – Slaiya's blow and the injection of the gowp-wyrm's venom.

In the hover booth, the commentators groaned in sympathy. "Wow! That was so hard it knocked Cuilean's leash out!"

"It was so hard it almost knocked *my* teeth out!"

"His leash is slowing him down! Why does the league make him wear the damn thing?!?"

"Because that's the only way to control his kind. He'd escape back to the Wayp without it."

On the sidelines, Focwaod Buttwater frantically tapped the handheld. "Cuilean! Cuilean! Fleece away from him!" (Advice that was, like most sports advice, self-evident, like "score" or "stop 'em" or *whatever*.)

"Can you adhere to me? Damn the Profit!" Buttwater swore. "His leash is out. He's not receiving any defections."

As the Focwaod's mic was relayed out as part of the streaming broadcast, the announcer had an opportunity to gloat: "I coulda told you that!"

The punch had staggered Cuilean, but more than the immediate effect of the clout was that the surprise blow lowered his defenses. Seizing the moment, Slaiya  followed up on Cuilean's apparent daze with two more potentially killing strikes – which, however, were ill-aimed on account of the obscurity of the ring, but the combination of which toppled Cuilean heels over head to the mat and displayed to all via the infrared cameras exactly what a Wayper wore under his kilt.

Which was not much.

And which caused much hilarity in the stands amongst the on-site audience of more than 500,000 fans and billions more watching on their screoins worldwide.

"Oh! TMI, Cuilean!" Fred Finkel chortled. "We came to see some ugly doings ... but not *that* ugly!"

On the stadium's overhead tote screoins, the odds shifted dramatically in favor of Slaiya's team, as last-minute bets surged in anticipation of a killer slam.

On the sidelines, Buttwater-Bates hissed impotently at BilWee, "Make him erectile! Make him erectile!"

The Zziippp studied the handheld in confusion. "Na lukluk straight," he complained.

Buttwater-Bates leaned close and shouted frantically, sprayingly. "Repossess it again. It's bottom side up!"

BilWee wiped Buttwater's slaver off his cheek and forehead and swiped the screoin of the handheld clean (or at least, not so clouded with mucus). A look of beatific revelation passed over the Zziipppaei assistant's face as he swiveled the handheld and exclaimed in amazement: "Haa! Lukluk straight now-aa."

Hearing the TokTok gave Buttwater-Bates a headache. He couldn't understand why these Zziippp-heads were allowed to breed. He had always thought that if they were only sterilized at birth, within a generation, a final solution to the problem they presented would be achieved. Then everybody would be Anboarnh, like himself, traits specially chosen, specifically selected for superior intelligence and fitness. *Why, why, dear Profit, are they allowed to replimate?!?*

BilWee's fingers poked sluggishly at the handheld.

"Move faster!" Buttwater-Bates sniped. "Move your hands more vapidly, you ratbrained immersible!"

The "ratbrain" protested that he was doing as well as he could: "Mepela no-aa ratbrain. Mepela mo-aa gudder."

"You've gotta be mo-aa mo-aa gudder!" Buttwater grew even angrier at being tricked – or so he felt it to be – into speaking the TokTok. "I mean, be more alactritous!" he scolded, his voice taking on the intonation of an irate old lady (as it did when he became angry).

None of which caused BilWee to move any more quickly. If anything, his bospela's ranting rattled him, scrambled his thinking, and thence his functioning. He let out an inarticulate squeal in protest.

Buttwater-Bates panted in exasperation. "Give him a blastification! Get him erectile! We're going to lose! And you know what that means!"

At the threat of ending up encased in a gowpaleen Melee Match ball (or at least his head), BilWee's finger trembled over the controller.

Buttwater-Bates violently rocked back and forth from the balls of his feet to his heels and flapped his arms to calm himself.

In the arena, Cuilean lay prostrate – though the length of time he lay stunned seemed much longer than it actually was. He was flooded with – he could hardly say what they were – visions? memories? hallucinations? (Had the pre-game cocktail of various stimulants and psychedelics – both artificial and natural -- been *laced* with something? Well, something besides the usual concoction of stimulants, intoxicants, mind-altering, performance enhancing constituents?) But whatever the ingredients were, his mind was over-washed with colors and sensations and sounds he hardly recognized. It was as if he were walking in a dream he'd already had, a *déjà rêvé*, a dream already dreamed and now visited for a second time.

No longer was the world a brackish brown, the accustomed tincture of barren sand mixed with oily gowp. He saw green, which puzzled him because the color did not exist, aside from that painted on walls, but here the green seemed to surround him, and even more confounding, overhead was an expanse of blue, whereas if anyone cared to look up through the domed top of any building in the DownBlow, they would see the true color of the sky, which was a dirty, orangish, gowp-tinged brown, the same color as the surrounding sandscape.

Cuilean had a momentary vision of walking through a living landscape saturated with greens and blues and reds and yellows and oranges, a ground cover of a green so deep it was almost blue, and a sky totally unlike the smudge-scape seen through the city domes here, but of a crystalline beryl. There was a smell in the air unlike anything he'd ever smelled – or remembered smelling – not the soot-infused aaire[37] that was pumped into the breathing devices and singed his nostrils but something unfamiliarly fresh and clean.

He heard a high-pitched buzz as a creature the size of the palm of his hand buzzed by -- something oblongish, and yellow with black stripes (or vice versa – it happened too quickly to tell for sure).

But that fierce drone was his being shocked back to the reality most immediately at hand as Buttwater-Bates had snarled at his putative assistant (whom the Focwaod was now regarding as more of an impediment, which prompted the suspicion: *Had the idiot*

---

[37] aaire – Artificial Atmospheric Inhalable Respiratory Environment

Zziippp been assigned to him as an act of sabotage?). "Bring him back, you idiot! Consort him back!"

His attention jerked back from spectating the cage match to his duties, BilWee blinked dully and squinted hard at his handheld's control panel.

"Ratbrain piss-head," Buttwater-Bates yelped in his customary tone of a dump-rat caught in a trap – and none too pleased about it. "Give him a shock!"

Prodded to awareness – such as it was – BilWee moved his finger over the panel and lowered it as slowly as a crane operator bringing up a load of bituminous gowp.

Buttwater-Bates ground his teeth, his lips writhing in impatient anger, but he restrained himself from snarling anything else.

"All done, bospela," BilWee reported with an exhalation of breath.

"Gratifications to *you*," the *bospela* snarled with a sarcastic grimace.

"Bospela tok tanks," BilWee told himself, gratified at the slight praise.

In the arena, Cuilean came back to himself – that is, his present self – just as Slaiya was in a midair leap, poised for a kill blow.

"Inspect him with aggrandizement!" Buttwater-Bates screamed.

Regaining his focus, BilWee located and pressed another command.

Cuilean felt the surge of radrenaline and dodged Slaiya's leap, and the Zziippp – remarkably agile for her size, nearly half-again as big as her human opponent – hit the ground and rolled to her feet.

The two Melee Match warriors faced off again, circling for an advantage. Cuilean held out his arms to get a feel for Slaiya's position. Touching the beast's fingers, he said just as the Zziippp was about to launch another assault, "Whop me. Or yupela weak sma-fella."

This, more than anything else could have, halted Slaiya in her lunge, so surprised was she by this ... this ... she couldn't even conceptualize just what he was: He wasn't an Anboarnh, and he certainly wasn't a Zziippp, but here he was addressing her in TokTok.

"Mepela no weak sma-fella," Slaiya protested angrily in TokTok.

To which Cuilean responded with a taunt in his tone, "Yupela weak sma-fella!"

"Mepela no weak sma-fella!" Slaiya screamed (in a voice that betrayed her innermost fear that she was indeed a weak sma-fella), and she clobbered Cuilean with such a strong wallop that he staggered backwards.

Cuilean steadied himself, shook his head, and stepped forward. "Whop me mo-aa har."

"This is amazing! Cuilean is daring the Zziippp champion to hit him!" Finkel broadcast breathlessly, telling the audience what they had just witnessed. "It's as if he's challenging Slaiya: *You can't put me out. Bring on your best. Hit me with your best shot!*"

Again, the Zziippp giant delivered a blow that rattled Cuilean's skull.

There was a flash of green in Cuilean's vision.

"Whop mo-aa," Cuilean said.

Another blow. Again: another glimpse of a world that wasn't.

"Wan time mo-aa."

And another apparition – but that faded too quickly to make sense out of.

"Mo-aa har," Cuilean told the Zziippp in the TokTok.

~~

Finish her!

Gaisgeach air ghaisgeach, 's laoch ri laoch.
Champion to champion, hero to hero.
Proverb from *Leabhar an Leaghaidh Mhòir* —
The Book of the Great Melting

A spinning roundhouse kick from the Zziippp catapulted Cuilean into the electrified fence but also must have jarred loose the connection between the leash and the base of his skull because he saw a splattering of sparks, which might have been the light show of the fence, but not just that, for he also saw something *else,* the vision again, but this time more clearly: a red-haired girl in a green land riding a huge horse-like beast with a lance-like horn growing out of its snout.

"BilWee!" Buttwater-Bates snarled into the Zziippp's ear. He was now slathering at the mouth – literally: white flecks ringed his lips.

BilWee wiped the
spittle from the side of his head.

"We're misplaying him! Bring him back! If we don't win, the Profit is incontinent, and we'll be delegated to the farm!"

Putting his finger to the earpiece that gave him a live feed from the field, Fred Finkel gloated: "Yep! That looks likely now," adding a schadenfreudish chuckle at the thought.

"Another ejection!" Buttwater-Bates screamed in a little-girl shriek. There was something about the desperation in Buttwater's voice that spurred BilWee to action. A series of buttons pressed, and Cuilean felt a surge of stimulant-induced rage that swept through the vision of green fields like a forest fire, burning it and melting it away.

Before the fence-flare went out completely, Cuilean saw a dagger hanging just within his reach -- long, sharp-pointed, with a bone-carved handle: another weapon that he was well familiar with, a *sgian dubh*. He grabbed it before the lights went out and jumped to his feet as Slaiya charged again.

Cuilean tucked the dagger away and planted his feet to brace against her charge, but though expected, the rush was unstoppable. Slaiya lowered her head and butted Cuilean with the force of a charging *mìneotarbh* – a wild bull-beast from the Wayp -- propelling the Port Denver player backwards like a dart from a kabloey and – unintended consequence – safely out of her reach.

Frustrated, Slaiya galumphed after the "Fight from the Heights," as Cuilean was known, but rather than meet the attack, Cuilean dodged away, again just out of range of the Zziippp giant's reach. Slaiya picked up her pace, and Cuilean dashed to the far side of the steel-cage ring. Slaiya moved with an ambling side step, cutting off Cuilean's path of escape. With nowhere else to go, Cuilean took to the one direction that was left to him – up! – and parkoured off the sides of the steel cage.

"What's he doing!?!" Finkel shouted in a mixture of puzzlement and delight.

Just as the announcers in the hover-booth were all atingle at the spectacle, the audience responded with laughing and cheering and booing and stomping their feet and clapping their hands and blowing vuvuzelas in a cacophonous symphony that sounded like the angry swarming of giant killer bees.

Fred Finkel segued his attention. "Listen to them," he called out, referring to the crowd. "They're going crazy!"

Slaiya lumbered forward and staggered to a stop. She put her hands on her knees, panting deeply. She reached wanly towards her opponent. "Stop run," she said. "Stay fight. Get done this cwazy. Let mepela kill yupela."

At this, Cuilean could barely restrain a chuckle. "Okay," he said. And spreading his legs shoulder wide, balancing on the balls of his feet, running his tongue along the outside of his teeth and making a smacking sound with his lips, he invited her with a sly smile: "Come on and get me."

At this, Slaiya drew upright, gathered herself, ducked her head, and rushed forward.

A stillness, a quietude of anticipation came over the audience, as if they had drawn a collective deep breath and held it.

Cuilean blitzed forward in return. The two seemed about to smash together in a massive collision – an irresistible force meeting an overpowering assault. But at the moment they met, Cuilean leapt at Slaiya and balanced for an instant on her outstretched arms.

With this surprising maneuver, Slaiya jerked reflexively upwards, adding propulsion to Cuilean's leap, and propelling him atop her. He wrapped himself tightly around her head and shoulders.

Stumbling off balance, she reached up to dislodge this irritating, vexing midge that was now impeding her vision, but the formidable bulk of her shoulder muscles prevented her from lifting her arms high enough to even scratch her ears, much less strip

Cuilean off.

The crowd laughed uproariously at this unexpected turn of events: The mighty Zziippp warrior bumbling around with her opponent clinging to her head – paradoxically enough, safest where he was most intimately close.

Slaiya's frenzy grew more and more frenetic as she squealed in what the crowd in the stadium took to be comical outrage. She circled awkwardly, lurchingly, in her frantic endeavor to peel off and smash this infuriating botheration to the ground and administer the kill-blow she had long practiced and which was a favorite feature of this sports hero's play.

However, before she could extricate herself from Cuilean's grip, he spun himself, propeller-like. The motion caught the giantess by surprise as her shoulders torqued, her upper torso coiled, her legs twisted over her planted feet, and her far-flung breasts, whirling like helicopter blades, accentuated and accelerated the spin. Her legs corkscrewed as she lost balance and teetered.

Cuilean threw himself downward across the Zziippp's back and grabbed her around the waist from behind. The sudden shift of weight toppled the Zziipppaei backwards. In the process of the fall, Cuilean had whipped out the *sgian dubh* – the "black" knife, though less the color "black," then "black" as in "fatal" or "fatefully concealed" – that he'd tucked out of sight at the top of his knee-high stockings.

Slaiya landed with a massive thud (amplified over the stadium speakers for the thrill of the fans), and Cuilean rolled through to come up between the beast's hiked hips.

Cuilean darted a glance at the scoreboard, which displayed the calculations of the teams' scores down to the thousandth of a point.

"FINISH HER! FINISH HER!" the fans in the stands roared, demanding a last-second bloody climax.

In the moderating hover-booth, Fred Finkel called it: "They've just got a few seconds left, and the score is tied, but Cuilean can set a team record with a final kill."

The lights in the arena flashed on in order to better light the coup de grâce. "Finish her! Finish her!" from the rabid fans, many of them standing now, so many of them punctuating their demands with the stomping of their feet that the stadium bleachers rocked and swayed.

"Do kwik, fren," Slaiya said with a nod, as their eyes locked.

Cuilean winked in response and jabbed the point of the dagger under Slaiya's championship belt.

At first, there was no reaction -- the crowd in the stadium hung in silence and expectation, and Slaiya held her breath in anticipation of the obliviation that was to come. Cuilean thrust again and this time slit sideways.

The hover booth camera caught the surprised expression on the Zziipppaei warrior's face at the exact moment the blade went home.

From there it was just a matter of Cuilean's rising and stepping to the head-ball.

"Over the goal, you slug-brain!" the head in the ball shouted, craning its line of sight to Cuilean's fallen opponent.

Picking up the head-ball, Cuilean walked it — as if out for a casual stroll -- towards the goal.

"Hurry up, you ratfucker!" the head-ball shouted. "I don't got a wyrm's life to waste on you."

There were only a couple ticks left on the clock as Cuilean, to the stunned silence of the stadium, placed the ball down on the ground in front of the goal.

The game-ending buzzer rattled loudly, breaking the hush, which had hung frozen in the air.

On the field, Cuilean gave an elaborate bow to the crowd, followed by a cute curtsy, accompanied by a dainty spread of his tartan kilt, followed by a Zziipppaei salute.

He raised the *sgian dubh* and pointed it to the highest seats in the stadium.

"He's saluting the audience!" the announcer interpreted, although in truth, Cuilean was pointing somewhere else, somewhere high above and far away and half-a-dimly-remembered-lifetime ago.

54

With the blade of the dagger clearly visible, contrary to the expectations of the audience, the knife was clean of the green ooze that sludged through Zziipppaei veins. There was a hushed confusion in the stands as it become apparent to all that the Zziipppaei Slaiya was still alive.

Buttwater-Bates spread his hands. Having looked forward to a last-moment victory, he squinched his face in quandary at the outcome.

Cuilean stepped back to his still supine opponent, reached down, and grabbing her by the arm, he yanked her to her feet.

A collective *Huh?* went up from the spectators.

Equally confused at still being alive and the score tied, alike, Slaiya turned to walk away, but as she did so, her pants plummeted to her ankles, and she wobbled, her feet caught in the tangle of cloth. The Zziipppaei struggled buffonishly to maintain her balance, if not her dignity. She lurched one way and the other and finally fell flat onto her massive, mangled, crenelated face.

The mob in the stands released a roar of laughter as the Zziippp she-monster, caught in a tangle of cloth and burdened down by her great weight, flapped her arms and squirmed like a doodlebug trying to right itself.

In the moderators' hover-booth, the commentary proceeded in bewildered speculation: "Cuilean must've thought his team was ahead. That's why he didn't score."

"Was this an illegal act of mercy?"

"The judges will be looking at that ..."

"Or a miscalculation as time was running out?"

"Definitely something for the League to look into."

"They'll be examining the playbacks."

"Right. There might be a fine involved."

"But there's no doubt about it. Even though Cuilean is one of the most valuable slaivs the League owns, this stunt today might get him sent to the territories."

"Maybe even to the Farm."

There were nods of wise assent from the old pros in the hover booth.

The announcer Finkel interjected: "Word just in! Under the *mmmmm* rule that the 'tie goes to the winner,' Fellatio Hibiscus has proclaimed themselves President, and as a special bonus treat for the audience at home and in the stadium (at least for those who bet *correctly*) ..." the announcer added this aside with a certain anticipatory pleasure before he continued ... "As I was saying, as a special delectation for the audience, the new President, Chief of State, Big Cheese, Head Honcho, CEO, COO, CUC, KUK, and General All-around BossPella! ..." (he was contractually compelled to repeat the entire title) "... Fellatio Hibiscus has declared that their first official act will be the eradication of their political opponents – not just the leaders, but all their followers in the stands!"

Up in the booth, Fellatio Hibiscus, the newly selected President, Chief of ... yada yada yada – you get the idea ... pressed a red button, which was mounted on the detached head of some grinning, former functionary that had just been brought to him.

Fred Finkel chuckled in amusement: "They'll think twice before buying those pricey seats again. Oh, no! They won't," he jokily interrupted himself, finishing with a gloating guffaw. "They won't have anything to think with!"

With that, the screoin displayed images of the armed PieceTakers of the Corporation moving through the crowd hacking at and killing panicked spectators, fans of (and voters for) the losing team and its owner, Goowhiggie Clawntrip. "What fun!" the announcer continued. "Ooh! Look at that! That head took a real bounce! Look at it go!"

This was before the audience was treated to the image of the surgical decapitation of the defeated challenger, "Grandma" Goowhiggie, followed by the equally careful encapsulation of her still living and smiling head (a politician must keep up appearances) in a gowpaleen sphere.

In the tunnel to the locker rooms, a Zziipppaei fan of the losing team who had somehow slipped past security, confronted Cuilean. "Tink ya tuf huh?" (which came out more as one single modulated sound — more like *tinkyatufhuh* — rather than a coherent sequence of decipherable words).

Cuilean eyed the creature. His system surged with a more powerful drug than any concocted by the Monstrato Corporation for administration to its workers (with stronger doses reserved for its fighters): The sheer intoxicating, mind-altering, sense-of-invincibility-endowing relief at still being alive. He couldn't resist a broad smile. "It doesn't matter how tough I think I am," he said, making a sudden foot faint towards the Zziipppaei as if attacking but pulling back his advance within a rat's whisker of the fan's face but without touching the muncaidh.

The Zziipppaei gave a startled *yip* and jerked back.

"Just how tough *you* think I am."

The Zziipppaei guards laughed in rapid monkey chirps and pushed a passage through the swarming throng so Cuilean could continue his way.

In the locker room itself, Cuilean collected a towel for his shower from BilWee, who also doubled as the equipment manager. BilWee noted, by way of making a connection with the hero of the moment, "Big knock Yupela head."

"'S nothing, BilWee." Cuilean spoke as if addressing somebody a couple feet to the Zziippp's right. "But who's your friend?" Cuilean tilted his head to the Zziippp's side as he took the towel.

"Huh?" BilWee blurted out in response, confused as to who or what Cuilean was talking about.

The little fellow worshiped the professional Melee Matchers. It was beyond his dreams to be one of them, for he was too small, too pudgy, and his hands were too weak and effeminate, although his years of working on the sidelines, assisting the head coach with the play calls, and in the locker room, handing out towels, washing the uniforms, repairing the armor, had brought him to the belief that he was -- *kinda, sorta* – although not a fight-baller himself but nevertheless, one of the guys. And when something happened -- like this -- that brought it to his attention that he really wasn't in on the joke, it disconcerted him to the point of spluttering and trembling.

Cuilean gave a squinting wink that included the corner of his mouth, what passed for a smile, or maybe not — there was no telling — and turned to the chem-showers.

But that wink wrapped BilWee warmly in an embrace of comradery that he so longed for. He got *it* -- or thought he did, he really couldn't be sure, but believing or wanting to believe, he laughed loudly to Cuilean's back -- too loudly, actually – and with a loopy grin, his eyes squeezed cockeyed, and his head cocked to the side, he announced, "Mepela savay. Yupela makim funny!" In his delight at being accepted, if only for a moment, as one of the team, *one of the guys*, he announced to all in general, although to no one in particular, "He makim joke mepela!"

With fond and worshipful appreciation, he crowed: "*Cooo-wonnn!*"

~~

What's a fren worth?

Na dìobair caraid san sabaid.
Forsake not a friend in the fight.
Proverb from *Leabhar an Leaghaidh Mhòir* —
The Book of the Great Melting

The PetrAle sports bar overlooked an expansive scenic vista outside the dome. A picture window which ran the width of the room overlooked an attractive view of sludge colored sand. The window box had been situated so as to frame in its middle a flaming geyser: "Old Firefull," as it was called, that would periodically spout jets of flame, one of the most spectacular natural phenomena in the DownBlow (very popular with lovers and tourists).

The structure which housed the bar was balanced atop a gowp derrick that supplied the decorative fountain of sludge-colored gowp in the center of the interior. The pool at the base of the fountain was stocked with tentacled gowp-wyrms of various sizes, which patrons could select for their meals and have them prepared – either boiled alive, or alternatively, sliced, diced, and fried at their

tables -- these being the more popular options (though once in a while, some inebriated partiers would challenge each other to eating the wyrms raw, which practice had resulted in more than one person having been choked when the tentacled wyrm would fight being chewed and swallowed and in its resistance clung to the face, mouth, and throat of the would-be eater, and choked him to death).

The room itself was hermetically sealed against the caustic atmosphere of the DownBlow by a series of air locks and opened up above with an overhead sky light – through which the sun could be seen setting off an orange glow through the ambient smudge across the skyline. After sunset, the moon rose bright orange through the hanging evening smut. At night, the fire-geysers sprouted up spectacularly on the surrounding hills like so many candles on a birthday ratbake.

Cuilean had already drunk a couple pitchers of PetrAle, chased by some shots of smodka (gowp-wyrms and potatoes being two crops that could still be grown in the American Pelago, aside from rats and cockroaches), and a few polydrug cocktails, his favorite being a mixture they called Liquid Lightning -- a barbiturate to help him relax (a necessary aid after a Melee Match), mixed with an amphetamine to speed him up (and keep the sedatives from putting him to sleep), with a kicker of radrenaline[38] leavened with an opiate to take off the edge, and with a dash of hallucinogen to create just the desired depth of experience.

He was sitting by himself at the bar. Puzzling. Since the fight-ball game, thoughts — memories, perhaps, or hallucinations, or just random fantasies — had been trickling into his thinking. He didn't know whether it was due to his leash having been short-circuited, or the whack on the head that Slaiya had given him ... or both, or neither, or whether his slaiv handlers had adjusted the medications delivered via the leash without telling him.

But whatever it was, he didn't know quite what to make of it. He'd catch a flash of an image. Of a green land. And clear water – far different from the brackish, gowpy liquid that filled the inland sea. And creatures he could not name but for some reason did not seem utterly strange, as if he were fantasizing a hallucination remembering a dream.

It was at times like this that Cuilean was overwhelmed with a sense of melancholy that could only be assuaged by drinking and

---

[38] Radrenaline - extracted from the rats' adrenal glands after zapping the male specimens in the testis with little electric prods, a job that required both a certain dexterity and a proclivity to inflicting pain upon small, defenseless creatures.

drugging himself into a stupor. The intoxication was an anodyne against the pain – much in the same way as the violence of the fight cage was. If he still had had the language – the FT – that the tentacled leash protected him against, blocked him from, he might have identified the yearning as that of *cianalas*,[39] but he didn't, so he interpreted the hole in the cockle of his heart rather as a *need for speed* – of violent action -- or a *desperation for the cessation* of all feelings, a respite offered by mind-numbing intoxicants.

In seeming answer to the urgency which was simmering near a boil within him – that is, something that would give him the opportunity and an excuse to forget, as he was lifting his mug to drink, Cuilean felt a sudden jarring of his arm which made the PetrAle splash against his face and over his front.

"What the ratfuck ..." Cuilean exclaimed, turning, just about ready to attack the idiot who'd jostled him (with little thought to whether the contact had been purposeful, malign, jocular, or accidental), but he was surprised to see the culprit was a little, old Zziippp with a particularly squinting look – eyes framed by bottle-bottom-thick glasses, his sight depleted from staring for so many years at tiny figures on a handheld screoin – who'd stumbled against him.

"Mepela sorry," the Zziippp said. "Mepela drink plenti too much."

But in righting himself, he happened to lean close to Cuilean's ear, and when he did, *sotto voce*, he said, "Here gowp-cred mepela owe," signifying that he'd transferred credits to Cuilean's account.

His perception shifted, Cuilean maintained the fiction of accidental contact and made a show of helping the old Zziippp right himself, loudly asked, "You okay there, fella?"

"Sorry, mepela drink much," the Zziippp apologized again, repeating himself, and just as he seemed to be pulling away, something stopped him -- a thought that had been niggling at him.

---

[39] *Cianalas* -- this word is probably due an extended note. It refers to what used to be called (in proto-Simspeek) 'homesickness,' that is an emotion of longing for a particular location. However, it is a term of rather broader application and refers not only to a physical location, but also to the people – friends, family, community, culture (and all the things pertaining to culture, such as the customs, behaviors, language, music, stories, social interactions, bonds, ties) of that locality. The word encapsulates not only the longing and the 'missing' of a place (and all its attributes) but also a kind of melancholy or dullness or dreariness that is incorporated into that feeling – as if being separated from that community, society, culture, and environment was akin to being apart from a loved one to whom one is inextricably bound, intermixed with a sense of permanent loss that augments that of "mere" separation.

A poorly-acted, pretend stagger: "How-aa yupela bet tie? Melee match never tie."

"Lucky guess," Cuilean whispered, with an inscrutable expression. *Was that a smile?* With a pat on the Zziippp's back, as if dismissing him, Cuilean said in a voice more for public consumption than private communication, "Maybe you should call it a night." Then, low again: "And not be asking questions that can't be answered."

The Zziippp nodded in agreement. "No mo-aa," before he achieved a remarkable recovery from his drunken stumble and walked straight away.

Before Cuilean could check his gowp-cred account, his ears pricked up at a commotion erupting at the other side of the room. There, a small gowpbarrel[40] of Zziipppaeis was pushing and shoving its way through the crowd amidst shouted objections:

"What're you doing here!"

"No Zziippps allowed!"

"You have your own place!"

But none of the protests seemed to have any effect, and none of the objectors raised the ante by actually standing up and physically confronting the phalanx of gladiatorially-hardened Zziippps.

At the front of which was Slaiya herself, who presented quite a different figure from that in the killing arena. As much as could be accomplished to make a wyrm-silk gown out of a Zziippp's leather hide (as the saying went), Slaiya came across quite delicately: She was decked out in a flowing gown of various shades -- pink, purple, garish red; her skull was framed with a tiara of tiny flashing lights; and about her formerly intimidating expanse fluttered delicate hand motions (that distracted and misdirected from her bulk). She could hardly be recognized as the same exterminator who had so often stood atop the bodies of adversaries on the fight floor. However, when she saw Cuilean, her demeanor changed, reverting back to the cage-killer so well known and loved by millions of bloodthirsty fans – thirsty, that is, for someone else's blood.

Cuilean shifted a sideways glance to see the source of the commotion but turned back, pretending indifference, or even ignorance of it. When the disturbance ceased, the aural space around him filled with an ominous silence.

Still not looking, Cuilean felt the proximity behind him — almost a gravitational presence, so intense was it, along with the hot breaths of the other mouth-breathers upon his arms.

Calmly — he had a bit of a smile on his lips, and an arch to his brow as if he were thinking this would be interesting, or maybe

---

[40] Gowpbarrel of Zziipppaeis – the term for a collective, or group, of the humanoids

even fun — he swiveled around and looked up into Slaiya's crenelated face and beamed woozily. "My friend ..."

"Yupela no fren Slaiya. I wanna savay. Whafor no killim die mepela?"

"Must've slipped my mind. I knew there was something I was supposed to do."

The smirk with which this was delivered infuriated the Zziippp-head, all the more so because even for a Zziipppaei, it made little sense. She puzzled for a moment over Cuilean's non-sequitur of a response, and as if the problem was that Cuilean had not heard her, she hollered: "I wanna savay! Yupela tok!"

Cuilean smiled tightly, because for all his apparent sangfroid, he was conscious – and a bit apprehensive -- of the notice they were attracting.

The prospect of a bar fight didn't faze him, but the possibility of drawing attention did.

Glowering at him, as if she were somehow insulted by having been spared on the Melee Match field, the Zziippp shouted in the high-pitched squeak that was typical of her kind, "Whafor no killim die! Slaiya hed daun shame. Spose killim losin pela die. Not killim die Slaiya. Whafor?"

By this time, Cuilean lost patience and blurted out through clenched lips. "Shut your cock pocket and sit the ratfuck down."

"Whafor sidaun?"

A wry smile. "Because it's a drink that you're owing me."

The answer took the Zziipppaei aback. "Huh?" She blinked repeatedly, rapidly, like a dump-rat caught in a hunter's spotlight. She'd been expecting a confrontation. An answer as hostile as the demand she had just flung at her Melee Match enemy. A punch in the face. A flash of steel. The finishing of the fight not settled on the game field. One of them bleeding out on the floor.

But not this.

Cuilean called out with a sharp bark, "Hey!" The bartend, a half-speesh, a mix of Zziipppaei and Anboarnh, turned as if yanked on a cord in Cuilean's direction.

Barely audibly, Cuilean told him: "I'd like you to be setting us up."

The bartend did his own puzzling out of the odd phrasing but caught the gist. And almost just as immediately, he balked. "I can't serve ..." He indicated the half-dozen Zziipppaeis bunched around Cuilean. "... those ramp-heads." This last word was nearly spit out.

The question came from somewhere down in Cuilean's chest, like a growl. "Is it throwing us out, you're thinking of doing?" And, following an ominous pause during which the server had been invited to think about what that might entail, "Really?"

Something like a snort came from Slaiya. All of a sudden, the Zziippp found herself siding with the man she had come to fight and destroy, or if not that, to die by his hand.

"No, no, it's ok." The guy didn't want a confrontation, certainly didn't want a fight. Not with the champion of the stupendous Electoral Bowl (or would-be champion, supposed-to-be champion, might-have-been champion, or co-champion, or ... *whatever*). "I'm just saying ... my *bosspela*. He might ..."

"If he says anything, you have him talk to us." Cuilean sucked his eyetooth and promised significantly. "I'll *explain*."

"Yeah, yeah, yeah ..." The non-breed evidenced relief at Cuilean's assumption of responsibility, and turning away, muttered, "Let me get those drinks for you now."

Cuilean snatched up the pitcher of PetrAle and chilled mugs that the bartend plonked on the bar. Without looking back at the server, as his hands were full, he was left to indicate an invitation to Slaiya with a head nod: "Let's find a table."

For all her anger and readiness to finish what had not been settled in the fight cage, and as accustomed as she was to striding confidently and forcefully and with deadly intent onto the killing field of the melee match arena, Slaiya hesitated at the expanse of tables in the bar.

Cuilean questioned her. "Is this alright?"

"Zziippps no can go dere ..." she offered.

"We'll see." Cuilean led the way to table at the far side of the barroom – one with a chair rooted against the wall and with a clear view of the area.

Three Anboarnhs were already sitting at it and saw the mob of Zziippps led by Cuilean, the now-famous almost-champion of the Bowl match. Who hadn't seen the come-from-behind victory? Who didn't have an opinion about Cuilean's refusal to take the *kill shot* at the final moment?

One called out, "Hey, chump!"

"What'd you say?"

"Your stunt reamed me in the ass."

"Maybe it's not your ass you should be betting."

Cuilean had a manner of saying a joke – if it was a joke – with a straight face, eying the other person closely like a sword-tooth tiger gauging the prospects of taking down a red deer, a manner that prompted the listener to question -- *Did he say that? Is he serious? Is he insulting me? Is he challenging me? Is he joking?* – but that gave no clue what the answer to those crucial, life-determining questions might be, although underlying it all was the impression that Cuilean was waiting in anticipation, as in, *This just might be fun.*

Cuilean tipped the import of his meaning: "But if you want to bet your *head* ..."

"Let it go, Arnau," one of the Anboarnh's friends warned him, giving him a tug on the arm.

"But I lost ..."

"Doesn't matter how much."

"Maybe you should listen to your friend, *Ar-noo*," Cuilean suggested with an exaggerated intonation, his eyes now slitted. He dug into the sporran that hung from his belt. He flipped his handheld out and casually transferred gowp-creds to the Anboarnh. "Here. Buy yourself some fun. Drinks, drugs, dawgs. *Whatev.* I can afford it. I didn't lose my head. Or my *ass* ..." This last with a mocking leer.

Arnau was just about to say something, but his friend pulled him back and thrust himself protectively between the two. "Thanks, thanks." he said, and pivoting rapidly, he spun Arnau around and pushed him back and away.

"But I ..." Arnau protested over his shoulder.

But whatever he was about to say, his friend cut it off in a hushed tone between clenched teeth. "Drop it. Not worth it. You wanna get yourself killed?" And perhaps of more urgent concern: "You wanna get all of us killed!?!"

The other two of Arnoo's drinking buddies backed away from the table with nods of appeasement and forced grins, in the process knocking over a couple of chairs.

Cuilean gave a suck to his teeth and a quick shake to his head and a subtle sigh, resigned to the realization that whatever game he might have gotten going with this bunch wouldn't have been that much fun, anyway. They were already sucking the Petrale dick. They would have fallen down with just breathing on them.

Switching to playing the gracious host, Cuilean motioned with his hand. "Looks like this table is open. Have a seat gentle-Zziippps."

Dumbfounded, Slaiya sat clumsily. "Wat-aa yupela wanna tok?"

"I'll be telling you." Cuilean reached for the pitcher of PetrAle and poured a mug, which he pushed across the table. He splashed a top-off into his own drink (his fine motor control not being all that precise after what he had already drunk) and slid the pitcher towards Slaiya's companions with a hand motion that said, *Help yourselves.*

"I wanna savay ..." This time, Slaiya's demand was more subdued, filtered between her being confounded by Cuilean's complete non sequitur of a response to her abortive assault, accompanied by the discomfort at being in a forbidden section of the bar. She gripped the mug with both hands as if it were the only thing holding her up from falling into the Grand Inland Catchbasin.

Cuilean flapped his hand as if to signal, *drink*.

Slaiya took a swig, and on another flap of the hand from Cuilean, took a deeper draft, finishing the glass and placing it down with a thump on the table.

Cuilean noted with satisfaction, "*Sin agad e* -- There you have it. There you are." The words had escaped him as a verbal/mental hiccup brought on by the head-banging he'd just received in the match. He had spoken under his breath before he could think, and not expecting to be heard or understood, and though he wasn't quite sure what the words meant, that ignorance did not excuse him. The gowp-wyrm registered the FT and shot a warning jolt into the base of his brain. Cuilean's eyes watered from the leash injection.

He went on quickly, reflexively covering the indiscretion of using the FT: "If it was killing you that I had done," Cuilean explained — knowing full well that what he said explained nothing — "you wouldn't be buying me the drink you owe me."

"Mepela no payim drink yupela!"

"Havta payim!" Cuilean retorted, slipping into the Zziipppaei's TokTok. "Yupela owe."

Doubly taken aback by Cuilean's code-switching and his insistence, the Zziipppaei protested with something close to a squeal. "No-aa!" But Cuilean could see the creature wracking her ball-bearing-sized brain for the memory of a debt owed.

"Let me be asking you this," Cuilean continued, betting it was not obvious he was making it all up as he went along — but even if it were, would a Zziippp-head get it? "What's the least your life is worth?"

The Zziipppaei squinted, not quite comprehending.

"Could you be saying a drink?"

"Yea-sa, bigpela."

"Well, then, who let you live?"

"Bigpela yupela."

"So, Bigpela givim yupela laif blong yupela when yupela lusim fight?"

"Givim," Slaiya agreed, although somewhat disgruntledly.

"So where is the payment for your life? What's your life worth?"

Slaiya felt the ground of certainty slipping out from under her. "Whafor payim life blong mepela?" The Zziippp had never considered that her life might be worth anything. She panted with the effort of contemplating such an alien idea before giving up.

It was only then that Cuilean let a twinkle of a smile crack the side of his lips. "Yupela payim wanna drink."

The sight of Cuilean's grin penetrated Slaiya's consciousness. "Bigpela tok funny!" she squealed in delight that this *whatever* it was that Cuilean was – *not a Zziippp, not an Anboarnh, but something else* -- was speaking to her as if she mattered, as if she were a person.

"A drink with a friend is not a funny," Cuilean said seriously.

The Zziippp asked incredulously, "Cuilean fren Slaiya?"

"Tru dat. Cuilean gudpela fren yupela." Cuilean gave a diagonal nod. "Then why shouldn't you be having a drink with the friend who gave you your life back."

The logic was overwhelming for Slaiya. Even trying to work it out made her head hurt. She grabbed the pitcher and slopped her mug full with the drink. "Well, mepela drink den!" she exclaimed, raising her glass. "Mepela gudpela fren Cuilean!"

"Mepela gudpela fren Slaiya," Cuilean rejoined.

After their second or third or fourth round (but *who was counting?*), Slaiya ventured, "Wan ting me wanna savay, gudpela fren."

"Wha dat?"

"How yu savay TokTok?"

Cuilean touched the side of his nose and allowed a warm smile to penetrate his usually pained expression. He leaned forward with a wink, "Wan day mepela tok yu. No-aa saif hee-aa."

Her tongue protruding from between her lips, Slaiya nodded conspiratorially.

At this point, it would be too much to say that Cuilean had a plan. But with the blow for which he had Slaiya to thank, the *whomp* that had rattled something loose in his mind, had come a glimmer of an intimation, like heat waves rising off the floor of the Plain of Desolation, an emanation in the penumbra. It wasn't a plan, much less an objective, but perhaps it was a vague inkling that could be grown into a notion, and from there nurtured into an egg of an idea, from which could be hatched a definitive goal, and out of that, be schematized into a full-fledged strategy.

Or, perhaps not.

With his gowp-cred account now bulging with his winnings, he had some options he hadn't enjoyed even the day before, even though he wasn't clear what those options might be.

But there was one way to find out, and even though that path had not appeared to him yet, he was thinking that he might have caught a glimpse of a glimmer of light that gave hope of an opening through the dense foliage of a dark forest.

~~

Go longlong cwaze

Is minig a thàinig comhairle ghlic à ceann an amadain.
Often has come wise advice come from the head of a fool.

Proverb from *Leabhar an Leaghaidh Mhòir* —
The Book of the Great Melting

Many drinks in, and half a dozen marches down the lines, as Cuilean and Slaiya were apportioning out the last dregs from the most recent pitcher, a Zziippp male appeared by the table. He was about half the size of Slaiya (though it was difficult to tell as she was seated, but even then, with her sitting and his standing, they were the same height). He was carrying a squirming, crying, Zziip-babe.

"Herpela wanna mumsy," the father Zziippp said, explaining their presence. The Zziipppbabe reached with an urgent squeal for Slaiya.

"Dis mepela lovpela," she said by way of introduction to Cuilean. To her Zziippp spouse, she said, "Dis mepela fren Cuilean."

"And who's this?" Cuilean said, lightly fingering the baby's hand.

"Dis uspela Zziip-babe," she said, and Slaiya, several-times all pro fighter, gold-ringed and gold belted champion of the killing ring, proud possessor of 32 plastisheen-encased challengers' heads, reached for the Zziip-babe, which was barely larger than her paw, and took it gently from the father and coddled it against her breasts, rocking it gently, and soothing it with a succession of birdlike chirps.

Presently, the Zziippp spawn stopped squirming and cooed contently. "Mepela tok fren mo-aa time," she told her lovpela. "Home sma time," she added as she handed the ZZiippp-babe back to the father. She made a kissy face, which looked more like the puckering of an aptrac truck tire than any invitation to smooch, and the two brushed lips.

As her lovpela made his way out of the bar with their baby, Slaiya lingered her gaze on them, and with a sigh, she leaked the admission of her emotion: "Mepela sad."

Cuilean scrutinized her intently. *Was that a drop of moisture in her eye?*

Slaiya shook her head as if to flick off an annoying pest that had just bitten her and concentrated on draining the last of her PetraAle.

Cuilean caught her eye when she set the mug down, and with an expression of sympathetic curiosity, he mouthed the question, *why?*

"Mepela no lukim lovpelas no mo-aa."

"What? Why won't you see them anymore?"

"I go longlong road," Slaiya announced.

Not quite understanding, for people – much less Zziippps – didn't go away, or go anywhere. "Where's it you're going?"

The Zziippp made an upward motion with her thumb and tilting her chin up, arched her eyebrows.

Unbelievable: "How is it you're going?"

"Mepela be trade ..."

"No! What! You were traded? Why? It's an MVP that you are." As long as he had been in the DownBlow, Cuilean's old habits of speaking had stayed with him, not necessarily the words, though sometimes those would erupt out of him in unexpected moments or filter through his dreams like ghosts, but the pattern was there, the rhythm of speaking, and hence of thinking. "It's a twelve-time All Pro Melee Matcher that is in you."

A shrug from Slaiya said more eloquently than she could ever have put into words that all that didn't make a rat-shit's worth of difference. "Mepela lose em," she explained. "No mo-aa gudpela dem."

What more could Cuilean say or do than offer a shake of the head? "Yupela no go bigfela garden?" he asked, referring to the euphemistically called *farm* (which was itself a euphemism). And then answering his own question, he followed up with a comforting suggestion: "Maybe they'll send you to war. Mo-aa gud than bigpela garden."

The Zziippp's countenance brightened hopefully at the prospect of going to war before it clouded with the reality. "No-aa farm. No-aa war. Mo-aa nogud."

"What's mo-aa nogud than farm?"

"Mepela go Wayp." The Zziippp made a face and chewed her lip.

"Oh, is that all? It's not that bad up there."

"How yupela savay dat?"

A good question. How did he know? Again, the strange image — a flash of green and with it the memory of a brazen trumpeting, and a word — *langanach* — though what it meant, he didn't know, but somehow the word went with the sound, which carried with it as if on a cool wind a longing, a yearning (though there was no wind in the desert islands of the Pelago except that which threw biting bits of sand and ground-down shards of glass and other detritus at anyone foolhardy enough to go outside without full protective face- and body-coverings).

The hesitation covered a multitude of disclosures.

"Al time mepela tink yupela TokTok blong nudderpela place." She flipped her wrist over his shoulder as if tossing a pinch of salt to indicate the past tense "thought."

A glimmer of an idea showed in Slaiya's expression as if somebody had switched on a dim bulb in a cavernous warehouse, and too quickly following up for Cuilean to answer, the Zziippp leaned her crenulated head forward, as misshapen as a run-over roadkill, as blunt as mammoth's skull, and probed Cuilean's countenance as if she would find the answer to her question there -- in his face rather than in his words -- and demanded rather than asked, "Where from yupela!"

Cuilean looked away, scanned the room, and lifted his chin and rolled his eyes up. A sideways nod: "It's a long time that it's been."

Self-satisfied in the confirmation of her guess, the Zziippp mouthed "Mepela tink dat." Leaning forward, she asked under her breath, "Whafor yupela hee-aa?"

Cuilean gave his friend a wry look – a slight twist to his mouth accompanied by an audible sucking of his teeth as if to say, *whadayathink*? He shifted to TokTok because even though the monitors could pick up that some non-Simspeek was being spoken, the computer algorithms were not capable of transcribing the words in anything but gibberish. Even then, he cast his voice in a low enough pitch so as to hide what he said under the cover of the bar's noise, "Watem yupela tink?"

A gasp of breath as if a child seeing Ratta Claws, the giant mythical rat that brought presents to all good Zziipppaei children. "You tok Wayp TokTok?" she asked in astonishment, and exclaimed in disbelief (such a thing was not possible): "No-aa!"

The only response from Cuilean was an arching of his brows. Then with a pained expression, "Hurt much ..." he motioned at the wyrm-leash around his neck. It hurt to think about it, to try to remember. Not some traumatic memory kind of hurt, but a real visceral, white-hot-spike-in-the-brain kind of hurt.

It actually wasn't that long ago, but with the medications and the wyrm-leash, it just seemed as long ago as ... a phrase came to him — *linn cogadh nan con* (though not without the concomitant penalty). He couldn't have told what it meant, though he *knew*: the *age of the wars of the dogs*, whatever *that* meant — although the gist of it being it was a long time ago. As long ago as the Great Melt, perhaps.

"Mepela wanna savay. Wat-aa like dere?"

An expression from Cuilean, as if to say, *you're not going to let this go, are you?*

To Slaiya's answering expression – a silent demand --Cuilean ventured, "Lot different from here, that's for sure."

"Wat-aa Wayp like?"

Cautiously, Cuilean ventured an answer as if sneaking out the memory and sliding it under the table to Slaiya. As he did so, a vision came floating down to him like a view through a mist. "It's green."

"So wat? Uspela got green." Slaiya grabbed the face of his newly-made friend, gripping and squeezing his cheeks so he looked like a puffer-slug. She swiveled Cuilean's gaze towards a woman walking by. She was the perfect image of female pulchritude: her plump breasts thrusting forward, supported by twin trusses so the eyes of her nipples stared straight out, and a tuft of green pubic hair-lush in the cleavage of her crotchless pants. The only thing that gave away her identity as an aiRep was her flawless skin, as smooth as porcelain and as white. Not that Cuilean could tell the difference in his present state. "Like dat," Slaiya said.

Cuilean fluttered his lips and blew a raspberry that sounded like a 12-Zziipppaei paddle boat skimming across the water. But he was on the track of an idea, and despite this momentary distraction, he would not be put off. "Not green like that." He winced from the effort of concentrating on the memory. *Was it a memory? A drug-induced hallucination?* He wasn't sure, couldn't quite tell, but whatever it was, he went with it: "It's like stuff growing ..."

"Like bigfela algae garden?"

"No, plants, trees ... and not even in a garden ... out in the ..." He struggled for the TokTok word.

Slaiya screwed up her face. "Watem?"

Cuilean hit on it: "Bigplais. In bigplais garden."

"No in-house garden?" Slaiya asked, not quite understanding, referring to the enclosed nurseries in which everything was grown to protect it from the toxic atmosphere outside the domed enclosures.

"No-aa, outside house garden. Outside dome. No-aa dome!"

Slaiya drew in her breath in astonishment "Outside no-aa killim die?"

Cuilean shook his head.

"Watem kind stuf kom up?"

Cuilean was at a complete loss for words to explain to his companion what kind of plants grew in the Wayp, for there were no words in TokTok or even in Simspeek to describe what he wanted to, so he resorted to "Big algae. Bigger than Anboarnh. Bigger than Zziipppaei."

And as an afterthought – "Animals, too."

"Uspela got amal." The Zziippp sounded defensive. "Mo-aa amal: rat, cockroach, deserliz, gowp-wyrm ..." She drifted off, having come to the end of her taxonomic list.

"No," Cuilean offered, "other animals ... big animals. Like you haven't seen ... like used to live on the earth before the Great Melt."

This was too much forbidden thought for Cuilean. His wyrm-leash tightened in warning. If he had considered it, Cuilean might have been surprised that the leash had allowed him to recount even this much.

A picture came to his mind that made him flinch: the image of a red-headed girl beside a lake. Oddly enough, he knew that it was a lake that he was seeing with his memory's eye, only that wasn't the word that came to mind. He winced again at the memory of a body of clear water stretching far away to the base of a snow-capped mountain, but each imagined sight of the scene was accompanied by a sting. He shook his head as if to flick off a carnivorous flying dragon wyrm, one that was burrowing into his ear with a high-pitched whine.

"*Loch* ..." he muttered, though he hadn't intended to be heard.

"Watem?"

"I just remembered something ... water. Fresh water ..."

Slaiya squinched up her face and cocked her head like a pet rat trying to understand what a person was saying: *What's that? "Weaedaarr?"*[41]

Cuilean enunciated: "Water ... *waa-tur* ..." Hitting the "t" hard for emphasis. "And it's clear, not brown like here. And it's in the ground. All over the place."

"In dirty groun'? No-aa in gowp?" Slaiya curled her lips in disgust at the thought.

Not to be deterred, Cuilean pressed on. Even though the memory burned like a dragon wyrm's stinger in his brain: "*Uisge.*"

"Watem?"

"It's what we ..." He faltered and lowered his voice even further, just for safety (he could never be sure what the wyrm-leash might pick up), before he continued: "What *they* call it."

"Whafor dempela makim dat?"

---

[41] Weaedaarr -- Waste Excrement and Excreta Derived Aqua Alternative Reprocessed Replacement

"They don't 'make' it. It just is. It's in the ground or it comes from the sky ..." To Slaiya's puzzled expression, he explained further: "From uptop ... from *a' mhàthair*." He winced as the leash delivered a shock for uttering a forbidden word.

"Wat-aa?"

He decided to chance an explanation. *In for a drop, in for a barrel of gowp*, as they said. "The 'Mother' – the 'Goddess.'"

"Wat-aa?"

"Like GAWD."

"Wat-aa com from uptop?"

"Rain."

"No tru. Rain fire hot."

"But this rain doesn't burn. And another thing, too. They don't talk Simspeek or even TokTok."

"No? Dempela no-aa TokTok?"

"Nope."

The idea was thought-shattering. "How-aa dempela tok den?"

"It's like they have a different word for everything."

Slaiya was shocked. Even though what Cuilean was suggesting was ridiculous in that it was impossible that any reality existed outside the one universal Wuarardd of Gawd[42] she was close to being scandalized. She'd never heard such heresy. Involuntarily, reflexively, she reached across the table and put her fingers over Cuilean's lips, lest her friend get himself arrested for blasphemy.

She was strangely, dangerously intrigued, too. She couldn't resist snatching at the bait. Although it was against her desire and self-interest to engage (lest she be accused of being an accomplice, aider, and abettor of apostasy), the idea was so outrageous that she couldn't help herself from blurting out her objection. "No-aa!" Which was by implication also an invitation to Cuilean to continue.

If Slaiya had been angry before at Cuilean's desecrating the sacrosanct rules of the Melee Match and not killing her, now she felt her temperature really rising like the bubbling cauldron of the Grand Inland Catchbasin. "Just wan wod blong wan ting. Wan ting.

---

[42] Wuarardd (WUARARDD) of Gawd -- Worldwide, Universally Accepted Reality Authorized by the Regulation of Dogma Division of Gawd (see Gawd).

A fact established by the great linguist Nimh Chimpsky (may his name be entered in the Profit's side of the Eternal Final Audit) was that there aren't any differences between languages: Every language is the same, and all undergirded by the Universal Fundaments of Language, which was what Simspeek and TokTok – the first for the Anboarnh and the second for Zziipaeis, whose intellects could not handle the more complicated structures of Simspeek -- were predicated on; and as the Monstrato Corps had these as the universal standard for communication, it was considered anathema to use any other than the WARWD OF GAWD (see ref. WARWD OF GAWD).

Wan wod. No two wod. Two wod pain hed. Mean em dat? Mean em dis? Ting 1? Ting 2?" She demonstrated with her two forefingers to show the difference between the two things. "Pain mepela hed. WUARARDD GAWD tok tru. Wan tru! No savay two tru!" She shook her head vigorously as if throwing off a bad dream.

Cuilean had been smirking mischievously, but his wicked glee dissipated when he saw how distressed Slaiya had become. Contrary to his usual inclination, he had no wish to further tease his friend. "I no-aa wanna go Wayp now-aa," the Zziipppaei whined disconsolately. "Nogud place."

Cuilean tried to smooth over the horror story he'd just told. "No-aa nogud place," he said reassuringly. "Good place."

"You makim mepela feel gud." The Zziipppaei pointed a stubby forefinger at Cuilean. "I go bad plais. Yu winim. No trade yupela. You no go."

A wry face came to Cuilean, as if a sudden taste of unseasoned wyrm. He shrugged, but it was a shrug feigning indifference as a wave of desire swept over him, not so much that he wanted to, that he was conscious of wanting, but there was *something* he couldn't quite identify.

Again, he heard that *langanach*, and this time it seemed to be calling him in the form of a memory of a day that came to him like a blow to the head.

He attempted to cover the vision that overwhelmed him by reaching for the pitcher, but there was a snap and a crackle in the cowl-leash as the circuits crisscrossed, commanding him to cease his *wrong-think*. The shock from the leash made his hand jerk as he was pouring the last of the PetrAle pitcher, slopping it over the table top. He clenched his teeth against the stabbing in his brain.

"Want to. Get to. Have to. Not much of a difference, is there?" for the obstacle to his returning to the Wayp was as a wall as high as the cliffs rising up from the sea. A conundrum. An imponderable, or if not imponderable — for it was, at that, ponderable, for one could ponder it -- but even if pondered, it would at bottom remain unfathomable, unsolvable, inscrutable (resistant to being scrutinized).

"Watim rong?" Slaiya asked. "Drink plenti too much?"

"I was just thinking about something else. Lost track."

It suddenly came to Slaiya -- an unusual and unexpected insight. Amazed at the totally unexpected wonder of the revelation, in a drunkenly theatrical whisper, she hushed: "Yupela wanna go!"

"Even if it was wanting that I was, it wouldn't be possible. No way to get out of the Melee slaiv contract."

"No-aa," Slaiya agreed.

As Cuilean glanced around for the waitress to order yet more

PetrAle to aid his forgetting, Slaiya's demeanor was a study in a search for understanding. Something unaccustomed to the Zziipppaei: a thought, which she strained to get out, as if she were passing whole a giant rat, one clawing with viciously long nails and biting with needle-sharp teeth as it worked its way through her intestines. Finally, she ventured, "Less ..." and left the word hanging there between her lips and Cuilean's ears.

There was something unfinished, irresistibly compelling to the phrase that prompted Cuilean to ask: "Unless what?"

"Less," she went on, stopping to process the idea that had come to her out of the gowp dark. (As it is written in the *Protocols of the Profit*, "From the mouths of Zziippp-babes ...") Slaiya leaned halfway across the table, and glancing around to make sure that no one else could see what she was thinking – as if her thoughts were blazoned across her non-existent forehead -- she lifted the PetrAle bottle close to her lips in order to cover them and muttered in a barely audible voice with a flicker of a glance into Cuilean's eyes, "Less Bigpela Cuilean go longlong cwaze. No gudpela dem no mo-aa."

And that was it.

That was when Cuilean's itch was transformed into an inkling, which would soon evolve into a notion (though not yet transmogrified into an idea, much less developed into a plan), but that was the beginning of it: *Go longlong cwaze.*

~~

For GAWD

[Global Access to Wealth Directorate]
All praise to the Profit!

Cha dèan cridhe misgeach breug.
A drunken heart doesn't lie.
Proverb from *Leabhar an Leaghaidh Mhòir* —
The Book of the Great Melting

The room was feeling just right, comfortably spinning like a slow merry-go-round. Slaiya and Cuilean had hunkered over their pitchers of PetrAle, arguing over the nature of reality, truth, and whether true love existed or if it was just the ass-explosions spewed out by screoin songsters.

You might wonder what views a mere Zziippp might have on such matters, but once you got to know them, they weren't as simple-minded as many of the Anboarnhs thought. For instance, Slaiya held some views that were quite unique, if not heretical, one of which was that there was more to life than accumulating barrels of gowp: "All wanna mo-aa gowp, barrelful gowp, fill house with much gowp-barrel, but no mo-aa happy." That it was possible for Zziippps and Anboarnhs to live together without one being lower than the other – that Zziippps and Anboarnhs were equal (a view perhaps encouraged by her experience in countless melee matches): "Anboarnh not mo-aa gooder den Zziippp." And most heretically, "Mepela dream," she said, leaning even closer, "what if no gowp? What if ocean not fire, air not burn breathe, but everything like in bigpela garden?"

But all these opinions, of course, were whispered across the table in the bar that was so noisy that the surveil screoins couldn't pick up the blasphemy being spoken.

By this time, however, if she were to be called before the Court of Inquiry and forced to give testimony against herself, there was little chance that she would remember anything she'd said. Her eyes had the opacity of an oil-blackened windshield in a gowp blizzard.

Cuilean wondered how the Zziipppaei could even see out of them. Not that his own vision was any clearer. Only, his own hazel eyes had the quality of somebody looking out through a blood besmeared facemask that had been caught in a flying cockroach storm and hundreds and thousands of the insects had smashed themselves against the no-longer clear gowpaleen. His gaze had the quality of a hunter – which was his position in Melee Match, so that made sense: You weren't quite sure who was behind there, just that there was somebody seeing, observing, calculating, measuring, stalking, aiming.

Cuilean weaved his head back and forth to keep Slaiya in focus, swaying in synchrony with her own pendulating, because for some reason, she obstinately insisted on going in and out of focus, splitting in two and remerging into one ugly, massive natborn Zziippp monstrosity. Not that Cuilean was prejudiced against the natborns, for where he came from, the Wayp (although he hardly remembered it, so effective had his memory-bleaching been), everyone was a natborn, unlike here in the Pelagoes where those who could afford it -- the Anboarnhs -- had their children manufactured to exacting specifications.

Cuilean's attention (as well as that of everyone else in the tavern) was diverted to the wall screoin, where Magnus Mugwump, The Chairman of the Chamber of Commerce Association for Securing Trade and Prosperity (COCASTAP) was addressing the 666th Virtual Meeting of the Corporate Congress. "We are gathered here," he read from a prepared statement, working his hands back and forth in front of him as if he were playing an accordion. He paused to ad-lib: "And a very good gathering it is, too, I think, one of the best ..." before continuing with his original thought ... "to prevent a massive violation of corporate rights." Another interjection: "A terrible violation, one of the largest in all of history."

He spread his hands and pinched his forefingers and thumbs together as if stretching a rat's cradle between them to demonstrate just how large the violation was. "Insurges operating under the banner of the Wayp Water League have infiltrated the major population centers of that beleaguered land and are even now subjecting the corporate owners of the privately held gowp properties to gross violations of their rights as corporate citizens," he said, adding, "And remember, corporations are hoomans,[43] too – very fine hoomans, some of the best. Even now, the Insurges are

---

[43] HOOMAN (as in Hooman life) – Humanoid Organically Originated (or) Manufactured (and) Artificially Nurtured

threatening to force the Wayp legislature to claim collective ownership of all water resources, preventing the Corporation from pumping the gowp out of the ground and accessing the gowp resources that belong to the Monstrato Corps."

Mugwump continued: "In doing this, they have violated the rights of the Corporation. Furthermore, they have terrorized countless Pelago citizens living and working there by assaulting them in the streets and public places with the sounds of their sneaky little Insurge language in clear breach of the International Conventions on Simspeek."

On the spur of the moment, the thought came to him to comment on his speech-writer's text: "A terrible fate! Such a terrible fate! Oh, the hoomanity!" He turned sideways from the camera and leaned forward so far that it appeared that he would teeter over. "This violation of the Universal Declaration of Corporate Rights will not stand! (Very bad to stand!) And that is why I am ordering an expeditionary force of the Monstrato PieceTakers to restore order and protect innocent property against these bad people. (Very bad! The absolute worst!)"

Evidently responding to the eyes-on-screoin data that the attention of the audience across the viewing world was waning, the image cut to another scene, one in which there were flashes of light, the sounds of massive explosions and of the rumbling of aptracs. The United Corporations' flag fluttered as a watermark in the background, and the words flashed on the screen amidst a blaring of processional music:

The United Corporations
of
The Pelagoes
Presents
Worldwide Operation – Liberating Funds!
(WOLF)

Ta-daaa! Blared the synthetic trumpets, and immediately the electric guitar riffs of the Corporation's anthem played loudly over the speakers. When the song got to "by the gowp-geysers' light," everyone in the bar was on their feet. And by the time the song reached the lines,

cluster bombs bursting in air
shock and awe everywhere,

the entire crowd had feverishly joined in.

While everyone else stood transfixed before the swelling music, the hypnotically strobing lights (interspersed with micro-second long bursts of print spelling out slogans such as "Fight!" or "Corporate Freedom!" or "Join Up!"), and images of Monstrato PieceTakers in uniforms the color of oil-drenched sand marching bravely towards battle to secure the rights to gowp  access and freedom from the tyranny of language terrorists, and images of brave Zziipppaei warriors running and shooting at an unseen enemy, Cuilean noticed something else in the background of the broadcast image: a green landscape and free-flowing water, heard -- somehow, though he could not have told you how, nor even what it meant – the beckoning like a whispering on the wind -- *Tiugainn dhachaigh* – Come home.

An Anboarnh next to Cuilean, noticing the tears streaming from his eyes in response to the shock he'd received on account of his outlaw thought, wrapped his arm around Cuilean's shoulders. "Hey, buddy, we all feel this," and picked up the song and sang more loudly than he had been.

The video clip on the screoin ended with the slogan emblazoned ... "CAGAAA!!!" and under it the written subscript of the words the acronym represented: "Creating Archipelago Greatness, Affluence, and Abundance Again!!"

"Yaay!" went the crowd.

"Uspela go take!" someone shouted from the Zziipppaei side of the bar.

"Yaay!" shouted the crowd. "Take!" The ability to articulate any ideas more complicated than that being at a low ebb, "Yay!" was repeated more loudly and more certainly, if not with more complexity.

Cuilean pushed his way to the front of the crowd and leaped up onto the bar. Demonstrably excited, frenzied, his hair standing on end, his eyes pulsing larger and larger, his visage that of an enraged demon, he shouted, "Take!"

The crowd in the bar shouted back: "Take!"

"Take!" he yelled.

"Taaayk!" the mob in the bar yelled in a response that transformed into a rhythmic chant: "Take! Take! Take! Take!"

Sensing growing trouble, Slaiya edged closer, and finally within range, she reached up and tugged on her friend's arm. "Cuilean. Yupela makim bad trouble. Kom down."

Which idea was echoed: "I need you get down there," a bartender called up to him. He was a natborn — a Zziippp, but of a higher order, one that could almost pass for an Anboarnh, that is, without the typical downwardly-ramping forehead of his kind. His face was the pasty white of a life-long dome-dweller, somebody who had never spent a moment scorching at the fire-geysers of the Great Inland Drains, and he was capable of a low, truncated, pidgin Simspeek. There was a controlled urgency to his voice, like someone who was afraid of losing his job and being thrown out of the dome for failing to maintain control. *I trying hold everything together, but this rat-nuts-cake jumped up top the bar.*

"I need you to get up from there," Cuilean retorted.

"I mean it!" the bartender called out, his voice taking on more and more the sound of trying to keep it together while it was all coming apart. "No business way up there!"

"And you have no business DownBlow there!" Cuilean shouted back with a broad smirk.

Cuilean yelled out across the tops of the drinkers' heads. "I'm way up!"

Several in the crowd, now noticing him, cheered.

The bar-Zziippp reached up for Cuilean, but the *killa from the hilla* skipped away merrily, scattering the assorted glasses, mugs, pitchers, bottles, and appetizer plates that were set up on the bar top. "Can't get me!" he giggled, running to the far end of the bar.

The bartender chased him from DownBlow. Other servers joined in, reaching up to pull him down, Cuilean running and leaping and skittering and scooting to avoid them, laughing – perhaps, closer to giggling maniacally -- the whole time.

Ginned up by the calls to exciting action by the broadcast, the packed mass in the saloon, their attention having shifted from the display on the screoin to the hilarious goings-on right in front of them, were cheering for the erupting chaos. They surged in an inchoate, frenzied mass, upending tables, throwing chairs, smashing glasses and pitchers, whatever they could get their hands on.

Behind Cuilean, the tapster-Zziippp climbed up on the bar and warily approached the skipping, coulda-been champion of the melee match. Other servers followed, and they advanced in a disorganized line, stepping sideways uncertainly, fearful of falling.

In the face of their faltering progress, Cuilean found himself cornered at the far edge of the bar. He looked out across the mass of cheering faces, swung his arms back and then forward and flung himself into their midst as if diving into a mosh pit.

No sooner was he set on his feet than a rent-a-PieceTaker security guard forced his way through the mob to him. This bouncer was a huge Zziippp with no neck, fingers as thick as sea-slugs, and a forehead that ramped directly from the high-peaked crown at the back of his skull down to his eyes. "Wad wrong?" he demanded in a typically squeaky Zziippp-head voice.

The bar-tend was right behind the guard and jabbed a finger from around the safety of the PieceTaker's bulk and yapped peevishly: "There is! That him! Big maker trouble him! Plenty too much drink. Start fight. No stand up straight."

Indeed, Cuilean was reeling from the PetrAle and assorted other substances he'd imbibed.

Almost casually, apparently thinking Cuilean at this point presented little threat (or that the greatest risk he posed was the likelihood of his falling down and having to be carried out, or worse yet, of his puking all over anybody and everybody within vomit-throw range), the rent-a-PieceTaker reached out to grab Cuilean by the arm, and in a flash – deceptively quick for somebody who appeared not to be able to stand up straight -- Cuilean hooked the outstretched arm by the tricep and dragged it past him. He swiveled around behind the rent-a-PieceTaker, swiping the kabloey nestled in the holster on his hip.

As if he'd just won a move in an exciting, consuming game of wack-a-rat, Cuilean cried out triumphantly, "Ha ha!" and swung the kabloey around. "I'll show you standing up straight." As was the practice, the weapon was primed, loaded, ready for the fuse to be lit, and fired. He leveled the gun in the direction of the bartender.

The movement froze the barkeep. Cuilean's fury was seemingly uncontainable. It had a voice and a direction of its own. "Now, whadaya say? You dickless wyrm licker?" he demanded of the bar-Zziippp, or in the direction of where he thought the bartender was, for there seemed to be a couple of them now where there had been but one.

Cuilean lost focus on everybody else in the bar as the faces in the crowd faded into the background, and he trained the sights of the gun first on one of the bartenders and then on the other, his aim wavering back and forth between the two.

Then there were four facing off before him: two rent-a-PieceTakers and two bar-Zziippps. They must have been two sets of identical twins. *Curious!* Cuilean wondered, *What're the odds?*

The twin bar-Zziippps screamed a little-girl shriek and froze in terror.

The crowd of stool huggers around the bar thought this outburst was funny and exploded in riotous, hysterical laughter, which was contagious and caught Cuilean up in it, dissipating his anger. With a broad grin, he triggered the lighting of the kabloey's fuse (it was outfitted with an automatic ignition), shifted his aim just enough to miss the hapless bartender -- and shot a round into the screoin above the bar, shattering it into a thousand shards of flying gowpaleen glass.

The room spiraled around Cuilean as he searched frantically for his target like a drunk who had misplaced his wallet. Thoughts tumbled against each other, fighting like dump-rats in a sack. It was here a minute ago ... *He* was here a minute ago. Cuilean cried out, "Where's that sonofaratfucker!"

The shattered screoin flickered with flashes of images of rampaging Water League Insurges ransacking the Monstrato Corps' pumping stations; and of horrified immigrant Pelago mothers holding their children's ears against the obscene sounds of the Forbidden Tongue. The narrator's staticky voice -- broken into fragments like the screoin itself -- crackled from the fractured equipment:

> *... calm fears ... not make bad situation worse ... risk to corporate associates ... no choice ... act swiftly and strongly ... let me be clear ... horrified by the events ... restore lawfully elected regime ... Insurge renegades ... not an invasion ... liberation of corporate assets ... the objectives ... not create chaos, but preserve it ... destroy Wayp to save it ..."*

And the like, so on and so forth.

Still, Cuilean's nemesis, the evil tapster, couldn't be located.

Somebody shouted, "He's getting away!"

The cry penetrated the fog of Cuilean's stupefied rage. He was puzzled. *Who was getting away? Getting away from what? Getting away* **with** *what? What did getting away even mean?*

"There!" somebody else whooped, and Cuilean alerted to what he imagined was a movement at the door. He leveled the kabloey, but its load had already been fired, and it responded with a futile fizz as the fuse failed to find a live round in the firing chamber.

Somebody incited him with a shove. "Go get 'im! There he goes!"

The crowd laughed as Cuilean ran to the door and burst through the airlock into the toxic outdoor air.

Outside, he drunkenly groped for his face mask as at the same time he wildly scanned the smog-filled street. *The fuck-stain wasn't there! No sign of anybody, living, or most to be wished for, dead.* He snarled.

He heard a voice behind him. "Go get 'im, Cuilean!"

There was laughter again.

More shouts of encouragement:

"Get him, Cuilean!"

"Chase him down!"

"Kill the slug-turd!"

Stirred, Cuilean searched the surrounding wafts of fog-thick smoke for a sign of where his prey might have fled.

"There he is, Cuilean!" An arm flashed pointing over his shoulder to a pathway into the thick smoke.

Cuilean felt a giddy laugh rising in his gorge. He gave an inarticulate war cry and bolted where the arm had directed him.

He raced along the narrow street, and as he ran, he was vaguely aware of the stampeding feet keeping up with him.

It was like a pack of bear-wolves chasing down a red deer. And he was the alpha!

Or was he the deer?

He tripped over a curb and splayed onto the sidewalk.

Several hands picked him up. "That way, Cuilean! That way!"

He felt hands spin him around.

"There!"

Cuilean raced off in the new direction he'd been pointed.

A half-dozen Anboarnhs — as pale and slim as the test tubes they'd been incubated in – united in an electrifying new entertainment, chattered and squealed like excited, blood-thirsty muncaidhs of Cuilean's native Wayp.

"Where'd he go!?!" one shouted in a high-pitched voice.

Their shouts prompted Cuilean's own thoughts and goaded him on.

"Where is he!?" another echoed.

Cuilean ran helter-skelter ahead of the chasing mob.

Slaiya lumbered after the pack of wild rats, unable to keep up. "Coo-wan!" she cried out in distress for her friend.

The Anboarnh pursuers mistook the import of her cry (as well as his name). "Yeah! Get 'im, Coo-win!"

"Show the Insurge rat-fucker, Coo-win."

~~

Your mission

(whether you choose to accept it or not)

Gluais cho luath ris a' ghaoth 's bi cho cruaidh ri stàilinn.
Ionnsaigh mar theine 's bi cho daingeann mar a' bheinn.
Move as swiftly as the wind and be as hard as steel.
Attack like fire and be as firm as the mountain.
Proverb from *Leabhar an Leaghaidh Mhòir* —
The Book of the Great Melting

Cuilean swirled in a circle, dizzy, confused, half-blinded by the PetrAle and the rest of what he had imbibed. Everything was a blur -- partly because of his own inebriated state, partly because of the low hanging smoke-and-soot-filled smudge that hung over the city and gave everything a gauzy, hazy, sepia sheen.

He ran smack into a street sign. He couldn't tell whether the obstacle was animate or inanimate, so he decided – so as not to offend – to take the safe course of action and apologize: "Sorry, I didn't see where I was going."

When the pole didn't answer him, Cuilean took offense. "You can say something," he slurred. "You didn't see me either. Least you can do is be a little polite."

The stanchion stood on the curb, stoic, looming threateningly.

"Gonna take that attitude, huh?" Thinking he'd heard a challenge, he amped up the antagonism: "No! You watch where you're going, ratfucker."

Cuilean tackled the post, which was (not surprisingly) unmoved by the attack. Only with his arms around it did he realize ... and apologize. "Sorry, I didn't ..." Realizing how stupid it was to apologize to a pole, he nevertheless gave it a conciliatory pat and stumbled on in his quest.

From above, the light of the moon refracted through the translucent dome and shimmered through the orangish-brown atmospheric haze and smog that wafted through the streets as it did this time of night. The orb seemed to be encompassed with a fiery halo.

The streetlights pirouetted around him as he himself spun dizzily. Finally, he stopped, and breathing in quick pants, he sagged to his knees. "I'll kill that ratfucker," he seethed weakly, his rage flagging in frustration, though by this time, he'd forgotten the precise reason for his grunge.

He was so tired. He slumped and said as much, "Tye-ard." He wanted to go to sleep.

As Cuilean had slowed, and now stopped, his pack of followers closed in on him. Giving up on the sport of seeing Cuilean catch the elusive prey that didn't exist -- maybe a stranger with the bad luck of having ventured out into the evening acid-smog (or the hapless street sign) -- they circled him, laughing and mocking.

"This is cockroach shit."

"The ratfucker's out of his head."

"Get up, Cuilean!"

First one, then the other kicked him. One pulled out a kabloey, lit the fuse, and unloaded a dart into Cuilean's butt.

The Melee Matcher let out an animal squeal, a feeble attempt at muttering an actual word, one that might have been *stop*, or *stay*, or *stand down*, or *stupid shit*, but instead just dribbled out as "Staa ..." which was unintelligible even in TokTok.

The kicks and the blows rained on him. Cuilean was no longer funny on his own account but rather provided entertainment only to the extent that the pack of Anboarnhs could torment him – something they would never have attempted if he were not so obviously helpless to defend himself -- all the while chanting a taunt over the hunched, incapacitated gladiator:

> "Turd on the tide!
> Turd on the tide!
> Shit smear a mile wide!"

Cuilean heard this, but what echoed with him were not these words, but a song that came to him as if on a smog gust from a distance through an open window. As he hunkered in the gritty artificial turf of the simu-garden, he tilted his ear to the tune playing in his head. It was faintly familiar, as if something he'd heard a long time before.

It was as if it were a punch that Cuilean felt, one that shook him out of his reverie, as another one of the Anboarnh mob surrounding Cuilean unloaded another electrified dart from the kabloey. "Let's see if this wakes him up!"

But instead of squealing in hilarious pain, from somewhere arose a deep-throated roar, a sound that started out as a rumbling growl that rose in volume to a rolling thunder and then to the howl of a Wayp sword-tooth tiger.

With one eye squinted, the other grown large, his hair standing on end like the scruff of his sword-tooth mother, his lips curled to reveal the full length of his teeth, his visage distorted in rage, one lip curled upward and the other curled under as if bitten by his own teeth, the tendon and sinews of his left forearm swelled and rippled, that shoulder humped with muscles, and the other by comparison appearing to have shriveled, Cuilean leapt the ten feet that separated him from the Anboarnh snark slammed him with the full force of a bolt from a gowp-canon. The Anboarnh flew into the crowd of his friends, and with a series of shrieks and roars, Cuilean laid into the tormentors, flinging them to one side and the other.

The assailed Anboarnhs let out a jumble of startled yelps and squeals, but one of the them, having been thrown to the wayside and observing the fray from the sideline, realized: "Hey! What're we doing!?! There's just one of 'im!" he shouted.

"Let's get 'im!" Somebody else echoed.

And with that, the small mob coalesced. The lead Anboarnh, a chinless, slack-muscled Level 9, took a step forward.

Cuilean stepped back.

The Anboarnh chief — for that is what he had become — checked to make sure he was being followed, for there was no way he would take on Cuilean by himself. "Come on," he said to those behind him. He stepped forward again when the mob crowded behind him, nudging him forward as Cuilean retreated a few steps.

"He's running away!" One of the Anboarnhs shouted excitedly.

Cuilean back-pedaled rapidly.

Sensing what they imagined was their prey's fear, the small horde crowded in a mass towards him, and at that, Cuilean turned and ran.

The pack of Anboarnhs, with various shouts and yelps, picked up their pace and ran after him. By this time, Cuilean was in full sprint.

He darted between two aptracs that were parked on the road. One had been towing the other, and a loose chain dangled from its rear hitch. Cuilean swept up the chain, which was about two Zziippps long, and as he ran, he looped one end of it around his arm between his hand and his elbow.

Emerging from behind the vehicles, pausing long enough to make sure his pursuers could see him, with long, easy, loping strides, he kept just a couple Zziippp lengths ahead of the pack.

In front of him, he spied an alley between two domes, and not sure what he would find there, not knowing if he himself would be trapped, he decided to chance it and cut abruptly into what turned out to be a cul-de-sac -- just what he was looking for, though in a moment, he would be boxed in.

But there was a geodesic ledge two Zziippp-lengths overhead, and he leapt for it, swung himself up, and hand-over-hand, he monkeyed his way to the alley entrance, just as the gang charged in beneath him.

As the Anboarnh pack crowded into the blocked far end. One turned and shouted in surprise, pointing up at Cuilean. "There's the ratfucker!"

Cuilean dropped to the ground just behind the chasers, who milled in confusion, the awareness sweeping through them that the hunted had become the hunter.

In a few deft moves, Cuilean uncoiled the chain and whipped it in a circle over his head.

The pack hesitated.

"That's cockroach shit!" the Anboarnh gang head shouted without full conviction. "Go on! Get 'im!" he ordered, tugging the nearest of his followers ahead and pushing him in Cuilean's direction.

Cuilean stooped, and whirling himself dervishly, he scraped the chain in a wide circle along the ground, and as he did, sparks flew up into the combustible atmosphere, making patterns of fire in the open space between the close-packed domes.

Cuilean made a figure-eight snake over his head to speed the velocity of the whipped chain and bent again to drag the chain on the gowphalt at his feet. Small lightning bolts flew from the chain links sparking on the paved road surface.

He advanced on the gang, spinning while he did so. The chain on the gowp-infused, hard packed road sent up a ring of fire around him.

Faster and faster Cuilean spun. A wall of fire encircled him and grew higher and higher. But the most frightening thing was the crazed laughter that came out of the midst of the circle of flame that sprang up to the top of the nearby domes, cracking the opaque windows high off the ground.

"He's making a chain re-action!" one of the Anboarnhs shouted. The realization caused the pack to retreat, as much from the display of pure madness as from the wall of flames.

Just before the conflagration combusted in the atmospheric gases and exploded in the enclosed space, Cuilean tossed the chain so it skittered like a flaming snake towards the throng of Anboarnhs, now crowding in the far end of the sealed-off dead-end.

Cuilean himself leapt high to one of the dome ledges and rappelled rapidly upwards away from the blast. The explosion rocked the twin domes and engulfed the swarm.

After the detonation: silence, and a gradual wafting away of the blast smoke.

Cuilean slid back to the now-charred ground. He stood alone, panting like a mad sword-tooth after a hunt. He trembled from the surge that had coursed through his body. He leaned against a nearby stanchion.

Slaiya, having been left behind by the speed of the runners, lumbered up. "Yupela okay, bigpela?"

Cuilean, unable to answer, his chest convulsing for air, nodded and held up a hand to signal *wait*.

"Les go way now-aa," Slaiya urged, tugging on his friend. "No safe hee-aa."

Before they could move, there was a flash of light: They started, startled, to look up at a tall presence that appeared like an ANGIL[44] of GAWD. The light from the moon-glow streetlamp (situated because the actual moon was hidden behind the bank of orange smudge that covered the land) refracted off the Anboarnh's white suit, which was so bright and white that it made Cuilean squint as if into a spot-light glare.

Cuilean straightened warily. He didn't like the feeling of being snuck up on.

The man in white stood before them: a slender Anboarnh with the pallid complexion of a bottom dwelling sea slug. His skin was not just pale, it was almost translucent, which gave him the appearance of a ghost, only with half the expressiveness. He had a pained countenance, as if he had a tack in his shoe, which, for one reason or another, he could not remove.

"I've been sent here," the man in white said.

"Who-aa?" Slaiya asked, sounding like the exhalation of an air

---

[44] ANGIL – Agent of Notification of GAWD's Instructions and Leadership (see GAWD)

intake-exhaust unit.

"GAWD," the man said.

Cuilean stared in stupefied, drunken wonder. People – both natborn and Anboarnh – spoke of GAWD, mused about GAWD, argued about the nature of GAWD, marveled about the miracle of GAWD's Wholly Presents (like on Listmus, when GAWD left lottery tickets for good pupae in exchange for their gowp savings); but for Cuilean, GAWD had always been so distant, essentially unknowable. He'd never been touched by his Wholly Presents before, not even in the HOUMH[45] where he'd been deposited when he was a child.

Doubting still, Cuilean asked, "What does GAWD want?"

"He wants to give you something." A smug *gotcha* smile.

Cuilean was only half-aware of what the man was saying. Everything was going around, and not in a good way this time. He tried to focus his sight, but everything still was a blur. The light from the moon and the reflection off the resplendence of the man's suit produced a glowing halo and hurt his eyes. He squinted into the glare. "What?"

"Your mission, whether you choose to accept it or not."

Cuilean cautiously noted the gowp-uniformed Zziippp PieceTakers, clothed in the regulation and unmistakable sand-colored coveralls of the Monstrato Corps, stalking ever more tightly around them.

"Me?" Cuilean was still struggling to understand.

"Yes. You." Was that exasperation in the ANGIL's voice? Irateness over having to explain himself? If it was, he restrained himself from any more overt display of anger. After all, this was a high-value taking of his. He'd acquired Cuilean on slaivers after his team owner had released him for apparently throwing the melee match – Cuilean and the entire team, as a matter of fact. And such a valuable property should be treated gently if he wanted to maintain the value of his newly acquired asset.

In the fog of Cuilean's drink-and-drug addled mind, he was well aware of where this was leading. He'd heard of such draft-gangs. They roamed the domed cities trolling for what they took to be able-bodied recruits – "volunteers," they called them – and snagged them up like so many sea slugs by an ocean trawler. Cuilean formed his words carefully, trying not to slur: "You can't draft me. I'm under contract with somebody else."

"Not any more."

Now Cuilean was doubly confused. He shook his head to clear his vision as if that would clear his mind. "Why?"

---

[45] HUOMH -- Habitation for Unhoused Orphaned Minor Hoomans (see Hooman)

"That information is classified. You won't know until ... well, until whenever it's revealed to you."

The sand clouds outside the dome were swirling. The sound of this man's talking was like the buzzing of a desert sand fly in his ear. He wanted desperately to curl up right where he was and go to sleep.

Shaking off this urge, Cuilean ventured a challenge. He had a vague idea of his rights, or proper procedures, or *something*. "You have orders?" Though even as he said it, he really wasn't too clear on just what the legalities of the situation were.

The man in white smiled and touched the breast pocket of his suit. "Of course."

"Can I see them?"

"A man of your obvious intelligence has to be aware that the information is classified above your security level." He displayed the screoin of his handheld towards Cuilean. "I can show you this, however."

Cuilean squinted at the warrant that the man-in-white had pulled up on the handheld, although it was all a blur. The Anboarnh read out the name he saw there which should have been *Cuilean Mac Tìgeir – Cuilean Son of the Tiger* in the FT -- but which he mangled in pronouncing; after a couple mouth contortions and an exasperated huff, the man in white managed "Calan Mac. Is that you?"

Without waiting for an answer, he continued, "You have the right to agree to go along with us peacefully or to be beaten until you do agree. Anything you say or don't say can be used against you. You have the right to a lawyer of our choosing, or if you can't afford a lawyer, or if your lawyer is not present, you have the right to have none. Is this clear?" Without waiting for an answer, "Good." And without glancing up from the handheld: "Is your lawyer present?"

Cuilean looked around dramatically, despite the seriousness of the situation, bemused by the stupidity of the question. He let out a loud breath as if to say – *whadayathink*?

The man in white noted for the record: "The accused signifies he does not wish to have his lawyer present."

The Anboarnh in white scanned the charges, the verdict, and the sentence that appeared in the appropriate spaces on the form. He read aloud quickly, with no intonation or affect, other than the evident desire to finish. "You've been charged with blasphemy against the Monstrato Corps and desecrating the Wholly Melee Match by refusing full competition, leading to an alteration of the legitimate point spread pre-determined by the properly designated corporate authorities. You have been found guilty of these charges.

Do you have anything to say?" (No pause for answer.) "Very well, the verdict is that you are to be assigned to the purchaser of your contract, CacaHed[46] Docherty ..."

Here, the man in white broke off from reading to interject, "That's me."

Picking up where he left off, Docherty went on: "And transported to the Corporation's outpost in the Wayp."

And to the PieceTakers, "Take the prisoner. He belongs to me." He flipped his fingers at Slaiya as if discarded leftovers. "And that one, too."

There was the sound of a rush in the air, and Cuilean and Slaiya were enveloped in a net that quickly closed around them, smothering them in its constrictions.

~~

---

[46] CacaHed (sometimes, CACA) -- the short version of the complete acronym CACAAAAAAHED, the acronym for Chief Administrator - Capital Acquisitions, Annexing, Abducting, and Appropriating – Antarctic Archipelago: Head of External Development.

3. Twilight dropping

'S an gaoth às an tuath a bheir cranndachd 's gaillinn.
It is the wind from the north that brings withering cold and storm.
Leabhar an Leaghaidh Mhòir —
The Book of the Great Melting

Wiktionary: Environmental Degradation in the Foretime

Death of the Antediluvian Environment
and
The Rising of the Modern World after the Great Melt

Professor Harold Harishchandra Higginsbottom (editor)

The people of the Wayp refer to the era of the ancient world as *an t-àm ro thìm* — "the time Foretime," or the Foretime. As a historian, though, I must be more precise (if less mythological and poetic) and mark it as the period prior to the Great Melt, approximately 9,500 years before the present time (BPT), when a series of ecological traumas led to the collapse of the previous global environment and (to satisfy the Monstrato Corps Truth Telling regulations), the rise of the present, even better business environment.

There were several aspects to the environmental collapse that the planet experienced at that time. From the extant records of the historical archives (which are at best fragmentary, having been either lost, destroyed, or so heavily redacted by the Monstrato Corps censors that they might as well have been lost or destroyed), and from the research of the cosmic-neuronal net "spelunkers," I have been to piece together that in the era of the Great Melt, the Earth's ecosystem underwent such a heavy and massive sequence of assaults that it could not be sustained in its then-state. The totality of such shocks to the environmental system destroyed the world known by the ancients and created the one which we now enjoy.

An event that preceded and precipitated the Great Melt was the super-heating of the globe. While some short-sighted ancient Casandras issued fear-mongering warnings of what they called "global warming," the far-seeing vision of the Monstrato Corps recognized and exploited the potential for profit that the natural phenomenon presented, for in creating an environment that was

92

supportive of only certain forms of life, those able to live in temperatures over the boiling point of water, for instance, or which could adapt to the changed environment in accordance with the iron law of *deprival of the fitless*, inferior  forms of life were eliminated from the planet – in other words, those which were incapable of adapting and evolving. In contrast, Hoomans, a species of superior fitness and adaptability, were able to construct and retreat to shelters either underground or underdome, a necessity that had the added benefit of stimulating the economy by leading to a boom in dome construction, solar radiation protection technology, and air purification device industries.

(Glory be to the Profit of the Monstrato Corps!)

~~

The Coven of the Sisters

'S mise bòidhchead am measg blàthan, bradan san amar, darach sa choille, 's seabhag air creag
I am beauty amidst flowers, a salmon in the pond, an oak in the forest, and a hawk on a cliff.
Proverb from *Leabhar an Leaghaidh Mhòir* —
The Book of the Great Melting

As they traveled out of the forest, Ròna heard a bird-like chirping that although she couldn't exactly locate the source, she knew came from somewhere in the tall grasses that fringed the tree line. She recognized the call as that of a *cat-ruith* -- a running-cat – a large spotted feline about half the size of the sword-tooth tiger. This hunter was long and graceful, which when it ran, stretched out, all legs off the ground like an arrow shot from a bow, and could chase down the swiftest deer. Whereas the sword-tooth lurked in the undergrowth and would spring out at its prey and take it by surprise, the *running-cat's* speed over longer distances made it in some ways a much more effective hunter than her larger cousin, for if a deer or a llama managed to evade the sword-tooth's first charge, chances were the intended meal was safe, for the tiger could not keep pace with it; on the other hand, the running-cat would chase its prey down or pursue it until the target of the attack dropped either from exhaustion or hopelessness.

Not that there was any danger to Ròna and her caravan (the cat would not attack anything as large as Dìleas), for the *chirrup* the girl had heard was that of a mother calling her cubs playing in the scrub grass to come close to her and out of the way of the passing cavalcade that Ròna was leading to *Taigh Mòr nam Peathraichean* — the Big House of the Sisters. This was a long, two-story building with stone walls and a thatched roof where the village council met (and many women lived, especially those who were not married, or who had — for one reason or another — chosen not to live with a spouse or anyone else).

The interior was open and airy, and by its design, it seemed larger from inside the than it actually was. It was well-lit, with the air flowing comfortably, though unobtrusively throughout, lending to a well-ventilated atmosphere despite the number of people who often gathered there.[47]

But this day, the house was empty for the most part. The People – at least, those who wished to attend the coven meeting – had gathered in the amphitheater set in a nearby wooded grove -- a clear space in a small, bowl-shaped valley. Whether natural or human-made, no one could have told since it had been thus for much longer than anyone could remember or had been recorded. Surmounting and circling the lip of the bowl was a ring of trees, which stood as if holding hands, keeping sentinel and bearing witness to the proceedings below: oaks, yews, cypresses, pine, fir; and fruit bearing trees, too: plum, apple, peach, along with a minority of citrus – orange and grapefruit (though these last two were stunted due to the sometimes-harsh climate of the Wayp).

Mairead Mhòr, Big Margaret, the *Àrd-Phiuthar*[48] -- the Big Sister in the FT – was a tall dignified woman of middle age. She stood before the congregation draped in a dark green plaid robe that reached to the ground, its cuffs, hem, and collar fringed with white fur. On her shoulder was perched an owl – *cailleach-oidhche* in the FT, "old woman of the night." When the elder woman spoke, it was in a melodic, soprano voice, the tone turning up at the end of the phrase, accompanied by a fluttering of hands that rose upwards like a flight of doves.

The declivity leading to the center of the bowl sloped gradually to a flat stage. The amphitheater was not so large that a person's voice couldn't be heard at the upper reaches, though deference was given to those whose hearing had faded; these people, more often than not elderly, were ushered to the front near the stage.

---

[47] Although it is beyond the scope of these Chronicles (as well as the ability of the chronicler) to expound upon the technology of the society of the Wayp, we can go so far as to explain in brief that the energy requirements of the interior lighting, heating and air-conditioning, and other applications were provided by a power grid with interlacing sources of energy, including wind, hydro, hydrogen- and solar-power technology comprised of microscopically thin solar cells applied to the exterior of buildings, which could by itself serve as an exemplar of the technological culture of the People of Wayp, which aimed for maximal efficiency with minimal perceptibility.

[48] Sisters of the Mother - A designation that was both formal and informal. Generally speaking, the term referred to all members of the community, even the men as representatives of the Mother and guardians of her garden in the Wayp (though males were more often referred to as "children" of the Mother). Formally and officially, the term indicated the leaders of the council and the appointed "little sisters" who were responsible for various aspects and functions in the life of the community.

The sides of the bowl were ringed with rough concentric circles or footpaths worn away by long use so as to form not only aisles but also on either side a low natural bench. These circles ran the entire circumference of the theater, so there was no "front" or "back," but created an arena in which anyone speaking could be seen by everyone else with at most a slight turn of the head, and the natural acoustics amplified the sound of a person's voice so to make anyone who spoke easily audible to everyone else.

This was the preferred meeting place for ceremonies and council meetings in all but the most inclement weather, the reasoning being that *Clann na Màthar* -- the Children of the Mother – should not separate themselves from the embodiment of the divine that was all around them lest they forget their connection with *her* -- the Mother, the goddess -- and her manifestation, the natural world that embraced them.

Typically, at the beginning of each assembly, the people would recite an invocation to the goddess, which served to help center their minds and reminded them of the divinity of everything, as all that was emanated from the Mother, and just as the Mother infused all things, even the non-living.[49]

> *'S mise bòidhchead nam blàthan,*
> *bradan san amar,*
> *darach sa choille,*
> *'s seabhag air creag ...*

> I am the beauty of the flowers,
> a salmon in the pond,
> an oak in the forest,
> and a hawk on a cliff ...

This business of the gathering was shaken askew when Ròna, mounted on Dìleas and dragging Morunx behind her, came charging down the aisle that ran from the top of the amphitheater to the center stage. Dìleas was snorting and huffing and puffing and throwing his head back and forth and up and down and making half leaps in his gallop. Behind her, Ròna tugged the struggling bundle of humanity that was the angry, stooped, mud-splattered, bruised, scraped, and venomously spitting Morunx ... unless he lost his footing and was dragged until he could right himself.

At the edge of the staging area, Ròna pulled Dìleas to an abrupt

---

[49] As recorded in *The Book of the Great Melting*, even the inanimate was a repository of divinity: *Tha a' bhan-dia na cadal anns na clachan* – The Goddess sleeps in the stones.

stop as the *Àrd-Phiuthar* – the Big Sister -- put up her hand as a signal to Ròna that she should stop and wait.

Morunx had just regained his footing and was running as fast as he could to keep up so he wouldn't be yanked down and dragged again, only to find the rope had gone slack with the unihorn's sudden halt, and the bound man ran nose first into the beast's not too aromatic anus. (*Dìleas*, unfortunately, had gotten his snout into a batch of fermenting, rotting tubers and was suffering from diarrhea).

Morunx had been angry before, and now he found himself furious – furiously indignant, indignantly furious, as frenzied as a tiger hornet whose nest had just been destroyed, as enraged as a mother sword-tooth whose cubs have been threatened, as ... well, you get the point: not only had he been prevented from doing what he believed he had every right to do – cutting down *mere* bushes (well, they were big bushes, but the same difference ...) that blocked access to his property (as he thought of it), and as well, presented him with the opportunity for a nice profit, but on top of all that, he'd been tied up like a salmon poacher, hog-tied like a unihorn calf, and dragged over rock-strewn ground, up hills and down, like a bundle of mammoth dung fertilizing the fields; and now – to heap insult upon indignity! – bound like a *Samhain*[50] truffle pie, with one boot one and one off, limping like a three-legged hell-pig, groaning like a diarrhetic glutton, he'd been run smack face-first into some damn monstrosity's asshole and had had his face smeared with a mask of poorly-digested excreta like a mammoth-leaper who fell the wrong way off the back of his bull!

The conventicle was wrapping up the trial of a man who'd been accused of rape.

A girl of about 15 years of age who was the accuser stood to the one side of the Big Sister, the accused on the other.

"What do you say to the accusation?" The Sister asked.

---

[50] *Samhain* – the end of summer/autumnal celebration of the equinox, when the two worlds, this one and the other came together and passage between them was possible

"I didn't do it. At least, not the way she said I did. She wanted it."

"Did she say that?"

"Well, it was the way she said 'no.' I just knew … I thought she was my girlfriend … I could tell. She wanted it."

The accused's protestations angered several members of the crowd, amongst whom were the girl's family and friends.

They shouted imprecations.

"*Breugaire!* – Liar!"

"*Neach-èigneachd*[51] – Rapist!"

Several shouted suggestions, including the perennial favorite (sometimes, no matter what the infraction – there were just those who reveled in the spectacle of the ultimate penalty, irregardless): "*An rathad goirid leis! –* The shortcut with him!"[52]

And as often in such cases, someone yelled out, "*Spothamaid e!* – Let's castrate him!"

Somebody else liked that idea and followed up in agreement with an invocation that was more direct: "*Geàrramaid a bhod dhe!* – Let's cut his dick off!"

This suggestion, as it seemed to be more appropriate to the crime, was taken up by several others in the crowd.

An older woman, who was standing with her arm around the girl, lending her moral support, and from the look of the child's trembling, a literal shoulder to lean on, as well, interjected. "Sister, I think we've heard enough."

"I agree," Mairead said. "It's time to reach a judgment."

Big Mairead turned to the other Big Sisters arrayed informally and loosely on the dais. These thirteen[53] conferred in low voices that could not be heard outside their circle, sometimes one to the entire tribunal, and sometimes two or three separately.

Presently, the conference broke, and Mairead turned back to the larger assemblage and announced generally, but also specifically to the man, "It's the consideration of the Sisters that we *not* return you to the DownBlow, where such behavior is tolerated."

---

[51] *Neach-èigneachd* – literally, 'one who forces'

[52] The "shortcut" – the "short way" to the sea thousands of lengths below, in other words, throwing somebody over the cliff; also, *an dòigh luath* – the "quick way" to the DownBlow).

[53] Thirteen -- In accordance with the belief of the people of the Wayp that numbers signified ideas, principles, concepts, and/or themes – that is spiritual values – and not just meaningless quantities, the Council of the Sisters – *Comhairle nam Peathraichean--* was constituted of 12 Sisters and one Big Sister. Thirteen being a "sacred" number as it represented the number of lunar months – as well as menstrual cycles – in a year.

For a moment – and just *one* moment -- the accused, who was evidently well aware of the manner in which the *returning* would have been brought about, was relieved. The miscreant smugly nodded to himself, and beaming a short-lived smile that spoke of his satisfaction at having pulled one over on the Sisters, the girl, and everyone else, blurted out, "Oh, thank you ..." At the same instant, realizing it might be considered inappropriate to grin in such serious circumstances, he forced a solemn and recondite expression to cover the smirk, an expression that was somewhat contradicted by the words he spoke immediately following: "Not that I did anything ... really ...." He suppressed a grin. "But, yeah. I'll be careful. I promise. But you know," he asserted smugly, not being able to stifle a bit of a chortle, "the girls can't keep their hands off me."

But the Big Sister cut him off with a decisive sweep of her hand in the same manner that she would employ if she were admonishing a child. "*Ist* – Quiet. How much trust we can put into your promise? You've been warned before, so I'm not sure I understand what exactly you mean. Do you mean, 'careful' not to do such a wicked thing again? Or do you mean 'careful' not to get caught again? And if that's what you mean, I don't want to even start to think about how you might ensure that. So, we're going to make certain you keep your promise."

The implication of the Sister's words struck him like a blow across the face. "But you said ..."

Again, an upraised hand silenced him.

"I said the Sisters wouldn't pass judgment. I didn't say anything about *them*." With a sweeping arm movement, Big Mairead indicated the people in the assembly, many of whom had risen from their seats in the amphitheater and were crowding towards the stage.

A change came over the man. As if he had been suddenly buffeted by a gust of glacial wind, a fit of trembling engulfed him. "I didn't mean to ... We were just having fun ... I thought ..."

He was swarmed by several people in the gathering – and these were pressed from behind by many others who strove to reach him. Those who could get their hands on him ripped and cut his clothes from his body.

"This isn't fair! I didn't do anything! No, seriously ... I'm sorry ... I ..." His attempts at exculpation transmuted into inarticulate screams.

The flaying happened so quickly that almost before he knew it, he had been lifted back to his feet and found himself again facing the Big Sister. One moment he had been standing fully clothed in the middle of the congregation, and the next he was *rùisgte* -- as

naked as the minute he'd been delivered into this world of the
Mother.

Stripped naked, he felt the blood rush down his legs from his
gashed loins. He shivered involuntarily as if he'd been left standing
nude on the icy mountain slopes that rose above them, or as if he'd
just been dipped in the glacial water of *Loch na Màthar* – the Lake
of the Mother.

He whimpered, "I'm sorry ... I'll never do it again ... I didn't
mean to ..." As if his plea could restore what had been ripped and
cut from him.

The Sister raised her voice to override his protests: "You have
taken from this girl that which can never be restored – her
integrity, her dignity, her autonomy – and can be repaired only
with time and difficulty. In committing that crime, you have
perpetrated a shattering of the network of trust that binds us
together as a community; and on top of that, an even greater
atrocity: a violation of the sacredness of the Mother."

She paused and let those words sink in. "From this moment
forward, you do not exist for us. No one will see you. No one will
recognize you. You are no longer one of the Children of the Mother.
Since you refuse to recognize the humanity of others, as of now,
you have no humanity: no rights to life, property, dignity, anything.
Leave. You have no place here. You have no rights here. You have
no life here."

She turned away from the quivering man as if from a clod of
excrement upon which her sight had landed and shifted her gaze to
face Ròna and her trussed-up prisoner. With a smile, she asked,
"What do we have here?"

There was something in the Big Sister's expression that looked
to Morunx like the grin of a bear-wolf before it gobbled down a
rabbit.

~~

It's mine, all mine!

Dèan math do dhuine fèineal, 's bidh e fèineal fhathast.
Do good to a selfish man, and he will still be selfish.
Proverb from *Leabhar an Leaghaidh Mhòir* —
The Book of the Great Melting

Rob Morunx's run-ins with Ròna's family had been going on ever since he'd arrived from the DownBlow. He'd claimed an ancestral relationship through his mother to *clann na Màthar* – the children of the Mother – and had been granted permission to settle, though some suspected that what he was really after were the water rights that came with the croft he was allowed to farm – rights to the water which he was eager to sell off to the Monstrato Corps, and it wouldn't make much difference to him if he sucked dry the entire Lake of the Mother.[54]

"They want to buy my water? I say let them!" Morunx had declared defiantly at the Council of the Sisters – *comhairle nam peathraichean* in the FT.

"It's not yours to sell!" rejoined a chorus of voices outraged at the idea that someone would claim ownership to the Mother's milk.

"You think I bought this land just to shovel mammoth shit? What profit is that water making just sitting in the ground? How do you people say it?" He was mocking them, throwing their own proverb back at them. "It's not worth a chicken's cluck."

"*Cha ceannaicheadh e gog na circe,*" Dòmhnall muttered under his breath, equally disgusted at the man's ignorance as he was

---

[54] One of the peculiar features of the socio-economic system of the Wayp was the lack of the concept of private land ownership. Land and indeed the natural resources attached thereto were considered "borrowed" from the "Mother"; it was incumbent upon each "trustee" to maintain and "return" the land in the same or better condition than it had been upon the inauguration of the transaction. Practically speaking, this custom resulted in the pseudo-legality of community ownership of property, as the "community" was regarded as the trustees or the protectors of the Mother's interests, a system much less efficient (I'm sure the reader would agree) than the law of absolute sovereignty of ownership enforced by the doctrine of Meemynism which was Constitutionally protected in the domains of the Monstrato Corporation.

angered at his arrogance in refusing to learn the language of the people who'd granted him sanctuary as a refugee when he'd come to them fleeing the persecution that he claimed he'd suffered in the poisonous lands of the DownBlow.

Indignation moved Dòmhnall to sputter between his clenched teeth: "The Great Mother gave us this water. To keep. To save. To guard. Not to sell!"

"It's my property!" Morunx had shouted back. "I don't see any document giving rights to my land to this great big mother of yours. It's mine! All mine! And I'll do with it whatever I want!"

"They'll suck the lake dry!" Dòmhnall had protested with a mixture of outrage and confoundment – *How could somebody even begin to think like this?*

"Suck it dry?! How can they do that? It's inexhaustible! You people say so yourselves. No lips in the world could suck dry the milk from the 'Mother's Teat,' as you call it," pronouncing the term with disgust. He puckered his lips and swung his head in the direction of the twin mounds frosted with snow that rose up over the lake.

The incomer's mockery made even Dòmhnall, who was not particularly religious himself, want to prick the man with the *sgian-dubh* -- the black knife -- that he kept tucked away in its sheath at his knee.

After this exchange, being of the view that there was no use in or good to come from talking to such a person, Dòmhnall simply went out of his way to avoid him whenever he could. But some interactions were unavoidable, such as the time when he had to ride over to Morunx's farm, hauling a hay baler behind his favorite mammoth, *Mo Chridhe* – My Heart. They were in the same collaborative farm -- *co-thuathanachas* in the FT, or 'farming together' -- that shared the machinery which baled various grasses and hay that fed the herds during the winter months. It was a huge contraption, run by its hydro-engine that extracted the hydrogen in water and burned it, expelling pure water as waste. And as Morunx happened to be next in line for the machine, it was up to Dòmhnall to pass it off to him.

Ròna's father was hoping to be able to avoid the man and just drop the contraption off, but as he came up on Morunx's farm, Dòmhnall saw him standing by the side of the road, and even from a distance, the man's impatience was visible and palpable. He was preparing and ready, Dòmhnall was sure, to pick an argument or make a complaint if the machinery was delivered late. (Though there was little concept of or use for *clock-time* in the Wayp.[55])

"*Seo agad e, ma tha* – Here you have it, then," Dòmhnall said, while he was uncoupling the device from *Mo Chridhe*'s harness, stating the obvious in the forbidden tongue, which he knew would rankle Morunx – and which is why he spoke in the FT to him.

"I could report you!" Morunx snarled.

Dòmhnall shrugged, and turning away to finish what he had been doing, he muttered "*A mhic do sheanar*," which had something to do with his being the son of his mother and his own grandfather, a considerable insult in a culture that revered genealogy. Although Dòmhnall figured that Morunx wouldn't understand the gibe – or perhaps *because* he knew this -- casting the slander gave him the pleasure of a secret, petty revenge, nonetheless.

Unable to respond directly, Morunx snarled, "I don't want it here! It doesn't do me any good here. You're supposed to deliver it to my field."

Dòmhnall stifled the urge to lash out at the man, and in a controlled voice, he said, "No, I'm supposed to deliver it to *you*, and this is where *you* are. So ..." Again, taking pleasure in the small goad, which he was well aware would cause Morunx disproportionate aggravation, "*Sin agad e.* – There you have it."

Dòmhnall turned away and pretended to be interested in the ignition switch on the baler. It was then that he saw the bear-wolf, mange-ridden, scrawny and ill-fed, lassitudinous with hunger and, no doubt, with loss of blood from the fleas and ticks that swarmed over her. Despite his resolution to drop the baler off and leave without saying anything more, Dòmhnall couldn't restrain himself. The words were out of his mouth before he could stop them. "You should take care of your bear-wolf," he snapped.

"It's my animal!" Morunx barked sharply. "I own it! I'll do whatever I want to with it!" He stared fiercely and defiantly,

---

[55] A joke in the Wayp went something like this: An incomer asked what was the word for "tomorrow" in the FT. After a moment of reflection, he was told, "We don't have a word that expresses such urgency."

primed for a fight, his bushy brows beetling, twin tufts of hair
sticking out from the sides of his head, just above his ears.

Dòmhnall restrained himself from saying anything more than,
"You keep treating it like that, it won't be yours for long." And
blurting out, as the anger rose in him, "*Am fear nach biadh an cù
aige fhèin, rachadh e gu galla air dàir.* -- The man who won't feed
his own dog can go fuck a bitch in heat."

"What!" Morunx shouted, certain from Dòmhnall's tone of voice
that he had said something nasty, which Morunx imagined as being
all the worse because he couldn't understand it. "What did you
say?!" He was wild. "Don't you dare use the Forbidden with me!
Talk in Simspeek! I could report you! What did you say!" he
demanded again.

"The language law applies only when we're dealing with the
Monstrato Corps – not amongst ourselves. And you claim to be one
of us, so ..." Dòmhnall trailed off, leaving the *rach thusa* – the "fuck
you" -- that he really wanted to say unsaid.

Abruptly, Dòmhnall collected himself and shifted his tone.
Smiling, he explained, "Besides, I didn't say anything bad. It's just
an old proverb my grandmother used to tell us: "Beautiful people
are not always good, but good people are always beautiful."

Morunx glowered in disbelief, but what could he say? He
himself had refused to learn the language of the People, and so it
was his own fault that he didn't know what had been said. Besides,
he was puzzling over how the saying related to him. He knew he
wasn't "beautiful," so did that mean that Dòmhnall was calling him
"good"? A strange thought, considering their ongoing
disagreements. Or was he saying the opposite of what he meant?
That he was neither good nor beautiful? In which case the proverb
didn't apply at all.

"It didn't sound like that," Morunx grumped. To explain his
rationale, he went on, somewhat weakly: "What you said was
shorter ... not as long as you explained."

"It's not exact. A lot gets lost in translation. But that's the idea."
And with that, Dòmhnall, not trusting himself to stay any longer in
the man's presence, swung onto *Mo Chridhe*'s back and rode away.

Leaving the baler right where he'd dropped it off by the side of
the road.

~~

Just a misunderstanding

Tha e ag iarraidh tròcair nach beireadh e.
He begs for mercy who would not give it.
Proverb from *Leabhar an Leaghaidh Mhòir* —
The Book of the Great Melting

The heat of his fury and indignation dampened by what he'd just seen, Morunx temporized. "It's just a misunderstanding, your honor ..." He fumbled for the correct word: "Uh, your mistress ... uh, your Big Sisterness ... your Big Sisteress ... "

Already tired of Morunx's explanation, as well as his insistence on communicating in Simspeek, the Sister pointedly turned away from him and addressed Ròna. "*A Ròna, a chaileag?* -- Ròna, my girl, what do you have to say?"

On her own part, in her indignation and her anger, Ròna was barely able to speak. She swept down off Dìleas's back and towed the stumbling prisoner to the center of the stage before the *àrd-phiuthar* – the Big Sister. The girl gave the rope that trussed the miscreant a tug, and Morunx was yanked forward. Indeed, there was only one way for him to go. Bound and tethered by his own rope, pinioned as he was between the immovable Dìleas, and from behind by the press of the council attendees who were crowding close, he was forced to the feet of the Big Sister. With another yank on the cordage that bound him, Ròna tugged him to his knees. With a surprised yelp of protest, he splayed face-first before the imposing Druidess.

There was a confusion of voices as many spoke, yelled, and exclaimed all at once, their voices rising and falling in competition with each other like rats in a bucket clambering on each other's backs to get out (or in this case, to be heard), but nothing anyone said came out as articulate, comprehensible sentences.

Ròna: "Desecrating the tabernacle..."

Morunx: "Had a right ... insufferable ... outrageous!"

A woman at the back of the crowd: "*Dè tha tachairt!?* -- What's going on?"

And another, a little farther towards the front: "*An e Ròna a th' innte?* -- Is that Ròna?"

Somebody else: "*'S i!* -- Yes."

And so it continued until the Big Sister raised her hand, and accompanied by the skirl of the bagpipe attendant who had marched up and was now blasting the screech directly into the mix and snarl of humanity that had gathered in the middle of the stage, the assemblage was called to attention, and although there was an occasional outburst here and there such as, "Can you see?" or "Who's that tied up?" the Big Sister slowly managed to bring some likeness of order to the confusion, and gradually, silence fell upon the assembly.

"Now we'll find out what this is about," the Sister began.

Morunx blurted out, "I was just ..."

"Quiet!" the Sister commanded in a voice that wasn't loud but was forceful and must be obeyed. More softly, she continued, "You first, Ròna, *a ghràidh.*"

Calmed enough now to be able to put her anger into words, Ròna –speaking in the FT -- explained how she had found Morunx and what she had discovered him doing -- cutting a path through the sacred grove of the Mother, and horror of horrors, strung up with a saw in the branches of one of the mother's trees and threatening her very life!

"I object!" Morunx cried out. "I can't understand a thing she's saying in your damn gug-gug talk. You know the treaty forbids it! You have to use Simspeek in any proceeding I'm involved in."

"You'll get your turn," the Big Sister said, ignoring the point of his protest, although speaking in Simspeek since, as she knew, for as long a time as he had lived among them, the man had never had the decency to acquire *Teanga Clann na Màthar* -- the Tongue of the Children of the Mother. With an expression that reflected the seriousness of the accusation, Mairead directed her interrogation to the accused, "What do you have to say to these accusations?"

Morunx spluttered ... "Outrageous ..." He was so indignant he could hardly put a sentence together. "Don't even know ..."

"You know what you did."

"I was just ..."

The mother cut him off with a slashing movement of her hand. "Is it true what Ròna is saying?"

"Well, yes ... but ... a right ... my property ..."

The Big Sister held up her finger, and even Morunx had the sense to realize his time for speaking was done and abruptly stopped his blathering defense. "When you came here, *a Raibeirt* – Robert -- and asked for sanctuary, even though you'd been ..." She paused and looked to one of the other sisters for help in translating, "... *rugadh 's thogadh* ..."

"Born and raised," one of the younger sisters offered.

"*Tha sin ceart* -- That's right," she continued, "born and raised in the DownBlow. Because you claimed kinship, you were allowed to stay." Her mind strayed as if into the underbrush by the side of the trail to the remembrance of that time and the controversy Morunx's coming had stirred up and the trouble it had caused her personally, but she quickly recovered her trail of thought. "And the conditions were explained to you, and you agreed ..."

"But it's my property ...!"

"No!" The *Àrd-Phiuthar* cut him off in a voice that spoke more of correction of a wrong-headed child than of argument. "Nothing is *yours*. Nothing is *ours*. It's all ... " She lifted her hands and moved them outwards as if to communicate the ineffable, that which could not be spoken.

"Damn ... damn ..." Morunx groped for the worst imprecation he could fling at the woman. "Damn *togetherist!*"[56] He nearly spit this word out, the worst imprecation he could think of at the time that fit the circumstances. "You think everything belongs to the hive and nothing to ... to ..."

"To you?" the Big Sister interrupted, holding her hand up flat towards his face as if to stop the flow of his words. She went on: "You're right. Nothing is ours. It all – all this ..." a circular movement of her hands ... "belongs to the mother, and we are her guardians ..." and with a motion that encompassed the whole assembly she finished ... "... her Servants."

"That's stupid!" Morunx blurted out. "You can't be the servant of a bunch of dirt and weeds!"

The mother gave a stern look as if to say, *are you done*?

In spite of himself, Morunx's outburst spluttered to a halt, and he quietened.

"None of us," the Big Sister explained in the patient but weary voice of a parent explaining something for the umpteenth time, "own any of this. It is given to us ... how do you say ..." Here she turned to a younger sister by her side and asked, "*air iasad?*"

"On loan," the younger one offered.

"On loan," Mairead said, sounding out the words like someone trying out a new food in her mouth for the first time, "from the mother herself ... and shame to us if we don't return it to her and pass it on to the next generation as we have found it. We thought you understood this. You said you did."

---

[56] Togetherist – along with "Togetherism," the system of social structure and belief ascribed to the People of the Wayp by those from the DownBlow. However, it should be noted that neither term is employed in any form or derivation by the People, perhaps (at least in part) because there is no enunciated or enumerated doctrine or dogma, per se, amongst them.

"But the trees were in my way."

"Then you need to find another way."

"You're putting *trees*," he said, enunciating the word as if it were a profanity, "over the Profit!"

"Yes," the Sister responded, as if this were obvious and she was pleased that he finally seemed to be getting the point. "Now you understand."

This was too much for Morunx. His indignation ramping up again, he angrily blurted out, "Oh, I understand you people just fine. You're lazy. All of you. You don't work. You sit around and tell stories and play music. You've got all this wealth at your fingertips, but you won't reach out and grab it. You just let everything grow wild. You don't plant crops. You don't mine what's under the ground. You ... you ..." he spluttered. "You just let everything be ..." He was brought up short while he hunted for the word, which, when he found, he nearly spit out as if even saying it brought a disgusting taste of filthy contagion to his lips: "*Natural*."

As if out of breath after a run, he settled into a panting silence.

"Are you done?" Big Mairead asked in a cool, unmoved tone.

Chastised, though she had said little, and perhaps even apprehensive that he had said too much too vehemently, Morunx nodded.

"You're right," the Big Sister said. "We don't dig in the ground for gowp. How could we cut into the Mother's flesh and suck out her blood? We don't cut down the trees and burn the wood so we can pile up more worthless stuff like the DownBlowers.  How could I cut off my mother's arms and legs? You accuse us of not working, of not always being busy. But people who work cannot dream, and wisdom comes to us in stories and songs from dreams."

She'd had her say, and that was an end to it. "But enough of this. However pleasant and edifying this conversation might be," she went on, "we'll have to continue it at another time."

Morunx couldn't tell whether she was being sarcastic or serious.

"What should we do with you?" she asked, though she did not expect him to answer, nor probably would she have taken as meaningful anything he might have said.

Finally, Ròna thought, this question furnished her an opportunity. She burst out, perhaps too eagerly: "Return him to the DownBlow! The quick way! Over the edge!"

Sister Mairead repressed a smile. Ròna had always been hotheaded. Always ready to strike. It was not for nothing that she carried the bow strapped over her shoulder. Well suited for her role as protector of the loch and the adjoining forest. The old Sister laid a calming hand on the young woman's arm as if to say, *not now, my dear*, or maybe, more ominously as far as Morunx was concerned, the implication of which was not lost on him, *not yet*.

She turned to level her gaze on the man, who was silent (or had been silenced). Morunx grudgingly conceded, though it wasn't clear whether he was responding more to the sister's moral power and her calm reason or to Ròna's demand to throw him over the edge of the cliff and return him the "quick way" to where he came from several thousand lengths below, "I'll find another way."

"I was hoping you would," the Sister said.

Dropping her jaw in stunned disgust, Ròna held her tongue. Not only could she not understand the people of the DownBlow who treasured their god Profit above everything else and would lie, cheat, steal, and ruin to attain it (the words from the *Leabhar Mòr* being etched in her heart: *'S fheàrr a dhol acrach na dhol an aghaidh Màthair na Cruinne-cè* -- It's better to go hungry than to go against the Mother of the World), but she couldn't understand the Big Sister letting this evildoer off so easily, without even a word of reprimand, a stroke of punishment, not even being hung *tòn-os-cionn* – butt over head – till he came to realize how upside down his point of view was.

"Is that it?" The Sister asked generally, although her glance landed pointedly on Ròna herself. "Do we have all the information we need to make a decision?"

Hardly being able to contain herself now that the time had come to shoot her arrow like at a bird at the crest of its flight, Ròna ejaculated, "There is one other thing," and thrust her hand out towards the Sister to show the mangled butterfly.

The older woman's countenance changed. Direly, she demanded of Morunx, "Did you do this?"

"What!"

Ròna punched her hand towards him, revealing the corpse lying in her palm with its broken purple, blue, and white wings, shortly before as iridescent as stained-glass window panes, but now deathly faded, twisted, and crumpled.

For the first time, Morunx flinched in fear. "No, I didn't do it! Nobody saw me! You can't prove a thing!" He babbled in starts and stops, "What if I did? I mean, it's just a ... You people ... As long as I live here ... I'll never understand ... You think some damned bug is more important than making a profit!" This last was spit out in disgust.

Mairead turned away from him and conferred with the other Sisters. There was evidently some disagreement. Some vehemently advocated severe punishment, accompanied by vehement pointing, and others suggested more lenient rehabilitation.

After some length, the Big Sister turned back. "We've decided."

"To the DownBlow!" someone shouted from the rear of the assemblage.

Although the shouter was hidden, the Sister gave a look in that direction as if to say, *I know who you are, and that's enough of that.* She held her arms in the air, and with her thumbs and index fingers formed a triangle. The hubbub subsided. She spoke: "We've decided to give you one last chance. You can go."

Morunx hardly believed what he had heard, or thought he'd understood. The expression on his face was the image of smugness. He wiggled his arms and torso and looked around as if to say, *Get these things off me.*

"What!" Ròna yelped. "You can't!"

Others in the crowd likewise protested.

"*Air ur socair* – Take it easy, all of you," the Big Sister told them. "We're not quite finished."

Oh, oh! Here it's coming, Morunx thought: the catch, probably some sort of probation, or similar mammoth shit like that.

"You can go, but not just anywhere."

"Where?" he asked petulantly.

"*Taigh nan gallachan leat*," Mairead said, breaking out in a broad, unambiguous smile. The Sister was well aware of the stigma that in the DownBlow attached to all things female, so she was – in spite of the seriousness of the moment -- playing with that belief to the discomfort of the accused.

Indeed, those words chilled him so that goose bumps raised on his arms. He knew enough of the FT to understand their import: literally, "to the house of the bitches with you," but more, the equivalent of "go to hell."

He looked around desperately for an explanation that might offer him some hope. Instead of shared concern from his two co-conspirators, his accomplices in the attempted murder of the oak tree -- *Biorachan Beag* and *Biorachan Mòr* -- Little Pointy Head and Big Pointy Head. However, instead of looks of sympathy for him or fear as to what punishment they might face, what he saw instead were puzzling nods of affirmation, and even a smile, accompanied by the puzzling phrase, "*Nach do rug do chat na cuileanan* – Hasn't your cat birthed puppies."[57]

Morunx couldn't help but react with an expression of thorough befuddlement: What his circumstances had to do with a freakish crossbreeding of cats and dogs he could not have told, even if he had had time to figure it out.

The Sister was not a cruel person, so she didn't let Robert Morunx dangle too long at the end of this rope over the abyss of his terror (as much as he might have deserved it). "Or, more accurately," the Sister went on, "*taigh nam peathraichean.*" She let that one sink in for a heartbeat before she clarified (knowing full well he had not understood the FT): "You will live in the house of the Sisters for a year and a day."

The relief flooding over Morunx was visible. He fought the twin urges to burst into tears or to break out laughing. *Is that all! That's not so bad! I can do that standing on my head!*

"At the end of that time, we will revisit this matter to see if your thinking has changed."

Returned to his usual smug self, he shrugged as if to say, *Yeah, yeah, yeah, fat chance of that.* Though these thoughts he wisely (for once) kept to himself.

"But before you go, we have a gift for you."

He was more confused than he had been before. Was this another trick? "A what?"

One of the Little Sisters stepped forward with a sapling, about a forearm's length in height, its root bulb wrapped in a rough gauze cloth.

"*Tiodhlac* -- A present."[58]

The younger Sister handed the small tree to Morunx.

"Thank you, I guess."

"'*S i do bheatha* -- You're welcome."

"But what is it?"

---

[57] *Nach do rug do chat na cuilleanan* – idiomatic expressions, proverbs, curses, swearing, etc., are heavily culture and language dependent. To unpack this expression, we have to understand first that as a herding culture (mammoths, mineotarbhs, sheep, etc), the People of the Wayp were dependent upon dogs and their "cousins" the bear-wolves to care for and mind the animals in their herds; for herding purposes, cats were absolutely worthless, so the meme evolved amongst the language culture of the People of a person who was so lucky that even the most worthless of their possessions (a cat) produced something of significant value (a dog). As comparison, a parallel expression is known to have existed in the DownBlow: "You're so lucky, you fell ass-backwards into a pool of gowp!"

[58] The word she used -- *tiodhlac* – in the FT could mean either "gift" or "funeral."

This time more definitively: "'S i do bheatha[59] -- She's your life."

A squinting, puzzled expression. He didn't know how to make *ceann no bonn* in the FT – head or bottom – of this turn of events. He could hardly believe his extraordinarily good fortune in getting away with little more than a slap on the wrist. After all, he could live with the women. It might even be a bit of fun. He cautiously ventured, "Is *that* all?"

"Not quite ... just one last thing," Mairead responded with a dramatic flair nodding towards the baby tree. "Do be certain you take good care of her."

"Sure. Of course," he shrugged casually.

"We hope that while you are living with the women, you will learn how to care for somebody else besides only yourself. She ..." the Sister continued, dipping her chin in the direction of the potted plant Morunx was holding carelessly, "She will demonstrate whether you have learned that lesson or not. This little one is a gift to you – a *tìodhlac* – but if she dies, it will be your *tìodhlac* ... your funeral."

With a swing of her head and a dismissive backwards flip of her hand, she signaled that the bound man was to be taken away.

~~

---

[59] Although the phrase signifies "you're welcome," it can be translated literally as, "She's your life," the "she," in this case being of ambiguous reference, signifying either the Mother, or the sapling.

The girl on the lake

'S fuar a' ghaoth a shèideas coimhich thugainn.
Cold is the wind that blows strangers to us.
Proverb from *Leabhar an Leaghaidh Mhòir* —
The Book of the Great Melting

Ròna could feel the thumping of the great heart of the shaggy one-horned beast as her legs pressed against its flank. Its huffing of breath shuddered through its body. It was early in the morning, and Dìleas was, like Ròna herself, still but half awake, though unlike herself, he had not been fortified by a couple cups of *bainne na màthar* – the milky tea of the mother in the forbidden tongue -- the hearty brew of mushroom tea, honey, and mammoth milk.

The mist lay lightly on the water rising like steam off a hot cup of that tea in the early morning chill. They, the two of them – Ròna, *piùthrag na coille,* the little sister of the forest, as they called her position and function in the FT (though her domain extended farther than just the forest), and Dìleas, her massive companion -- had paused on a low rise overlooking the shore of the *Loch na Màthar* – the Lake of the Mother.

The girl set her sights on the small skiff waiting for her on the shore. Also responsible for monitoring the health of the lake, she'd been notified that this day she was to have a ride-along, a visitor from *an Tìr Ìosal* – the DownBlow.

Not that the prospect of an observer changed much of anything. As on any other day, she'd readied her supplies, packing a case of little bottles with rubber stoppers, each in its own pouch in the case, a few sleeves of labels on which to mark locations where the water was collected, and a full set of markers -- variously-colored pens, a different color for different areas of the *loch* (or, lake, as she reminded herself in preparation for her ride-along, as the DownBlowers very often took offence at the use of the FT, so that even the thought of it or in it was dangerous, as the thinking in it might lead to a slipping of the tongue into it, and that uttering, however brief or fleeting, to a treaty violation charge.

And tucked into the outer pouch, a flask of tea and whatever she'd brought with her for lunch -- a sandwich, a bit of left-over fish-and-chips, or a meat pie she'd picked up from a shop in the village of Balnabane on the way to the dock.

She sat back down into the saddle, nudged Dìleas awake from his standing doze, and rocked forward with a soft, "*Thalla, a bhalaich* -- Let's go, boy," and they ambled on down to the lake shore.

She left Dìleas browsing contently in the bush by the water's edge, and once she'd stowed her supplies away in the side compartments of the *curach* – the small boat she was taking out -- she hoisted the sail. The ropes were stiff from the cold and stuck in the hooks of the mast, but after a couple of tugs, the sheet ran up easily enough.

She slipped the rope that secured the boat to the dock and pushed off. The only break in the quiet of the morning chill was the lapping of the water against the prow of the dinghy.

The silence seemed to move across the surface of the water like a palpable presence -- almost as if it were a living spirit exhaling from the forest across the lake, gliding across the crystalline water, and engulfing her and everything else before soaring up the steeps of the mountains.

Gliding over the water, she paused a moment to let the great silence wash over her. Her eyes lost focus, and she saw everything while looking at nothing specific – the slope of the forested rise on the shore; the circling hawk above; the ripples cascading across the lake surface. She heard everything, while listening to nothing in particular -- a faint cry of a gull that had wandered south from the sea to the north, its squawk punctuating the silence; the murmuring of the leaves in the trees of the forest; the coughing roar of a sword-tooth tiger sunning itself on a look-out rock.

She breathed deeply and turned her attention back to her work. She adjusted the sail and guided the prow of the small boat to the dock a short distance across the waters of the *loch*, remembering a moment late that she wasn't supposed to use that term. She thought defiantly in the FT, *Thoir dhan tìr ìosal leotha! --* Screw 'em, or literally, *To the DownBlow with them!* They had no rights inside her head. Her thoughts were still free. She could think whatever and however she liked. She'd think *loch* and guard her what she said.

By the time she reached the pier, the morning mist had already begun to burn off, although the clouds overhead still threatened a stiff rain.

The pier-master (grandly called, considering the small bit of boarding that jutted out into the water) was waiting. It was a well-rehearsed and often-practiced routine. She would toss the end of the rope, and he would catch it, and with a couple of quick, looping movements, he would lash the small boat to one of the pier stanchions.

"*Tapadh leat, Eòghann* – Thank you, Ewan," she said.

"'*S i do bheatha* -- You're welcome," he responded.

An exchange that was as formulaic as the docking of the vessel.

It was then that she noticed the ride-along waiting for her. It had been arranged that this visitor from the DownBlow, as she'd been informed, would be hitching a ride across the water with her, but she observed that she'd be transporting not only this tourist on his way to Trayton -- the Corporation's not-too-inventively named trading town at the lip of the cliffs and the entry way to the Wayp -- but also the child who sat perched on the top of several boxes, which evidently were to be carried across the lake, as well. None of which pleased Ròna, for she had more important things to do, namely, monitoring the well-being of the forest and the lake, but about which, she decided, there was little she could do, especially since this accommodation seemed to be part and parcel of an effort by the Council of Sisters to maintain an accord with the incomers from the DownBlow.

The visitor was a large, middle-aged man, soft-handed and pear-shaped from half-a-lifetime, she guessed, of sitting hunched over a screoin. He was wearing a too-thin windbreaker, evidently something he'd brought along with him from the scorching DownBlow. The light covering was stretched over a plump body, his stomach pushing out and stretching the flimsy fabric bought for the size he had once been, not the size he was now (and which if it could animate, might have groaned under the strain of holding in his massive belly). He had zipped the garment futilely all the way to the top, little good that it would do him, Ròna thought, against the cold wind tumbling down from the snow-covered mountain peak.

Atop his head, he sported a plaid-patterned cap that had the word *Wayp* emblazoned across the front.

Has to be from the Pelago, Ròna thought. Only a Pelagan would come to the Wayp and wear a hat that announced where he was.

Beside the man was a scrawny *caileag* – a girl -- probably about 10 years of age, and likewise dressed more appropriately for the searing heat of the Pelagoes than the Wayp. However, the child didn't seem to mind the brisk breeze that wafted her shock of light-colored hair – or at any rate, didn't seem to notice it, so involved was she with the handheld she scrutinized with an intensity that caused her to bite her lower lip, a gesture that only accentuated her gap-toothed overbite.

"I really appreciate your doing this. Well, both of us do. It's really very nice of you. You see, I'm new here ..." (as if that were not readily apparent). "I'm moving here. I got a job!" a statement that might have been taken to be a boast, but actually emanated out of joint amazement and delight at his good fortune. "Just teaching," he hurried to add self-deprecatingly. "But a full-time position!" He said this as if he expected her to be as impressed as he was.

Not knowing exactly what that meant – how difficult it was for an instructor in mere Hoomanitais[60] (as he was) to land any paid teaching job – Ròna was at a loss to say anything other than, "*'S math sin* – That's good." A comment which she managed with as much verve as she could muster for something about which she was indifferent, and a slip into the FT, which the stranger either didn't catch or, if he did, let pass.

The man spoke in odd halts and starts, Ròna noticed, as if he had a thought he wished to enunciate, then thought better of his original approach, abruptly changed course, and started afresh, only a few phrases later to revert to his original idea.

"I was just appointed to a teaching job," he rushed to explain, omitting the fact that he'd been hired at what was considered the butt-end of the world because he didn't qualify for any more prestigious position in a location more central to the Corps' operations, and because nobody else wanted the job (as the Hooman Properties manager hiring him had made clear); facts he neglected to mention to save some face (one can be too self-deprecating, after all), preferring instead to pass himself off as a university *professor* (if not via committing a lie, then by omitting the full, painful truth).

"Really?" Ròna asked, more out of politeness than interest, or more out of a desire to stop the nervous rush of more-than-wanted information. "What're you teaching?"

---

[60] Hoomanitais – the study of Humanoid Organically Originated (or) Manufactured (and) Artificially Nurtured -- Intercommunication Tween Anboarnhs and Infected Sentiences

"Simspeek as a second language?" Oddly, this came out as a question, as if he were anticipating an objection or a correction. "Or," immediately realizing the issue of language was a fraught one, and as he was just an academic, and not an advocate, and didn't want to offend in either case, he added as a correction, "communication."

Ròna restrained herself from posing the question that had popped immediately to the tip of her lips – *Is that, like, talking?* She simply asked, "Where?"

"In the Monstrato Skypiercer Academy? In Trayton?" This he added as if she might not be aware of the black tower in the trading town at the end of the long trail up the cliff from the DownBlow -- an eyesore that many of *a' Chlann* – the Children – of the Wayp saw not as symbolizing the Monstrato Corps' wealth and prestige but instead as raping the Mother's empyrean.

He held out his handheld and offered, "Here." There were displayed his credentials on the screoin he'd just pulled up:

Harishandra Higginsbottom,[61]
Faculty of Hybrid Academics and
Education of Communication and Culture,
Department of Hoomanitais

A distinction that carried with it the acronym of FHAECC, and while impressive to those outside the educational industry, his credentials, such as they were -- and as he was so painfully conscious of that he could not avoid the persistent, nagging guilt of engaging in charlatanry – had not earned him credibility amongst his peers — at any rate, not amongst any but the most credulous, certainly not among those academics who were ostensibly his peers but were so far beyond him in acumen and academic standing in more important fields, such as those involved in the study and development of extraction of gowp from under the world's oceans or of augmenting the profit from the corporation's other operations, endeavors that led to increasing revenues and otherwise glorifying the Profit.

He added, it suddenly occurring to the man to explain the child by his side, "And I thought I'd show my little girl around before I had to start." Apparently struck with the doubt that perhaps he wasn't being clear enough about which little girl he was referring to (but not that he thought Ròna was defective in her

---

[61] In order to maintain intellectual and academic objectivity, throughout this history, Higginsbottom, the putative editor and compiler of this chronicle, will be referred to in the 3rd person.

understanding, but that he had been deficient in his explanation), he pointed to clarify any possible confusion between the only little girl standing next to him, and some other, random little girl in existence somewhere else in the world. "This is her."

Taking advantage of an exit avenue from what was pretty obviously turning out to be an awkward line of conversation, Ròna turned to the little girl standing quietly beside the man on the dock and asked, "And what's your name?"

Plethora

'S fhèarr treabhadh anmoch na bhi gun treabhadh idir.
Better late plowing than none at all.
Proverb from *Leabhar an Leaghaidh Mhòir —*
The Book of the Great Melting

Higginsbottom had shifted into his academic career late in his working career. After several stutter-steps and stumbles in his early adulthood, he had gone back to his studies and earned substandard degrees at the school where he now taught, such that (he was painfully conscious) he lacked all but the most basic skills to succeed in the education industry, and so was relegated to earning his living by teaching superfluous topics to dispensable populations of students in the most out-of-the-way franchises of the corporate territories.

Besides that, he had a tendency to be possessed by the most unfashionable interests, enthusiasms over which he apparently had no control. He seemed to be unable to concentrate on the more popular fields where one could earn plaudits, prestige, and Profit (blessed be its name). He didn't want to pretend to be something that he was not, but on the other hand, it would be humiliating to go around broadcasting how inferior he felt himself and his qualifications to be. So, his usual tactic was just this: to simply deadpan his position and to let others infer what they might from his apparently highfalutin title, which often impressed those who didn't know better; those who did, to his chagrin, saw him for what he was, or at least, what he felt himself to be: a failure and a charlatan.

"Pau,"[62] the little girl pled, looking up from her handheld, "are we going yet?"

"Pretty soon," *Pau* said mollifyingly.

The girl glanced up in Ròna's direction and nodded with a huff of satisfaction as if to say, as only an imperious child can, *it's about time.* She turned back to her parental unit and asked, "Think we'll

---

[62] Pau – "baby talk" in the DownBlow for Parental Unit.

see the monster?" although she didn't wait for her *Pau* to answer but quickly turned to gaze piercingly out across the water.

The *Pau* shrugged. "I don't know."

The girl's face scrinched in disappointment.

"Well, maybe, that we will," Ròna said. "But it's out onto the water we have to go before we know for sure."

"You talk funny!" the little girl blurted.

The child's abrupt candor made Ròna smile. "Well, maybe it's you who talks funny, and you just don't know it!"

"Huh?"

"What's your name?"

"Plethora," the kid answered.

"That's an unusual name."

"Well, maybe," the child conceded. "It comes from some ancient code. My parental unit told me it means 'too much.' You see, I was *extra*." The girl spoke with an enthusiastic brightness. "A defective unit cuz I was a girl, and an overrun on top of that. I was ready to be *retired* ..." She gave an odd emphasis to the word, the enthusiasm in her speech dwindled, and her expression grew glum with the contemplation.

However, as she turned her attention to the happy part of her history, she brightened and exclaimed, "But my parental units saw a sale from the unbirthing factory, and here I am!"

"Well, I'm glad. And here I am, too," Ròna replied. "I'm Ròna."

"*That's* a weird name!"

"Not where I come from. Which is here, where it's your name that is ..." a pause to consider her phrasing: "...unusual," which the young woman uttered so gently that what might have been taken as a snappish retort, the child received as it was intended – an invitation to think about the idea, but Ròna interrupted that opportunity for reflection by adding, "My name comes from a word that means 'seal.'"

"Why'd they name you that?"

Ròna didn't want to go into all the details so she just left her explanation at, "On account of my hair. It looks like a seal's fur."

The little girl peered intently at Ròna's hair as if seeing it for the first time, or really seeing it.

Ròna continued, "But we can talk about all that later – names, and unexpected ..." The Simspeek word eluded her for a moment. "*Leanabhan*," she said, and to the child's quizzical expression, she recovered the word she'd been looking for: "Babies, I mean. And *uilebheist*."

"What's that!"

Ròna explained, "That's what we call water monsters here. You see, we've got all sorts of different words."

At that, Ròna turned back to the business of the moment. "*Uill, Eòghann* – Well, Ewan," she told the pier-hand, "'*S e an t-àm nuair a feumaidh sinn falbh.* – It's time we have to go."

"*Bi faiceallach* – Be careful," Ewan replied, "*nach bàth thu an t-amadan seo* – that you don't drown this fool."

"*Nì mi mo dhìcheall* -- I'll do my best," she said, though leaving it ambiguous whether her "best" would be to drown him or not to drown him. "*B' i tè laghach a' tha anns an nighean bheag, co-dhiù* – It's a nice one that the little girl is, anyway." This last she uttered as a shrugging, ironic excuse for not drowning the larger passenger.

At first, the exchanges between Ròna and Plethora, and between Ròna and Ewan were just background noise for Higginsbottom, the conversation blending with the accompanying sounds from the lake and forest – the rush of the wind through the trees, the calls and cries of various unseen creatures in the shadows, the purling of the water along the shore and its lapping against the side of the small boat.

After a few back-and-forths between the two Indiginoes, however, the sun rose in his thinking: He was hearing something unlike anything else he'd ever encountered. He edged closer to listen to what they were saying while pretending to concentrate on the panorama at the far end of the lake. He tilted his head to point his ear towards the two. Maybe it was the boatwoman's accent that confused him, a strange way of speaking — he'd heard of such a thing. Simspeek in far reaches of the Corps' demesne sometimes adopted or evolved non-standard pronunciation, but this was something totally different. Something that was not accounted for in the academic literature of the Corps: It was as if there was a different word for everything, a concept alien and contrary to the theories of Simspeek.

Ròna noticed the man's interest, and as she was readying the skiff to launch, she examined him more closely in her peripheral vision. Lines were etched in his brow as if he were emersed deep in a perpetual, profound contemplation, either that, or regularly entangled in puzzling out a riddle (which perhaps amounted to the same thing).

He struck her as a man who couldn't walk out of a door and turn to the right without jerking to a halt and abruptly reversing himself completely to head to the left, only to stop after a few steps to reconsider where he was going, or to consider for the first time which direction he really wanted to take, and only then recollecting his original intention of going to the right.

Higginsbottom sensed he'd been caught eavesdropping. The watcher watched, as it were. "I'm sorry," he apologized. "I didn't mean to offend, but ..." Having lost track of what it was he originally intended to say, he drifted to a halt. So uncomfortable was he under Ròna's steady, noncommittal gaze that she'd turned on him when he began to speak that he'd grown palpably heated in the chill air. Droplets of sweat were forming on his forehead and dribbling down the side of his face.

Doubt overwhelmed the professor. Perhaps, his broaching (or thinking about broaching) the topic of the FT had somehow put him in jeopardy of violating the BABLE[63] laws (which were not enforceable so far from the domains of the Monstrato Corps, anyway); either that, he feared, he had infringed on some social protocol that in his ignorance of the society of the Wayp he wasn't aware of.

To his relief, Ròna turned from him and continued her dialogue with little Plethora, "But come on, let's get you on board." Ròna gave the girl a hand and a boost onto the one-sailed skiff.

"Pau, too," the little girl urged.

"Yes, of course," Ròna said, and with Ewan's injunction not to drown her fat visitor bringing a smile to her lips, she offered a steadying hand to Higginsbottom.

He waved away her offer of a helping hand. "I think I can handle this myself," he said with the tone of somebody still holding on to the image of himself as the young man he used to be, one who nobody would think required the assistance of a little girl barely older than his own daughter.

"You think so?" Ròna wasn't too sure, so she held her arms behind him out of his line of sight, not touching him but hovering, waiting, in case he proved as unbalanced as he appeared.

Steadying himself with outstretched arms as he stepped into the gently rocking boat, the fat man teetered on one leg. After a tenuous moment, he settled with a satisfied *oomph* on the bench, rocking the skiff from side to side.

The thought crossed Ròna's mind that the fellow was as likely

---

[63] BABLE Act: Binding Articulatory Basis for Language Expression; law that established Simspeak as the sole legal form of language expression within the domains of the Monstrato Corps

to sink her small vessel with his bulk as he was to tumble out of it.

When the water stopped sloshing turbulently against the hull of the *curach*, Ròna followed, making barely an impression on the vessel's stability in the water.

She untied the skiff, pushed off and seated herself at the tiller, but neither the change from stasis to movement nor any consideration for Ròna's being occupied with navigating the *curach* deterred the "Professor" Higginsbottom from his ongoing rush of verbiage, so taken up was he in his enthusiasm over the possibility of uncovering a long-lost treasure of knowledge.

"You see, I'm interested in different communication styles, and I couldn't help noticing ..." He felt that he was verging on being intrusive, offensive, so he cut himself short, but even in his hesitation, concerned that he wasn't being clear enough, he plunged ahead with a blunt question: "What was that?"

"What?"

"What you were saying to that fellow there." He tilted his head towards Eòghann on the dock, now diminishing in the increasing distance between them.

"I was just telling him ..." Ròna paused to construct a plausible fiction around what she had said.

"It doesn't matter ..." Higginsbottom interrupted her. "The point is, it wasn't in Simspeek."

He could see her closing off. He'd just intimated her involvement in a speech crime.

"I have to ..." Her voice either trailed off as she turned away or was lost to the wind in the sails, and so he missed, if she had ever said it, just what she had to do.

"I didn't mean ..." Higginsbottom apologized.

He was not a total dunderhead. He could think quickly when it came to his own field of interest. His own game. He saw a possible move: He could trade his secret for hers. "You see, I've got a teaching job with the University ..."

"So, you said ..."

"But I'm developing a research project on the side."

"Me too!" the girl next to him interjected.

The man gave the child an indulgent nod before returning to Ròna. "I thought while I was stationed here, I would conduct some of my own research. A private project. In my spare time." He stopped himself, not sure what more he should disclose, but with a quick decision, he figured, *in for any, in for many*, so he tentatively continued, "You know what they say in academia ..."

Ròna shook her head. *No*, she didn't.

"Reap the farm or buy it."

Something about his tone implied there was a meaning more

ominous underlying the phrase than was apparent on the surface, something Ròna didn't want to get into.

All this time, she'd been busying herself with adjusting the sail and managing the tiller to position the craft to sail across the wind and out onto the water. Her attention seemingly focused on what she was doing, her gaze averted from him, she intended to subtly communicate her small interest (and thus discourage further discussion), but at the same time not wanting to appear rude, she went back to what he'd just said a moment earlier and threw a question over her shoulder. "Research of what?"

The visitor was so full of enthusiasm about what he evidently saw as a grand opportunity, that he couldn't restrain his excitement about the prospects afforded by this undertaking. Indeed, contrary to the beliefs of many of his peers (nearly all, truth be told), this new posting, rather than constituting a professional exile to the academic hinterlands (or uplands, as the case may be) might have just presented him with a career-making project. He burst out with "Primitive cultures" and winced immediately afterwards, belatedly realizing how offensive that phrasing might have sounded.

Ròna's face froze. Having made an effort not to offend, she was on the verge of being offended herself.

The man sensed he'd said something wrong, or if not "wrong," then something whose import he didn't quite understand. (*Didn't the people of the Wayp pride themselves on preserving the ways of their ancestors?*) Seeking to make the situation better, he explained, "By that, I mean 'ancient.' I mean, you people have maintained your culture for thousands of years."

But that rephrasing hardly made things any less awkward. Just what everyone wanted to hear -- that they, and everyone and everything they held dear and near had been classified as "primitive."

So animated was Higginsbottom by his passion for the topic that he plowed right through Ròna's balking. "While I'm stationed here, I was hoping to find some people who still speak the local language and keep to the old ways."

Ròna couldn't help but be a little suspicious. Was this an obvious sting? "You know that's against policy, don't you? Your own corporate policy?"

"I've got a research permit," he hurried in justification, fumbling with his handheld to locate the documentation that certified his bona fides. "In the interest of scientific knowledge ... it's somewhere here ... I could show it to you ..."

Her fat passenger was evidently one of those people who – however well meaning, or perhaps because he was so well meaning felt the need to fill uncomfortable gaps of silence with his own *bleadraich*; Ròna knew no other word for it, certainly no word in Simspeek – meaningless babble, blethering, yapping, words that seemed to mean something but really didn't; noise that made as much sense as the nattering of *feòragan* – the brown squirrels which chattered continuously without respite, and without purpose, and which alone of the Goddess's creatures seemed not to have the Tongue.

"It's here someplace." Higginsbottom gave up trying to find the permit and tapped the screoin off. "I don't want to cause anybody trouble … it's just that … I have a great respect … and from a scholarly perspective … I have a lot of interest …" Here he became aware that he was blabbing incoherently, and he stopped to collect his thoughts and consider his words.

The single sail stopped fluttering as the wind filled it, and they glided farther onto the calm water. Seated at the stern of the skiff, Ròna steered them on a straight course up the *loch.* This portion of the lake – before it widened into the vast continental sea -- was situated in a cleft between two ranges of forested hills, a verdant cover that occasionally revealed an abundance of life that thrived under the protection of the Mother.

"*Na dragh ort* -- don't bother about it," Ròna said finally, pointedly using the FT – "*'s coma leam* -- I don't care" -- though stronger than that, perhaps more like *I don't give a shit*, but without the profanity.

Though she didn't translate the phrase for him, he caught its gist, and wave of relief engulfed him – although even that phrasing might not be totally accurate because putting it that way would imply a positive thing. In this case, it was more a negative, as in the abatement of an atmospheric compression that unbeknownst to him had squeezed him all his life but which he had never been aware of because it had been so ever-present.

He felt like what a deep-sea creature, a gowp-wyrm itself, must experience upon being brought up to the surface of the ocean from its life-long habitat on the soul-crushing sea bottom. What he felt was akin to psychological bends of having risen too quickly from the pressurized depths of this very *loch* itself (lake, he corrected himself with a singe of alarm that so little exposure to the Indiginoes of the Wayp had already infected his thoughts and his tongue).

But that anxiety was replaced by a dizzy giddiness of hope and anticipation by the time the *curach* had made its way towards the center of the loch.

~~

mìcheal dubh

Just because you can't see it

(doesn't mean it's not there)

'S math a dh'fhaighnicheas pàiste còrr 's ceistean an tiotag na b'
urrainn duine freagairt an seachd bliadhna.
> It's a good thing when a child asks more questions in a
> moment than a grown person can answer in seven
> years.
>> Proverb from *Leabhar an Leaghaidh Mhòir* —
>> The Book of the Great Melting

Those who were used to the Wayp — either natives or long-accustomed visitors – would let the scene pass by without remark, but the little girl was amazed. She'd never seen a green landscape nor living creatures aside from the rats and cockroaches that infested the domed cities of the DownBlow, and the sea slugs and giant ocean worms in the aquariums her Parental Units had taken her to. But upon entry into this strange and magical land, she was encountering such a profusion of life that had been only dimly pictured in her child's phantasmagorias and only vaguely alluded to in her history textbooks.

"What's that?" The little girl pointed at a soaring bird, resplendently lighted by the sun, its wings stretched as it glided far above. Its back and wings were black as if it were wearing a cape, and its head was crested as if with a white hood.

There was something about the innocence of the child's eager inquisition that lured Ròna from her usual caution with incomers. "'*S e iolair-iasgaich tha th' ann*," she said.

"What?" in a tone that said the answer was more bizarre than the sight of the never-before-seen feathered creature.

Ròna thought for a moment. She'd never been asked to put these things of her world into the Simspeek, which was a clumsy language, anyway, useful for functionalities of buying and selling, but little else, certainly not to describe the Mother's world (for instance, there were any number of small, mammalian, skittering creatures in the DownBlow, but only one word, "rat," to describe them all).

126

"*Iolair*," Ròna said, but enunciated slowly, *ee-oo-lar*.

The little girl flipped the pages of her handheld, found what she was looking for and swiveled it around for Ròna to see. "That?"

The young woman glanced at the page and nodded.

The child scrutinized her resource. "That's an eagle!"

"Yes," Ròna confirmed, for the word in Simspeek had eluded her. "A fishing eagle."

The *iolair-iasgair* – the fishing eagle – its wing span nearly as wide as a woman was tall, with a deep brown back and snowy white breast, tucked its wings against its body and arrowed into the water.

The little girl gasped, her breath caught in amazement. "What's it doing?" she asked with an outrush of air.

"He's getting dinner." Ròna directed the little one's attention to where the bird had disappeared. "Watch!"

In the span of time that it would take to draw three deep breaths, the predator arose from beneath the surface, flapped its wings in open air, scattering drops of water in a flurry, and took flight, a struggling salmon – nearly half its own size --caught in its talons.

With a deep inhalation of amazement, Plethora looked up at Ròna: "And what's that thing it has in its feet?"

"*Bradan*," Ròna said, adding with a shake of her head, "I don't know what the Simspeek word is."

The child slid her fingers across the screoin of the handheld. She was adept at the device's manipulation and quickly found what she was looking for. She swiveled the apparatus around to show Ròna what she'd come up with. "Salmon," she announced. Her voice dipped to a conspiratorial tone. "But I like your word better." She tentatively tried saying it: "*Bradan*."

But the show was not yet completed. Ròna pointed. "Keep looking."

The fisher-bird rose high above them and soared to the pinnacle of one of the many trees that stood sentinel over the *loch*. There it hovered above a clump of twigs and branches that had been woven together to form a nest in the very tip-top of a pine tree.

"What's it doing?"

"Feeding his family. *Ist* – quiet. Pay attention."

The bird dropped the fish into the nest, and another bird – almost as big, though not quite – rose from the recesses of the roost, and hovering, the two faced each other, beating their wings.

Plethora was mesmerized by the scene played out before them – so much so that she let out a series of *oohs* and *aahs* to communicate her wonder.

"It's like they're dancing!" the little girl exclaimed.

As the boat skimmed across the water's surface, Ròna tilted her head from time to time to glance at the youngster, whose eyes were raptly shifting from the handheld screoin to the surroundings.

"Now, what've you got there now, *a ghràidh*?"

"I'm looking for the *monster* ... but my pau says there isn't one."

Ròna shrugged. "Just because you can't see it all the time doesn't mean she's not there. Sometimes, she doesn't come all the way up to the surface. So, you have to look under the water ... and maybe you'll see a shadow, a dark patch, moving."

The *caileag* – the little girl -- scrutinized Ròna closely. "Have you seen it?" she asked.

"We don't say 'it.' Vessie is a 'she.' And we don't really call her a 'monster', either."

"What do you call her then?"

"*Uilebheist* – not quite the same thing." Ròna leaned in and lowered her voice. "And I can't say that I've seen her. They don't want me scaring our visitors."

Higginsbottom, the parental unit, chuckled softly.

Ròna lowered her voice conspiratorially. "But I won't say that I haven't seen it, either." She winked.

The little face opened in amazement. The girl took a deep breath and asked, "What does it ..." but corrected herself, "What does *she* look like?" Before Ròna could answer, Plethora swiveled the handheld tablet around and flicked it open to a well-studied page and held it out for Ròna to see.

"Like this?" She pointed at a picture of a shark finned, thick-bodied, long-necked aquatic dinosaur with needle-sharp, rapacious teeth set in its disproportionately small head. As she touched the screoin, the image was animated, showing the creature swimming in a long, looping circle and darting its head forward to snatch at a small fish swimming by. "I think she's a Plesiosaurus," the kid said.

"That's what they used to call ..." She paused as she thought and continued, "... her."

"Like I said, I can't say, but ..." Ròna looked significantly, and directly into the child's eyes and nodded subtly --- *just between you and me.* "If you see her, that's what she'll look like."

"See!" The daughter's triumph was one of a long-running dispute between her and her parental unit. "I told you!"

"Let me show you something." Ròna opened her case. "Part of my job is to go around the *loch* ..." She caught herself. "Lake, I mean. Sorry. I must have caught something in my throat." She continued with her explanation: "And collect water samples."

"What for?"

"To take them back to the lab where we test for various things -- oxygen levels, acidity, salinity, pH factor, and toxins ..." She noted the kid's brow scrunch. "Poisons," she explained. "Things that aren't good for Vessie."

Listening intently, though trying to appear that he wasn't, Higginsbottom grunted in interest, and the *caileag* nodded sagely. It made sense to her, even if her parental unit might regard what their guide was saying as merely a "cultural artifact."

"So, I collect these." Ròna's hand made a pass over the assortment of tiny bottles, each no bigger than the kind people swigged *teatha na màthar* – the tea of the mother -- on the cruise ships that ran up and down the loch. In fact, back at the lab, the running joke was that they should fill those bottles with the brew, and before collecting the water samples, they'd have to first drink the magical tea from each one.

Ròna went on: "So, I collect samples at different depths. Right at the surface, at ten lengths, a hundred, and a thousand. We want to make sure that Vessie's home stays a healthy environment for her."

"An interesting metaphor ..." Higginsbottom, now the observing researcher, muttered.

Both Ròna and the girl alike ignored the muted interjection. "How deep does the lake go?"

"Some say just a thumb of the moon's transit, but others say ..."

"It opens to a sea in the middle of the earth!" the little one interrupted enthusiastically.

"*Tha fìrinn agad, a bhalaich* – You have truth, dear," Ròna nodded. "That's why they can never find Vessie when they look for her."

And so it went for the entire trip: "What's that?" followed by a terse though indulgent answer interjected between her duties as sister of the lake and the next rapidly fired "What's that!" The child inquired into the identities of every passing creature seen slinking through the underbrush, including the *mathan-madaidh* – the bear-wolf — spotted standing on its rear haunches and gazing curiously out at the passing sloop.

Higginsbottom's attention drifted from the two girls' chatter. (Though Ròna was entering into her womanhood, to him – sagging, as he was, into his middle years – she appeared to be of a youth so far distant from his present age that he could barely see her as anything other than a child.)

The wind wafting across the surface of the water and flapping the sail carried the words of the girls' conversation in wayward directions, so he couldn't pick up everything – or even a significant portion – of what they were saying. So, prompted to curiosity by his own little girl's wonder – *what was all her fuss about?* -- he looked out from the sailboat. In so doing, for the first time, he actually saw their surroundings, and the sight snagged his attention like a dump-rat on a barb-wired fence (the closest simile he could think of). He barely dared move as if in fear of disturbing the resplendence, of shattering the still sanctity of the scene. He felt — a phrase drifted to him from his studies as an undergrad in ancient literatures -- "like Cortez standing with a peek at a rear end," though neither he nor his fellow students, nor even his professors had been able to make out just who this mythological Cortez might have been, nor where the rear end happened to be, nor why this person would be so struck with amazement at the sight of it, but enough was grasped of the general import that it expressed the wonder of someone who had just seen for the first time a vision marvelous but heretofore unknown, albeit not exactly clear just what.

Ròna secured the tiller, and standing up in the gently rocking craft and while still negotiating the boom that secured the bottom flap of the sail, she drew a length of weighted line out of a side compartment of the boat. She unraveled the weighted plumb line, revealing at the end of it a metal container, about the size of a large man's finger.

The little girl's mouth gaped open with astonishment and admiration as she watched the older female – who, despite being barely out of her teens herself, seemed mature and wise beyond comprehension.

When Ròna noticed the girl's intense open-mouthed wonderment, she suppressed a smile. "Do you want to help me?" she asked, and when the child nodded vigorously, Ròna gave her the tube to hold while she secured it to the long wire which would carry a pulse to the sensor that would read out to her the depth of the container.

"If you watch, you can see the bubbles when the air comes up,"

Ròna told the kid. "You see this flap here?" The child nodded again vigorously. "Well, when it's deep enough, this opens and lets the air out and the water in."

They dropped the weighted bottle into the water and waited as the line played out. Ròna glanced at the readout on the computer screen and to the child, whose gaze was locked where the line had disappeared into the water.

"Watch this," she told Plethora, steering her gaze to the computer readout. "Tell me when it reaches a thousand."

"Okay!"

The numbers ratcheted higher as the plumb line plummeted lower.

The wire trailing across her palm and through her fingers, Ròna could feel the descent slowing as the weight of the bottle reached an equilibrium with the density of the water. "Is it there yet?" Ròna asked, getting a little kick out of prompting the girl with her own impatient query.

"It's going so slow," the little one complained. She counted off: "A hundred. Two hundred. Three ..." and so on, until, finally, wiggling with excitement, she exclaimed, "It's almost there!"

"Just let me know."

"One thousand!"

Ròna stopped the wire's slide. "You want to push the button to get the sample?"

"Oh, yes!" the *caileag* shouted so suddenly and loudly as if nothing in her short life had ever given her so much joy.

Ròna guided the child's hand to the screoin, which the little one touched gingerly.

"How do you know if it's getting the sample?"

"If you look over where the line goes into the water, you'll see the bubbles from the air coming up. Then we'll know that we've got the water sample." Although Ròna well knew that the tiny bubbles dissipated in the rise to the surface hundreds of lengths above the collection bottle, and would not be seen -- could not be seen -- she was counting on the child's imagination and eagerness.

The young woman wasn't far wrong as the little one exploded, "I saw them! I think I saw them!"

"*Sin agad e!* -- There you have it," she said, sufficiently relaxed with the girl to switch in and out of the FT. "Let's bring it up," and she offered the screen to the little girl to activate the ascent.

They waited through the winding whirr of the line. The bottle clanked against the hull.

"There it is!" The youngster's sudden shout startled both Ròna and the parental unit. Ròna smiled in amusement at her own and the man's reflexive reactions. "Let's pull it up, then."

Ròna reeled the bottle in, and cocking her head, she directed the girl to pull out the towel tucked into the side compartment. "Dry it off," she said.

The youngster applied the towel, and Ròna affixed a label to the tube and scribbled the coordinates on it and at what depth.

The professor's daughter watched intently, it dawning on her that the moment was fading away even as Ròna stowed the cylinder in her pack.

The young woman noticed the *is-that-all-there-is-isn't-there-something-else?* expression on the child's face. "You've done such a good job, how'd you like it if I appointed you Special Assistant?"

This was a delight and an honor almost too magnificent to be believed! It was all the child could have hoped for, more than she had ever dreamed of. She rose up off her heels in a half-jump. "Yeah!"

"You have to understand, I can't appoint just anybody. It has to be someone special. Somebody who promises to take care of Vessie's home and never let anybody hurt her. Do you promise?"

The little girl nodded her head zealously. Barely able to hold herself in, she squirmed with the agony of waiting.

"Okay, then ..." Ròna wrote the words "Special Assistant" on one of the labels and held it out, stuck to her forefinger. "Where would you like it?"

The child tucked her chin and scanned her torso as if there were a huge expanse of choices there, before finally deciding, "Right here," pointing to a spot on her chest below her left clavicle, just above her heart.

"Alright, then." Ròna patted the sticker in place. "You're now my Special Assistant, protector of the home of Vessie and all her friends."

Without a word in response to Ròna, the kid turned to her parental unit and announced triumphantly, "See, Pau!?! I'm Special Assistant!"

Ròna bent over the side of the boat and skimmed her hand across the top of the water. She brought her fingers to her lips. Was that *blas an t-sàile*? – the taste of salt? Or something worse, *ola* – oil?

Something that would have to be confirmed by *Peathraichean an Locha* – the Sisters of the Lake -- but troubling to even speculate about.

~~

Twilight dropping

Chan eil càil cho math ri snàmh ann an loch reòite.
There's nothing as good as swimming in a frozen lake.
Proverb from *Leabhar an Leaghaidh Mhòir* —
The Book of the Great Melting

After all was done, came the time of day that Ròna lived for when away from her duties as "little sister."

She docked the boat and whistled Dìleas to her. Together, they rode along the shore of the *loch na màthar*.

After a short while, she pulled her companion to a stop, and they paused, he standing patiently still, she atop his back listening to the slow dropping *ciaradh* -- the twilight of the evening; when she could sit embraced by the warm lapping of the water against the lakeshore. The stillness and the quiet were disturbed only by the lone caw of a heron calling for its mate from across the water in one of the tall pines that ringed the loch. Drifting through the dropping mist of the oncoming evening floated the ghost-like apparition of a long necked white swan -- an *eala-bhàn* in the language forbidden by the Monstrato Corps, which, however much it attempted  to assert its authority, lacked any real (or moral) sway over the people of the Wayp.

Listening to the soft breathing of the world, she absorbed the tranquility. From somewhere, there came to her the bleat of a sheep, and the *langanach*[64] -- the bellowing -- of a red-deer stag on

---

[64] *Langanach* - there was no word Simspeek that translated the meaning of this word, for it contained within it the meaning of the sound of the yearning lowing of a bull-deer; its searching and its desire not just for a sexual partner but even more, as Ròna imagined, its longing for a heart-mate.

a mountain ridge above her. A trout's long speckled body rose up out of the lake and fell back into the vague whiteness again with the slapping of its flank on the face of the water.

She heard a call that sounded like somebody clucking or knocking their teeth, followed by a rapid, ratcheting trill. Above her, she caught a glimpse of an *oidhche-gabhar* – the night taker -- a brown and black bird, little bigger than her hand, with tufts of feathers atop its head that looked like the swept-back ears of a wildcat in flight. It rose up from where it had been perched on a low branch and swept out into the dimming sky, swooping and swerving, catching its insect meals on the wing, and dipping down to the water to drink on the fly and soaring up again.

She dismounted, and she hiked, and Dìleas plodded behind her. Although the day was growing late, it was still pleasantly warm, and within a short period of time, even at the gentle pace they took towards the tall trees on the upslope, beads of sweat were forming on her forehead and upper lip. She felt trickles of perspiration running down her sides from under her arms. Her heart beat soundly, and she breathed vigorously, deeply.

Trekking farther through the woods up a steep incline where spray and mist was thrown up by the falls from the upper loch to the lower, she came to a giant oak tree – its trunk gnarled and weathered, its branches dripping with mistletoe vines -- the Grandmother Tree, which legends told had stood there for thousands of years, maybe even since the time of the Great Melt. She placed her palm upon the withered trunk of the ancestor.

"*Ciamar a tha thu, a ghranaidh* -- How are you, granny?" Ròna crouched next to the ancient personage and placed her hand flat on the earth to listen to the colloquy carried along the roots and synapses and mycelium of the forest sentinels. She stood and smelled the air.

She and Dìleas went on
and came to the far shore.
After slipping out of her
clothes and folding them
and tucking them into a
neat pile on the sandy
beach, she mounted the
unihorn and eased them
both into the water as

softly as she could, as if even a splash would desecrate the holy sanctum of the *loch*.

Away from shore, she slipped off his back and swam down to a fathomage where the light from the world above was dissipated and blotted out and absorbed by the water above her, and there she floated, carried by the gentle current that flowed from the incoming melt of the snow pack on the mountains above the loch, and there as if floating in interstellar space, borne up so that she had no weight, no presence of her own, almost as if she did not exist except as a droplet of the great sea that rose up from the womb of the world. In absolute silence except for the rhythm of the occasional bubbling exhalation from her gills, she felt the presence of a massive latency beneath her, one that dwarfed her, as if she were but a water flea on its flank, and they -- she and this thing, this unfathomable ubiquity -- floated as if in communion, until it flowed off and away from her like a giant, elegant subterranean ship. When cleared of her, in a sudden movement that she sensed but was not able to see, faster than breath, it flashed away.

Coming to the surface, she gazed out across the loch and upon the mountain rising precipitously from the level mountain valley, sloping gradually away from her to disappear into a wood of conifers and pine.

She called Dìleas to her, and they made their way towards the beach, where they waded through the shallow water and crossed the narrow *machair* – or sandy strand.

Walking ahead, she guided her "faithful" into the woods, and they hiked along a narrow trail, up a steep incline and came to the ruins of an old house the color of greyish-blue, or *liath* in the FT, the color of an overcast sky or an old woman's hair -- that stood alone near the shore.

She'd mused on trips like this how lovely it might be to fix up the tumble-down and live on the quiet shores of the loch -- the sweet smells rising from the water to the south, the cool breezes blowing down from the heights of the *Beinn na Màthar* – the Mountain of the Mother -- to the north, but for now, even though she could probably get permission from the Council, the thought was no more than the wafting of a pleasant, inconsequential breeze.

They proceeded a short distance farther, and the different plants became more distinct -- grasses low lying, ferns sticking up and arching above those, and a few saplings growing out in the sunlit areas, taking advantage of the refuge from their taller cousins' deep shade. She passed by these, careful not to trample them or brush against them and break them, until after a few hundred lengths, she'd passed into the relatively bare ground of the shaded forest, where moss lichens grew on the rocks and against the sides of the trees in the shade and on the damp soil. She passed through a copse of birch trees, white trunked with black-streaked fringes streaking their bodies -- friends of hers, as she thought of them.

A little farther on, she came on a faintly marked path, having to turn sideways at a couple points in the dense underbrush. When she neared a stream, the sharp-thorned berry bushes grabbed at her clothes, threatening to stab her with their miniscule needle-teeth. She stepped to the cliff which fell precipitously to the DownBlow and perched on the "lip of the world" -- *bile an t-saoghail,* as the Children called it.

She unpacked her flask of lukewarm tea and unwrapped her meat pie. A bank of brown smoke billowed a thousand lengths beneath her like a great blanket of woolly mammoth down -- the under-coat of lanolin-rich and fluffy soft mammoth's fur. It was on account of this, that sometimes they called their mountain land not Wayp (which was the term the Corps had settled on them and not their own, anyway), but rather, *an tìr os cionn na smùide* -- the land above the smoke.

As she sat munching slowly on her meal, she went back on her earlier consideration: How, after all, she didn't need the results of the water analysis to tell her that the lake was low, lower than usual, lower than it should be. It was more than a suspicion that the cause of the falling levels was the Monstrato Corps' pumping of water over the cliff to get at the gowp reserves below the lake floor; it was more than speculation – she could see it.

Neither did she require any lab report to confirm what she already knew: that the effluvium from the mining operations were leaching into the lake, and slowly – or perhaps not too slowly – killing it.

Because this seemed all too clear to Ròna, she didn't understand why the Council of the Mothers had agreed to the arrangement that had allowed the Corps access to the lake (and even if she had completely understood, she probably still would not have agreed). There were those who had argued the contract was lucrative, those who had been resigned to acceding to the power of the Corps in the face of the threat of the PieceTaker troops, and those who had referred to the arrangement as a "dynamic partnership" – though the scheme had not been without its critics. "Rogues and scoundrels," one opponent of the deal had put it, "selling out our heritage, our homes, our lives, the heart-blood of the Mother, for a few pieces of silver."

Ultimately, the vast reserve of gowp beneath the Lake of the Mother was too great a "natural resource" – no mention of the resource of the water that covered it – too great a temptation for the Corps to forgo acquiring either by purchase or by force. Besides, no doubt went the reasoning in the high reaches of the Monstrato black spiral in Trayton, as one of the last wells on earth rich with valuable and easily accessible reserves of gowp, why shouldn't the Corps monetize the oversupply of this valuable resource that was of no worth or use to the People of the Wayp? Wasn't it the moral obligation of every Corps associate to maximize revenues? (All praise to the Profit!) If they did not, the precious gowp would just be wasted, destined to lie in the ground for an incalculable number of years, not being put to productive, profitable use, so in the end, the benefits being too attractive to turn away from, the threats too present and real, the persuasions of the Corps prevailed, and the Council of the Sisters agreed to a trial period.

Which period, Ròna well knew, as did all the Children in actuality, was a "trial" nothing. But was a marriage until death – the death of the life-blood of the mother.

As Ròna ruminated the cold meat pie she'd packed for her midday meal, she also contemplated how the Mothers had not foreseen the methods that would be employed to extract the all-too-precious gowp: To clear access to the subterranean, subaquatic sludgy black gold, the Monstrato Corps had taken to pumping the water of the lake over the cliff as useless by-product. They were even now in the process of erecting a dam to further strip bare the body of the Mother to more efficiently extract the gowp.

Already, vast stretches of former lake bed had been pumped out, dried out, and were left covered with caked dirt, coated with the residue of rotting fish corpses, blown over by bitingly sharp granules of sand, and swarmed by vicious, flesh-eating gnats. The Lake of the Goddess had supported the Children of the Wayp for thousands of years, but now in the face of the incursion of the Monstrato Corps, how much longer could the Mother's blessing of life last? How long could this desecration be sustained?

The trees behind her bent away from the cliff and the cold, stiff wind that typically blew from the north. The *smùid* stretching out before and below her glowed an orangish red. Turning her eyes over that expanse of nothingness, of sheer air and cloudbank that stretched farther than she could see over the DownBlow, she gazed upon the play of red and reddish-brown lights in the growing dark - - *fùirneis-iarainn an donais* in the FT, or the devil's forge -- that

137

filtered through the smoke that blanketed the lands below, alternately with a infernal effulgence smoldering long and softly,

and then blazing up suddenly and brilliantly.

She turned away from such thoughts and from the sight of the black Skypiercer, which rose in the distance from the Monstrato outpost of Trayton, spearing up over the intervening ridges and hills to cast a shadow on the land, seeming to rape the yielding veil of the Wayp.

It was time to turn back. She had to make it down the west shore and finish ahead of the storm clouds blowing down the steep mountain sides around and above her. She took a last swig of her lukewarm tea and packed up the remains of her lunch.

4. Across the sludgy sea

Bha mi nam choigreach ann an tìr chèin
I was a stranger in a strange land
Leabhar an Leaghaidh Mhòir —
The Book of the Great Melting

Wiktionary: The Gowp Slick

Professor Harold Harishchandra Higginsbottom (editor)

It must be remembered that the ecological catastrophe that occurred in the lead-up to and the following of the Great Melt was not directly connected with the heating of the planet alone, but the global warming and the subsequent melting of the polar icecaps compounded the complex of shocks to the environmental system.

In the centuries surrounding the Melting – a process whose date cannot be pinpointed because it spanned centuries – the oceans of the world acquired their current protective covering – a combination of gowp flowing upwards from the deep-sea drilling and a mono-molecular film formed from a complex of saturated long-chain polymers generated from the vast quantities of industrial wastes discharged into the oceans.

The inorganic blanket of plastic micro-beads and gowp created an oxygen-impermeable membrane that prevented the evaporation of surface water into the air. This intact seal would be broken only when water was violently disturbed by  storms or the occasional passing ship or a falling satellite.

The shroud over the world's oceans was augmented by billions (trillions? an immeasurable amount?) of tons of industrial wastes, whole or broken merchandise, industrial and commercial equipment, tools, engines, mechanical devices, furniture, textiles, packing material, sized in scale between the frames of aptracs, the exoskeletons of appliances such as refrigerators and stoves, the floating wrecks of boats, ships, cars, and the assorted and indistinguishable rubble of various sizes down to plastic micro-beads; and those were just the detritus that was visible; much was not, such as sewage runoffs or direct and purposeful dumping from cities, agricultural regions, mining operations, and industrial facilities. These filled the seas of the world, and their residue crusted along the shores like brown, hardened scum around the bowl of a toilet.

There were sporadic efforts at the beginning, in the midst of, and in the immediate aftermath of the Melt to break the seal. Each measure proved more futile (and sometimes more fantastical) than the previous: These included plans to ply the seas in giant paddleboats to churn up the covering and release the water below to the evaporative process and return the oceans to the ecological circulatory system of the world. Another proposal entailed trailing giant reams of absorbent material like giant rolls of paper towels or toilet paper behind aircraft carriers and other large naval or cargo ships to clean up the excreta of the world's societies.

There were many other proposals and abortive attempts, none of which proved effective in exposing the festering, rotting infection that was sealed under the thickening scab that closed off the world's seas to the healing offered by the natural circulatory system of the environment.

Or which garnered enough support to be fully implemented.

Each method either suggested or attempted was short-lived, not fully committed to, or rejected as impractical from the outset. Various stakeholders (which effectively included everybody on the planet) argued against the efficacy of a particular approach, or complained that this one or that unfairly imposed a burden of cost or implementation on them, or that it pointed the finger of blame at one party when another was a much worse actor.

What about those people over there? They do worse than we do. They're not doing their fair share. It's alright for you, you've already got yours, but we're just coming along; once we've developed our economy, we'll gladly join in. Who's going to pay for all this? It's not that big a problem. The predictions can't be proven right. You can't prove today what tomorrow is going to look like. It's all just projection and conjecture.

And so on.

Likewise, endeavors to implement a world-wide scheme met with resistance or backsliding. *Why should we pay to clean up somebody else's mess?*

While one party might adhere to agreements to cease dumping effluvia, or strip mining, or clear cutting, to name just a few examples, another found it in their self-interest to take a shortcut and steal a portion of the commonly held wealth of the earth, figuring, *Everybody else is looking out for the planet, it won't hurt anything if I just make a little Profit for me.*

~~

Across the sludgy sea

Cha tig buaidh no piseach air duine a bheir cat dhan uisge.
He will not profit who takes a cat into the water.
Proverb from *Leabhar an Leaghaidh Mhòir* —
The Book of the Great Melting

The old song went "loud carrier keeps on churning," and indeed the "carrier" -- or the ship -- that was transporting the contingent of Zziippp PieceTakers was both loud and churning as it forced its way through the flotsam that crusted the sea between the Merican Pelago and the cliffs of the Wayp.

> *Sailing, sailing o'er the browny deep*
> *Plowing through the boiling sea*
> *of debris and shit and pee.*
>
> *Sailing, sailing across the sea we go*
> *Mining all the Profit's rights*
> *In the ocean's fiery glow*
> > Cheerful ancient sailors' sea shanty,
> > mined from the Cosmic neuronal net

The face of the dun-colored water sheened and shimmered with rainbow swirls of oily gowp – at least that which was visible beneath the layer of jetsam and flotsam that coated the surface. Like a pot that had been left on a low simmer, bubbles boiled up to the surface, popping and releasing the acrid stench of an oil fire, which burnt the eyes, stung the nostrils, and prickled the skin – or would have, if the people on the ship's deck had not been wearing their atmopuro masks and sun-screening veils.

Undoubtedly, the vista of the sparkling sea lighted by the arcing electrical storms that were set off by the methane and methane-hydrate geysers shooting up from the underwater mining operations that blanketed the ocean floor would have inspired aesthetic awe in anyone who had had the leisure to enjoy such a sight, but the Zziippps in the engine room of the flat-bottomed paddleboat that had been making its slow, painful, hard-won way from the Pelagoes to the shores of the Wayp had no such sweet time to enjoy the spectacle.

For more than a month, the ship and its crew of PieceTakers had been slogging through the sea, its scoop-nose splitting the surface as it furrowed, plowed, shoved, and bulldozed its way towards its destination.[65] The massive vessel – its paddlewheel plowing the debris through which they traveled, scooping it up and dropping it behind them, and thus propelling them through the viscous seas -- was driven by the most modern dual power-plant technology – the gowp steam furnace and the twelve-Zziippp-powered rotary engine, a marvel of modern technology.

All around them raged nature, dripping gowp in heap and scum. As the ship thrust its way through the Straights of Spoliation, on one side, the waves of fire rose up a hundred feet, and on the other side, a crater opened up, and the debris fell in a cascade into a whirlpool that had no bottom.

During the voyage through the Great Sulphurific Garbage Patch, one of the chief pastimes of the travelers – officers, service staff, engine room crew (when they weren't working), and passengers – was standing at the back of the ship and watching the massive paddles churn through the muck of the ocean.

What particular item of debris disposed in the oceanic cesspool would the paddles churn up next? All grist for speculation – both intellectual and wagering.

Tables were set up on the deck for betting, and tote boards were hung listing the odds – if of not every conceivable eventuality, of at least the more common and popular: the odds that the next refuse scooped up by the giant paddles would be a plastic container – and of what size (there was a betting line on that, too); a piece of

---

[65] If these seem like strange words to use for the sailing of a ship, consider that much of what the barge had to do was to actually push its way through the assorted debris and detritus of millennia's worth of garbage that had run or been dumped into the waters of the earth. Ancient legends record that this body of liquefied semi-solid detritus was once called the "Pacific Ocean," though nowadays it is called much more appropriately the Great Terrific Garbage Patch. The surface of the semi-permeable sludge was sometimes so thick that a man – whether Anboarnh, Zziipppaei, half-speesh, or muncaidh -- could walk across it. (Your author takes the position as stated in the International Declaration of Humanoid Rights, "that we hold these truths to be self-evident that all Anboarnhs, muncaidhs, sentient aiReps, and others of humanoid form -- known, unknown, discovered, undiscovered, or not yet mutated, created, or manufactured -- are endowed by the Monstrato Corps with the right to a slice of life, the possibility for bootstrap mobility, and the pursuit of profit.")

furniture, appliance, or machinery (or a whole item); or a gowp-mummified body – and whether animal, Anboarnh, or Zziippp.

CacaHed Docherty, the Monstrato Corps executive officer of this operation -- the man-in-white -- did not bother himself with such frivolities but rather spent the greater part of his time leaning against the railing on the bridge of the scoop-nosed barge – straining against it, sometimes bouncing against it -- as if the meager force of his slight weight would speed the ship all the faster.

The soan[66] of Magnus Mugwump, mayor of Richerton, Docherty had been imbued with the certainty that because his father was widely regarded as a "great man," so must he, the soan, be. Adding to this sense of superiority, he had been endowed with a preternaturally high forehead – though one couldn't be sure whether it were naturally or prosthetically so. Nevertheless, he prided it and had his barber cut his hair back to augment the appearance of his brow's height, and to apply a lacquer to enhance its sheen, for he felt it signified the obvious fact that he was the smartest person in any room, office, suite, apartment, accommodation, house, space, area, alcove, joint, or cubbyhole.

Not only that, but he was imbued with the conviction that anybody who didn't recognize his brilliance was an idiot, which led to him speaking in a tone that asserted his superiority in expectation that everyone else would be quiet and listen to him, and precluded (along with his father's wealth) anyone from disagreeing or otherwise gainsaying him.

He wore a drawn, pained expression to his countenance, as if a sand wasp were continually burrowing into his ear, which decorum would not allow him to root out. A tall man – indeed, he had always been taller than his peers, even as a boy -- he had grown up literally looking down on others, which physical peculiarity had transmuted into an assumption that he was perched higher -- morally, intellectually, spiritually – than others. As such, he had developed the habit of looking at people with an expression of barely

---

[66] soan – Spawn of Anboarnh.

tolerating distaste – whether other Anboarnhs, Zziippps, refugees, or slaivs from the Wayp – as if he were regarding from a height a cockroach that had just invaded his meal of algae salad and rat meat, tilting his head back as if to escape a stench that offended his nostrils and his fine sensibility.

When he smiled, it was a smile without humor, more like the cold-eyed gaping maw of a sea-wyrm stretching wide its mouth to engulf a tasty prey.

Meanwhile, DownBlow, in the belly of the behemoth, the Zziipppaei engine assets trudged the wheel that powered the paddles of the sea-going vessel. There were six spokes on the mill wheel and two Zziippps on each. A smaller detail of two Zziippps shoveled loads of gowp into the furnace, which glowed eerily while slowly burning, thus completing the most up-to-date dual-engine rig.[67]

The temperature inside the engine room was soaring – a combination of the body heat thrown off the toiling workers in the close quarters, the slowly burning fire in the boiler, and the feverish temperature radiating up from the sea on which they sailed. Shimmering waves of scorchitude distorted vision and miraged the imagination.

Whether plodding around the drive-gear or shoveling gowp into the slow-burning engine furnace, the Zziippp crew intoned a work song that synchronized their movements:

> Wok day
> Wok night
> Not wok
> No gud life
> Get pay
> Get gowp
> No more try

---

[67] Part asset-driven — the Zziippppaei wheel drive, consisting of a spoked wheel with a Zziipppaei asset pushing each handle; and coupled with that, the furnace into which a couple other assets scooped shovelfuls of gowp, the slow burning, black-smoke-belching petroleum product which was the only propellant that would not ignite the combustible atmosphere in the DownBlow.

Uspela drop
Uspela die

Repeated ad-infinitum.

Standing on the circumference of the endlessly rotating wheel with a long taser-whip, Buttwater-Bates – Monstrato Corps Focwaod Massdaoer Priamus Thorben Beezow Doo-Doo Zipitty-Bop-Bop Buttwater-Bates, that is (of the genetic line of the West Virginia Isles Buttwater-Bateses) -- would lash one of the Zziippp workers or another as regularly as a metronome, responding to the inevitable grunt, cry, squeak, or squawk of pain with some inspirational corporate slogan, each one followed by another crack of his whip and another moan or groan or yelp from the "inspired" worker.

So, it went like this:
Whip!
"Ouch!"
"That's it, my Zziipppaeis!"
Snap!
"Ou!"
"Working rigor mortisly rewards remonstrably!"
Crack!
"Yee-ou!"
"Have relief in yourself!"
Slash!
"Aahh!"
"No shot in the butt to succession!"
Pop!
"Ayee!"
"Work makes you freeze!"
Thwack!
"Ratfucker!"
And so on and so forth.

Cuilean was placed diagonally from Buttwater-Bates. He was also armed with a whip and also under orders to drive the wheel-rats, although he made it a point to crack the whip in the air above their heads and not on them. So far, his sabotage of Corps discipline had gone undetected as he'd perfected the art of making a snap, crackle, and pop with the long lash, which, however impressive as it sounded, touched no flesh; though his fellow-conspirators would shout out mock cries of pain: "Yupela cruel, Cuilean!" or "Too much hurt, Cuilean!" or "Yupela natborn of ratbitch, Cuillean!"

In between Buttwater's inspirational (if bewildering) encouragements and the metronomic snaps of the whip, the Focwaod kept up a running flux of verbiage in Cuilean's direction – it would be inaccurate to refer to it as "conversation." He was one of those people – albeit, an Anboarnh – who despised the sound of silence, which meant space (figuratively speaking) for  thoughtful, perhaps unnerving, reflection, time unfilled by talk – though certainly you couldn't call the interior of the engine room "silent."

"So, where do you spectacles our deportation is, frotch[68] boy?" he yelled at Cuilean across the engine room. Though technically a question, because it was yelled to pierce the grinding of the mill-wheel, it came out as more an angry demand.

Either way, Cuilean ignored the question/demand, whichever it was.

"Wouldn't it be isotonic if it was the Wayp!" Buttwater-Bates yelled, knowing full well that was where Cuilean was rumored to have come from.

Cuilean pretended not to hear the question, although he had heard it, and the flash of an image of a red-haired girl triggered a jolt from the tentacled cowl that made him wince.

Even though he most likely could see nothing across the smoky haze of the engine room, Buttwater-Bates sensed Cuilean's discomfort caused by his words and pressed forward relentlessly.

"That's your original have-a-hat, isn't it! I mean, the place you used to in-hav-it."

Cuilean was caught by surprise. He went from trying to figure out what the Focwaod was saying one moment to the realization of what he meant the next. A forbidden memory flashing through his thoughts without warning induced another electro-chemical jolt before he could guard against it. Cuilean gritted his teeth to keep from crying out, which would only have encouraged the Focwaod

---

[68] Frotch boy – the ethnic epithet applied to natives of the Wayp, derived from the observation of the common (though by no means universal) red hair on their heads and (presumably) their crotches; ie., an abbreviation of "fire crotch."

further.

Though there was such a cry – for a split moment, Cuilean had to check himself – *That wasn't me, was it?*

But then Cuilean heard the cry again – *It wasn't me!* -- this one not as sharp but definitely a cry of pain. Searching through the hazily oscillating air, he caught sight of one of the Zziippps writhing on the ground.

Buttwater-Bates was standing over him, screaming, "Get up! It's not that bad an injunction! It can't be deletionary!"

Cuilean moved to where he could see BilWee lying prostrate under the wheel arm. "What happened?" Cuilean demanded of no one in particular. Just a question thrown out for anyone to field.

Which Buttwater-Bates did: "I hardly touched him. He's faking." Fear had crept into his voice – fear of being charged for damaging Corps property. "Get up!" he shouted at BilWee, "or I'll have you shipped to the farm!"

Cuilean ignored the man and kneeled at BilWee's side. "Can you get up?"

"Don't proper him any assessment!" Buttwater-Bates yipped. "'Helping hurls,'" he added, mouthing one of the Corps slogans. "It's a viola of the Code: You have asservations about chairing the Profit with him, now?"

"You'd better hope he's able to go back to work."

"He's okay," Buttwater-Bates insisted.

"Mepela okay," BilWee repeated. "No go farm."

"See! You can lay all your dots alongside."

Nevertheless, Cuilean pointed BilWee to a bench at the side of the engine room. "Sit down there for a bit."

"Hey!" Buttwater-Bates protested. "Who's gonna do his work. We won't meet our ricotta."

Cuilean stepped close, uncomfortably close.

Backing away, but trying to maintain some semblance of authority, Buttwater-Bates muttered to Cuilean, "Never figured you for a ditch-digger lover."

"Never figured you for a Buttlicker."

Cuilean had evidently struck a nerve. The junior Focwaod objected, correcting immediately: "The correct aperitif is Buttwater-Bates."

"That's what I said – 'Buttwanker.'"

What came out now was an inarticulate stream of spits and snorts and rage as Buttwater-Bates strove to formulate an answer. Finally, "I'm your superlative officer! You have to show me some reject even if you don't mean it." Buttwater-Bates raised the whip threateningly, though unconvincingly.

Materializing out of the smudgy haze of the engine room, Slaiya stepped between Buttwater-Bates and Cuilean. "Nopela hurt lil fren."

Buttwater-Bates pulled up as if he'd just come up to a wall -- like one of those people who were driving along, oblivious to a barricade that had been visible a half-mile down the road stretching across the highway and was surprised to have it appear right in front of them all of a sudden as they came up on it, as if to say, *Whoa! What's that!?! Where'd that come from!?!*

"Mepela not let," Slaiya added.

"Hey," Buttwater-Bates said, letting the whip drop to his side in a suddenly limp arm. "Just choking. Merely a mini-school of gesticulation amongst friends. Nothing to be relegated seriously."

Slaiya grunted.

"I appreciate the back-up," Cuilean offered as Slaiya was turning away, "but I don't think he'd do much damage."

"Nopela *try* hurt lil' fren."

Endeavoring to maintain some semblance of authority, Buttwater's voice sounded above the din: "But what about our coda!?!"

A deep rumble from Slaiya: "Mepela take place." And she motioned BilWee's partner to move away from his place on their spoke.

"But it's a two-man shaft!" Buttwater-Bates protested, obviously still worried about the quota.

"Mepela do two Zziippp work," Slaiya said, as unconcerned with the little man's yelping as she would have been by the buzzing of a flying cockroach. Without another word or sign, the giant Zziippp heaved her chest against the wheel-spoke and started the engine again.

"Just make surety you do ..." Buttwater-Bates warned, unconvincingly.

In a neutral growl of ambiguous import, Slaiya muttered, "Yes, bospela, Buttwad, sir."

"Don't appellation me that!" He raised his whip again, this time with more conviction – as it was only a Zziippp he was facing.

Cuilean stepped between Buttwater-Bates and the Zziippp. "Let's cool the gowpfire here," he urged in a calm voice. "Just to clarify. What should they call you?"

"My no-man closure is Buttwater-Bates. Massdaoer Buttwater-Bates."

"Massdaoer Bates?"

"Yes."

"You're Massdaoer Bates?"

"Yes."

"Massdaoer Bates all the time?"

Impatiently Buttwater-Bates answered -- as in, *what else would he be all the time, or other times when he wasn't what he was?* "Yes!"

A general snigger went around.

"Well, no."

"So, not Massdaoer Bates."

"No!"

"Why not?"

"I don't like it."

"You don't like Massdaoer Bates?"

"Well, yes."

"You're not proud of Massdaoer Bates?"

"Sure, I'm proud."

"Then say it loud. Say it proud. I Massdaoer Bates!"

"Yes ... no!"

"Just to clarify: When do you like ... Massdaoer Bates?"

"All the time."

"Where you like ... Massdaoer Bates."

"Here. Home. All place." Then he caught himself. "Nugagation. I don't mean it like that. I'm preempting to say I don't like how you usurious the name."

"What's wrong with how I use the name? It's your name, isn't it?"

"Well, yes. It just sounds like ..."

A puzzled, expectant look. "Like what?"

"Just not how you're fruitifying it. Not like that."

"Why not?"

"It doesn't feel good."

"Massdaoer Bates doesn't feel good?"

"No. Not feel ... *Sound.* It doesn't *sound* good."

"How does it *sound* when you Massdaoer Bates?"

"It just sounds funny."

By this time, the Zziippp workers had yet again left off from turning the wheel and had crowded around the two in order to listen. Somewhere at the rear of the audience, a jokester imitated what he imagined Massdaoer Bates sounded like – somewhere between a squeal and a series of whoops: *eeee ... woooo ... wooo ... woo ... wo.*

Massdaoer Bates shouted angrily, "You're misapprehending my words! You're misdisfiguring my meaning! The circumevolution of your expansiveness implicates dismissiveness. It's like you're saying ..." Deep breath: It was difficult for Buttwater-Bates to get the word out. "... *masturbates.*"

"Well, *you* are Massdaoer Bates. What's wrong with that?" Cuilean asked innocently.

Which gave Buttwater-Bates pause as he couldn't tell whether

151

Cuilean was mocking him or if there was a fundamental misapprehension.

Anything Buttwater-Bates wanted to say right now was drowned out by the raucous laughter. "Okay!" Cuilean called out above the din. "Everybody calm down." He posed the question to Buttwater-Bates, "Let's start all over again. Let me ask you. What would you like to be called?"

"Call me Buttwater-Bates. Or, maybe Focwaod Buttwater-Bates. Yes, my official title. Focwaod." As if this were better.

"Okay!" Cuilean announced definitively. "Everybody hear that!?! Buttwater-Bates. Or Focwaod! But not ..." He paused for dramatic effect. "Not the *other* thing."

Cuilean checked with Buttwater-Bates with raised eyebrows. "So, is that okay?"

The Focwaod gave a resigned nod, and noticing the gathering around them for the first time, he snapped, "Destruct them to return to their deployment."

"Yessir, Focwaod, Sir," Cuilean said with a Zziippp salute. Then he announced, "Everybody back to work."

At that, Slaiya picked up the cue and gave out a squeaky command: "Go-oo!"

With a few last chuckles, the work crew of Zziippps returned to their stations at the wheel. Then the chant resumed, this time a little different than before:

> "Wok day.
> "Wok night.
> "Buttman say
> "Wok right.

"Not the least bit humus!" Buttwater-Bates whined. "It's not Buttman. It's Buttwater-Bates."

> "Wok hard.
> "Wok till sweat.
> "Buttwanker say
> "Not done yet.

"Seize and persist! That's enough!"

But his command had no effect, and the crew improvised further as they trudged on, slipping in Buttwater's mangled name and inventive variations of it every few lines

Fuming impotently, Buttwater-Bates stood outside the circle. There was little he could do: To discipline his squad further would impede the output. As it was, the work was getting done, the quota would be met, the profit target would be attained (or as Buttwater-Bates himself would put it, "abstained"), and he would reap his share of the Blessed Profit.

Glory to the Profit of the Wuarardd of Gawd![69]

~~

---

[69] *Glory to the Profit* – included here and elsewhere in these chronicles as an obligatory (which is to say, mandatory) acknowledgment of the source of all highlife, prosperity, and the salute of grabbiness.

The staircase of the Goddess

'S fhasa tearnadh na direadh.
It's easier to go down than to climb.
Proverb from *Leabhar an Leaghaidh Mhòir* —
The Book of the Great Melting

The ocean-going paddleship had entered the southernmost reaches of the Great Sulphurific Garbage Patch, where the accumulated flammable sea-snot had been blown their way by the currents of the world. Outside the approach to the harbor, the paddle-ship churned the muck of the sea to keep them stationary as they waited for the firestorm to break and a lane to open in the sludge.

Even then, as they made their way through the fire-free corridor, flames reached up in an insurmountable wall on either side, and the inferno formed an arch over their heads. Finally, however, the transport ship docked at the narrow strip of level ground that comprised the small colony of Portafire that fronted the cliffs of Wayp, the Zziippp engine crew let off their Sisyphean, circumnavigational trudging and their endless shoveling, and the squadron of PieceTaker guards let off enforcement duties as they all crowded expectantly at the massive steel door that encased the interior of the barge.

Before they were released from the belly of the behemouth, the PieceTakers were issued breathing apparatuses to enable them to step outside – the first time off the ship during the month-long journey from the Pelagoes to the shores of Wayp – and transfer to the aptracs they were assigned to. The gangplank of the ship lowered with a groan and a rumble and a great yawing creak that could be felt trembling up through their feet and shuddering through their bodies.

The corporate officers walked down the gangplank to direct the embarking of the aptracs. Among them was Cuilean, serving as a junior officer. He had been assigned as foreman of the Zziipppaei crew for no better reason than no one could figure out exactly where he fit, and he did seem to have a rapport with the creatures.

He wasn't a Zziippp-head, that was obvious both from his appearance and his speech (though it was expected that he'd been "born" in the manner of a Zziippp, though somehow not infected with the ZZyzx virus), but neither was he an Anboarnh. As an indentured slaiv, he inhabited some intermediate zone between free Anboarnh and Zziippp.

Crowding down the gangplank came the officers and after them, the galley hands and the armed PieceTakers, celebrating their landfall with excited hoots and high-pitched chattering in anticipation of setting their feet on land after the seemingly interminable sea voyage from the Pelagoes. These numbered nearly forty Zziippps, including PieceTaker guards, gear-turners who cranked the engine wheel, and stokers who shoveled the bituminous gowp into the furnace of great cruiser, a fuel that smoldered slowly rather than burned so as to not ignite the methane-heavy atmosphere of the Downblow that permeated the *Tìr na Smùid* (though accidents had been known to happen).

Around Cuilean, his fellow "volunteers" – conscripts like him drafted into this PieceTaker expeditionary force, a mixed assortment of Anboarnhs, Zziipppaeis, and other slaivs "freed" from territories outside the domains of the corporation -- milled about on the verge of this new land.

Before them was the harbor and behind the caravan of aptracs parked on the verge they caught a glimpse of the small town nestled in the bay. Above them loomed the sheer cliff that rose abruptly from the shore and disappeared into a candy-cottonish, brown smoke bank.

They wore breathing apparatuses against the toxic, soot-laden smog that piled up against the cliffs, and cresting their heads were spotlights to facilitate sight more than an arm's length in front of them. Those head-lanterns, combined with the asynchronized whooshes of the oxygen tank regulators, gave the impression of spectral ghosts of so many asthmatic, wheezing, gleaming-eyed cyclopes hovering in the fuliginous gloom, which was so dense that even at a short distance, the halos of their headlamps seemed to float disembodied in the infernal mist.

Slaiya sidled up to Cuilean. Her face was grimy from working the engine room, only the halos around her eyes showing their natural coloring through the goggles. The headlamp dripped with a condensation of gunk. "Dis smoke mo-aa bad den blong Pelago," she offered.

Cuilean gave his signature sideways nod. Behind the goggles and the mask of his breather, and the enwrapping tentacles of his leash-cowl, his gesture was inscrutable.

"No gud hee-aa. I go bak inside. Lilpela mo' better come too,"

Slaiya added, using her adopted name for Cuilean.

Cuilean wasn't ready to give up on whatever it was that he was about. "Mepela come sma time."

Slaiya was about to say something else, but there was an implication in Cuilean's voice that came through even the staticky voice box of his breathing app. "No wait long long time. No gud hee-aa," she repeated. "Mepela no like."

Relieved of Slaiya's presence after the Zziippp retreated into the belly of their assigned aptrac, Cuilean felt an overwhelming impulse to kneel down and kiss the ground, something he'd never thought of doing before, not here, not anywhere, not in actuality or contemplation.

He resisted this urge, for that would have called attention to himself and perhaps have given an indication of his thoughts and motivations, which would have triggered a punishing shock from his leash, though he did kneel -- ostensibly to tighten the straps on his boot for which he had to remove his glove. With his bare hand, to steady himself as he pretended to wobble out of balance, he touched the rocky soil, as if venerating a holy body.

"That's an amplitude of that!" Buttwater-Bates snapped, his voice crackling thin and reedy through the breathing apparatus.

Cuilean smiled at him – the grin which a sword-tooth tiger makes before it eats a sheep, but which expression was covered by his cowl.

Unnerved, the Massdaoer Bates moderated his tone, and looking towards the others, he announced generally, "Everybody back to your stationaries."

Just as they were mounting the ramps to the half-dozen aptracs lined up on the landing strip, Cuilean stopped to look up at the brown-smog draped cliff, trying to remember, and failing that, trying to imagine, what was at the top. For which thought he was rewarded with a sharp pang from the tentacle leash around his neck and a hard glare from the man-in-white who stood resting his hands on the railing of the ship's deck, who said nothing and did not move except for an admonitory inclining of his head before he redirected his gaze from Cuilean below him to the heights of the cliff they were about to climb.

From sea level, the escarpment rose up precipitously, eventually disappearing into the smoke. A serpentine trail was etched into the wall of igneous rock, shale, and basalt, which had risen at the time of the Great Melt when released from the weight of the continental ice sheets. It would be glamorizing what was actually little more than a mountain goat track to dub the only entry way and trading route to the mountain uplands of the Wayp a "road." Called the Staircase of the Mother – *Staidhre na Màthar* in the FT – in some places, it narrowed to a single lane as it snaked and zigzagged in intestine curves up the precipice, as if the hand of the Goddess herself had etched out a twisting DNA spiral on the face of the rock.

The aptrac was normally propelled by a dual-engine similar to that which powered the sailing sea-barge: Zziippp engine-hands pushing and pulling in alternating up-down-motions on either end of the seesaw gear driver; that, and the Zziippp stokers shoveling gowp into the maw of the furnace.

However, the grade of the climb was too steep to allow this self-propulsion alone, so the engine-room crew got a much-unused-to assistance in the form of mammoths brought down from the uptop to tow it on their ascent.

As they made their way up the ribbon of the zigzagging trail, the aptracs rocked back and forth perilously. Inside one of the vehicles, squished onto a bench, facing off with other Zziippps and a couple junior executives, Slaiya whimpered each time the treads of the boxish vehicle went off track and teetered over the ledge, and again when it banged against the cliff wall, reverberating like an empty gowp drum.

The trip was not any less excruciating than Cuilean remembered. Only the last time, many years before, right after he'd been "liberated" (as they called it), it'd been in the other direction, descending to the DownBlow, a long, slow trudge, stuck behind a convoy of three other aptracs, their smudge engines coughing out a thick fog of black, smothering exhaust.

In the *smùid* that was so thick that it was difficult to see across the interior of the aptrac, Priamus Buttwater-Bates was going on about his playing the gowp-cred market and how he planned to make a killing mining and trading the contracts.

"Yupela dig gowp?" BilWee asked.

The contempt in Buttwater's answer was audible, but so, too, was the pleasure he took in that scorn: "No, dumbraybious. I don't *dig* it. I just perchance the *contract* to dig it."

"*Then* yupela dig-dig`?"

"No, you ignorant anus" accompanied with a contemptuous shake of the head. (As much as he presented vexation with the line of conversation, the chance to actually exhibit disdain was gratifying for him.)

"Why yupela get 'n' no dig?"

An audible exhalation of exasperation at having to explain: "I wait till the contract abbreviates its value. Then I sell it. Thus," he added with a grand flourish, "realigning a profit."

"What if no go up?"

"It always alleviates in value."

"And then you buy much goods?" BilWee asked, pleased at the good fortune of somebody he imagined to be his friend.

"No, that's not the objection. You don't want to dispense the Profit. You roll over on the Profit and choir more! And assembulate

till they go up. And then you discharge for Wholly Profit!"

"*Then* yupela get mo' mo' goods?"

Buttwater-Bates slowly shook his head for dramatic effect. "You still don't underestimate, do you? But I suppository that's why you'll always be a small head."

"I no sma-head," BilWee grumbled, turning away in a sulk and putting an end to that conversation.

Not able to let it go, Buttwater-Bates pursued the topic. "Oh, you sma-hed, alright." He normally disliked dipping into the vernacular of the Zziippps, but in this instance, he felt he had to in order to get his point across. "You get more gowp-creds!"

Despite his reluctance, BilWee was pulled back into the conversation. "And then you get goods?"

"No! No goods. The Profit almighty. Get this through your sloping skull. You rollover in your mess of winnings and get even more gowp-creds."

"And then goods?"

"No! More! Get more. Zillions of gowp-creds. Gazillions of gowp-creds! Gagazillions of gowp-creds!"

By this time, the Zziippp didn't dare ask the next obvious question, which was probably just as well.

Having heard enough, Cuilean interjected himself into the conversation. "Leave him alone, Buttsniffer," he warned.

A sore point with the Anboarnh: "Buttwater-Bates. You are well ascertained of that. Priamus Thorben Buttwater-Bates," adding haughtily – as if this should mean something (as it did where he came from), and as if it were any better – "Priamus

Thorben Beezow Doo-Doo Zipitty-Bop-Bop Buttwater-Bates of the Isle of West Virginia Buttwater-Bateses, to be exact."

"Sure, sorry, Throbbing Buttwanker."

Before the junior associate could rise to the challenge, the aptrac hit a divot in the single-laned road, rocked violently, and tilted precariously towards the ledge. There was a moment of silence, a collective inrush of breath, and an exhalation of relief as the vehicle rocked back.

Slaiya groaned.

"No be fraid," Cuilean said to his Zziippp friend between Slaiya's whimpers.

Which only made Slaiya whimper more forcefully. "Whafor uspela go longlong uptop?" she protested by way of an answer.

Buttwater-Bates blurted out at the botheration. "What is deviated with these slantbrows? Can't they lurch to talk Simspeek?!" His voice dripped with open, sneering derision. As if Slaiya weren't sitting across from him and couldn't hear or understand anything he'd said, he'd addressed the question to Cuilean.

Slaiya didn't pick up that she hadn't been included in the conversation. "Whafor?" The plaintive whine in Slaiya's voice hinted that she was about to break out in tears.

"Wholly Profit!" Buttwater-Bates execrated. Though it wasn't quite clear whether he was swearing or giving an answer to the question.

"The Corps wants the gowp," Cuilean offered, shifting into Simspeek so as to not attract the ire of Buttwater-Bates, who was, after all, the detail officer in charge.

"Mo' plenty gowp DownBlow!" Slaiya protested.

"Why am I the one numerated to extricate to these small heads!" Buttwater-Bates spit out rhetorically.

"Mepela not sma-head!" Slaiya protested.

"Look," Buttwater-Bates went on, ignoring Slaiya's objection, "the Indiginoes of the Wayp are in postulate of gowp." Here, he code-switched to make his point even clearer to the Zziippp. "But they are too 'sma-head' to understand how rich in Profit they are. It's that simplex." With a period. Full stop. As if that explained everything.

Distracted from her fear of flying over the cliff edge, Slaiya offered, "If they no have gowp-creds, give 'em." She beamed with pride as if she'd hit upon a solution that no one before had thought of, and which would justify their turning the caravan around and heading back to the DownBlow.

"They won't celebrate, you cockroach-brain slanthead."

A wail as the aptrac hit another pothole on the trail. "Whafor!?"

Whereas previously, Buttwater-Bates scorned discussing anything with a mere Zziippp-head, his revulsion for the backwardness of the people of Wayp overflowed his despisal of the benightedness of the Zziipps. This new topic had redirected his ire – albeit in absentia -- towards those who refused gowp to the Corporation. "Because they're invertebrate sam-wedges!"

Omar Shawn, a hyperkinetic junior officer, jumped up from his seat, squeezed into the crammed walkway in the middle of the aptrac, and danced jiggily-piggily. He squatted and shot upwards, jumping as high as he could, banging his skull on the overhead armor. He yelped in pain, clutched his head, staggered a step, but continue his antic, rapping,

> These red-haired freaks
> Give me the creeps
> Makes me wanna eat
> The soles of my feet!

Anboarnhs and Zziippps alike laughed.

Through his petulance, even Buttwater-Bates managed a smile. However, not willing to give up elucidating the subject that he felt so passionately about and in which he piously believed, he continued more calmly. "You asked why the Waypers just won't sell us their gowp. Because they have no idealizations what's really impotent!"

As an afterthought, he added, "And they hate us!"

"Whafo dempela no like uspela?"

Slowly, as if explaining to a child: "Because we're well trees. And devolatized. And free to devolve gowp-creds anyway we can!"

"And then sell for Wholly Profit!" BilWee inserted, proud that he'd finally gotten the point.

Buttwater-Bates, tired of explaining and correcting and still not fully convinced that the muncaidh-man really understood, he lifted his brows at Cuilean as if to say, *Why do we have to put up with this lunkheadedness*?

With a sudden lurch, the aptrac swung out over the ledge of the narrow trail, throwing the passengers against the portholes and to the terrifying sight of the plunge straight down. With a discord of shouts, screams, and half-intelligible instructions, Slaiya and the others on the cliff side flung themselves in the direction of mountain to tilt the vehicle back and regain purchase on the narrow, single-laned trail.

Likewise, Buttwater-Bates swung back to his single track. "Besides, we're impartializing them a flavor – pumping all that water out of the way of the gowp. After they see the benefits of the

Profit, they'll be perpetuated of the rightness of our way of life!"

The Focwaod settled back onto his bench, convinced that he'd triumphed in his exegesis (or as he would have put it, "extra geezis").

~~

It's sweet

Os cionn tìr na smùid 's fìorghlan 's blasta an t-adhar, oir 's e deò na Màthar.
The air above the land of smudge is pure and delicious because it is the breath of the Mother.
Proverb from *Leabhar an Leaghaidh Mhòir* — The Book of the Great Melting

Mounted at the trail's end on the lip of the precipice and at the entrance to the plateau of the Wayp was the trading enclave unimaginatively named Trayton. It was here that the remaining aptracs finally made landfall after the ascent up the Staircase, although more than half their deployment had either been lost in the plummet from the narrow track or stranded on the down-hill side, with no way to advance.

In spite of being at less-than-optimal strength, the three troop transports that were all that remained of the original expeditionary force were impressive, a sight designed to awe and shock any who might stand in their way or by the wayside. The wheels inside the rolling treads alone were three times taller than the wan Anboarnh men and the thick-set muncaidh-men who worked inside the bellies of the mechanical behemoths.

As soon as the great rolling treads, designed to grip a purchase in the dry-packed, sandy dirt of the desert islands of the DownBlow, touched the boggy ground of the Wayp, they slowed to a sloggy, churning crawl, spewing the mud and decayed vegetable matter of the bog in all directions, and eventually, unable to obtain a purchase on the mucky ground, moiled to a complete stop.

Focwaod Buttwater-Bates yelled out from behind the control portal beside the aptrac door – or tried to yell as his voice broke and drifted upward in pitch after the first couple syllables, and he had to start over again: "Lightning the load! Everybody! Get your Zziippp asses out and push!"

There was a general scurrying as the assorted Zziipppaei troops and their Anboarnh organizers rushed to the aptrac off-ramp to lighten the load as ordered and shove the vehicle out of the clutches of the soft ground.

Cuilean, as the ranking lieutenant, stood at the exit at the front of the squad, waiting for the ramp to lower. In preparation to enter the atmosphere, whose character, condition, and quality were unknown to the PieceTakers, he fiddled with his breather-mask.

The gate dropped open while he was still adjusting the apparatus, and he was caught in the rush of PieceTakers who crowded behind him and pushed him out into the open air of the Wayp.

So urgently did the contingent take the command, that not one of them gave a thought to the conditions of the ground on which they were situated, it not occurring to any one of them that the same bog which had clenched the aptrac to a standing stop, might also encumber them as they dashed out, only to end up wallowing in the mud, trapped up to their knees and hips in the sticky goo.

Most of those serving in the expeditionary PieceTaker force were Zziipppaei natborns. Only a few were Anboarnhs, and these were the managers – the Focwaods and, of course, CacaHed Docherty himself -- certified fresh and pure from their manufactory, albeit with a grayish pallor to their skins and a fragile, twig-slender posture to their bodies.

But whether hulking, ramp-browed, natborn Zziipppaeis -- tufts of hair sprouting from beneath their sleeves or collars, or upon their ears or knuckles -- or the Anboarnhs -- the taller and slighter, ashen-toned supervisors -- the PieceTakers found themselves floundering in the black, boggy land, which at first appeared to be firm, but as soon as a foot touched the surface, the mud and peaty gunk crept into the crevices of their body armor like fibrous tentacles and sucked them down until several of the soldiers, flopping about in their heavy body armor, sank up to their knees, weighted down as they were by their robotic exoskeletons (synced by computer to the soldier's movements), their packs, their ammunition, their body armor, their oxygen tanks fitted into the helmets to enable breathing in harsh exterior environments, their infrared night goggles, and whatever other equipment, paraphernalia, or apparatuses they might be carrying.

Some attempted to continue towards the rear of the aptrac to fulfill their assignment of pushing, and some gave up and floundered either to dry or dryer land, or back to the aptrac ramp itself, and there they hauled themselves up onto its solid base and turned to help those who were still wading through the mud and seeking the haven it offered.

Contrary to the expectation that the lightening of the load and the pushing from behind would free the vehicle from the sticky, oozy grip of the slush and allow them to continue, in the confusion, as all the engine-hands had abandoned their posts to help in the pushing, the aptrac heaved to a stop, pitching CacaHed Docherty against the turret wall.

The CacaHed looked down on the scramble from the safety of the bubble-turret atop the vehicle. "Somes the times I wish I could retire 'em all to the farm," he muttered to no one in particular with all the intensity of a spoiled child. And with a snarl that chilled Buttwater-Bates to the bone, he added, "You, too! There's no one in the engine room."

"Not tall and sundry, you pine heads!" Buttwater-Bates yelped – doing his best to roar the relayed command, purposely and unconvincingly pitching his voice unnaturally low, which in any case, still came out more as a petulant complaint. His face distorted with the effort. "Engine hands: Back to your propositions!"

With that command, the PieceTakers who had rushed out to push turned around and crowded their way back up the gangplank, bodies on the way up cramming against those who were still coming down, and all of them clogging the door so it was impassable in either direction.

After a melee of confusion, which consisted of more shoving and pushing, shouted contrary orders, all the PieceTakers piled back inside, and the aptrac ramp-door slammed shut.

Leaving Cuilean alone outside, fumbling with his breather-mask.

"I didn't signify everybody back! Somebody's got to push! Cuilean! Where's Cuilean!" Buttwater-Bates demanded. "He's supposed to be organizing this!"

By the time Cuilean had retraced his steps back to the aptrac, the landing platform had already been withdrawn. He banged on the hatch door. The metal resounded hollowly.

The face of Focwaod Buttwater-Bates peered out the porthole at his junior officer, and he jabbed a thin finger angrily. "Cuilean, sonofaratfucker, affix your mask!" He whined, "I don't want to be confiscated for your damage!"

"It's jammed!" Cuilean yelled back, his fingers, smeared with mud, fumbling with the controls.

Buttwater shouted something that could not be heard through the thick gowpa-glass. He repeatedly yanked on the exit lever control.

Nothing. No response.

He thought to hit the intercom button. His tinny voice came through the speaker as he complained to no one in particular (and everyone): "The controls are not repercussing!"

BilWee shouted, "Ca-won, look out eyes blong yupela!"

Cuilean dramatically clamped his eyes shut against whatever

new toxins might be in the atmosphere of this strange land (that is, in addition to those known in the DownBlow).

"No pull in wind!" BilWee warned.

Which admonition only prompted Cuilean to dramatically gasp in hyperventilation.

Heads and faces crowded and jostled for a line of sight out of the portal: some not to miss the spectacle of Cuilean's tortuous demise in the unknown atmosphere of the Wayp, and some in genuine concern for the impending suffering of their friend.

The two-headed Zziippp, known by the twin names of Piddleday and Piddledoo; Kowok, the muncaidh-man with a probiscus (could hardly call it a "nose") that dangled like a mammoth's penis; Owerouchie, the Zziipppp with a huge mammoth ear on one side, matched with a mouse ear on the other; and Nardilfarf, whose nose had somehow migrated to the side of his head in the womb of his mother (an argument, an Anboarnh eugenicist would say, against so-called "natborn" births).

"Override, you ... you ..." Buttwater-Bates stuttered.

"Ratfucker?" Owerouchie suggested softly.

"Rat-dick licker?" came another prompt from Piddleday in the rear of the group crowding around the porthole.

"Oh, that good," Piddledoo squeaked in approbation.

Even BilWee thought to throw in a helping hint (perhaps forgetting for a moment that the insult was aimed at himself): "Stupid idiot sma-hed!"

With a mental eyeroll, Buttwater-Bates ignored all the proposals. "Just do it," he said.

"Did, but long long time wait," BilWee pled in expiation.

Buttwater-Bates, again to whomever was standing next to him: "Override!"

And the answer from BilWee in an exasperated plea: "Nogud. Not work!"

"Hold on, bigpela!" Piddleday called out the portal to Cuilean.

"Hold on!" Piddledoo echoed.

"I can't 'hold on'!" Cuilean's voice was strained and creaky as he expelled the last air from his lungs. "Whadoldo?! Not breathe?"

Buttwater-Bates observed to no one in particular, "It's of no abuse telling him not to expectorate," and added, when no one responded (which he hadn't expected, anyway), "He *has* to expire," and as an afterthought, as if on reflection he was not quite sure, "doesn't he?" He followed with another question, "How long can he embroil!?" Although Buttwater-Bates phrased this as a question, it sounded more like a command. "How long can he keep from inspiration!"

On the bridge of the aptrac above them, the man-in-white,

looked down as still and apparently as dispassionate as a ghost. Which is not to say that he was actually without emotion. He was filled with feelings of all kinds: a quaking fear that his investment would be lost; a sinking dismay that his primary asset – the Melee Match champion whom he still intended to re-enter in the fightball competitions -- would be ruined; a dark dread that his venture into the Wayp to recoup his capital would come to naught; and a raging anger that all this would happen because of some supplier cutting corners.

Hell! Not even talking about "corners," talking about the whole goddamn slice of the cake! All to increase profits by .01 percent if they used a lower grade of material -- in this case, a gowpaleen that dissolved on contact with oxygen -- their engineers' calculation being that that since there was so little oxygen in the earth's environment, there was no danger of that happening.[70] Which design hadn't taken into account the atmosphere of the Wayp.

Which Docherty knew was a good idea – no blame attached to the Profit-taker for doing that. He was just pissed off that he hadn't thought of it first.

Greedy dump-rats.

Meanwhile, Cuilean was reaching the point where he couldn't hold his breath anymore. Like a man drowning, he gave in to the reflex and took a shallow breath.

He had had a vague memory that the air would be alright to inspire. Unlike in the Pelagoes, where if you breathed outside the pressurized atmosphere of the domed city, the air would sear the insides of your lungs as if you had taken in a deep breath of fire, here, for some reason, the air didn't burn.

Cuilean took a deeper breath.

"What himpela doing?"

"Himpela pull in wind!"

"Sorry sonratbitch. Bigpela go tox shock."

"Don't breeze!" Buttwater-Bates shouted angrily. (He would have told you that his fervor had more to do with the prospect of losing a valuable member of his corporate team and that he would be held responsible and perhaps even required to reimburse the Monstrato Corps for the loss than with any concern he had for Cuilean himself.) From the interior of the aptrac, the Focwaod pounded on the thick gowpaleen of the portal (even though the pounding could not be heard outside nor have any effect inside).

---

[70] And indeed, following this innovation in cost cutting, the company's stock had soared, the CEO who'd engineered that bit of cost cutting had been bonused with billions of gowp-creds and eventually got himself elected to the Senate of the Agglomerated Conglomerates of the American Archipelago.

His voice came across the speaker tinny and mechanical, not at all as commanding as he would have hoped and intended. "Discommence that, PieceTaker!"

"No pull in wind, bigpela Cul-win!" BilWee echoed, his voice rising childishly despite his massive bulk.

From inside the locked hatch, his eyes darting between the sight through the pane and his dials beside him, Buttwater-Bates shouted, his voice sounding tinny across the communicator. "Hold on! We're almost there."

Cuilean filled his lungs with a deep breath.

"Himpela give up!"

"It's almost spherical poisoning!" Buttwater-Bates diagnosed. "It's getting to his brace!"

Another breath. An expression of peace came over Cuilean's face.

"Wholly Profit! Himpela ending it!" Omarshawn exclaimed in horror.

"Cul-winnnn!" BilWee screamed. "Noooo up give!"

Cuilean's body slumped into a seated position on a tree stump.

Because the view from behind the portal window was occluded by a smoky vapor, it was difficult for those still in the aptrac to see exactly what was happening with him.

Helpless faces peered out the quadruple-paned gowpa-glass at him. Inside, Buttwater-Bates ceased banging on the controls and shoved BilWee, the usual operator, to the panel, with the command, "You do it!" as if someone else on the handle would make a difference.

With a couple of adjustments on the Zziippp's part, a robotic voice emanated from the panel speaker: "Cycle activated. Please wait for decompression of entry passage."

The door mechanism proceeded with the involved process of completing the closing, securing, readying for opening, and opening.

There was a gush of air like a loud sighing, the ramp clanked open and down, and the crew rushed out.

Cuilean pushed away the helping hands of the helpless, hapless Zziipppaeis and jammed his own hand into the helmet, and while his Zziippp comrades might have thought he meant to reconnect the tubing, he instead yanked it out. "Damn cheap piece of shit! It's coming apart!" he shouted over the communicator.

"Quick!" Buttwater-Bates ordered from safely inside the airlock. "Get him into the hypersonic chamber!"

Cuilean's demeanor changed. He grinned broadly as if it had all been a prank. "Guys … don't worry. You can breathe the air."

A bigger grin.

"What fuck himpela saying?"

"Cwazy talk. Hurry up!"

"No, I mean it. I can breathe. *You* can breathe." Cuilean laughed. "Look!" He took his air mask totally off and tossed it up in the air like a long-suffering PieceTaker cadet at graduation. He did a backwards somersault into the boggy ground and landed on his feet with a splat. He beamed in delight. "You can breathe the air!"

"Himpela crazy?"

"Himpela almost over."

"Himpela die sma time."

"Himpela dead soon!"

"Himpela down fall."

But when he didn't fall over, and much less, did not die, even the most extreme doubters questioned, "He not pull in wind?"

"I'm serious, guys," Cuilean told them. He waved cheerfully, encouragingly. "The breathing's fine! BilWee, look at me. You don't need it!"

They heard Buttwater's tinny whine through their helmet mics. "Somebody resubordinate him," though obviously that *somebody* would not be him.

Clicking over to the intercom communicator, Buttwater-Bates ordered to some unseen operative still inside the aptrac, "Ready the equinox chamber. We've got mass-diffusion!" Back to ordering the men: "Put your wear-masks on!"

Which had the same effect as his previous orders.

That's when Slaiya, who in addition to her fabled career in the fightball arena, was also a veteran of the 23rd World War, survivor of the Insurge massacre in the Valley of Armageddon, who'd been the spearhead of the invasion of the Arctic methane fields, who had served three tours in the Military Operation of the Amazonian Desert, and two more in War of Eternal Peace (during which she'd survived on rats and cockroaches as she and her soldiers fought island to island in the chain of the Andes Isles for a full fourteen months, and which name had proved to be only one-third right – the result of the campaign turning out to be neither "eternal" or "peaceful") – overcome with anxiety for her friend (though corporate psych-ops still disputed whether Zziippps could experience such refined emotion), bellowed, "Air make cwazy!"

She charged through the bunch of PieceTakers – Anboarnhs and Zziippps, alike – tossing them aside as if they were just so many dust bunnies floating across the desert like a tearanado *tearing* (hence the name) towards a domed city in the Pelagoes.

She lunged forward with a roar. "PUT BREATHER!"

"Look, big girl," Cuilean said, stopping her charge with an upheld hand. With a mischievous smirk, he said, "It's alright," and he did what no one else would have dared to do. He snatched off Slaiya's own breathing app. She swiveled and instinctively lunged at Cuilean, who bounced nimbly away.

The Zziippp giant charged again, her arms flailing ineffectually, reaching for the missing breather mouthpiece, and like a virtual matador, again Cuilean dodged away, this time with a taunting laugh and a teasing wave of the app.

Slaiya stopped and glared. This time, death was in her eyes. Though admittedly, she was conflicted. Normally, she'd squash somebody who did something -- *anything* -- like this like a flea on a dump-rat's butt. But Cuilean was her "fren," and "no want hurt."

And besides, she'd already been *there*, tried *that*, and it hadn't worked the first time.

"Look," Cuilean reassured the giant Zziippp, "you don't need it." Cuilean himself drew a deep breath. "You see, you're breathing too. Go, on," he told the Zziippp, whose face was glowing red from holding her breath, sweat drops beading up on her forehead. "It's *sweet*."

One by one, the other PieceTakers - the few Anboarhns and the several Zziipppaeis -- took off their breathing apps. It was the strangest thing they'd ever seen or experienced -- or even heard of -- unlike anything they'd ever imbibed.

One laughed hysterically: "Cuilean right! Air sweet!"

This was too much for the massive Slaiya. She was outraged at the thought that she'd lose control of the whole squad in one moment. "What do! Allpela cwazy!"

The muncaidhs around her were smiling uncertainly, their brows lifted tentatively. They were nodding and grinning in encouragement of themselves and each other.

Slaiya glowered and sniffed the air.

It *was* sweet.

Still angry and from long habit needing to assert control lest all mayhem break out and the Zziippps start doing *whateverthehell* they felt like (which could only end badly), Slaiya reached into the breast pocket of her utility belt and took out a gowp-gar. Then with a flourish, she flipped out her mini-torch lighter.

Even those PieceTakers most convinced of the safety of the air shouted and reflexively either flinched back in anticipation of the atmosphere igniting or reached forward defensively to grab the lighter and prevent the spark in the open air that would set off a chain reaction that would combust everything and everyone for an acre around.

"NO!"

"Zzyzx disease!"[71]

Even Docherty cursed from on high in anticipation of seeing the greater part of his investment conflagrated in a firestorm. "Ratfuck!" he exclaimed, referring to an act of sexual engagement with the only living land creature in the Merican Pelago larger than a cockroach.

But before anyone could stop it, the flame sprouted from the lighter.

There was a collective gasp, some screams, a couple of the Zziippps threw themselves into what they imagined was the safety of the boggy mud, but aside from that, nothing happened.

No combustion. No explosion.

The flame just flickered atop the tube. Slaiya grinned superiorly as she calmly lit the cigar. "Lil fren, yupela no fool Slaiya. Mepela know all time air goodsafe." Jamming the tube of dried gowp and cured algae leaves between her teeth, she giggled squeakily.

And after a few moments, recovering from their terror at the prospect of instant immolation, so did the other Zziippps.

---

[71] ZZyzx virus (pronounced zeez): contagion thought to have been released from the melting permafrost during the Great Melt and spread by mosquito vector. Contagion caused widespread (which is to say, universal) birth abnormalities and defects, which were congenital and transmissible across generations. See Zziippppaei.

You're shitting me

'S draghaile caraid amaideach na nàmhaid glic.
A silly friend is more troublesome than a wise enemy.
Proverb from *Leabhar an Leaghaidh Mhòir* —
The Book of the Great Melting

The first full day they were vaycay in Wayp, Cuilean and his squad were deployed to guard the dam at the head of the lake. Chatter had been detected that indicated there might be some Insurge activity to sabotage the corporation's gowp mining and water disposal operation[72] (though actually, in the other order – disposing of the water first, and then mining the more valuable gowp).

Standing atop the turret of the aptrac as it plowed along the verge between forest and field, Cuilean, his head and face still encased in the tentacled leash, braced himself against the gunwale. Across from him, the ranking Corps officer CacaHed Docherty proudly surveyed his new acquisition.

Docherty, as was his usual practice, was dressed entirely in white, his suit made of brilliantly shimmering, reflective gowpaleen poly-fibers. If the sun caught him the right way and if somebody was standing at the right angle, the light flashing off him could literally be blinding. At night, that suit would sparkle like a star. But as they passed through the countryside, the only thought that came to him was, *what a waste of good real estate.* Just the trees themselves -- the last remaining stand on the planet -- was worth a small fortune, which was only a bonus in addition to the huge profit to be made from exploiting the gowp in the mountain valley ahead of them.

Come the early spring in the Wayp, after the last snowfall melted into slush under the warming sun, leaving just a gossamer film of ice on the ground, and the water seeped downwards towards a seed that had fallen, perhaps blown by the wind, or

---

[72] *gowp mining and water disposal operation*: actually, performed in the other order; that is, disposing of the water first, and then mining the more valuable gowp.

dropped from some fox's fur; or that of a mammoth; or an *aon-adharcach* -- the one-horned, horse-like creature that pounded the plains of the Wayp; or a *leomhann-claidheamh* -- a sword-tooth tiger; or a *lunndaire-craoibhe mòr* -- a giant sloth, slow-moving, hairy, bear-like; or the *mathan-madaidh* -- the bear-wolf; or any of the numerous smaller animals: badgers, hedgehogs, or carnivorous hares -- *a' maigheach fheòl-itheach* -- that roamed the mountain slopes, sheltered in the heather, burrowed in the moor, or nested in the forest.

However it was transported, the seed was lightly silted over by the rich loam as an infant put to bed. Sensing the warming of the soil, the seed pushed embryonic baby root hairs out into the interstices between the granules of the soil, suckling on the dribbles of moisture leaking down, and swelled, pregnant with its new life. The seed in a few days more sent up a tender tendril -- the embryonic cotyledon – which squirmed its way to the surface and poking a tentative sprout -- a fragile plumule, the precursor to the stem from which the entire plant would erupt -- through the topmost layer of soil, breaking the last diaphanous veil of frost, and reaching into the air and the sunlight.

A few days after that, chlorophyll activating its influence colored the fragile shoot with a light green. A single small leaf spread its wings to absorb yet more sunlight, and the petiole from which the entire plant would erupt curved upwards, orienting its leaves (now there were several), and pushing out a bud from the topmost arch of that branch, and others that opened into a triumphant display: a row of tiny downward-hanging, trumpet-mouthed blue-bells, the purple-blue color of lapis lazuli.

It went unnoticed by all but Cuilean when the tank-treads of the aptrac crushed through the bed of blossoms.

In front of the expeditionary caravan as if it were beckoning them, rose the *Cìochan na Màthar* in the FT – or, in Simspeek, the Tits of the Mother – the twin mounds topped with white nipples of snow which constituted the crown of Wayp that fed the pure springs and swelled the waters of the lake below.

The aptrac shuttered to a halt, throwing the two PieceTakers forward.

A moment later, Buttwater-Bates shoved his head through the turret hatch. The Focwaod had watch down in the engine room, and now he was reporting the reason for their stopping. "My apoplexies," he said, climbing up onto the deck. "A sly grinch in the mechanism," he explained. "The gowp fire went out. We're working on re-iglighting it. We'll get running in just a couple snakes of a rat's tail."

Buttwater-Bates slipped beside Docherty, crowding the

commanding officer's space, attempting to leach even a little bit of his power. In this, he shifted from a report to a conversation opener: "This is just ratfuckin' creeping. All these things moving around!"

"They're called animals," Cuilean noted dryly from behind the two.

"Yeah, whatever they are. And when the aptrac stops, you can't hear anything except the ..." He was at a loss. What was it that he heard? It certainly wasn't the rumbling of an engine, nor the whooshing of air compressors and atmospheric purifiers that filled the aural spaces in the DownBlow. "Just so Gawd-awful *qwerty*," the Focwaod went on. "Gives me the loose juice!"

Listening, if you paid attention, you could hear the symphony created by the voices and the silences that combined, mingled, and harmonized in the song of the Wayp: the rustling of grasses; the blowing of the leaves caressed by the wind; the *ceileireadh* -- the twittering and singing of the various birds -- the sparrows, the larks, the thrushes -- in the concealment of the bushes and the branches; the sharp, fierce cry of an eagle; the warning bellow of a bull stag; the mewing bleat of a mammoth calf calling for its mother, and the mother's reassuring, long trumpeting in reply. All this, un-meliorated by any clang or clank or rumble or roar of human-made mechanism.

Taking a break from their exertions as the vehicle's powerplant, a couple more Anboarnh junior officers and Zziippp PieceTakers crowded into the narrow space of the turret.

The incomers from the DownBlow stood atop the bridge and gawked upon the surroundings with their mouths agape. Below, in the engine room and the hold, those who weren't engaged in restoring the motor wheel to working order pressed together and ogled out the portholes with their eyes ajar.

The abundance of life was strange and wondrous to the newcomers from the lands under the cloud of *smùid* which blanketed the dead lands of the DownBlow. Used to a land inhabited only by rats, cockroaches, various desert lizards that could survive in the fiery landscape, and assorted species of sea wyrms in the gowpy seas, they had never seen anything like the abundance of life that seemed to swarm before them now: Eagles soaring, wild unihorns grazing, and in the dark shadows of the thick-as-grass forests, a sense of ominous beasts slinking. A sword-tooth tiger spread out unconcerned on a boulder sunning herself. In the stream by the side of their track, a salmon leapt from the water. Everywhere were the midges -- fierce little flies that bit pertinaciously and mercilessly.

The Zziippps and Anboarnh PieceTakers alike wore Cuilean out with all their pointing and demanding, "What dat? What dat? What dat?"

"I don't know," Cuilean protested again and again. "Why do you think I know?"

"Cuz you come here," BilWee said.

Summoning the words and names pained Cuilean by triggering the wyrm-leash. He resorted to making up facts that were safer, less painful to utter because he wasn't actually accessing his memory. Made-up names like "big flying thing," or "lazy giant rat thing," or "eat grass amanal."

Unexpectedly, suddenly, pointing to a massive elephantine creature with sides looming like giant walls and tree-trunk legs, and hair draping over it in long, rastapharian dreadlocks, and two fierce tusks protruding from its mouth, BilWee shouted "WHAT DATPELA!?!"

The exclaimed question jolted Cuilean, and without a chance to reflect or deflect, the word came to him with a shock of recognition: "*Mammoid* – mammoth," and a shock of a different sort from his leash.

The resultant jarring shot of pain knocked the breath from him, made his head spin, and brought tears to his eyes.

"What do!" BilWee asked in awe.

Before Cuilean had just been going along with the childlike curiosity and awe, but the blow both angered him and made him fear its repetition.

"See those big teeth?" he started to spin his tale. "That monster stab you with those. And then ..." he stopped dramatically and shook his head. "You don't want to know what happens next."

"What? What? What? Tell BilWee."

Seemingly reluctant – taking a deep breath as if he were to commence the delivery of bad news -- very bad indeed -- Cuilean went on. "And then long finger ..." he poised his forefinger to dangle from his nose before he continued: "Longfinger pull you apart."

BilWee and the other Zziippps huddled around him gasped in horror.

"And then it eats you while you're still alive! Pulling you apart like a barbequed rat!"

Imagining the horror, a couple of the Zziippps set to weeping in despair. "Why uspela here?" one whimpered.

"But no afraid," Cuilean said, lapsing into TokTok. "One way safe."

A chorus: "What dat? What dat? What dat!?!"

"It's not nice. You won't like it."

The refrain from the chorus: "Tell. Tell. Tell."

Cuilean made as if he were going to start explaining ... "Well ..." He stopped with a pained expression. "I can't ..."

"Whyfor? Whyfor? Whyfor!?!

"The people of the Wayp don't like it if I tell. It's secret."

Several voices: "Tell! Tell! Tell!"

He leaned forward, and in a low, barely-to-be-heard voice, he confided, "The mammoths won't eat their own."

Curious stares as the Zziippps tried to figure out where he was going with this.

"So, if you make them think that you're a baby mammoth ..."

The light dawned. "How do dat?"

"What do babies do?" Then he shifted to the TokTok word. "What newpelas do?"

A puzzle. One of the Zziippps ventured: "Thempela cry?"

Cuilean shook his head and then explained: "They shit themselves."

"You say we shit us?"

"No, no, no. That won't do. You'll still smell like ... well, like you. There's only one way to protect yourself from them."

"What?!? How do dat!?!"

"Make yourselves smell like baby mammoths."

"Huh?"

"You have to rub mammoth shit all over yourselves."

"Where get mammoth shit?"

Cuilean pointed out to the field.

"No way!"

"Yes way," Cuilean re-assured them.

Faces lit up in revelation!

BilWee was the first to break. He flung himself over the side of the turret and

clambered down the handrails of the aptrac. It was only a moment later that a couple more Zziippps followed. All of them who had heard Cuilean's disquisition, and -- as word spread to the engine room below -- `what was left of the working engine crew swarmed up through the turret and over the sides.

Even Slaiya, the captain of the Zziippps, wavered on the bridge. Finally, she broke her hesitation and followed, soon to be seen scooping up mammoth paddies and anointing herself with the feculence.

Cuilean stood beside Docherty and Buttwater-Bates watching as nearly the entire crew of Zziippps scampered across the field, locating mammoth shit-paddies, and smearing themselves with them.

In the field, a couple of the Zziippps moved closer to the grazing mammoths, and jumping and waving their arms, shouted things like, "No eat mepela!" or "Mepela newpela bignosepela!"

Focwaod Buttwater-Bates gripped the wall of the turret so hard it looked like he was trying to break it.

Docherty coldly examined Cuilean's countenance for a hint that might betray him, but Cuilean stood stony-faced, placid, and expressionless.

"What in the name of the Wholly Profit are they doing!? We're behind schedule already," Docherty spoke between his teeth, barely moving his lips, but his displeasure was clear and loud.

Spurred into action, Buttwater-Bates screamed from atop the aptrac. "Get back here! This is unauthorized slugfest and reparation! You are commandeered to overturn to work!"

By this time, the shit-pedition had run its course since most of the troop had gathered all the protection they felt they needed. The troop of Zziippps came galoomping back.

As they clambered back up into the turret and crowded around the hatch to return to their work stations in the engine room, Buttwater-Bates exploded at the Zziippps, "Get away from me. Your smellification is omnivorous!"

BilWee beamed. "But uspela safe now!"

"You won't be if you don't get the engine up and gunning again!" Buttwater threatened.

The Zziippp engine-hands disappeared down the hatch. Buttwater-Bates turned on Cuilean: "Don't be feeding me defenestration!"

Cuilean had to think for a moment about what the officer might mean. "I shit you not, Buttwanker," Cuilean replied placidly. "I keep you tucked away with all my other crap."

Just as Buttwater-Bates was swelling up to react – a response that he should have known wouldn't turn out well for him – Docherty interjected, "Buttwanker ..." The CacaHed corrected himself, although not before his slip was noted by both Cuilean (with a barely dissembled smirk) and the junior officer (with an all-too noticeable glower). "Focwaod Buttwater-Bates, go DownBlow, hose those Zziippp-heads off, and get us rolling again."

With a kill-you-later look at Cuilean, Buttwater-Bates grumbled something inarticulate and climbed down the ladder to the bowels of the brute that was transporting them.

The smidgen of a smile that was discerned in the corners of Cuilean's eyes was not lost on Docherty before he turned back to scanning the surroundings.

The silence and song of the forest was shattered into a thousand million pieces by the start-up roar of the aptrac engine, and stygian smoke pierced the air above them, wafting down and stinging their eyes, noses, and lungs.

A flock of redwinged blackbirds soared up and away; a rabbit found cover in its leaf-hidden bower; squirrels fled to the highest branches and shivered in their hollows; a giant beaver, as large as a human child, waddled to the stream bank, slipped into the water, and swam to the underwater entrance of its lodge. A red deer, whose ancestors had been carried thousands of years before to the new continent that had risen up out of the ice, leapt back into the safety of the forest shadows.

Docherty breathed in deeply the black, sooty smoke that rose from the exhaust funnels of the aptrac, and like a music aficionado enjoying a favorite melody, he closed his eyes to savor the clamor of the engine and the clank of the vehicle's gears. "I'm not a religious man, but praise the Profit!"

mìcheal dubh

No can pain newpela

*Far a bheil tròcair, gràdh, 's co-fhaireachadh, 's ann an sin far a
bheil a' Mhàthair.*
Where mercy, love, and compassion are,
it is there where the Mother is.
Proverb from *Leabhar an Leaghaidh Mhòir* —
The Book of the Great Melting

The aptrac was making a slow go of it, slogging across the
boggy landscape, alternately through the tall grasses and over hip-
high stands of heather, with its file of PieceTakers strung out ahead
and behind, trudging uncomfortably through the boggy ground on
the side of the narrow path (it would do the concept of "road" a
disservice to use that term to refer to whatever this was).

Periodically, the column's forward movement would chug to a
slog and a halt, and the troop of Zziippps and Anboarnhs would
have to move forward to unwedge the vehicle from the boggy soil
or disentangle it from the underbrush.

CacaHed Docherty stood atop one of the aptracs. He was
dissatisfied with the progress of his contingent. The vehicle wasn't
going what might be called 'fast' at all. Excruciatingly slow, to be
strictly factual. He leaned forward over the front turret wall as if
his slight weight (comparatively speaking) would propel the aptrac
forward faster (although he well knew it wouldn't).

His greyish-whitish skin – the color of a sea-bottom wyrm –
was offset by the blazing, sparkling white of his habitual suit, which
was itself made from material that gathered, reflected, and
accentuated light so you had to squint to look at him. His hair was
the same shade of white as his suit and in some ways seemed to be
a continuation of that garment.

"Why they allow all this water on the land, I don't know!" This
last, Docherty said repeatedly, sometimes shaking his head in
disbelief, or amazement, or disgust (the words muttered under his
breath, exclaimed out loud, or sworn vehemently, depending on his
mood). He was implying a comparison with the vastly superior –
and much more easily traversed landscape of the DownBlow, with

its parched, hard-packed, gowp-topped surface. "This is just not efficient."

Docherty's detachment was on its way to investigate reports of Insurge activity near *Loch na Màthar* in the FT – The Lake of the Mother in Simspeek, or, as he'd come to call it, the Lake of the Motherfucker.

BilWee pointed excitedly towards the line of trees. "Bospela, lukim!"

Thinking that they'd chanced upon an Insurge nest, Docherty's chest contracted as a heaving of bile welled up into his throat. He swallowed the upsurge, lest the rise of emotion be discernible. He rasped hoarsely, "Where!" and squinted around and about with a pinched, pained expression into the foliage across the meadow.

"Longway! Longway!"

But Docherty couldn't make out what the half-brain was going on so passionately about. It irked him to even acknowledge the ramp-head's excitement, but his curiosity overcame his disinclination. He demanded coldly, "What." Docherty had an odd way of expressing his questions, his intonation never rising at the end, but rather coming down, as if he had just issued a threat.

"Dere!" came the animated response, the Zziipppaei himself now growing as irritated with Docherty's inability to understand good Zziipppaei TokTok as Docherty was with what he heard as the PieceTaker's inarticulate gibberish.

Buttwater-Bates thought he'd help out, or score a point by chiming in. "What do you meme? What are we suppository to be looking at? I don't see anything."

"Oh ..." In his excitement, BilWee had forgotten that whatever it was he had spotted that had so stimulated him he'd seen through his binoculars. "Hee-a," BilWee said, handing the field-glasses over. "Lukluk hee-a."

Ignoring Buttwater-Bates, BilWee thrust the glasses past him to Docherty, and as the Monstrato Commander raised the spectacles to his eyes, the PieceTaker pointed towards the upper reaches of the forest. "Lukluk up long way."

"For what!" This was more a demand than a question, though at this point, it might have been unclear whether Docherty was truly not comprehending what the Zziippp was saying, or if he couldn't see what was being indicated.

"Flyfela!" BilWee pointed, his hand wagging excitedly. "Newpela flyfela an' mommy!"

They really were too simple, these Zziipppaeis, but to humor the creature -- it was hard to think of them as people -- Docherty looked where BilWee was directing. And sure enough, there was a large eagle bent down over a chick, the baby's skin showing pinkish under its downy white feathers. The larger bird poked its beak into the gullet of the smaller one, which gulped the masticated offering greedily.

"I've heard what the Indiginoes[73] do with these things. Whadaya call 'em?" This last he directed to Cuilean.

The only word that came to Cuilean was one drawn from the deep well of his long-term memory, a word that he once knew (though if you had asked him, he wouldn't have been able to tell you he knew it now) and that he blurted out without thinking – "*Eòin*," he said, and rapidly corrected himself, "Birds," but not before the leash zapped him for the effort.

Cuilean tried to hide the effect of the jolt by looking watery-eyed away, but Docherty did not miss the flinch and smiled in amusement. (He must have been the kind of child who enjoyed pulling the legs off cockroaches or gutting rats alive.)

"Yes, *birds*," Buttwater-Bates interjected. "We studied ForeTime live storms in school."

Docherty mused. "They used to train the predators to hunt. I'm like that." This was in a self-congratulatory tone. "A hunter. A predator." He wasn't so much talking to anybody in particular, for who was there to talk to who would understand other than himself? An Indigino slaiv or a shallow-brained Zziippp? *Don't make me fall down laughing.*

He held out his hand to BilWee. "Hand me a kablooey," he told BilWee, and then in the gap between his instruction and the Zziippp's non-response, he snapped, "Sometime soon." Still no response. "Like, *now!*"

"Yea-sa, CacaHed bospela." There was some fumbling before the Zziippp untangled the weapon from his shoulder, and then some more as he attempted to hand it barrel first to his superior officer, retracted it from Docherty's outstretched hand, and swiveled it around and poked it into his commander's chest, butt first this time.

With an arch of an eyebrow and arms spread as if to say, *what am I supposed to do with this?* Docherty reminded the Zziipppaei that he had not loaded the weapon.

Hurriedly, BilWee took the weapon back and primed it, muttering in his sweaty, anxious haste not to make a mistake, the mnemonic under his breath –

> Clean the tube
> Pour the gowp

---

[73] Indigino (plural, Indiginoes) = indigenous residents of the Wayp; the People, the *Sluagh*

Drop the slug
Ram the plug
Clamp the fuse
Ready to use.

He stopped himself with an "Oh!" and lifted brows as he remembered just before he got to

Light the fire
Shoot when desire.

He thrust the stock into the man-in-white's chest. Perhaps a little too hard, BilWee realized after the fact, for at the thump against Docherty's body, the Zziipppaei mumbled, "Mepela sorry, bospela."

Responding with only a glare, the CacaHed sighted through the scope atop the weapon. BilWee stood by, moaning softly and shifting nervously from foot to foot.

Docherty carefully lit the fuse that activated the firing, and with some satisfaction, he watched the larger bird alert to the sound of the weapon's *kablooey* (hence its name) and then just a moment later collapse and fall off the branch adjacent to the nest.

He shoved the rifle back to BilWee. "Go retrieve it."

"Wot?"

"The bird." Slowly so the words did not zoom too quickly for the Zziippp-head's comprehension. "Get. Bird."

"Bospela want flyfela?"

No answer except a cold glint.

BilWee raised a shout to rally a troop of his fellow snorters, and in a spirit of adventure, the Zziipppaeis sallied out of the aptrac and crashed happily through the meadow.

As they reached the base of the tree, BilWee victoriously held up the carcass of the dead adult eagle and came whooping back, followed and surrounded by his whooping comrades, the band of Zziipppps.

"I don't want the dead bird," Docherty explained with forced patience. *They really have to do something about raising the IQs of these creatures by a few points. Just a few. So they're not complete idiots.*

BilWee scrunched his face. Before, he thought he knew, but he wasn't sure what it was that his Commander wanted.

Buttwater-Bates thought he'd help. "The Commander wants the chicanery."

Even more confused.

Leaning towards BilWee, his eyes fixed on the tree line but his mouth near the Zziippp's ear, Cuilean offered in an undertone so as to not be heard by anyone else, "The baby bird. Newpela flyfela."

"Ooh!" BilWee let out in a long breath, at last understanding. "Newpela flyfela!"

"Yes," Docherty confirmed, as much as the TokTok was bitter in his mouth: "Newpela."

"No mommy now," Cuilean added. "All lone."

"Yeah," Buttwater-Bates chimed in, not wanting to be left out. "We can't just panda it. Somebody's gotta take careful it."

With that, BilWee's whole demeanor changed. While he had not been happy about the shooting of the "mommy flyfela," he was elated at the idea of caring for the baby eagle.

"Newpela! Get newpela!" BilWee shouted as he scrambled down the cockpit ladder. "Alfela!" he called to the others. "Alfela! Com long mepela. Hariap!"

A few of the Zziippps who had been in the hold of the aptrac peered out of the open gangway door to see BilWee scurrying towards the copse of trees.

"Com!" BilWee shouted back over his shoulder. "Hariap! Alfela com!"

There was a hubbub of exchanges back and forth and a gathering like a wave of scum mounting on the open sea.

"BilWee wanna us go ..."

"Himpela wanna us get som ting ..."

"Go wi BilWee."

"Himpela wanna uspela go."

A scramble down the gangplank, and the drool[74] of Zziippps rushed after BilWee into the forest, and he, for his part, excitedly leading the way, continually intoned to himself, lest he forget his mission: "Gat newpela flyfela, but no can pain. Newpela, newpela, newpela. No can pain. No pain. Newpela, no can pain."

"PieceTaker Cuilean ..." Docherty spoke without bothering to turn his head even a smidgen to see whether Cuilean was attending to his words. He just assumed that, of course, his subaltern -- his property -- was.

Cuilean didn't verbally respond but did shift to face the CacaHed.

Docherty continued. "You'd better go with them. Make sure they all get back in one piece."

Cuilean swung down from the turret, half-dropping, half-catching himself on the rungs of the ladder to slow his descent.

He landed on the gangway just as the last of the Zziipppaeis

---

[74] Simspeek had retained special terms for certain groups of things, such as a mischief of rats, a slime of slugs, an creeping of cockroaches, and as used here – a *drool* of Zziippps.

were coming out. They ambled with a scampering gait, rocking forth and back as they propelled themselves forward.

Breaking into an easy jog of long, loping strides, Cuilean caught up with the drool of Zziippps, who were scurrying along like a giggle of excited school maggots.[75] In spite of their misshapened legs, they could move quickly. BilWee shuffled eagerly ahead of the pack.

They reached the tree, the whole dribbled of them, and swarming around the base, they variously attempted jumping up to catch the nearest branches – even the lowest of which were quite out of reach – and the Zziippps were too ponderous for their stunted legs to propel themselves to that height, a fact which seemed to elude the Zziipppaeis as they leapt again and again, only to fall to the forest floor again and again.

A couple attempted scaling the trunk, sliding to the ground after just a handhold or two.

The idea flashed across BilWee's mind that teamwork might be just the answer to the problem, and he instructed, "Help. Help himpela!" And one gave another a boost to reach the nearest tree limb, but the branch was still too high up.

"BilWee!" Cuilean shouted over the melee. "Tell them to stop that. They're not getting anywhere. That's sma-hed. Make a ladder."

BilWee pushed his way into the melee, shouting and shoving and swatting, and managed to bring some order to the small mob. "Hed-sma, hed-sma, hed-sma!" he shouted. "Yapela hed-sma! Make lada!"

"Huh?"

"Lada! Go ontop lada!"

He grabbed Piddleday and Piddledoo and another Zziippp, Kowok, and yet another – Nardilfarf -- and he pushed and tugged them to the base of the tree. There, once he had them in a bunch, he pressured them down with his hands on their shoulders – "Daun, daun ..." -- until they understood to hunch over and form a base for Owerouchie to mount atop the others, urging, "Up, up ..."

After that, the ascent was relatively easy, almost like mounting an actual ladder, as BilWee stepped up, first on the bottom rung, or Piddleday's foot (or was it Piddledoo's?), and on the next rung, pulling himself up hand-over-hand on Kowok's nose (accompanied by grunts and stifled complaints), and on Nardilfarf's head, bracing on his ears, and clambering up and hoisting himself high and higher.

So BilWee labored up the pyramid to the lower bough, grasped

---

[75] Maggot – the official and accepted Simspeek word to describe the stage of development of a Zziippp between birth and sexual maturity.

that, and with difficulty hoisted himself astraddle the thick branch, his tongue sticking between his teeth out the side of his lips in concentration so intense that the sweat beaded up on his face and ran down his neck and soaked his shirt front under the body armor that he'd forgotten to take off and that he was now unnecessarily hauling many Zziippp-lengths up the tree.

Far above him, the plaintive peeping of the nestling elicited reassurances from BilWee: "No cwy, newpela flyfela. No cwy. BilWee com."

He climbed higher, lifting his weight through levels of ever thinning branches that now bent under him, straining to support him.

Far below, the other Zziipppaeis called out encouragement and advice.

"Luk aut, BilWee!"

"No fa' daun, BilWee!"

"Twy har, BilWee!"

"No!" another Zziippp called out, intending even better advice. "Twy mo' har!"

Finally, BilWee was close enough to reach up for the nest. His fingers groped around inside it. At their tips he could feel a downy presence nudging away just out of his grasp with accompanying, protesting, frightened peeps. Beneath, he sensed the branches supporting him breaking away. Desperately, he lunged his hand blindly towards the last contact in the nest and grabbed. His fingers closed around the baby bird.

"No fraid, newpela flyfela," he said, bringing the hatchling to his chest just as the branches snapped beneath him, and he plummeted to the ground.

At first, the slenderer branches did not break his fall but rather slowed it, though whipping his face and hands. He did not try to grab any of the branches as he descended because he was intent on shielding the precious, fragile treasure cradled against his chest, and so he fell through the thinner branches, which whipped him viciously, and as he descended farther, and the branches grew yet thicker, they clubbed him fiercely before breaking under the force of his fall (force having something to do, of course, with momentum, weight, mass, and probably intellectual density as the poor Zziippp didn't have the presence of mind to cushion his impacts in anyway – perhaps by moderating his fall with his arms or legs, or by maneuvering to hit an oncoming branch with a soft, fleshy part of his body rather than a bony bit), and reaching the level of thigh-thick branches which were too sturdy to break under him, he bounced from one level to another -- hitting a branch, attempting to grab it with his upper arms (the bird still clenched tightly between hands, forearms, and chest), but unable to do that, bouncing up like a pin-ball and plunging to the ever-stronger, heavier branch below that, until he reached the bottommost rungs of the tree, and he ricocheted off the thickest limb of all, and as his fellow Zziipppaeis (or Zziipppaei, depending on which style guide one follows) scrambled this way and that, guessing and misestimating the direction of his dropping in their endeavors to catch him, shouting a plethora of confusing, confounding, and contradictory instructions.

"Hee-a!"

"No, hee-a!"

"Ova hee-a!"

And running first one way and then the other, bumping into each other, knocking each other over, as they scurried around the tree in opposite and conflicting directions.

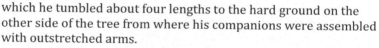

BilWee rebounded high and flipped in the air, after which he tumbled about four lengths to the hard ground on the other side of the tree from where his companions were assembled with outstretched arms.

Once landed, he sprawled awkwardly and horribly, one leg protruding at a bizarre angle.

His Zziippp comrades stood in open-mouthed astonishment – both astonished at the sight of their friend splayed out on the ground and boggled that they had so miscalculated so as to miss him altogether.

Then came the sharp peep of the baby eagle.

This cry was greeted with much enthusiasm. "Newpela flyfela al-rite!" one of the Zziipppaei shouted.

And the cheer went around.

"Newpela al-rite!"

"Flyfela al-rite!"

They rushed to BilWee and grabbing at him, they tried to pry the chick out of his hands. "Let lukim!" one shouted.

"Let mepela lukim," urged another.

This is when Cuilean stepped in, tugging and pulling and pushing the Zziipppaeis aside. "Yupelas pain newpela flypela!" he warned them loudly. "Bak. Bak!"

This was the one consideration that would calm the small mob, though there were still muted appeals, much like the pleading whimperings of pet rats.

"Let lukim."

"Wanna lukim newpela."

"You'll see," Cuilean reassured them. "But you have to be careful. No pain newpela," he added in TokTok for emphasis.

He stepped close to BilWee and gently opened the Zziippp's hands that had clutched and shielded the eagle chick on the tumble from the upper branches. In the Zziippp-head's open palm, the chick was displayed for all to see.

A series of *oohs* and *ahhs* went up from the drool of Zziipppaeis.

"Nais," one said.

"Nais-pela," another agreed.

It's only then that they turned their attention to BilWee, who sprawled brokenly on the ground.

"BilWee al-rite?" one asked fearfully.

"Mepela tink BilWee die," another one ventured.

BilWee groaned in pain.

Another Zziippp contradicted: "BilWee no die!" adding hopefully, "Mepela tink."

But as they lifted BilWee, his left leg still jutted out awkwardly. He screamed in pain and collapsed over it when he tried to stand.

"Be careful," Cuilean called out, stepping into the midst of the fray. For the benefit of those Zziippps who had trouble comprehending, he added, "Be lukaut. BilWee pain."

There was a universal *ooohh* of understanding.

"BilWee pain!" one of the Zziipppaeis sagely observed.

"BilWee pain!" the cry went up.

"No can wak," one of them observed, and recalling the Monstrato Corps policy towards injured assets, he added somberly, "Himpela go patch-place."

"No!" Cuilean interjected forcefully, and slipping into the Zziippp patois, he added, "No go pasture. Dat sma-hed tink. Yupelas carry. Al yupelas carry."

Hurriedly, muttering and chiming to themselves as if to keep the idea in the forefronts of their small frontal lobes, "Uspela carry, uspela carry," the Zziippps gathered up their friend, whose hands still cupped to his chest the chick, whose peeps carried above the yelps of the Zziipppaei Guards. Hoisting BilWee on their shoulders, they quick-marched (or, quick-bumbled) out of the grove of trees and across the open field to the aptrac, all the time shouting repeatedly, "BilWee pain! BilWee pain!" to keep constant in the forefront of their attention the plight of their friend and fellow.

Reaching the troop transport, they stopped and set BilWee upright, supporting him on either side while he steadied himself on his single good leg.

"BilWee get newpela flyfela for bospela," BilWee reported, wobbling unsteadily between the two Zziippps who stood on either side.

"BilWee al-rite!" Ges announced for Docherty's benefit, though unintentionally calling attention to the fact the BilWee was *not* al-rite.

"Himpela no pain," Piddleday announced.

Piddledoo added, "Himpela no break leg."

"What!" Docherty demanded.

"They say they got the chick the Commander wanted, but BilWee hurt his leg."

Buttwater-Bates pushed in: "How by the Wholly Profit do you even commencify to comprehensive what these mutants are talking about?"

Cuilean shrugged. "Well, I understand *you* ..." Leaving the rest unsaid.

CacaHed Docherty peered down at the leg. "What's wrong with it?" he asked, though the question was mostly rhetorical as he could well see what was wrong: The lower part of the leg was twisted so that it jutted at a right angle from the upper.

"Leg no lukim al-rite," BilWee said. "Maybe brukim"

"We'll have to send you to the pasture to get better."

A shock went through the assembled Zziipppaei Guard. This was the one Simspeek word that was universally understood.

BilWee blurted out impulsively -- though it was far from him to countermand his bospela. "No!" he said before he could think. "No bigpela patch-place!" He softened his outburst with the plea, "Pwees."

The other Zziipppaeis, shaking their heads vigorously with short, spasmodic jerks, shifted from foot to foot and alternatively edged closer to their friend to support him, and away from him to avoid being clubbed by the descending, feared hammer of being "retired" to the pasture.

"But I can see ..."

"BilWee no pain," BilWee said. "Lukim ..." he shrugged off his support, and with a free arm (still clutching the bird with one), he pushed his friends' assisting hands aside. "BilWee not hurt," he repeated.

"BilWee al-rite. BilWee al-rite!" came the repeated refrain from the others. Heads nodded frantically in unison. "BilWee okay."

"We notice you're not al-rite," Buttwater-Bates asserted. "Any wonder can see that. You necessity go to the pasture."

"No bigpela patch-place. Pwees. Cul-win, tok Bospela. Big pwees! You tok mepela no go patch-place. Tok Bospela. BilWee alrite."

All this time, the Commander had been standing aside, observing the conversation with distaste. Looking past Buttwater-Bates, Cuilean turned his appeal to Docherty. "Commander CacaHed Docherty, sir."

Expressionless, Docherty regarded Cuilean. "What!" Not a question. More a sneer.

"You want the bird, right? How're you going to take care of it? It's just a ..." Here Cuilean balked, or rather his speech did, for he'd run up against a wall. There was no word for a young bird in Simspeek – in fact, as there were not even any birds in the DownBlow, and even the word had passed into obsolescence. An expression came to him out of the fog of forgetfulness forced upon him by the leash – "*Isbean*," he said, but then the Simspeek term coming to him, he rushed to cover, "Baby bird, I mean," but not quickly enough as almost immediately he flinched from the jolt that followed accessing this forbidden memory.

Buttwater suppressed a thin smile and a chortle.

Cuilean blinked off the brainshock, and ignoring the Buttwanker, continued his plea to Docherty: "A baby bird. If you want to keep it, needs to be taken care of. How're you going to feed it? Who's going to do that? Not *him*," he added, with a tilt of the head towards Buttwater-Bates.

Cullean's words stirred up a storm in BilWee's thinking – which considering the shallow brain pan of the Zziipppaei, was less a tempest in a teacup than a mild dabbling of condensation in a petri dish – but nevertheless, an idea that in his desperation, he could cling to. He exclaimed, "BilWee no go bigbela patch-place. BilWee luk aut newpela flypela!"

"What?" Against his inclination, Docherty was shocked into responding. *This might actually be a good idea.*

"BilWee luk aut newpela. BilWee like newpela. Newpela cam up bigpela flyfela. Bospela wanna flypela get amals. BilWee learnim newpela get em."

The CacaHed, who like most of the Anboarnh caste had resolutely refused to learn TokTok,[76] raised his brow and looked to Cuilean for a translation.

"He says he'll take care of the ..." Cuilean watched himself here,

---

[76] It was widely believed amongst the upper caste Anboarnh that admitting to knowing of another language code besides Simspeek – much less, even knowing how to speak it – incurred a loss of status or was a cause for shame, if not disgrace.

less he be jolted again ... "baby bird."

"Yassa, bosfela!" BilWee blurted out in TokTok; although the more advanced Zziipppaeis were able to understand more simply constructed and more slowly spoken Simspeek, they were congenitally unable to master the more complex syntax, grammar, phonology, and vocabulary. "BilWee luk aut newpela flypela!"

In his desperation, though perhaps not by premeditation or calculation, but more by accident, much as somebody who'd never thrown a dart before might by chance hit a bull's-eye (or, as they called it in the DownBlow, a rat's-eye), the Zziipppaei had piqued Docherty's interest, had touched exactly what it turned out he might want (though he would not have been able to tell that wish before this moment). He'd heard how the locals -- the clann, as they called themselves, the *Children* -- trained these predators to hunt for big game, sometimes as large as a small mammoth, even.

BilWee breathed hard for several gasps to recover from the exertion of speaking. (For anyone else, the gap would have constituted a strategic pause for effect before the delivery of the bottom line, the key bargaining point, but for the Zziipppaei, though it had that effect, the drama of the pause was entirely unintended.) "But no bigpela patch-place."

"Alright," Docherty agreed. "No pasture."

BilWee strained to form the word: "Na pa ... pa ..." The effort raised a sweat on his ramped brow. He finally formed the words and expelled them as if spitting a dead fly from his lips: "Na patch-place."

"Na patch-place," the hushed murmuring of relief was passed from Zziippp to Zziippp, as if no one had heard Docherty say it a moment before.

"But ..." Docherty hissed.

The whispered celebration stopped short.

"Do something with that leg." Docherty made a face at BilWee's leg, and which in all the discussion of the bird, he'd completely forgotten about, but which now that the issue of the care of the eaglet had been settled, pushed its way to the forefront of his consideration. "It's disgusting."

Cuilean stepped back in. "We'll take care of it."

"Yassa, Bosfela, uspela care," BilWee assured Docherty.

With a couple of hand gestures, which the Zziipppps understood, much like pet rats can learn simple signals, Cuilean directed the Zziipppps to carry their friend to the back of the aptrac.

Once there, knowing there was no other remedy, he told them to hold BilWee down, and he positioned the leg against the rear bumper without saying what he was going to do besides warning BilWee, "This gonna pain."

Up front in the turret and below in the belly of the transport beast, a yelp, a shriek, and a howl were heard as Cuilean jumped high and landed with full force on the broken leg, re-breaking it and then forcing it relatively straight with a series of violent yanks and successive blows (or as straight as it would ever be – albeit with a slight bow that would ever after give BilWee a distinct sideways lurch whenever he walked).

After that, Cuilean bound the leg tightly with thick, all-purpose field tape.

"BilWee okay, gudpela Cuilean," the Zziipppaei exhaled with satisfaction before passing out.

5. The girl who rode the unihorn

Cuimhnich iad às tàinig thu.
Remember those from whom you came
Leabhar an Leaghaidh Mhòir —
The Book of the Great Melting

Wiktionary: In the Beginning

"Toiseach an tòiseachaidh"
(translated from the FT)

Professor Harold Harishandra Higginsbottom (editor)

It has been postulated that every society conceives some creation myth, a "story" which is more often than not an amalgamation and blend of history and legend, fiction and fact, actuality and downright fabrication, which the people of that culture accept as a real or symbolic representation of the beginnings of all things, which in most cases is taken to be "real," no matter how fanciful it might seem to those outside the belief system, although in all cases, it is heavily weighted with symbolism as to the true nature of reality.

In other words, each culture conceives of the origination source not in accordance with "reality," but in its own image, which is thus held to comprise its DEITI.[77] This conception of the universe guides and informs in myriad ways how people should interact with each other, how society should be constructed, and how humans should regard their relationship with the natural (or "natural") world.

For the people of the WAYP, the universe is organized around the principle of the Mother -- a universal intelligence, an actual entity, a ubiquitous, all-pervasive being that is manifested in the "reality" we know as the material world. In this conception, "she" is not only the source (as the "mother") of the universe itself, but also the body and heart of all reality. What's more, "she" is not an ineffable, non-material principle, but actually comprises all being – all intelligence, all spirit, all material, and all life itself. In short, the mythology of the people of the Wayp have it that all existence, which is to say all things *in* existence, is actually the "Mother" herself.

---

[77] DEITI -- Defining Existential Instigatory Triggering Incident.

Which is, this editor does not need to remind the reader, completely contrary to the findings of Pelagoes supercomputer calculations which have clearly demonstrated and proven that known "reality" is actually the holographic calculation of the Wholly Profit, which in order to achieve ever-increasing ROI (Realization of Increase) demands constant, unregulated manipulation and domination of the macrocosmic algorithm that creates the holograph in which we imagine we exist.

But this entry in the Wiktionary is not intended to argue which mythology is "true" or "false," but to describe the shaping philosophy of the People of the Wayp.

Although the Wuarardd of the Profit very clearly teaches us that the universe arose from the primeval Gowp of GAWD that then congealed into planets and stars -- the stars themselves being nothing more than balls of Gowp that had caught on fire, and life itself being the immutable impulse towards the seeking of Profit from nothing), adhering to the irrational worship of what they call the "Mother," the mythos of the People holds that the known (and unknown) universe was born in an event they call the Big Birth – *a' Bhreith Mhòr* in the FT.

Supposedly, in this "birthing" event, the universe emerged from a "black hole" -- an empyrean birth canal out of which the cosmos was born. The pangs of this celestial natal event resulted in the innumerable stars and planets in existence today and contained the seeds of all life that now populates the universe.

This fabled ontology is variously represented skematically by any of numerous and various icons, four of which are duplicated below:

mìcheal dubh

Don't mean nuthin' to 'em

'S e àicheadh spiorad chàich a' chiad cheum gu fìreanachadh an an-ochd dhaibh.

Denying the spirit of others is the first step to justifying cruelty to them.

Proverb from *Leabhar an Leaghaidh Mhòir* — The Book of the Great Melting

Holding himself upright by leaning on a makeshift crutch crudely formed from a fallen tree branch, BilWee stood to the rear of the aptrac turret platform behind CacaHed Docherty, First Adjunct Cuilean, and the Anboarnh helmsman who steered the vehicle.

BilWee had wrapped a cloth around his arm, and on that perched the eagle chick he'd rescued. He frequently turned to the eaglet and squeaked to it.

Already the heat was rising, raising with it dust and midges -- tiny, fiercely-biting beasties that swarmed like a horde of fiends out of the firey pit of the DownBlow. Those on the platform slapped futilely at the nasty creatures, which in actuality were too small to see and too numerous to swat.

Which didn't stop the PieceTakers from trying.

When the "band of bothers" (as Buttwater-Bates put it) finally hauled within sight of the lake, Docherty swung the breathing apparatus away from his face, but the atmosphere of the Wayp sent him into a coughing fit, so he replaced the piece over his nose and mouth. The smudgey, smoky air of the ventilator -- a mixture of gowp dust, carbon dioxide, carbon monoxide, methane, and ozone that duplicated the atmosphere of the DownBlow -- swirled up to his nostrils and down into his chest, and he took a deep, satisfied breath.

Ahead of them, the mountain at the back of the lake rose up higher than they could see, disappearing into a wreath of silky white clouds. To one side, a flight of ducks, some capped emerald green, and others a dull brown, skittered across the surface of the water.

195

A tight smile etched itself across Docherty's lips, like that of a Melee Match gambler confident of a sure thing. Spacing his words between the lurching over the rough ground, and speaking loudly enough to be heard over the engine's growl and the reverberating of its wheels as they whirled for a purchase in the marshy surface, he called out in a voice meant to be conversational but which didn't really elicit a discussion: "Wholly Profit! The last untouched gowp reserve on the planet, and they want to stop us from bleeding it!" He pursed his lips in disdain for the backwardness of people who would commit such a sacrilege. Largely musing to himself, though his voice was audible, he went on: "It's just sitting there. Not doing anything! Not of any use to anybody! Like it says in the Wuarardd of Gawd, 'What good is it to a man to gain sole rights if he loses the profit?'"

Unclear whether the question had been rhetorical or if he was expected to comment, Cuilean groped for an answer that wouldn't anger his commanding officer or trigger a reprimand from the leash.

But he took too long, and irritated by the lack of response, Docherty snapped, "You're from here. Tell me."

"I don't remember much from those days, CacaHed, Sir." Which was always the safe answer and true enough in its way. In addition to the memory-obliterating leash, with all the time he'd spent in the DownBlow, his remembrances of this land were hazy even when they were clearest.

"Don't give me those rat droppings." Only one thing could have disgusted CacaHed Docherty more than a Frotch, and that was a Frotch who pretended he wasn't – that he was just a normal Anboarnh. In all veracity, though, the commander wasn't expecting an answer from Cuilean, for as dependable as he was, the man never said much, perhaps because when he did, his strange way of speaking, his accent, and sometimes odd phrasing betrayed his non-Pelago background, which in itself drew scorn from those in the DownBlow and oftentimes a painful reprimand from his leash.

But the Adjunct made a convenient listener if what was wanted was less a conversation than the feeling of talking to someone (without the annoying inconvenience of having to listen to anything they might have to say back). "What do these people think? Aren't they rational? What use is something if you can't dig it up, cut it up, package it, and sell it on the market? Make a Wholly Profit on it?"

Gathering that he wasn't expected to respond thoughtfully to his commander's musings, but rather just nod in agreement from time to appropriate time, Cuilean allowed himself to be distracted by the vague familiarity of the vicinity. To the others, the plush green surroundings were strange, other worldly, but for Cuilean, it was as if he found himself revisiting a dream.

Reaching back into his memories, or as far as it was safe to delve, he dimly remembered that somewhere, sometime long ago, he'd known the answer to the CacaHed's question, but that knowledge had been wiped from his memory by innumerable jolts from the leash that strangled him – both his breathing and his thinking. In spite of the forced forgetting, however, he knew there was a reason why it was somehow wrong to shave the trees from the skin of the planet, dig into the bowels of the earth, and drain her water: *Bainne na màthar* -- the milk of the mother — was phrase that came to him, accompanied, as might have been expected, by a shock.

Yet he persisted with his tentative gropings for recollection. His gaze skimmed the vista of trees and grasses and bushes and the rushing water that flowed towards the lake where they were heading. It was funny, he thought — though not funny in a way that would make him laugh — but odd, strange: The language betrayed him as if the words that had been taught him in the DownBlow were not adequate (which idea in and of itself constituted a sacrilege against the Wuarardd of Gawd).

Words that did fit teemed in his mind like a heavy fogswarm of nasty imps pestering him, pricking him, biting him with their subversive suggestions, each biting and then flitting away before it could be grasped.

Aibheasach -- remarkable -- he thought.

Anabarach -- unusual --came to him.

Neònach – strange -- flitted by.

And *iongantas* - wondrous.

And with each one of these came a jolt as the leash detected his accessing the portion of his memories in which the FT nestled. Accompanying the words, as well, came what was either the remembrance of something that had actually happened or was the flitting by of a recollection, as vague as it was, of a dream. A nebulous mirage in which he was himself but not quite himself -- more a little, ignorant, unthinking, unreflecting animal that was barely capable of knowing anything except the smell of wet fur, the welcoming body into which he pressed himself, and the sweet milk he greedily suckled from the hairy teat. These were the only things he knew, things for which there were no words, but to which he might now ascribe names: milk, food, warmth, others, safety.

That was him. He who knew nothing because he had not yet begun to know. He who had no thoughts because he had not yet begun to think. He who had no words because words had not yet formed in his mind. A *he* who lacked all the things that made him who he was now, and yet it was him.

The flash of revelation brought the reward of a blinding shock from the leash.

Atop the aptrac, Cuilean lifted his bleary, teary eyes to the world that presented itself to him afresh.

The tall pines.

The arching ferns.

The squat grasses.

The multi-colored pheasant in the brush.

The fox slinking in the shadows.

The sword-toothed tiger lying lazily, fearlessly, on a boulder in the sun.

The mammoth in the distance.

The eagle far above.

The twittering mavis – an azure caped, brown vested bird -- in the high branches.

And lighting on a quivering branch, another bird probably no larger than the palm of his hand – though it was difficult to be certain at this distance: brightly yellow-breasted, red-cowled, with wings splashed with scarlet and black framing a bright yellow core.

Something ached him. Only this time, it wasn't the jolt at the base of his skull; it was the struggle with the significance of all that he saw. The idea came to him as if a white-hot flash in the periphery of his vision — like something he wasn't even quite sure he had

seen, and yet more certain, more real than an image observed on a handheld, a flickering of light and shadow made to amuse the casual screoin-watcher, or a wayward digression of a hyperactive imagination, but rather a recognition of a time before this time, and imparted to him a unaccustomed desire to be as he had once been though he had little idea of just what or who that was. That and the revelation of the Mother: These were all her children. These were all *his* brothers and sisters.

A rumble of the aptrac around a bend in the trail brought his mind back to the watch-turret. Rounding the turn, the vehicle emerged from the cover of a small hill and came within view of a crowd of Indiginoes. It was difficult to say how many, but the mass covered the ground nearly as far as could be seen between the aptrac and the lake.

There was an organized chaos to the assembly: a happy milling about, small groups circling for dancing, children running around freely and wildly with high squeals, and festive swaths of cloth hung from the trees that circled the clearing.

The people gathered in the open meadow were a motley agglomeration — not so much because of their physical appearances, though they were nothing like the misshapen Zziipppaeis nor like the wan, elongated Anboarnhs. They were fair-skinned, and in some cases, even softly pinkish. Many of them sported wild, red hair and were dressed in garments that presented a kaleidoscope of colors, nothing like the uniformly drab garments of the PieceTakers. Their clothing appeared to be comprised of patches and stripes and checks and patterns of all different colors, mostly that resembled or blended into the surrounding landscape – earth tones and foliage-colored: shades of green of the leaves of the bushes and the trees and of the grasses; and reds, yellows, blues, and purples of the flowers blooming across the landscape.

It wasn't just people on foot either. Several of those in the gathering were mounted on strange beasts: one that looked to the Zziippps and the Anboarnhs, who had nothing with which to compare the creature in the DownBlow, to be a giant furry rat the size of an aptrac with an elongated nose and two long, curving, protruding teeth; another one, a slender mount with a single lance-like horn emerging from its forehead.

The PieceTaker contingent was still at a distance from the mob, but strains of never-before heard music wafted to them -- high pitched melodies intermixed with long skrills and pulsing drumming beats – all indistinct, but mixed and in some ways harmonizing with the sound of the wind through the branches of the trees or its rush down the steep mountain sides that the *loch* backed up to, all blending with the various pips and cheeps and squawks that emanated from the birds that filled the basin.

Between the aptrac and this festival of color, sound, and movement was a barren patch of ground where the water had already been drained to clear the way for the gowp-pumping operations that stretched out on either side of them, leaving a soggy mass of mud composed of boggy soil and putrefying fish bodies. As the aptrac advanced, the PieceTakers could see the dead fish skeletons protruding from the boggy mess, and if they listened carefully, they could hear the bones crunching under the wheels of the vehicle.

Some distance off, on the other side of the crowd, was the skeletal frame of a derrick rising from the dried lake bed, and behind that, the bone-white wall of the new dam that the Corps was building to block one of the streams that flowed into the lake basin -- a barrier the Corporation was constructing to denude the land of the useless water that obstructed the mining of the valuable black gowp that lay underneath.

All that was left of this arm of the lake that used to slake the thirst of half the Wayp, feed the crops, water the fields, and provide sustenance and habitat to innumerable wildlife was now just a shimmer of rising dust and a haze of heat waves off what used to be the surface of the loch — a wavy mirage that stretched as far as the dam, which loomed like the fossilized remains of an ancient behemoth over a fabled mammoth burial ground.

The aptrac sloughed through the muck, sporting a banner that read

The cooling mountain PetrAle of the Monstrato Corps.

The transport vehicle struggled up the narrow path that wound through the woods to the clearing. The way was more cramped than was comfortable for the PieceTakers of the Corporation, as most of them came from domed cities where the streets were a hundred lanes wide, but here, the trail was one which had not been gouged from the Mother's flesh and scabbed over with unliving, unforgiving, calcified gowp, but had been worn away gradually over the centuries by the foot traffic of the comings and goings of the various creatures who inhabited the land, including the *sluagh* – the people of the Wayp – who gathered here for the summer *cèilidh* – and not for military vehicles the size of buildings.

The aptrac's treads became bemired in the muck near where the path they were following ran up to the edge of the cliff that delimited the border of Wayp.

Slowing to a creep, the PieceTakers found themselves hemmed in: to one side, by their uncertainty about the rabble who had for one reason or another assembled here; in front of them, by the cracked, dead lake bed; beyond that, by the bone-white dam; and farther away, by the green field, behind which rose a forest; and on the other side, by the cliff-brink of the Wayp, which fell away thousands of lengths through the enveloping smutty clouds that roofed *Tìr na Smùid* — the Land of Smoke.

The mission had been that the aptrac was to advance impressively and imposingly through the crowd, and as the squad proceeded, they were to dispense favors of PetrAle lending to the impression of their being munificent representatives of the beneificient Corps. Finally, they were to take up an authoritative position opposite the gowp derrick.

Contrary to those plans, however, the aptrac chugged and lurched goofily, periodically lunging Docherty or the others in the topmost turret against the surrounding wall of the deck.

It was partly the grabbing muck and partly the crowd of people massed around the pathway that brought the aptrac to a complete halt. It crouched at the edge of the meadow, the low rumble of its engine sounding like the rough cough of a tubercular dragon belching fiery, black smoke.

"Keep going! Keep going! Keep going!" the CacaHed shouted to no one in particular. He asked the same unknown personage: "Why aren't we moving!"

Popping his head up through the hatch in the floor of the vehicle's tower, Buttwater-Bates called up: "We're stuccoed, Commander!"

Docherty took a moment to process what his junior officer was telling him. He blasted the angry order back, "Well, get us *unstuccoed*!" Even more perturbed that he had to use a word that didn't even exist.

Up top, BilWee nuzzled the chick, "Be al rite, lil flypela," he cooed. "We go no time." He pulled a piece of dried rat flesh saved from his own breakfast out of his pocket, popped it into his mouth and chewed it. He extruded it through his lips and offered it to the eagle chick.

The bird grabbed at the meat and gobbled it down. Then it fluffed its feathers in what might have been interpreted as a gesture of satisfaction, gratitude, and perhaps, filial affection.

With the momentary cessation of the feeding of the furnace DownBlow in the gut of the transport carrier, the cloud of black fumes that had been belching from the belly of the beastly machine and enveloping the command tower dissipated, and the PieceTakers could see more clearly across the terrain before them.

Several people in the crowd headed their way.

Docherty decided quickly that now was the time to demonstrate his contingent's friendly intentions. *What better way than to unpack the gifts brought along for just this purpose?* Keeping a wary watch on the mob, the same way he might have eyed a rabid dump-rat, he directed over his shoulder, "Pass out the samples."

Buttwater-Bates echoed down the hatch, "Bring the examples!"

An Anboarnh PieceTaker by the name of Claver Kshaf clambered up the ladder and out the hatch. He turned and called back down. "Pass sose up." (He had a bit of a lisp.) Hands attached to unseen bodies hoisted the cases through the hatch, and three

Zziipppaei assets hurriedly unpacked the Monstrato Highland Spring PetrAle and started tossing the bottles into the crowd.

"What's this?" Cuilean asked.

"Pubic rations! Ha, ha!" Kshaf told him. He was an Anboarnh junior officer with an implacable, smashed-in face, which looked as if he'd been beaten with a baseball bat. (Rumor had it that he'd once gotten into the losing end of a tussle with a Zziipppaei fightball player, which might just have been the story that he himself passed around to conceal the fact of his having been deformed in his manufacturing process.) He punctuated every statement with a nervous chuckle as if everything he said was meant as a joke, although his eyes bespoke constant fear as if his Zziippp nemesis might reappear out of the smog of time.

Docherty adjusted a megaphone and shouted in his thin voice, the sound of which hissed through the loudspeaker system. "Welcome to the grand opening and ribbon-cutting of the Monstrato PetrAle Pumping Plant." His arm swept awkwardly out of sync with his words, as if inviting the people in the crowd to admire the cliff-high sides of the dam behind them and the vista of gowp derricks in the now desiccated lake bed.

"This is a great day for the people of The Wayp," he announced, his voice amplified by the loudspeaker system wired into the aptrac, which was better suited to ordering people to G*et out of the way*! and *Pull over*! and *Stop or we'll kill you!* Threats to force compliance rather than sweet reasoning to persuade of the benefits of a new product or way of thinking.

"In cooperation with the Monstrato Corps, the citizens of Wayp are embarking on a great adventure of converting their naturally occurring reserves of gowp into an exportable, monetized commodity!" This was read from a prompt on his handheld screoin with the brittle enthusiasm of a game show host who expected his audience to erupt into cheers.

Instead of cries of acclamation, the CacaHed was answered with dead silence.

Set back over the absence of the response he expected, he continued. "Let me explain. We're converting a natural resource that until its discovery by the engineers of the Corps ..." (pause for applause -- nothing ...) "... uh ..." He faltered to find his place. "A resource that ... uh ... has been completely un-utilized, but we are now monetizing it so it can bring wealth and prosperity to the people of The Wayp!"

Another pause in expectation of a wave of grateful appreciation.

Again nothing.

Someone in the crush of Indiginoes – it sounded like a woman

– shouted what seemed to be a translation of Docherty's words into the FT.

There was something about the voice that caught Cuilean's attention and impressed upon him a shock of *déjà entendu* – something already heard, something heard before, but where or when he could not have told.

He looked hard and at first couldn't figure out where the voice had come from, but after scanning the crowd, he found what he was looking for. It was a girl — a young woman, perhaps — slight of frame and sporting a shock of red hair that flowed down her head and onto her shoulders like a mantel. She was astride a furry quadruped that had a single horn growing from the middle of its forehead – a unihorn, or as the word came to Cuilean with a painful jab, *aon-adharcach*. She was half-draped in a colorful patterned garment — a sash thrown over her shoulder and wrapped as a skirt around her lower body. She held a half-body-length bow in her hand as comfortably as if it were a part of her arm.

Somebody shouted: "*Chan eil sinn ag iarraidh am beartas agaibh!* -- We don't want your prosperity!"

Another yell came up, also in the language strange to the PieceTakers of the Corps: "We want our water!"

Although Docherty had no exact comprehension of what had been said, from the tones of the voices and the gesticulations of those in the mob surrounding them, he understood enough of the gist of what the response was to his suggestion of shared wealth: A resounding *No!*

In a shout that attempted to be persuasive but at the same time sounded as if he were speaking to children, he pressed on. "You don't understand."

He focused on a nearby man who was riding a mammoth and was therefore nearly at the level of the turret. The Indiginoe was astraddle the animal's thick neck, and his legs were tucked behind the floppy ears of the pachyderm. With a long shaggy beard and an unruly mane, the fellow was nearly as woolly as the animal he was riding, and his hair was of the same brownish-reddish color – *ruadh* in the FT.

Docherty pressed on with his explanation. "We dispense with something that's worthless — the water — to get at the valuable asset, the gowp, which we sell for a profit." And as if this settled the matter, "Which you get a share of!"

"*Tha iad ag iarraidh oirnn bainne a' mhàthair a reic* – They want us to sell the Mother's milk!" the girl shouted, passing Docherty's words on to the crowd.

Docherty observed that whatever it was she had said angered the flock of Indiginoes even further.

"You can't sell what's not yours," a man shouted angrily in the FT.

Ròna relayed this in Simspeek back up to those on the aptrac.

CacaHed Docherty felt his ire rising. "It is too ours! International corporate protocols for the claiming of unregistered natural assets ..."

But his words were cut off by the girl on the unihorn swiveling in her saddle and crying out to those behind her. Her call was not as bellowing as that of the fellow on the mammoth but could be heard by those in the throng not because it boomed a bass, but because it piped above the low roar of the gathering riot. *"Chluicheadh na creutairean seo an strìopair airson na màthar aca fhèin* — These creatures would play the pimp for their own mother."

The comment raised a laugh from the motley horde.

And then a chorus of angry, inarticulate shouts.

"What!" The Monstrato commandant craned an ear to catch the words, even though they had already flown past him, and he wouldn't have understood them even if he had heard them clearly, so he was left like a hunter who was vaguely aware of a flock of birds taking flight off to his side, but left to guess at what exactly they were or where they arose from; he knew only that he had missed his shot at whatever it was that had just flushed from the brush.

"You understand the FT!" Docherty shouted, taking out his anger at not understanding on the Adjunct closest to him – which, in this instance, happened to be Cuilean. "What'd that creature say!"

Cuilean had winced as the words of the girl had triggered an electric jolt. He had heard what she'd said, and surprisingly to him, he'd understood – though if you'd asked him before this moment, he'd have told you that he had no memory of the FT. Even so, partly to avoid a further disciplinary sting, he excused himself with a dramatic shrug that said in the universal language, *I dunno.*

"Idiot!" Docherty grumbled. "Why am I surrounded by fools!" Less a question than an imprecation.

Cuilean shrugged in mock helplessness, in professed ignorance. (Though he could have ventured a guess.)

The Commander snarled, "Useless!"

Cuilean took glanced up the steep side of the mountain towards its peak where storm clouds were brewing.

Before there was any chance for him to reflect on what he saw, the crowd pushed even closer to the aptrac.

Another shout from the assemblage. "We want what's ours. Not yours!"

That damned girl again, Docherty thought. Of all the things that mystified the Commander — the strange "religion," the infestation of nature out of control, the complete disregard for the Wholly Seize of the Profit,[78] this one thing puzzled him the most: the abundance of females, not just as breeding stock, as suppliers of eggs, but (as strange as it might seem to the Anboarnh of the DownBlow) as actual members of their society.

The PieceTakers threw bottles of PetrAle as far into the crowd as they could. But this only brought those at the back of the mob pressing forward to the aptrac, pushing upon it, rocking it back and forth.

One of the distributors threw a whole case of PetrAle into the throng. The brick of encased fluid hit a child, and further cries of protest and anger went up.

Somebody in the mob threw a bottle back -- not a gentle lob but rather a forceful, aimed hurl.

The container hit Cuilean in the back of the head.

BilWee squawked, "Gowp-bomb!"

Panic spread like an electric shock through the aptrac.

Another PetrAle-filled projectile flew up from the throng and grazed Docherty's temple. For someone who presented such a fearsome front, the Corps Commander let loose quite a little-girl squeal.

The shower of bottles increased – first one, then a couple, then a few, then a rain of them.

Another voice from the crowd demanded, "*A-mach às an seo!* -- Get out of here!"

It was then that Cuilean heard the pops from the Zziipppaeis' kabloeys. The Guards of the CacaHed's troop were priming their pneumatic rifles and firing shot after shot. The normally regulated and coordinated sequence of firing became disjointed and sporadic. Rapid staccato bursts split the tumult like sharp claps of hands.

Cuilean called out for the shooting to stop, "They're not gowp-bombs! They're throwing our own PetrAle back!"

But Cuilean's cry went unheeded, for Docherty's attention was pulled to the shaking structure of the derrick at the far end of the field. He could see the gowp scaffolding tottering, its frame rocking back and forth like some massive beast being felled. He squinted to see more clearly. "What the ratfuck're they doing!"

If Docherty had had the words, he might have been spared

---

[78] Wholly Seize of the Profit -- the inalienable right of the Monstrato Corporation and affiliated and subsidiary bodies to seize any and all profit-making opportunities as its own, wholly and without regard to any other claims, within or without its domains and jurisdictions.

surprise by the reflection that *an uair a thig aon rud, thig a h-uile rud* – When one thing comes, everything comes -- but he didn't possess that proverbial reference, and so he was shaken by outraged shock at the sacrilege, as in, *With everything else that's happening, now this!?!*

His voice trembled in astonished fury. "They're tearing down the derrick! They can't do that. It's Corps' property!" His articulations came out as outraged splutterings of sentence fragments and disconnected phrases. Intending for his voice to carry down the hatch to the engine room, the man-in-white shouted, "Get us over there! Everybody on the engine wheel!" Within a few moments, half a dozen Zziippp PieceTakers were scrambling into the cave that housed the power plant of the troop transport. "Get us moving! Don't stop! Hit it!"

Docherty raised one arm, leaving the other poised on the mounted, high-caliber kabloey. "Remember, we're not stopping. If you see something, shoot it," he ordered, referring to the watch words of the Monstrato Corps, equally applicable to this situation as to any other in everyday life, but now even more so as unknown, only guessed at, and horrifyingly fiendish schemes swelled in their imaginations: a trip wire that would snare the aptrac or a mid-road pit that would cripple the lumbering monster truck, and in either case make it vulnerable to further attack; a DIY mammoth-manure bomb; an explosive PetrAle piss-off cocktail; an Insurge sniper's nest – any of these leading to the slaughter of the PieceTaker contingent, their torture, their immolation, perhaps even their being dismembered alive.

"Blast the muck out of it!" Docherty screamed, desperation in his voice. "Get us out of here!" With all the Zziippps manning the motor wheel in the engine room – except for those few frantically shoveling gowp into the furnace – the treads of the vehicle gripped the ground, and sure enough, the aptrac pitched forward with a deep-chested rumble, lumbering into the crowd.

BilWee was huddled against the wall of the turret casing, whining inarticulate pleas and whimpering. "No fraid, lil flypella," he reassured the hooded eagle chick, who perched on its caretaker's arm, undismayed by the melee going on around them.

Docherty swiveled the dart-firing kabloey canon towards the crowd, pumped the pneumatic action, took sight, and fired a series of darts, and the people, who had just moments before been gathered in a festive celebration, scattered in general confusion in cross-currents, some running away from the fired projectiles and some towards what they took to be the cover of the PieceTakers' own transport.

In front of the aptrac, an old woman groped blindly and

stumbled. Her feet seemed to have gotten tangled in the mud and the muck and the bog-roots of the heather. Confused as to which way the sound of the grinding wheels of the aptrac were coming from, she dithered indecisively in her panic, turning this way and that as the monster truck bore down on her.

For some reason, the sight of the *cailleach* – the old woman – triggered an eruption in Cuilean of the FT, a spewing of words that sprung to his lips so quickly that he had no control over their ejaculation and that came out before he realized what he was saying: "A *mhaighster, mas e ur toil e, stad!* -- Sir, please, stop!"

Cuilean was chastised for his cry of warning by a stab in his brain. His eyes blurred from the leash's jolt, he staggered. Nevertheless, as the aptrac pitched forward, he managed to gulp out in Simspeek, "There's people there! We're going to kill somebody."

"Don't worry 'bout it," Docherty responded without looking back from his charioteer perch, following up with the contemptuous stereotype held by the rulers of the DownBlow, "Don't mean nuthin' to them!"

Quickly upon that observation, he shouted the general command: "Full smoke ahead! Don't stop! You fuckin' fuckheads of fuckers!" (Which didn't make any sense – even Docherty himself could not have explained what it meant -- but it sounded emphatic enough at the time).

"Don't stop, or I'll stop you for good!" (A threat which *did* make sense and which was not an empty one: He was known to have shot those who had defied, impeded, or even too slowly obeyed his orders.)

The CacaHed pulled out his kabloey-sidearm to punctuate the point.

Below deck, the Zziipppaei crew set to pumping furiously on the crankshaft which powered the tread-enwrapped wheels. The aptrac lurched forward with a deep-throated rumble and grumble and straining and complaining.

Before he knew what possessed him, with a single movement, Cuilean thrust the helmsman out of the way and sent him toppling over the side of the turret, a tumble that left him hanging onto the side, clinging on by his fingers and spewing a string of Simspeek curses.

Cuilean gave the tiller a sharp twist that buckled the wheels, turned them sideways upon themselves, and brought the aptrac to a lurching halt.

Docherty blurted out, "What the ...!" but before he could finish the sentence (if it was going to be a sentence), he himself was thrown by the aptrac's sudden heave and abrupt stop into the sidewall of the gun turret and nearly over the side himself.

The girl who rode the unihorn

Tuitidh a' h-uile rud a thèid a chrathadh.
Everything falls that is shaken.
Proverb from *Leabhar an Leaghaidh Mhòir* —
The Book of the Great Melting

The aptrac, as large as the House of the Sisters in the village and belching black smoke and soot, perched on the path that ran along the edge of the cliff that overlooked *Oir an t-Saoghail* — The Edge of the World -- which fell thousands of lengths through the clouds of mist and smoke to the rocky shore and the ocean below.

The throng in its horde-fury was pressing against the massive transporter and rocking it on its tracks, while the Monstrato PieceTaker Distribution Agents in their gowp-colored uniforms and "Have a Happy Monstrato Day" sashes had locked themselves in the belly of the monster transport and were peering in swelling dread out the portholes upon the gathering storm of the motley mob that was arrayed in a semi-circle behind the young woman with shocking red hair and tattoos banding her bare arms. The people in the gang were dressed similarly, and they carried vicious swords, long pikes, or various other evil-looking instruments that looked like they could be effective if employed to cut or maim or disembowel.

The Zziippps inside the belly of the aptrac looked out in horror at the four-footed monster that was nearly as large as their own aptrac. Two tusks – each longer than a Zziippp -- protruded from the sides of its mouth. The furry giant reared up off its front legs, pointed its twin lances in a threat and in defiance of the even larger beast it faced, and came crashing down with such vehemence that the ground shook all around it, lifting those closest a full three fingers off the ground.

The young woman shouted. "Leave our water!"

Docherty gripped the side of the turret wall with his tentacle-like fingers. "You're in violation of corporate policy!" he shouted in rage at the sacrilege. His indignation was palpable. He'd never encountered such disobedience to the policies of GAWD. "We have rights to that water!" Even though his actual voice was tinny, over the sound system of the aptrac, it was amplified to a bellow. Out of sync with his utterance, he pointed at the lake that shimmered in the distance.

Ròna shouted back in the peculiar pidgin of Simspeek that was common to the People of the Wayp, her voice rising above the tumult. "It's not anybody's that's the milk of the mother!"

CacaHed Docherty, his white suit now flecked with dirt clods from the tossed mud and smudged from the deflected bottles thrown back at the PieceTakers, turned to Cuilean, who was just then tugging uncomfortably at the leash apparatus that tightly bound his neck, and demanded, "What the ratfuck is this Frotch bitch talking about? Who's this 'Mother'?"

"CacaHed, sir," the young man explained, "it's their religion."

"Their what?"

"You know, like for the Wholly Profit ... except for ..." Cuilean paused, searching for a non-offensive phrasing.

Docherty had little patience for waiting for the complete explanation. "But the Profit's real!" he blurted out, incredulity writ large in his countenance, an anger rising in his voice against the blasphemy. "You can see it! It's there on the screoin. You can see the numbers! That's a ratfuck more real than some imaginary spirit."

Adjunct Cuilean shrugged his shoulders and lifted and spread his hands, as if to say, "I'm just saying ..."

Docherty steadied himself against the turret gunwale as the mammoth butted the aptrac, making it shake. "That's just superstitious theory."

Cuilean shrugged. He wasn't going to argue the issue, not with a Commander who had the power to increase the controls of his leash. He wasn't going to point out that the anger of the horde they were facing was more than just *theory*.

Still, there was something familiar to Cuilean about the young woman astride the great beast's back, her red hair flaming brightly in the unfiltered light of the mountain sun. There was that shock of color that impinged on his memory, and after that, though she was some distance away, he could make out that she carried herself with a fierce intensity. Which seemed, in and of itself, queerly familiar. He squinted, but he couldn't make out nor bring to mind what was so familiar -- perhaps because of the glare of the sun in the thin air of the Wayp, nothing like the dull, hazy atmosphere in the DownBlow where he'd spent so many years of his life.

Added to that, he had no more than a moment to puzzle out the faint recollection — if it was that. For below them, the one-horned beast she rode was so agitated, straining to charge, taking some steps forward, then stopping, controlled and restrained only by its rider's guiding it in circles by the taps of her heels on its flanks.

In a single movement, the young woman leapt to her feet on the back of the strange animal, and pointing with her bow, she shouted a command to the PieceTakers inside the aptrac: "Come out!" Another shout from the girl. "You'll not be harmed."

Docherty shouted a caution of his own at her. "You're not authorized to damage Corporate property!" His voice quaked with the contemplation of the blasphemy of such an act of sacrilege.

The girl answered only with, "Your last warning ..."

"No! I'm warning *you*!" Docherty barked back, though the confidence in his voice seemed to be waning, marked partly by the quaking tone of voice, and partly by his response having been reduced to a mere repetition of her words back at her.

Raising her bow over her head, Ròna let out a wild cry, that sounded — if the corporate representatives in the aptrac had been familiar with any other animals beside sewage rats and sludge slugs — like the screech of an enraged sword-tooth tiger, a cry that echoed a fierceness that would not have been guessed at by her slender frame.

At the other end of the mob, the furry fellow atop the woolly mammoth shouted "*Thalla*! -- Go!" and gave a couple prods to the back of the animal's ears. His mount lumbered forward, picking up speed like a freight train transitioning from the dead stop of an immovable mass to the speed of an irresistible force.

When the mammoth hit it, the aptrac rocked on its treads.

The hairy man directed the tusked beast to retreat, which the animal did with ominous backwards steps.

The man leaned forward towards the ear of his mount and exhorted, "*A charaid!* — Friend! *A-rithist! Thoir ionnsaigh air!* — Again! Attack it!" The beast dipped its head, aimed its thick skull at the aptrac, and charged.

It slammed into the rolling fort, which this time slipped sideways and teetered on two wheels, as if just about to topple over. Various members of the mob cheered or screamed or gave out loud whoops, and they swarmed towards the vehicle and added their collective exertions to that of the mammoth.

Once again, the mammoth retreated and charged, but this time,

rather than delivering a single, bone-rattling, teeth-shaking blow —
it did that, right enough -- it also grabbed a purchase on the rocky
cliff top, plowed its feet into the ground, and leveraging its tusks
under the aptrac, lifted one end of the vehicle. The aptrac slid
sideways, teetering more precariously on its two cliff-side wheels.

In the innards of the transport, the terrified faces of the
Anboarnh PieceTaker supervisors and their Zziipppaei drones
stared out of the portholes.

Several banged on the thick semi-transparent window,
mouthing inarticulate screams — unheard because of the thickness
of the gowpaleen panes.

The soundless, pantomimed terror of those trapped in the
interior grew more frantic as the cliff loomed even closer, which
those tethered to their workstations on that side of the rolling
fortress saw out their windows.

"CacaHed, sir," Cuilean gripped the turret sidewall to keep his
balance. "Gotta get the ratfuck outta here!" He'd already made up
his mind what he was going to do; he was just poising for the right
moment.

The aptrac shook again. It was teetering on its two wheels —
as close to being horizontal as it could get without toppling over.
Cuilean clung to the bridge wall, barely keeping from tumbling out.
Without having to bend his neck, he peered straight across the
small structure to where below, the cliff fell away past where the
eye could see.

Commander CacaHed Docherty creaked his directions, his
voice breaking in the middle of the command. "Stay at your posts!"

Totally ignoring the reality that their posts, having slid away
from them in the topsy-turvey innards of the aptrac, had not stayed
with *them*.

"Commander!" Cuilean pleaded.

The Commander exclaimed, defiant of the actuality of what he
was even now experiencing, "They wouldn't dare!" (although this
was mostly to himself, with Cuilean overhearing his soliloquy).
Gripping the turret wall to keep from sliding away, Docherty lifted
the megaphone to his lips and blasted out a dire threat to the
assembled rioters: "This is the property of the Monstrato Corps! If
you damage it, you'll be liable for the damages!" (A little repetitive,
to be sure, but consider the exigency of the situation.)

That seemed not to impress anyone, least of all, the mammoth,
which was by this time working the aptrac towards the edge of the
cliff. Nor did Docherty's warning impress the dense crowd of the
Wayp folk, who themselves were pushing *en masse* against the
transport, adding to its slide. The angry shouts of the mammoth
jockey melded with the beast's fierce trumpeting as it butted time

and time again into the side of the aptrac.

At the same time, the one-horned had added his weight to the cause of toppling the PieceTaker carrier. Urged on by the slim, red-head girl astride his back, he had locked his horn into the side of the vehicle and was churning his feet in the boggy ground.

The PieceTaker troop truck, lifted by the mass of people, levitated, as if floating, to the edge of the cliff.

Those trapped inside the metal casket pounded desperately on the portholes.

Docherty primed, loaded, and shot his kabloey.

Which had the unintended consequence of causing the people in the crowd to flee under the cover of the aptrac itself, and once there, to add to the lifting of the monster truck yet closer to the quick way to the DownBlow.

Having given up on waiting for the order to save themselves, several Zziippp and Anboarnh PieceTakers clambered up from the lower deck into the turret – rats fleeing the slip over the brink -- and flung themselves off the teetering aptrac where they scattered

pell-mell in the boggy grass on the lip of the cliff.

Himself, CacaHed Docherty clung tightly to the gunwale, as if his determination alone would hold the mechanical monster erect.

Cuilean made a jump that surprised the people of the Wayp as it would have done justice to one of their own mammoth leapers, although it admittedly wasn't amongst the best leaps ever seen, for the young man didn't quite make the target he was aiming for, but he did manage to hit on a ridge that jutted out from the rocky face of the mountain, and it was there that he secured a grip of sorts on a narrow ledge somewhere between the aptrac and the DownBlow.

Which was good enough.

As he clung to the cliff face, over his head, the massive piece of machinery, belching smoke from the twin funnels on its flanks, passed the tipping point and toppled over. Everything before had been as if in slow motion, but now the monster truck accelerated from stasis to velocitous plummet in a beat of a dragonfly's wing and disappeared into the thick bank of clouds several thousand lengths below.

The rush of wind sucked Cuilean along with it by the force of its gravitational pull. He grappled for a clump of soil and a bush in a frenetic series of grabs, each frantic attempt to seize a handhold failing to secure a purchase, and he slid off the tenuous perch.

~~

He's my stray

An nì a tha caillte gheabhar a-rithist e.
What is lost can be found again.
Proverb from *Leabhar an Leaghaidh Mhòir* —
The Book of the Great Melting

A general lull — a silence of shared awe -- followed in the wake of the monster vehicle's toppling over the edge of the cliff. Then a realization drifted amongst the Zziipppaei assets sprawled out on the grassy knoll where the aptrac used to be. Eying the Wayp folks warily, they drew together into a tight drool, and more tightly and tightly, a general and seemingly coordinated wail rising from them, surging into a crescendo, accompanied by a wringing of hands and squinting of eyes as if to blot out what horrors they imagined were to befall them.

Each Zziipppaei PieceTaker pushed towards the center, seeking to gain the safety of the enveloping troop, so there was a constant flux in the formation – a sucking towards the vortex as if a whirlpool. As the PieceTakers at the outer rim pushed in towards the middlemost, they forced the ones there to the rim of the circle, and these in turn immediately strove to regain the safety of the nucleus.

All the while, the Zziipppaeis were trembling, crying, moaning, wailing in mindless fear. One refrain could be heard arising above all the inarticulate ululation: "No eat! No eat!"

Seumas, for once taken aback, muttered, "What's gotten into them?"

"They don't want us to eat them."

"Where'd they get that crazy idea?"

Seumas shouted angrily. "*Chan ith sinn sibh!* -- We're not going to eat you!" There was no response, for how could there be? The Zziippps did not understand what he was saying, did not understand anything except that it had been said with such a force that was not in the least reassuring, but just the opposite. The vehemence of his shout only added to the general impression that eating was exactly what the strangely dressed inhabitants of the

Wayp had in mind for the Zziippps.

Seumas thought perhaps they hadn't heard him, so he raised his voice and shouted even more forcefully: "WE'RE NOT GOING TO EAT YOU!"

But his yell only inspired greater terror and louder wails of distress.

The people of the heights looked around, one to the other, no one being able to offer a suggestion how to assuage the terror of the Zziippps.

Ròna, on her unihorn, pushed to the front.

In fear at her approach, the Zziippps wailed even more loudly – or rather, not so much at *her* approach, but because they could hardly see her through their blinding terror inspired by the massive unihorn, at what they were certain was the coming attack of the sword-snouted, Zziippp-stabbing monster upon which she was mounted.

Sensing they were afraid of the one-horned, she slung a leg to the side and slid down its flank and walked towards the Zziipppaeis, who cringed as if before the approach of the horsewoman of the apocalypse.

Ròna stood quietly before them. After a short span of time, the wailing diminished to a low sobbing.

When she thought the ones closest to her could hear her over their own moans, she asked softly, "What bad?" (Like many people of Wayp, she was fluent in several languages, including the languages of the Pelagoes, both high and low -- Simspeek and TokTok.)

Uncovering his eyes for just the moment it took to whine, BilWee offered — "Uspela fraid."

"What are you afraid of?" Correcting herself, she immediately rephrased the question, "What fraid yupela?"

"Uspela ..." Here he made a motion with his hands to indicate his entire group. "Uspela fraid yupela eat uspela."

"I'm not going to eat you. What gave you that idea?"

"Wayp all time eat Zziipppaei."

"Not true." She reached out to touch the Zziippp who stood so tall that he cast a shadow that enveloped her. He bent his head down and squinched his eyes shut against the impending doom that he imagined was coming for him, like a child screening its eyes to blot out something terrible lurking in the shadows. "Go 'way, go 'way," he shuddered, flinching like a terrified mammoth before a mouse.

"Mepela no eat Zziipppaei," Ròna reassured him.

The gentleness of her voice mollified the Zziipppaei foreman enough to encourage him to peek out from behind his hands. There

216

the Wayp girl was, still standing calmly in front of him, her hand on his arm, looking at him with what to him was a strange expression on her face. Rather than the usual hate and disgust he was accustomed to in the countenances of his Anboarnh superiors, instead, hers was -- he was nonplussed; he didn't have a word for a not-Zziipppaei who wasn't revolted by him or didn't want to strike him.

"Yupela not eat?"

"No, mepela not eat," she replied, dipping into the Zziipppaei's TokTok again.

However, Bilwee was only half soothed, not totally convinced. Suspecting a trick, he lifted his chin and pointed doubtfully with it at the one-horned. "Himpela eat?"

"Himpela no eat," Ròna reassured the Zziippp, and whistling, she summoned her giant mount to her.

With a snort, Dìleas clomped forward and stopped beside the young woman.

A high-pitched squeal emitted collectively from the Zziipppaeis, along with renewed sobbing and whining. The drool cringed together even more tightly.

Ròna uttered a soothing reassurance and lifted the Zziipppaei's hand toward her mount.

BilWee stiffened, and half resisting, complying only grudgingly, fearfully, he allowed Ròna to guide his hand jerkily towards the unihorn's flank.

Ròna placed the Zziipppaei's hand onto the furry side of her one-horned. "See," she said and moved his hand to stroke Dìleas. The animal grunted softly and let out a breathing noise between its loose lips, which flapped with the gust of air.

"See," she said. "Himpela like yupela."

"Like mepela?"

"Yes."

"No eat?"

"No."

BilWee ran his hand over the furry side of the one-horned. The words came from him almost without volition, in amazement: "Himpela soft."

Dìleas turned his head and nuzzled his lips into the Zziipppaei's face and flapped a slobbery raspberry.

A look of consternation came over BilWee, but Ròna interpreted the unihorn's meaning before another wave of panic could set in. "He kissed you."

The Zziipppaei was astounded. "Himpela kiss?"

"Yes."

BilWee announced loudly to the other Zziipppaeis, "Himpela

kiss BilWee. No eat BilWee. Uspela fwiends!"

The others looked upon BilWee as if he were a god of sorts, destined to be remembered in the legends of the DownBlow: the Zziipppaei who hadn't been eaten by the one-horned!

"Come! Touch!"

After that, a pet-fest ensued, as one by one – at first slowly, cautiously, reluctantly -- the other Zziipppaeis came forward to caress the one-horned, which snorted contently as it had not been regaled with so much attention in a long time.

"What himpela name?"

"*Dìleas*," Ròna told him.

"Name funny," BilWee ventured. He was warming up to this strange Wayp girl.

"It means 'faithful,'" Ròna told him.

"Full fay?"

Seeing the Zziippp didn't quite understand, Ròna offered, "'True,' in a way."

BilWee breathed out a long *ahhh*, as if he'd seen the light of revelation. "Trueway," he told the other Zziippps with the tone of someone delivering the good news of the Wuarardd of Gawd. "Himpela name 'Trueway.'"

Right at that moment, a shout from the edge of the cliff pulled Ròna's attention away. Atop his mammoth, leaning forward as far as he could, his heels locked under his ride's ears and his hand propped on the animal's brow, Seumas gazed intently. "There's something down there!" he shouted.

With a quick leap upon the one-horned's back, a heel tap, a knee nudge, a cluck, and "*Thugainn, a bhalaich* — Come on, lad," Ròna guided her two-ton unihorn to the edge of the precipice.

As she lifted herself out of her seat and leaned forward, there was little to see, or much, depending on your point of view.

The rocky, grass-covered cliff descended nearly vertically into a thick, dirty-orange bank of smoke that covered the *Tìr na Smùid* — the Land of Smoke — a blanket that stretched out to cover the entire globe below the risen land.

The girl swung off her mount and warily approached the precipice. Standing at the edge and peering straight down over the side made her dizzy, so she laid down, and poking her head out, she peeked out over the cliff.

A multitude of creatures swarmed the rocky wall. Gulls and gannets returned to their perches after the startling flight of the monster transport truck past their sanctuaries. Little mountain badgers scurried away from the chock-full nests which they, taking advantage of the parents' sudden absence, had sought to raid for the unexpected treat of a few eggs.

Ròna eyed warily a small floating form soaring far in the distance. At least, it appeared small — just a speck against the gray-blue sky — what the People of the heights called *adhar liath.* Without perspective or comparison, the figure appeared as tiny as a sparrow. But she knew it was more than it seemed. Soaring majestically the *iolaire bhuidhe mhòir* — the great golden eagle — three times as big as a man, and a wing-span twice as long, kept sentinel for prey. And well she knew, she could be its next meal, if she were not careful.

As she looked over the cliff, nowhere did Ròna see any sign of the plummeting vehicle or any of the remaining men who had been in it. The entire vehicular megalith had been swallowed by the smog bank.

"I don't see anything," she said over her shoulder at her brother and was about to turn away, when she did see something. It was just a dim shade, the color of the soil beneath the grass.

But it had moved.

She peered more closely and intently. *There! There it was! The movement again!*

She quickly returned to her mount and unlashed the lasso that was hanging from the saddle pad. With a few deft movements, as fast as a dragonfly on the face of the Lake of the Mother, she whipped the rope around Dìleas's neck and shoulders and tossed the unsecured end over the edge of the rocky heights. Seemingly forgetting all the caution she had evidenced just a heartbeat before, she dove after it, catching it in mid-flight, and rappelled her way down the escarpment.

"*A Ròna!*" shouted Seumas, her thick-chested brother. Rushing to the verge himself, Seumas leaned forward and peered over and called after her even after she was no longer to be seen, "*Dè an ifrinn tha thu a' dèanamh!?!*[79] — What the hell're you doing!?!"

Ròna was already rapidly descending, hand over hand on the rope, and then like a cliff-goat, leaping, bouncing off rocky or dirt ledges, she parterred down, aiming for the spot where she'd spied the stirring in the cliff grasses.

Several others crowded up behind Seumas. "*Ayy!*" he screamed as they pressed him to the very curb of the cliff. "*Thoir an aire! —*

[79] *Ifrinn* – an etymological note: some authorities hold that the word has roots in an ancient, mythological, imagined "place" of punishment and torment of the souls of people after they have died – know in ancient proto-Simspeek as "hell." In the FT at the time that these chronicles cover, the word had become another name for the DownBlow, a place of eternal torment, a land of fire, sulphur, toxic gases, and brimstone, where poor tormented souls of the living resided as punishment for the sins of humankind. Accordingly, the inhabitants of this DownBlow were sometimes known as *ifreannach* or "hellspawn."

Be careful!" he cried out, the shout of alarm probably being motivated more by his concern not to be sent tumbling after his sister than any deep concern for her well-being.

"What's she doing?"

"Where's she going?"

"She can't be climbing all the way down!"

But the girl had no intention of descending all the way to the base of the cliff that was lapped by the brown waters of *Cuan Mòr a' Chaca Ghoiliche* — The Great Sea of Boiling Shit,[80] as the people of the Wayp called it.

When she heard a rustle, caught a glimpse of the sand-colored PieceTaker uniform, so out of place in the green land of the Wayp, she braked to a sudden halt.

Careful — for she well knew the sound could have been made by one of the mountain goats — *gobhar-beinne* in the FT — that hung on the vertical cliffs overlooking the ocean thousands of lengths beneath the topmost heights, and that so fiercely guarded its territory that it would butt an intruder -- man, woman, or any other beast, they were all the same to it – and send the trespasser tumbling into the clouds below.

Ròna ventured closer, suppressing her breathing, for the unusualness of the sight alarmed her. She was about to retreat when she saw a boot-covered foot, and then, a swatch of dark soil, damp as if oil had spilled on it, and she saw the flies buzzing around the viscous red-brown coagulation.

Pushing aside the veil of cliff grass, she stepped through to a shelf on the precipice. There she saw the man. The ledge had broken his fall, though he might well have broken his back or his neck on striking it.

---

[80] The ocean was known in formal Simspeek as The Great Sulphurific Garbage Patch.

No one in the massed bunch on the bluff from where she had come saw what she could see: The indistinct form she'd spied from above was now more clearly delineated as a man in the dun-colored one-piece uniform of a corporate asset.

Her eyes traveled to the damp but already clotting blood that surrounded him.

She stepped closer to where the PieceTaker -- whether unconscious or dead -- she could not tell -- had landed after he'd been thrown out of, or leapt from the aptrac.

She of course noticed the strange cowl that was attached to the man's head. It seemed to be formed of a hard, shell-like cap, that was clamped securely over his eyes, was anchored over the top of his skull, and running down the back of his head to the nape of his neck, was secured by a pulsing tendon around his throat.

But what riveted her attention was a shock of hair that peeked out from beneath the hood: *ruadh*, or chestnut red; then on the other side, another lock of hair – *dubh*, or black; and draped over the man's forehead, a strand – *bàn*, or blond.

She crouched beside him and gripped his shoulder to turn him over. As she did so, and his arm flopped, the sight of a scarred ridge that extended from the wrist to the crook of his elbow gave her heart-stopping pause. In the *priobadh na sùla* – the flash of an eye -- that followed the moment of her sighting that scar, she was struck as if with a slap of recognition – of *faicte a-roimhe*: She'd seen this before.

It took her a moment to recognize and process what it was she was looking at. Her breathing stopped, and at the sound of a groan and the movement of the man, it quickened to a hyperventilating pant.

She rapidly turned her attention back to the living helmet that encased his head and face, leaving only narrow eye-slits to see out of. The headgear was cracked and fitted askew on his head. She tried to shift it, tweak it, twist it, and torque it, but it wouldn't budge more than a finger's width, and when she did manage to inch the cowl one way or another, it sprang alive, its tentacle grips tightening and choking the man, and a fierce serpentine mouth released from the base of the fellow's skull and threatened her with an angry hissing and bared fangs.

So startled was she that she pulled her hands back in alarm, and the thing – whatever it was -- quickly retreated to the back of the neck and bit more deeply, sending a paroxysm through the man's body that elicited a groan.

In a way, she was thankful for the torment she'd caused him because the fact that he felt pain meant he wasn't dead.

He was still alive!

However, there was no time for her to revel in relief.

She felt the ledge shifting under her.

She quickly and deftly girdled the rope under his arms and around his torso.

And at long last acknowledging those above her who were craning over the edge of the cliff to see what she was doing – if indeed, she was still there, for she had been lost to their sight -- she stepped into their view and called out urgently: *"Tarraing!* — Pull!"

The order came as a surprise, but it was only a moment before the people responded. Seumas turned rapidly and shoved his way through the mob, pushing through the throng to Ròna's hairy one-horned steed. With a word and a gesture, he swiveled the animal around, and responding to the order *"Rach!* – Go!" sure-footed Dìleas pulled.

The line went taut just as the berm gave way, leaving Ròna and the strange soldier from the land of smoke dangling several thousand lengths above the dun-colored sea below.

The unihorn and the rest of the people hauled Ròna and her prize up the scarp. At the edge, grasping hands helped her and the limp figure over the lip.

Finally, Ròna and her find were sprawled on flat ground.

Seumas pushed through the crowd. Having been struck numb with fear before, having seen Ròna disappear over the side of the cliff without a word of explanation, he was now all the more angry that she'd returned safe with this strange burden: *"Dè cac mòr a' mhamoit a bhios seo mu dheidhinn!?* -- What the giant mammoth turd is this all about!" he demanded. *"Carson a tha thu a' bodraigeadh ris a' chat-seachrain damainte seo?* -- Why are you bothering with this damned stray cat?"

Ròna looked up at him calmly, but no less sternly — with that look of hers that said, *na cros mise* — don't cross me. She snarled in as close to a growl as a human throat could muster. *"'S e cat fuadain agamsa a th' ann.* -- He's <u>my</u> stray."

~~

A song heard before

An uair a thig tionndadh na h-aimsir, tillidh gach eun ri ealt aige fhèin.

> When the change of season comes, each bird returns to his own flock.
>
> Proverb from *Leabhar an Leaghaidh Mhòir —* The Book of the Great Melting

"Who is he?"

They gathered around him, murmuring speculations about the man with the strange cowl over his head – a device that seemed half alive and half mechanical -- a solid cap that fit over his skull and covered the top of his face, and tentacles that wiggled and slithered, pulsed and twitched around his neck, securing the ... *thing* ... whatever it was.

Trying to get a fix on him, to figure out who he was, before they could know what to do with him, the people gawked at him as if at a specimen in a zoo — though they didn't know what a zoo was, the concept of keeping animals in cages against their wills never having occurred to them; or like at a strange creature washed up on the shore, a never-before-seen monster of the deep or some far-away sea.

The Big Sister Mairead gently pressed forward. The others made a path for her.

"'*S e saighdear a th' ann*," she said. "It's a soldier that he is."

"What's that?"

Even the Big Sister was hard put to explain herself. She knew the word but to go further taxed her knowledge and her experience, not to mention her sense of decency. And even then, how to explain it? With a deep sigh, she said, "They fight."

The word went round as the people repeated amongst themselves what she had said.

"*A Phiuthar* -- Sister," one of them put forth the question. "Fight what?"

"Other people."

It was strange to many of them that a grown man would be

described as doing that — fighting, that is -- although fighting of a sort, they knew. It was something the mìneotarbhs -- wide-horned, long-fanged, ox-like creatures -- bear-wolf cubs, and boys did, until they grew out of it or learned better.

But to Seumas it was clear! "It's wrestling that he does, then?" He felt himself warming to the poor fellow. He himself used to wrestle when he was a boy. Out in the bog flats, where the mud and the muck near the lake was a couple inches deep, the boys would tussle with each other when they weren't testing themselves against the mìneotarbh[81] calves. The loser would be evident as he rose up from the wrestling pit plastered with boggy mud, and the relatively unmired victor was greeted by the cheers of his friends.

"Oh's" and "Uuh's" of recognition went through the assemblage, as each one repeated it to another who perhaps hadn't heard on account of their being farther back.

"He looks like a big fellow, there, *a Sheumais*! '*S dòcha gun gleac e air do dhà ghlùin thu*! -- Perhaps he could wrestle you to your knees!" A laugh went round, partly because of the gentle reference to and ribbing about Seumas's renowned prowess. Partly because of the ridiculousness of it: that this slim, unimpressive stranger would best Seumas, champion in his time of the Wayp!

The Sister shook her head, gave her hand — the one not gripping the knobby cane — a slight wave.

---

[81] Mìneotarbh – An ox or bovine creature, with thick fur, well adapted to the cold winters of the Wayp. It is large, ominverous species with wide-spread horns and long canines. It is typically larger than a unihorn but smaller than a mammoth, and of a quick, violent, and aggressive temper. The species is of uncertain orgin and was unknown in the ForeTimes. Like almost all other animals of the Wayp, it is certainly the result of the attempt to populate the once barren environment of the risen continent, in some cases through DNA replication, mass cloning, or the comingling of DNA strands from various genetic precursors. In these early experimental attempts at gene replication and cloning, it has been suggested, the first settlers of the Wayp sought to create a domesticable animal with the the the docility of a cow, the woolen fur of a mammoth, and an intelligence approaching that of a human. Instead, what emerged from the undertaking was a hybrid creature with perhaps the worst traits of all three: the intelligence of a cow, the size of a mammoth, and a human propensity to predation. Another theory (speculative, of course) regarding the mìneotarbh's origin is that the species evolved out of a runaway medical experiment seeking to develop a resistant gene therapy for the then rampant ZZyzz virus through the comingling of various genetic materials, including human. The resultant forebearers of the now-existing animal escaped from the lab into the wild and established the basis of the current population in the forests of the Wayp. *Etymology*: the FT word is thought to derive from the name for a mythological creature in the ForeTimes, the "minotaur," compounded from the words *Mìneo*, or Minos, and *tarbh*, bull.

"It's not like that."

Which was puzzling. Seumas was the first to broach the mystery: "What, then?"

Ever since those from the DownBlow had first perched their trading town on the lip of the Mother's Staircase, the Big Sister had known the day would come when she would have to tell *Clann na Màthar* — the Children of the Mother — of the facts of life: The knowledge that had been passed down to her by her own *Àrd-Phiuthar* – her own Big Sister -- and to her by hers, and all the Big Sisters before; the knowledge about what it had been like in the ForTime, and what it was still like in the DownBlow. "It's not wrestling that he does," she began.

The hesitation was born of her reluctance, her desire to delay for even a moment what she knew was now inevitable. "These soldiers of theirs ... they kill people."

Stares of incomprehension.

"What'd she say?"

"She said he kills people."

The words rippled through the small assembly as the children of the Mother struggled with understanding. Some repeating the words to others or to themselves as if they had been uttered in a different tongue, and others shifting their stupefied gaze to the man lying on the ground before them as if the answer to their confusion lay somewhere on him.

"No, it's impossible," one finally ventured.

The Sister nodded to confirm what she had said. "*'S coltach ris an tìgear claidheamh-fhiaclach a tha e.* -- It's like the sword-tooth tiger that he is."

Those nearest the fallen man edged back. The ferocious, giant cats they knew: ravenous, rampaging, rapacious, killing beasts, who obeyed only one law – that of their own will: to kill or be killed.

The mind revolted against such a possibility – that a man could be no more than a tiger to other men. "A person can't ..." one started to protest, but he was stopped short when Mairead swiveled her attention to Robert Morunx, who was standing reticently at the edge of the crowd.

Around Morunx were clustered several children whom he'd been given the responsibility of caring for while he was on probation in the House of the Sisters.

"*A Raibeirt* – Robert," the Sister called out. "What do you have to say about this?"

Robert stepped forward. He spoke tentatively as he was still under the supervision of his probation, and he didn't want to jeopardize that. "Tha ceart i – Is right she," he burbled in broken FT, before dodging to the safety of his native Simspeek. "Yeah, no, I mean, the Mother is right," he said.

As he spoke, those who understood the Simspeek translated rapidly to those who didn't.

There was a tone to Robert's voice that sounded cathartic, as if an exhalation of relief at being able to lend a word of support to the Big Sister, on whom he depended for a favorable judgment of his case. "I've seen stuff in the DownBlow ..." More he hesitated to say. He looked to the Big Sister as if for permission to continue.

Mairead nodded her head, signaling for him to go on.

"They do kill people. Sometimes for fun."

"No!"

"Not possible!"

"I don't believe it!"

Robert was at the center of attention now, which he actually relished. He was being listened to, heeded, not being scorned. He nodded firmly. It was as if his turn to sing at the *cèilidh* had come around, and he wasn't about to give his place up. Though he spoke mostly in Simspeek, he was picking up a bit of the FT, so he stumblingly tried a phrase. It came out awkwardly but punctuated his point: "*Mi tha fìrinn agam.* – I is truth at me."

Seann Teàrlach -- Old Charles -- spoke up. The sharp-eyed, wizened man had been around for such a long time, there were those to whom it seemed that he'd always been an old man. His voice rose sharply. "It was so long ago, I hardly remember, but it's once that we had somebody come into the Wayp like this one ... when I was a boy."

"No! I don't believe it!" A teenager blurted out.

"It's true!" Old Charles insisted.

He'd taken the bait. The lad who'd challenged him nailed him with the punch line: "You were a *boy*!?!"

This jibe elicited a laugh from the surrounding people.

Old Charles smiled good humoredly. "In the ForTime, before the Great Melt." He spoke in jest, of course, though he had a wit that did not give away readily. He would look at you hard, squinting seriously, his lips pressed tightly (or maybe it was a glint of a smile, waiting like a sword-tooth in the brush to see if you caught the joke).

Returning to a tone of seriousness that brought their collective attention back to the issue at hand, namely, the unconscious *saighdear* splayed out before them, Seumas pressed, "What'd you do?"

"We put him on an island in the *loch na màthar* -- the Lake of the Mother -- and left him there until the madness left him."

"What do they do with people like that in the DownBlow?"

Robert inserted himself back into the exchange, unwilling to relinquish his claim on the center stage – after all, this was *his* story. "They reward them," he announced to the astonished crowd, "make them their leaders."

"They like what these *saighdearan* – these soldiers -- do!?!"

Robert didn't answer the question directly but rather continued with the line of thought he'd started on: "That's not all -- *idir idir idir* -- at all, at all, at all," emphasizing not with the tone of his voice but with the repetition. He'd picked up that much of the FT. "I haven't seen it, but I've heard of terrible things."

"Like what?" Seumas demanded.

"How they steal children."

The protests were loud, outraged, disbelieving — or refusing to believe.

"No!"

"It's not possible!"

"How could somebody ...!?!"

"Why!?!"

Robert pushed on, nodding vigorously. He'd been restraining himself for too long a time. At least for a moment, he was no longer the pariah, he was the messiah. He'd quickly been catapulted from the disgraced to the embraced. He was the bearer of *gusgal, sgudal* – gossip, rubbish – and as such, he was the center of everyone's attention. This was too tantalizing an opportunity for him to pass up. "They don't have children themselves."

"What?!?"

"Or it's very hard for them."

A man next to Robert shook his head rapidly. "That's crazy! They never have ..." He wiggled his fingers rapidly. "*You know?*"

Robert shook his head eagerly, with perhaps a bit of a mischievous smirk, like that of a 9-year-old telling his younger brother how babies were made. He was getting into this. "Well, they do sort of. But the men don't have sex with women. The men are what they call INCCEEL[82] in Simspeek."

One asked the obvious question: "They don't know how?"

"They think it'll save them from the ZZyzx contagion."

The question stumbled out: "What ... do they ... do ... then?"

---

[82] INCCEEL: Individuals Ceasing Copulation with Everyone ELse.

Old Charles pushed back into the discussion. It was as if the two of them – he and Robert – were collaborating as a gossip tag-team. He eagerly volunteered the real dirt: "*Bidh iad a' faighinn seirbheis o robotairean.* -- They get service from robots."

"*Dè sin? Robotairean?* -- What's that?" The word was unfamiliar. "Robots?"

"Like giant dolls ..."

"Dolls?"

"Only they move. Like real women."

"Not like Maggie!" Seumas guffawed, referring to his wife. "I'm sure of that!"

When the snickers dissipated, it occurred to Moire to ask. "But what do they do about children?"

"They grow them like plants in a pot."

"What!"

"How can they do that!?"

"Or they ..." Here Robert made a sweeping motion with his two open hands in the direction of the children clustered around him.

Moire gasped in recognition of the connection. "*Thugad an seo, a bhalaich* – Come here, lad," she said, summoning her own small son closer to her where she could hug him protectively.

"It's true that this is, then?" Seumas demanded.

Robert confirmed the suspicion with a single nod and downcast eyes, and old Charles confirmed. "*Chan iad na sìthichean a bheireas ur clann* -- It's not the fairies that take your children. It's these ones that steal them in the night and ship them to the DownBlow like chickens in cages."

Moire pointed at the man on the ground. "*Ach an rud seo?* -- But this thing here? What do they do with the likes of him? This killer of men and reaper of children?"

"'*S e gaisgeach a th' ann dhaibh.* – He's a hero to them."

It was in a wholly different light that they looked upon the stranger stretched out on the ground.

Ròna felt the urge to defend the man. "We don't know that *he* ..." She broke off, not even wanting to say the words again, to repeat the slander, lest just saying the words would confirm its truth.

But the revelation about the nature of the creature that had fallen into their midst could not be ignored and sparked even more heated debate over what to do with this monster who killed other men and stole children.

There were those who argued he should be sent away ... after he was well, of course, it being contrary to the teachings of the Mother to allow a person to suffer or die, if something could be done about it, and especially while he was a guest, however much his presence was unasked for.

Others thought the same should be done to him as he would do to them, but this was a minority opinion, and the suggestion was met with such outright opposition that it was not brought up again.

"It could be dangerous to keep him. *Gu dearbh* – indeed -- we have to be careful. Like when we found that sword-tooth cub ..."

"Yes, but what did we do?" Ròna argued. "We tied him up and fed him ... until he was well... and then, we let him go back to his own. We can watch this one -- *this* sword-tooth. He can't be any more dangerous than that."

"They came here to drain the blood of the Mother! To make the Wayp a desert like they've made the DownBlow! And steal our children in the process!"

There were those who stood off by the side and said nothing, even though there might have been one position in the discussion they favored over another; those who did not know what they thought or believed, but wanted others to decide; those who were passionate in their hatred of *na goill* – the foreigners who were not of the Children of the Mother like themselves; and there were those who believed in adhering to the teachings of the Mother, to love all, be kind to all, foster all, and nurture all, as She nurtured all life.

Mairead caught a movement at the edge of the crowd, and perhaps mistaking its import – thinking that the man who had shifted his position had something to say -- she asked, "*Dè do bheachd, a Raghnaill* – What do you think, Raghnall?"

But the small man turned his head as if seeking assistance from his twin brother Eòghann, an officious man, as tall and straight as a caber – the long, straight log the people liked to toss end over end. The bigger brother took the nod, and with a bustle of energy, he pushed forward.

When he was making an argument, as now, he had the habit of counting off his points by tapping his forefinger into the palm of his other hand. "There are three things we have to keep in mind," Eòghann began, raising his voice to be heard, and tapping his finger finger so vigorously, you'd have thought he was going to drill a hole in his hand: "First, we don't know what this stranger's intentions are. Second, what if the incomers find out that we have him?"

From his position a half step behind his brother, Raghnall nodded reflexively in agreement.

"Then," Eòghann continued, "who's going to take care of him and feed him? It'll take more than it's worth to do that."

"That's the same thing your mother said when you were on her tit," Ròna called out.

The outburst of laughter flustered Eòghann, but he recovered his composure and pressed on. "And besides that, *tha e ro chunnartach!* -- It's too dangerous! And if we take care of this one, pretty soon, we'll have more. We'll have to take in every stray soldier who wanders into the Wayp."

"No, you don't," Ròna countered. "Where'd you get that?"

"Make an exception for one," Eòghann asserted with the definitiveness of someone pronouncing a universal law. "Have to make it for all."

"No, you don't. That's why they call it an exception!"

There was a scattering of chuckles.

Ròna followed up quickly. "Besides, that's five things."

"What?"

"You said, *three* things, but you listed five. You don't even know what you're talking about. *Chan eil do cheann ach na bhrochan* – Your brains are just a mess of porridge. Besides, they aren't going to come up here – climb the staircase of the mother to take our tea and mammoth wool, just to get themselves thrown over the cliff back to where they came from!"

But however valid a point Ròna's was, the argument went on.

"They don't give *cac a' mhamoit* – a mammoth's shit – about our tea. You saw what they're after. They dump the water to pump their gowp out of the ground!"

"Yeah, well ..." Ròna felt the foundation slipping out from under her argument. "When they do that, we throw them out."

Seumas jumped on that idea: "And that's what I say we do with this one! Get rid of him. One way or another. He came with the PieceTakers. He's a killer like the Sister says. It's only right that we do to him what he would do to us."

Ròna stood aside, as it were – not literally, but ducked her head and figuratively stepped back, stepped out of the fray. Although she was unconvinced, a suspicion lingered that there was more to the situation and to the *coigreach* – the stranger – than appeared on the surface of things. There was something -- the scar on his arm, the multi-colored mane that poked out from beneath the strange cap -- that reminded her of something she couldn't quite put into words, or if she tried to, that whatever she said would come out sounding silly, and that she'd be contradicted again, and that the contradiction would win out.

Though she didn't say anything more, she held with those who pushed for refraining from a decision in the face of uncertainty, caring for him until they reached a consensus on who he was, what should be done with him: either to be allowed to stay or to be sent away.

Besides, there was something about what she herself had said just a little earlier. How had she phrased it? The words reminded her of something not lost totally to her memory although it was buried deeply in the recesses of her remembrance of long ago.

There was a proverb recorded in the *Leabhar an Leaghaidh Mhòir* – The Book of the Great Melting – that touched on what might have influenced Ròna's behavior; not, of course, that she consciously referred to the saying, but as a meme that had long been imbedded in the culture, it might well have informed her thinking:

A' chiad shealladh, leig seachad.
The first time, let it go.

'S a-rithist, an darna, ma feumaidh tu.
The second, again, if you must.

Ach an treas cothrom, ged nach rachadh clach ceann-a-mheòir an aghaidh gaoth a' tuath a' tighinn a-nuas bho Chìochan reòite na Màthar, tilg le d' uile neart.

But the third chance, even though the storm is blowing so hard that a stone wouldn't go a tip of a finger against the north wind coming down from the frosty nipples of the Mother, throw with all your might.

So it was for Ròna: The first sighting was the hair poking out from under the strange, wiggling cowl. The second was the scar that ran up the man's forearm. And the third, *her own words,* which though she didn't recognize them, per se, and couldn't tell where she'd heard them before, affected her with a strong sense of *cluinnte a-cheana* – "already heard" – and struck her as prophetic. Like a song she'd heard before but just couldn't place – *He's my stray.*

But why? Why was she so stirred to the bone with certainty that she must protect this strange foreigner from the DownBlow?

But in the moment, there was no time to contemplate the conundrum but only time to act before the chance was lost – only an opening of time wide enough *to throw with all her strength against the north wind.*

Ròna tapped Dìleas on the snout and whispered into his ear, "*Crom air do ghlùinean* – Down on your knees," and while the others were still arguing, and before anyone realized what she was doing, with a heave and a ho! she'd levered the body of the stray DownBlow PieceTaker onto the animal's back.

Situating herself atop the unihorn, she issued a quick command of "*Seas, a bhalaich!* – Stand, lad!" and Dìleas lurched to his feet.

There were shouts of consternation as she squeezed Dìleas's

sides with both her legs and the beast heaved forward.

Ròna guided him through the crowd – accompanied by protests and shouts to stop!

But it was too late. By the time any coordinated action could be taken to impede her getting away with her loot, she was already out of the midst of the throng, and a moment later, galloping away, her prize slung across the back of her mount like a sack of just-picked mushrooms.

~~

Blood, killing, and death

Ma ghabhas tu cùram ris a' Chruinne-chè, gabhaidh i cùram riut-sa.
Ma fhasaicheas tu i, fasaichidh i thusa.

If you take care of the earth, she will take care of you.
If you lay waste to her, she will destroy you.
Proverb from *Leabhar an Leaghaidh Mhòir* —
The Book of the Great Melting

While Ròna was leading the demonstration against the agents of the Monstrato Corps, her father, *Dòmhnall Camshron*[83] -- Donald Cameron -- sat in his home's sun room – so-called because it collected electrical power through its array of window panes coated with transparent solar cells. The house was situated just outside the village of Balnabane, which flanked the Lake of the Mother. The multi-colored cottages of the village presented a rainbow swath of red and blue and yellow and green and white and brown, and even purple, that spread along the shore of the lake and scattered up the hill leading from the water's edge. Some of the homes were close packed and some separated a bit on outlying roads and paths that led to the various crofts that were not owned by those who worked them, but were annually redistributed by the Council of the Sisters – *Comhairle nam Peathraichean*, in the FT – so that everyone shared equally in the bounty of the mother.

The room was furnished simply but comfortably. A pair of chairs upholstered in lush mammoth-wool throws were situated before a large picture window and looked out onto a small garden, that had just a short time before glistened all the brighter and greener for the recent rain – though now darkened by the shadows thrown by the enveloping trees and the towering slopes behind which the sun was sinking.

The walls were decorated with occasional family pictures and

---

[83] As he was known in the FT, literally, Donald 'Crooked Nose' – the legacy of some long-forgotten ancestor who must have gotten into a fistfight or some similar altercation and had been disfigured in a memorable way (though Donald's nose did not betray this part of his heritage).

233

portraits. Hanging in a nook was a copy of a painting featuring the climactic battle a few thousand years ago when the People of the Wayp won their independence from the Monstrato Corps. Displayed prominently over the fireplace was the family heirloom, the man-length claymore (*an claidheamh-mòr an t-solais*, or "great sword of light") that had been in the Cameron family for millennia.[84]

Dòmhnall was a tall man, lean from his having worked the farm all his life. His hands were large and roughened to the texture of tree bark. By this time in his life, his once-dark hair was flecked with white and mounted the top of his head like *canach* – bog cotton – a tall reed-like grass that grew in the bog lands of the Wayp and that in spring sprouted wild, unruly white tufts. He carried himself with an upright stiffness, common to men of a tall, thin frame who labored in the fields, but when he relaxed, all his muscles went slack and loose in full resting mode.

He set aside for the moment his worry about the Monstrato TACS[85] that would come at the end of the month like a curse that followed a blessing, the benediction being, of course, the gift of water from the Goddess, and the curse, the Corporation's claim on what flowed naturally and freely from *Her*.

But for the time being, his few dozen mammoths were already out munching the rich grass beside the copse of conifers across the meadow. Farther beyond that lay an arm of the *loch* that protruded into the acreage of his farm, the waters cool and pure, placid and clear.

There was something more pressing on his mind. He was waiting impatiently, although up to this moment, he had restrained himself from saying anything. However, finally, he could contain himself no longer, and in a mixture of annoyance and concern, he called out to his wife, "*A Shiùsaidh*! -- Susie!"

To his relief, it was just then that his wife, hobbled by a bad knee and weighted down with a tea tray in the one hand and

---

[84] Family legacy had it that this sword had been brought to the Wayp at the time of the migration during the Great Melt, having had been wielded by an ancestor of the Cuilean family at the disasterous *Blàr Chùil Lodair* in the old country, and by another ancestor to significant (and more successful) effect at *Blàr Bealach nam Mamotaichean* – the Battle of the Mammoth Gap -- a millenium before during the War of Independence from the Corporation. It wasn't the original sword, not the whole one anyway, for every few hundred years, it had to be repaired or restored – its blade strengthened, its handle bolstered, so what remained now was a sword inlaid with the pieces of the original – hardened from its original steel with metal forged from meteorite found in the risen land of the Wayp – hence its complete name, *claidheamh-mòr na beur-theine* -- "the sword of the flaming star."

[85] TACS - Toll of Aqua-pura Cost Survey

encumbered with a cane in the other, emerged slowly from the interior of the house. "*Tha mi a' tighinn, a ghràidh* – I'm coming, Love," she answered, nudging the door open with the handle of her cane.

Siùsaidh was a head shorter than her husband. Where he was calm musculature, she was a *gille-mirein* – a spinning top of nervous energy, it seemed to Dòmhnall sometimes, incapable of sitting still or resting – even *while* sitting still or resting. When she was younger, she'd taken pride in acts of beautification – arranging her hair or painting her nails, but her now graying hair – *liath* in the FT, actually more of a bluish gray, the same color as translucent clouds through which the blue light of the sky penetrated – straggled straight down from her head – brushed but otherwise untended -- and her fingernails curved like eagle talons over the tips of her spindly fingers.

When they were by themselves, they would use the FT between one another. It was the language they'd grown up with, and the language they'd first spoken to each other, and the language they'd first made love in. It was natural to them, and even though forbidden in business dealings with the Monstrato Corps, *what was the harm if they kept it to themselves?*[86]

The tray that Siùsaidh was struggling with was stacked heavily with a pot of *tì na màthar* – tea of the Mother – and fruit, scones, and butter for the both of them, and a single bottle of Monstrato Mountain Spring Water™ for her.[87]

---

[86] Increasingly, the Indiginoes – that is, *Clann na Màthar*, the Children of the Mother -- seemed to be giving up on the FT, or if not giving up on the old tongue, then using it less and less, partly because of the inroads of the media from the DownBlow, the convenience of their imported products, and the prospect of doing business with the Monstrato Corps, which insisted that all transactions with it be conducted in Simspeek. This requirement was in accordance with the Bable laws. It wasn't so much that it was illegal to use the FT, but using it while attempting to conduct business with the Corps could result in being fined or blacklisted. It might be supposed that since many found it more convenient (or less taxing) to simply use Simspeek in their non-Monstrato Corps activities than to have to be constantly on the alert as to what was more appropriate according to the time and situation, some of the Children of the Mother in the Wayp found themselves shifting to Simspeek in their everyday usage, using words and phrases of the language of the DownBlow even when it wasn't necessary

[87] Even though the real thing lay just a few hundred yards away in the *Loch na Màthar* – the Lake of the Mother – to Susie, buying water in bottles seemed to be a more sophisticated or advanced way of obtaining the commodity* than pumping the water from the lake itself or lugging it home themselves. Besides, *It was the same thing, wasn't it?* They were just paying for the convenience of having it neatly packaged and delivered.

* Footnote to the above footnote: The reader is here directed to a subtle shift brought about by the Monstrato Corps in so simple an action as bottling water:

Her insistence on the Monstrato Corps' bottled commodity was a source of ongoing (though low-level) conflict between them – "I can just get it for you in a bucket," Dòmhnall would complain, "from the loch. And for free!"

"*Tha fios 'm* -- I know, but it's more convenient in the bottle," she'd respond in a conversation that would loop repetitively. "And they sterilize it, or do …" -- she was a little vague on this point -- "whatever they do with it."

So it would go round and round, until Dòmhnall gave up. "Yeah …" he'd invariably concede with a wry, tight-lipped smile that ruefully conceded she'd bested him again. "Whatever they do with it."

"That's what I said."

Shame-faced for his impetuous outburst just an instant before, and prodded by a jab of guilt over his unthinkingly making her lug the tray across the room, Dòmhnall moderated his tone to one gentler. "*Leig leam*," he said. "Let me," and he jumped up – well, not literally "jumped" because he was past the age of jumping anything or anywhere. Although his knees were wobblier than they once had been, his shoulders and arms still retained considerable strength, so he pushed himself up as quickly as he could in a way that simulated a *leap* to his feet.

He crossed to where Siùsaidh was awkwardly balancing the tray on the handle of her cane. She was well used to her man's innate impatience. Though he was no longer the youth she'd married (*How long ago was that? It could have been a hundred years, when time stretched so far back that it seemed to fall off a cliff into an undifferentiated canyon that was the past*), and he was thickening in the waist, and grey hairs were spreckling his head, and his hairline was pulling back like the tide from a sandy shore, he still retained a bit of the boyishness she'd first known in him.

When he called out for her in his urgency and his voice rose insistently, calling for her to come and sit beside him because he wanted her *there*, in her chair where she *belonged*, next to him, as if it were that presence which made his world right and ordered and safe, well, she forgave him his impetuosity, for it was that same boyish impulsiveness which had won her to him in the first place -- his barely restrained desire for her (though in a different way back then), and his need for her (though of a different sort, back when).

He lifted the tray and proceeded to the center of the sun room ahead of her. There, he placed it on the little table between their seats. He quickly laid out their evening tea and returned to fetch

---

from precious, if not holy, *bainne na màthar* – the milk of the mother – is reframed as a commodity, a thing.

her, to make sure her tottering steps brought her safely to her chair. He nearly trembled with impatient anticipation as she took her slow steps.

"Are you all set?" he asked as she seated herself.

"*Deiseil*," she replied. "Ready."

He breathed in relief now that everything was as it ought to be and sat opposite her.

Siùsaidh caught Dòmhnall staring quizzically at his plate, as if searching for something that should be there but wasn't. There was something missing.

He'd started with the scone and worked out and around from that. There was butter, the kind the people of the Wayp made from mammoth milk – thick, sweet, and creamy.

"Do you have everything?" she asked in a worried tone.

Finally, he figured out what was lacking. "Is there any of that jam left?" Their daughter-in-law, Maggie, had brought some over the other day, made fresh from berries she'd picked.

A wave of guilt engulfed Siùsaidh over having forgotten: "I'll go get it."

It was Dòmhnall's turn to feel guilty. To make his wife hobble back to the kitchen was a burden he could not put upon her. "No, no, no," he insisted. "*Na dragh ort* – Don't you bother yourself. You sit." He said this with firmness though he knew that if he simply offered and did nothing, she would strain to rise in spite of his "command," so he pushed himself up quickly from his chair. "I'll get it," he said, pushing himself up quickly and disappearing into the kitchen.

He returned in a minute, waving the jar cheerily. "I found it. Just on the counter."

"I was going to bring it. I didn't mean for you to have to …"

"*Tha fios 'm*," he said. "I know." He bent over her and gave her a light kiss. "You've done so much already."

He re-sat and happily opened the jar like a child opening a treat. He scooped a spoonful of jam onto his plate. Then he remembered he should share. He reached the preserves over to her. "You've got to have some before I eat it all!"

It might be putting too much freight upon it to say that this was his favorite time of the day, but it was certainly a necessary part, for as the proverb said, *Brìgh gach cluiche aig an deireadh* -- The essence of a game is at the end -- the same was so for a day. Without a right ending, the day itself would not be right.

This period, when they sat in the sun room, however bright or gloomy it was outside, however dark the night, whatever drenching rain might pour, whatever snow, hail, or sleet might befall, here they were protected alike from the heat of glaring sunshine and cold blasts coming down from the glacial heights above them; this hour they shared at the close of the day, with its ritualistic scones, cheese, fruit, and *tì na màthar* -- the "mother's tea" -- this hour was sacred.

Dòmhnall turned on the screoin-cast news of the day, part of the interweb feed from the DownBlow. Suddenly appearing, larger than life-size and much larger than was comfortable, was the newly appointed Chief Operations Commandant (COC) of the Monstrato Corps, Magnus Mugwump. He'd popped out in full size in the hologram that floated out from the wall -- totally lifelike with his shock of white hair and pasty skin; "lifelike" in the sense of being verisimilitudinous, which is to say, accurately lifeless in his corpse-like pallor and face devoid of any human emotion except perhaps the gaping hunger of the grave, the rapaciousness of a money lender, or the rage of the killing field, and with his arms waving and spittle flying from his mouth so realistically that Siùsaidh's first impulse was to wince backwards to avoid being splattered. Mugwump was ranting about events near and far -- most recently what various pundits referred to as the "Insurge."

Dòmhnall and Siùsaidh had heard rumors of young hotheads in the Wayp instigating acts of resistance against incursions of the Monstrato Corps, though they hadn't paid much attention. When the old couple did happen to speak on they topic, just to be safe, they would revert to low voices and speak in the FT, because they'd heard -- though one could never know for sure -- that the ever-listening NSSA -- Network SpiderWeb Surveillance Agency -- operators behind the screoin did not understand the old language.

Mugwump promised to root out what he called a rebellion,[88] "Leaving nothing except bloody stumps!" which declaration he'd accompanied with a pantomime of curving his hands and forearms inwards, making a silly face, and gesticulating as if he were a helpless man with nothing but stumps for arms, in a manner that would have been comical if he had not been threatening such havoc. "I figh' wi'ou' aa-nee arms!" (Evidently, he imagined that a person with maimed limbs would also have a speech impediment.)

He dropped the mimicry and continued: "I will root out the last Insurge," he reiterated (though not clear whether for emphasis or because he had lost track of where his ramble had left off) – "demon cockroaches!" adding, non-sequiturly (never one to miss a product placement opportunity), "How d'ya like this PetrAle! It's the best, isn't it! Much better than the toilet swill sold by our

---

[88] Though dictionary fundamentalists might argue that a "rebellion" required a defiance of recognized authority, and whatever *authority* the Monstrato Corps' claimed over the Wayp was recognized by no one but itself.

competitors!" (Every sentence seemed to be an exclamation, even the questions.)

"Last source of pure gowp on the planet! Precious!" and to demonstrate its preciousness, he lifted the bottle high and poured the liquid over his head. It flowed through the strands of his hair, coursing in mucky effluvium over his face. He licked his lips. "Not only is it the best shampoo gowp-creds can buy, but it's delicious, too! A limited resource, available only while supplies last! Worth the premium price! More than worth the premium price! You're actually getting a bargain! Cheap at half the price! BUY IT NOW!"

With his stream of vomitus diverting back to the main river of thought he had been navigating, Mugwump again promised to root out the Insurge troublemakers and maintain the corporation's supply of the gowp to the "last, delicious slop!"

Worried, Siùsaidh turned to Dòmhnall. "Is he talking about us? How can we be Insurge? This is our home. They're the incomers."

"It's just for DownBlow politics," Dòmhnall reassured her. "There's no way he can do what he's saying. We're too far away. It's impossible."

Though whether he totally believed what he was saying could be questioned.

Despite his dismissing the threat as little more than political bluster, Dòmhnall found it disturbing enough that he switched the screoin-channel. As they sipped the refreshing *tì na màthar* and nibbled on their snack of biscuits, cheese, and fruit, they watched a short segment about a rat-pup pet that had found its way home across the Inland Seas of the DownBlow after it had strayed away on a family vaycay; and a report about a girl who'd fallen asleep in a stolen hovercar and when she was discovered, had led police on a wild chase, finally crashing into a wall (making her a bit of a hero in Dòmhnall's imagination).

But this *feasgar* – early evening -- there was a special edge to Dòmhnall's urgency to have his wife seated close beside him. Speaking in a low voice in the *seann chànan* -- the old language, "Have you noticed anything about Ròna?" he asked after a pause for a sip of tea.

"Besides the tattoo of *uilebheist an locha* – the monster of the lake -- on her breast?"

"What!" That certainly wasn't what he was talking about, and besides, it was totally new to him, and it was beside the point he was trying to make, and besides even that (the third or forth *besides*, if we're counting), he felt uncomfortable contemplating his daughter's breasts. He turned his face away in embarrassment.

When Ròna had first shown the tattoo to her mother, she'd explained it as body art like that of "*ar sinnsirean* -- our ancestors."

"*Ist, a nighean*," Siùsaidh had whispered. "Quiet, girl."

Siùsaidh been a bit of an advocate for the forbidden tongue in her own day -- which is why she'd insisted on going to the local college, *An Saoghal Mòr Ùr* (*the new barn*, named with some fondness after its predecessor in the old land, which was now sunk beneath the brown scum-caps of the rolling Northern Sea so far away), but that was before the Bable Edict, the Language Laws, before their beloved language (and everything a language contains and implies) had been declared an Insurge weapon of terrorism and so had been prohibited from use by anyone who did business with the Monstrato Corps. (Her own name, which she'd insisted on holding onto, had been a last, feeble act of Insurge, being close enough to the Simspeek so as to not draw a penalty). Siùsaidh regretted her youthful rashness, not for herself (she was past caring about anything on that account) but because of the ramifications it might have on the girl.

"No, not that." Dòmhnall didn't quite know how to broach the topic delicately so as to not raise an alarm, so he just launched himself into the deep end of the thoughts. "Is she in her room at night?" Meaning, *is she in her own bed at night?* "Does she go out?" He felt uneasy to be inquiring into the nighttime activities of his growing daughter -- but she was nearing that age when she was looking more and more like a young woman than a girl (actually, well past *that* age, but sometimes we see what we expect to see, what we're used to seeing rather than what is really there), and when her eyes seemed to scan the boys on the neighboring crofts more with interest than annoyance; but more was at stake than an indiscreet prying into her private affairs.

"If I remember correctly, you weren't so particular about my nighttime whereabouts when you used to come and throw pebbles against the window of my father's house."

A smile of remembrance and an arching of his brows from Dòmhnall. "*Tha fìrinn agad* -- You have the truth," he said, a momentary wave of pleasant remembrance sweeping through his mind.

For Siusaidh, this recollection reminded her that there were areas of Ròna's life which were increasingly being kept from her, as if the door to that room were being gradually shut -- not from any estrangement between the two of them -- the girl and the woman -- but simply as part of the younger one's establishing the boundaries of her own life outside parental control. Just a natural part of her growing up and away, Siùsaidh realized, though not without some nostalgia for an earlier time when they'd done everything together until the day when the girl had pulled Siùsaidh up short: "*A Mhamaidh!*" Ròna had exclaimed in exasperation, "Mom! If I were going to an orgy, you'd want to organize it like a play date."

Siùsaidh had blushed, not at the scandalous reference, but at the exposure of her meddling. "I can't help it. I'm a *mom*." After a laugh: "But I'd be very good at organizing such a thing."

"*Tha mi cinnteach*," Ròna had said with a wink. "I'm sure."

Siusaidh's reminiscence was interrupted by the heavy *clomp clop clump* of Dìleas outside. "*Thig an sìthiche ri iomradh* – Here comes the fairy we're speaking about," Dòmhnall said, glad for the change in subject.

Indeed, there was the sound of feet landing from a height – no doubt, Ròna jumping down impetuously from Dìleas's back, as she always did – the sound of hurried footsteps towards the cottage and the bang of the door bursting open.

"Well," Siùsaidh said, "we were just talking about you. How was *a' chèilidh* – the ceilidh, the gathering?" Without waiting for an answer, Siùsaidh immediately followed up with, "Your dad and I were just sitting down. Can I get you something?"

To forestall any undue effort on Siusaidh's part, Dòmhnall interjected, "No, she's fine. She can get it herself. She's a big girl."

"I'm just trying …" Siùsaidh protested.

Soothingly: "I know, but please … it's easier for her."

Ròna had heard this song before. "It's alright, *a mhamaidh*. I'm not staying."

"You have to eat!" Siusaidh protested.

"I'll get myself something later," Ròna reassured her mother. "Right now, I have a couple things to take care of."

"Like what?" Siùsaidh asked, or began to ask, but the question was not even out of her mouth. They were startled at the flushed and urgent look on their daughter's face as she blurted out, "*Thug mi fear dhachaigh leam* – I brought one home with me" -- apropos of nothing, relevant to nothing, relating to nothing.[89]

"*Thug mi anns an t-sabhal e*," she said. "I put it in the barn." She hurriedly added: "It won't bother you."[90]

None of this was surprising. They'd had a long history – well, as long as it was since Ròna was little – of her bringing home strays, wounded creatures, and various abandoned cubs, whelps, and

---

[89] *Fear* – at this point, they were speaking in the FT, and one of the peculiarities of the language is that the word *fear* could mean either a "man" or a grammatically gendered creature or thing – an "it." It might be too much of a stretch to suggest that Ròna was being purposely ambiguous – perhaps, occluding by omission – but that was the effect of what it was she had said.

[90] The same that was true about the word *fear* was also true of the pronoun *e* (he or him) – since there was no word for "it" in the FT, the pronoun could refer to any person, place, creature, or thing that was grammatically gendered masculine.

chicks.

"Okay," Dòmhnall said, resigned by this time to his fate of living with such a save-every-wandering-creature-that-had-lost-its-way daughter, simply admonished, "As long as it's not a sword-tooth or a bear-wolf that'll put the mammoths into a panic," albeit weakly and without much conviction, for well he knew that such a caution would do little to curb his daughter's penchant for saving foundlings.

Ròna nodded. Though it wasn't clear what she was nodding to. *That she'd heard her father? That she was in agreement? In confirmation that the creature wasn't of the sort that would disturb their herd?*

"It's not, is it?" Dòmhnall pressed – aware his stipulation had not exactly and clearly been addressed.

"*Chan e,*" she said with a shake of her head, and she expanded upon her answer with a purposely narrow, "No, it's not a sword-tooth or a bear-wolf."

Dòmhnall felt some relief (which was not total, to be sure), and Siùsaidh attempted to clear the tension from the room by asking, "Are you sure you don't want to stay?"

"*Duilich,*" Ròna said. "*Feumaidh mi falbh.* – Sorry. I have to go."

And just as quickly as she had come, she was gone.

"Close the door!" Dòmhnall called after her, his voice trailing off as it was apparent that she was already out of the cottage and away.

Dòmhnall and Siùsaidh sat quietly as the door swung with a creak in the night breeze.

Dòmhnall sighed in exasperation and heaved himself up. "You'd think she was brought up in a barn," he complained as he stiff-leggedly crossed the room to close the door.

"Well, she was ... sorta," Siusaidh smirked. "You know, we do live on a farm."

Dòmhnall snorted and made a funny face at her.

He stood at the verge of the room, the door in his hand, paused in thought. "Maybe I'll go check on her. Just to make sure everything's alright," he ventured.

The cold air gusted in his face, blowing down the sides of the mountain from the glaciers locked on the tips of the twin Cìochan na Màthar – literally, the nipples of the Mother -- that is, the twin snow frosted peaks of the mountains.

At this time, the Children of the Mother had returned from the upland summer pastures to the lower valleys of the Wayp, where they could winter in their well-insulated cottages.

The larks were gathering pine needles and grasses that they shook to mix with soil and their saliva, and that they would pack together to make their mud-bowl roosts.

Wagtails, slender ground dwelling birds known for their dog-like tail wagging -- *breacan-buidhe* in the FT, or "yellow plaid" after their patterned coloring of black and yellow -- were weaving cobwebs they had stolen from spiders together with blades of grass to make filigree nests.

Crows and ravens – *feannagan* and *fithich* – were plating twigs, grasses, and even stolen pieces of fabric to build their refuges.

Turkeys were digging and fitting out their burrows.

Squirrels – *feòragan* -- had been gathering and storing nuts all through the warm months.

Foxes – *sionnaich* – were now retreating to their dens.

The great bears – *mathanan mòra* -- a full two-man lengths tall, were withdrawing to their accustomed caves to hibernate.

The sword-tooth tigers were moving down the mountain to the warmer zones.

Dòmhnall was making his way to the barn when he heard voices farther out in the woods beyond the pasture. He followed the sounds and finally caught up close enough that he could hear Ròna speaking a short distance ahead. He crouched behind the trunk of a spreading yew tree to avoid being seen, but by that time, the girl had turned back to the house, and the two men she'd met with had continued down the trail.

His curiosity piqued, his apprehensions raised, the father shadowed the two men deeper into the surrounding forest and up a steep hill. A fog was settling at this time, and if it were not for his familiarity with his own land and the path he was on, he might very well have found himself tumbling into a ditch and perhaps drowning in the boggy mud by the side of the path.

Dòmhnall was not a complicated man -- which is not to say that he was stupid, for he was not -- just that his intelligence ran to the practical. He knew how to make and fix things. He could jerry-rig a plow blade with a piece of metal he'd dug out of a pile of rusty debris out back of the barn.

He had birthed a mammoth calf during a blizzard, crawling up into the birth canal of the bellowing elephantine mother to carefully extract the breached babe so as to leave both parent and offspring intact, and he had kept the newborn warm and alive by burrowing into a snow drift where the two of them waited out a driving storm, sheltered equally by the frozen blanket and the heat-radiating body of the giant mother.

He had climbed a steep crag to retrieve a lost unihorn calf, a foolish creature who had wandered onto a cliff ledge had gotten stuck where more sensible angels trod fearfully. Dòmhnall had scaled the rocks and carried it on his back to safety off its perilous perch, and then had splinted its broken leg before lugging it home.

And he had built and installed new rooms on the house for their once-growing family.

All these things he could do with his hands, but when it came time to talk to his daughter, whom he dearly loved, he found her as mysterious and distant as the *Sgrìob Chlann Uisnich* -- the path of the sons of Uisneach, as they called the Milky Way in the Forbidden Tongue.

He was at a loss to guess what had she gotten herself into. He'd heard that these so-called Insurges were increasingly rallying against the Monstrato Corps' water grab, or rather, its water spoilage. Indeed, he'd seen on the InterNews that in the city of Trayton there'd been demonstrations and even bombings, which had caused the PieceTakers to move in and set up check points, but out here in the country, there'd been none of that. *Cha robh sgeul no guth ann* -- not a "story" nor a mention, not a hint nor a breath.

While he had been thinking about these matters, his imagination perhaps all the more lit up by the shrouding mist and the darkness of the night, for as the ancient proverb had it, *Tha tuisg a' mhamoit nas motha anns a' cheò* -- The tusks of the mammoth are larger in the fog -- Dòmhnall had heard a branch snap in the darkness, and imagining that a nocturnal sword-tooth cat was stalking him in the pitch black shadows, he had dodged to the side of the trail, lost his footing, and tumbled into a pitch-black ditch with a startled and (if anyone had been around to hear him) embarrassingly girlish cry.

He was uncertain what the inky dark was hiding. From the recesses of the pit, he peered into the black shadows in the direction of the sound but could see nothing. It was that kind of moonless, lightless night in which you could not see a tree in front of your nose until you had run smack into it, or as it was said in the FT, *cho dorcha ri do cheann ann am bucaid de bhìth* – as dark as your head in a bucket of gowp.[91]

He climbed out of the ditch. He heard first one voice and then another. He felt arms around him, and he struck out, a solid, straight, right punch at what he guessed (as he had to, for he could not see) was the attacker's face. He felt tissue collapse under his massive fist and heard a satisfying crunch of cartilage and bone.

---

[91] Certainly, the most obvious interpretation of the word *bìth* indicates a substance of impenetrable darkness, or "gowp." However, it might be noted that many words in the FT possess a polysemic quality – that is, are able to express multiple or alternative meanings, so here, the word that is translated as "gowp," could also indicate hatred or malice.

And a shout: "*Bòd a' chac!* -- Dickshit! -- *Bhris e mo shròn!* -- He's broken my nose!"

Dòmhnall took advantage of the momentary distraction, and twisting out of his attacker's grasp, he hammered down in the general direction of his assailant. The old man was disappointed in having landed only a glancing blow, but it must have been telling, for the stranger went down under his fist.

Dòmhnall caught a glimpse of slender shadows. He reached out and gripped one and the other. He might not have been able to follow the convoluted, clever thought mazes of his much foxier daughter – he was, after all, as he himself would admit, just a man, and a mammoth farmer, at that -- but however simple his path of thinking was, it was straight and clear. He knew how to deal with poachers and mammoth thieves.

The two men strove to resist his bear-grip, but they weren't from the crofts, and they weren't men who worked in the fields all day long, nor were they the sort that wrestled mammoths on a farm. They were skinny men from Trayton if he could tell by their accents, and from the sound of their voices, they were young, around Ròna's age, he would have guessed.

They struggled vainly against his vice-grasp.

Dòmhnall barked: "Tell me what you're doing here. Before I turn you over to the Council of the Sisters for mammoth rustling."

"No ... we weren't doing anything with the animals," one protested.

"Then what!?!"

"The water."

"The *loch*?" the word escaped him before he could think. He caught these two clearly in the wrong, but he had to be careful lest they turn the accusation back on him for speaking in the Forbidden to representatives of the Monstrato Corps, if that's what they were. "The lake?" The idea was too absurd. "You're stealing the lake!?!"

"No," the one under his right arm protested. "*They* are."

"Who?"

"Who do you think?" The young man's voice took on the supercilious tone of a teenager explaining something *oh-so-obvious* to a head-thick adult, although not the tone you necessarily want to take if you're being choked under the arm of an angry mammoth herder.

Dòmhnall tightened the grip.

The young man choked out, "Sorry. Sorry. The Monstrato PieceTakers."

The kids writhed helplessly in the older man's grip. (At Dòmhnall's age, anybody under 40 was a "kid.") Finally, one yelped an explanation: "We're here with Ròna."

The utterance of his daughter's name dashed cold water on Dòmhnall's anger, and his grip slackened in surprise.

The interlopers, sensing the opportunity of the moment, seized it, slipped his grasp, and fled into the woods.

Perplexed, Dòmhnall made his way back to the cottage. As he came in, Siùsaidh scrutinized her husband in expectation that he tell her what he'd found out. When he didn't say anything, she prompted him: "What happened? What'd you see?"

Dòmhnall thought better of blurting out the details of the strange encounter. "*Chan fhaca mi dad,*" he said. "I didn't see anything."

But he was a poor liar, and from the look of him, Siusaidh suspected there was more than what he was letting on, for she'd known him long enough to be certain that something had happened, something he'd seen, something he wasn't telling her.

Realizing that he'd probably already said too much for his own good and Siùsaidh's peace of mind, he became inordinately interested in his cup of tea, and mumbling into it, he muttered, "Just Ròna and a couple of her friends."

"What'd they say?"

"I was too far away. *Cha chuala mi càil* -- I didn't hear anything," although his voice lowered even further if such a thing were possible, swallowing the words. "Just kids ... *a' gabhail spòrs 's mireadh* – having fun."

However, the words he had overheard from the apparition of Ròna in the night echoed in his memory and strangled him: "*Fuil, 's marbh, 's bàs.* -- Blood, killing, and death.*"

~~

246

A monkey's shit

Mur' eil tu a' tuigsinn ron tuiteamas, 's dòcha gun tig eòlas dhut às a dhèidh.

If you don't understand before it happens, perhaps you'll come to know after.

Proverb from *Leabhar an Leaghaidh Mhòir* — The Book of the Great Melting

With her foundling secured and secreted in a safe place where she was sure no one would find him until she could ascertain whether her suspicions were true or not, Ròna had an opportunity to turn her attention to some things she'd neglected, one of which was wrangling a wild *mìneotarbh* bull that'd been bothering her father's herd.

She found the animal in the pasture that abutted her father's *croit* – croft, or small farm.

Riding up carefully behind the bull, she lassoed *an ròpa* – the rope -- around the creature's neck and lashed her end around the horn of her own mount. She tapped her heels into Dìleas's sides with the command, "*Greim*! – Hold!"

Her one-horned had participated in enough round-ups to know  what was coming and what was expected of him: The wild one would bolt. It was up to Dìleas to stand fast, and sure enough, although the wild young bull had not been concerned upon hearing the one-horned come up behind him, the unaccustomed feel of the rope around his neck had startled him, and he did take off, managing to gallop a few lengths before the rope tightened and jerked him in reverse. It might be difficult to imagine such a large creature flying off its four legs, but that's what he did -- flipped and landed flat on his back.

Before the bull could react -- even as he was still in the air -- Ròna was leaping from the seat on her steed and rushing to where she anticipated the wild one would come down, a length of rope in her hand.

No sooner had the giant beast touched down with a ground-shuddering thump than did Ròna lash his legs -- first one with a loop and then with a quick swing, the other, opposite one, and quickly the two others, and the young bull was hogtied firmly.

"*Fuireach an seo, a bhalaich* – Wait here, kiddo," she told him in a soothing voice. "*Bidh a h-uile rud ceart gu leòr* -- Everything will be alright."

The young bull thrashed against his bonds and then amidst deep heavings of breath took a respite in his struggles.

Dìleas moved close to reassure the young bull, his placid stance slowly calming and quietening the untamed male's struggles.

It was then that Ròna heard a familiar voice calling out.

"Looks like you've caught a lively one!"

Ròna looked around and found her sister-in-law Maggie standing at the edge of the clearing, a mushroom basket dangling from her hand.

With a tilt of the head towards the *mìneotarbh* strung up in the middle of the field, Maggie asked, "What do you do with the bull once you've caught it?"

"You're a better one to answer that than I am." This reference to her brother – and Maggie's husband -- came with a wry smile. Which she followed, as she walked nearer, with a dropping of her tone of voice into a more casual reference to Maggie's gathering: "Getting a good batch?"

Maggie held out a couple mushrooms to show her friend. "Look at these ... nice and plump! I'm sure they'll be tasty – maybe in a soup with lentils and a few wild onions. Some bread and *teatha na màthar* – tea of the Mother ..." She drifted to a connecting thought, "You should come over."

Ròna made a wry face.

"I'm not sure if I should say this, but I know you and Seumas never really got along, and maybe if ..."

"It's not that I never wanted to ..." Ròna began.

"You could try ..."

"It would take a lot of trying."

"I know," Maggie relieved her friend of the need to explain further. "He can be such a *bod a' chac* – dickshit – sometimes. Sometimes he ... well, you know ..."

Ròna gave a quick nod in assent. Yes, indeed, well did she know.

"He ..." Maggie thought how to phrase it: "He gets out of control sometimes." She paused as if she didn't know quite where she was going along this path of thought, but in a moment, she saw the through-line. She tilted her head in the direction of the hogtied *mìneotarbh* lying in the grass a short distance away. "What do you do if you have a wild bull that makes too much trouble?"

Ròna tilted her head and lilted her voice comically. "*Bidh thu ga spothadh* – You cut his balls off."

The women laughed.

"I can't do that!" Maggie exclaimed. "I need 'em myself!" More seriously, she added, "But is there any reason you can't ..." She trailed off before picking up the question and finishing it ... "get along?"

As for Ròna, was there really any use or good to come from explaining, from going back over the thousand pricks and nettles inflicted by her brother on her -- from the time that he placed an actual thistle with its needle-sharp pricks in her bed to the time he set his dog on her cat?

Maggie turned away suddenly and called sharply after her toddler of a son. "*A Sheumais Bheag*! – Little Seumas!" He was named after his father, *Seumas Mòr* -- Big Seumas. "Come away from there. You'll prick your finger. Then you'll be sorry ..."

As if on cue, a wail rose up from the boy – a tossle-haired, dirty-faced little one, his face smeared with the berries he'd been picking and cramming greedily into his gob – and standing pitifully, crying, he raised his finger as the object of his misery.

Maggie went to him and lifted him. "I told you, didn't I? You never listen, just like your father!"

"Only eventually, maybe this one will listen," Ròna said with a wicked grin.

Maggie chuckled and kissed the child's tears away. She checked the finger and pinched the nettle out. She gave the miniscule wound a kiss. "There. All better!"

She set little Seumas on his feet and gave him a soft pat on his bottom. "Go to *Antaidh* Ròna. Maybe she can keep you from getting into trouble."

Ròna held out her arms. "*An seo, a laochain* – Come here, my little hero. You want to go for a ride on Dìleas?"

The boy's eyes went large. At first, it was all he could do but to nod eagerly before he burst out with, "Can I!?!"

Ròna lifted him to the beast's snout, whereupon the animal snorted.

"He's funny!" Little Seumas said with a squeal of delight.

"He told me it'd be okay if you rode him a bit." She lifted the little one onto the back of the hairy animal. "Hold on tight," she told the boy, placing his hands into the thick matted fur.

Keeping a hand on the boy's leg to steady him and to be ready to catch him should he slip off, she nudged Dìleas forward a step. "*Sin agad e! –* There you are!" she oozed. "'*S e maraiche mòr a th' annad --* It's a great rider that you are!"

Maggie had been watching intently, but when Ròna looked back, she dipped her head to avoid looking directly at her friend as she asked the question that had been on her mind, what she'd really been driving at with all her allusions to an uncertain, untamed, wild bull. "What're you going to do about that *coigreach –* the foreigner -- you brought back?"

Seumas teetered on his high ride, which gave Ròna a welcome distraction. She caught his leg and took a bit longer than absolutely necessary to reseat the child.

Finally, when she'd stalled long enough, she shook her head and shrugged, which, of course, was a non-response.

"You don't know! That's not an answer."

"I don't know what to tell you ..."

"Well, a lot of people are going to know what to tell *you* at the *Coimhairle nam Peathraichean –* the Council of the Sisters. Some have questions about whether what you did is right. And others go further than just questions. They're afraid it's dangerous."

Ròna's felt as if she'd been slapped. "Just something that ... I can't put it into words."

"Well, you'd better think about how you're going to explain it because the time is coming soon when you're going to have to." She punctuated her pronouncement with a line from a proverb: "*Thig gaillionn 's sian –* A storm is coming."

More softly, teasingly: "Do you even know what you have? *Chuirinn-sa airgead air nach fhaca tu fon chochall.*[92] -- I'd put money on it that you haven't even looked under the hood." A sly wink and a one-sided smile gave a hint as to the innuendo.

"It wouldn't come off," Ròna answered in a flat timbre, giving

---

[92] *Fon chochall –* It's always problematic to try to explain a joke, especially when the humor depends on a play on words that exists in another language, but this is too delicious for the editor of this history to pass up the attempt: The denotive meaning of the wood *cochall* is "hood" or "husk" or "sheath" or "capsule" or "encasing," so it is not a far stretch of the imagination to see the double entendre that Maggie is employing here: the "hood" that encases the stranger's head, and the one that encompasses his other "head."*

Footnote to footnote: The editor apologizes for his pedantry, but probably due to his career as an academic, such things do amuse him and seem to him (if to nobody else), worthy of being mentioned.

away no sign whether she got the full import of what Maggie was implying.

"So, it's the mystery of it all ..." Maggie lifted her voice insinuatingly, teasingly, leaving the implication of her statement open ended.

Though it was true that the stranger's face was hidden by the tight-fitting cowl, and Ròna had no idea what he looked like -- not that that mattered -- nor even who he was, there was something that impinged on her memory insistently like a calling of her name from out of a thick fog. But it was all too complicated to get into, so Ròna didn't respond. Admitting the truth would be embarrassing, and denying it unconvincingly would entail giving away too much.

"Well, they always say that you can't get a man any other way," Maggie said with a sly smirk, "except to rope him and hogtie him and drag him home behind your unihorn."

This sparked and stung. Ròna demanded, "Who says that!?!"

Which was maybe the reaction Maggie was looking for. She waved away the topic. "I shouldn't have said anything. Forget it."

Perhaps to divert from where the conversation was going – or had already gone -- Ròna gave Dìleas a little flick at his lower leg just above the fetlock where he was ticklish, where his funnybone was – if he had had a sense of humor. The unihorn lifted his leg, giving Seumas the sensation of a small jump.

The child squealed in amazement and delight. "Dìleas jump!" he cried out in glee.

"Yes, he did!" Ròna confirmed.

Maggie went on. "I hope you know, I'm on your side no matter what. Whatever you do, it's fine with me."

Ròna grimaced as if withdrawing from an unpleasant smell. While she'd avoided the subject even in her own mind, now that she was being forced to think about it, the issue having been thrust under her nose, well she knew the truth of what her friend was saying.

She reverted to Seumas. "Well, little man, I think you've tired Dìleas out. Time to give him a rest."

She lifted the boy up and set him down on the ground.

"More!" he demanded, lifting his arms.

Maggie scooped him up from behind. "'S fheàrr a bhith a' fàgail a' phàrtaidh nuair a bhios an spòrs as àirde -- Best to leave the party when it's the most fun," she said.

Then – "Here give these to auntie," she told Little Seumas, scooping a couple handfuls of mushrooms into a small basket.

"I couldn't ..."

"Nonsense! I've got too much. You'd be doing me a favor, get rid of 'em for me. I picked too many. I'd just throw them out, anyway."

"Love you," Ròna said, taking the basket, "*eadhan ma bhios tu nad ultach teine uaireigin* -- even if you are an armful of fire sometimes."[93]

"You're one to talk!"

Ròna bent down to Little Seumas and said in a high voice she'd use for a baby or a dog, "Love you, too ..." and with a leap, she vaulted up onto her *aon-adharc*'s back and swiveled his head around to face the hogtied bull *mìneotarbh* she'd left in the middle of the field.

"Ròna!" Maggie called out so as to be heard at the slight distance between them and over the rustling and the snorting and the clumpty-clombity-clomb of Dìleas's hoof beats.

Ròna pulled back on Dìleas's reins and nudged her ride half-way around to face her sister-in-law.

"I don't know if this is a silly question, or what," Maggie broached, "but ..." Again, she hesitated to finish the thought before she blurted out what was on her mind: "*Carson a bheireas tu cac a' mhuncaidh dha?* – Why do you give a monkey's shit about him?"

Good question, *why did Ròna give a monkey's shit?*

The *why* would be clear enough if what she suspected were true: the result and cumulation of a number of incidents that had started several years before the reaping, which itself had changed everything.

~~

---

[93] *Ultach teine* – an armful of fire, perhaps referencing an armful of slow-burning peat; but here, even the translation needs a translation -- in other words, "a pain in the ass."

6. Who wrote the book of love?

Far am bi do chràdh bidh do làmh; far am bi do ghràdh bidh do chridhe gu bràth.

Where your pain is, your hand will be; where your love is, your heart will always be.

Leabhar an Leaghaidh Mhòir —
The Book of the Great Melting

Wiktionary: The desertification of the planet

Professor Harold Harishandra Higginsbottom (editor)

As strange as it might sound to the modern reader, water that was drinkable by humans and supportive of animal and vegetative life forms was once abundant on the surface of the earth. The twin processes of the draining of all sources of fresh water, on the one hand, and on the other, the hydrocracking of gowp and the mining of other mineral deposits with the accompanying leaching of that substance into what water sources remained, resulted in the depletion of natural reserves of water and the necessity for humans to depend on manufactured or artificially purified fluids if human civilization were to survive.[94]

During the time preceding the Great Melt, people of the world witnessed the disappearance of water sources on which they had previously depended. This depletion of water was particularly devastating to the world economy because water at the time played a crucial role in sustaining agriculture, ecosystems, industry, and human life, acting as the planet's "life blood" that sustained various aspects of our environment.

---

[94] Ancient sources tell of an old saying – "Gowp and water don't mix" – but they do, and in the process create a liquefied substance that is drinkable, burnable, and spendable – in other words, that provides ultimate, all-in-one value.

The shortages of this vital resource were the result of

Overuse:

- the maintenance of lush gardens in desert-like environments (and the water usage those gardens demanded);
- overpopulation – the settling of arid regions and the insistence on maintaining lifestyles and water-consumption practices inconsistent with natural supplies;
- agricultural applications – widespread planting of crops that were "water guzzlers" to a degree that was unsustainable by local natural water supplies;
- the draining of aquifers -- underground naturally occurring water supplies -- faster than those reserves were naturally replenished;
- the general depletion of natural water resources to the point that formerly dependable naturally occurring water reservoirs had been drained to non-existance.

The spoilage of existing natural water supplies:

Paradoxically, even after the melt, when one might have expected the volume of potable water to have increased on account of the dissolution of the world's icecaps, usable water reserves further diminished because of the tainting of available reserves by

- the co-mixture of the fresh-water icecap runoff with the salt-laden sea water of the surrounding oceans, the salt content of which had been increased by rising temperatures, and which had been further compromised by the industrial and agricultural spillage mentioned above;
- the rising sea levels flooding and tainting heretofore fresh water lakes, rivers, streams, and underground acquifers;
- accidental run-off or purposeful dumping of agriculturally and industrially tainted chemicals or water polluted with such chemicals into existing natural reserves of water, which spoiled and made them unfit for any human, animal, or further agricultural consumption;

- mining mineral and gowp deposits in ways (for instance) through the use of chemicals or by means that caused the mineral/gowp residues to leach into natural water reserves (thus rendering those unfit for further use).

Rising temperatures

Adding to and aggravating the above listed conditions and circumstances was

- the phenomenon of rising temperatures to heights which made life unsupportable;
- the drying out and depleting existing water resources through naturally occurring evaporation.

Not only were droughts severely destabilizing to the world economy but so, paradoxically, were floods, as they made previous population centers uninhabitable and agricultural practices untenable. Furthermore, flooding exacerbated the contamination of what water resources remained, distributing agricultural and industrial runoff, including heavy metals and other toxic elements from mining operations, further tainting naturally occurring water resources.

Coastal population centers became uninhabitable because they were inundated with rising water (partially caused by the melting glaciers and ice caps, the swelling volume of water under heating conditions, and the erosion of coastal land due to increased storms and eradication of wet-land protective zones).

Even inland, low-lying areas found themselves flooded with tainted waters from the worldwide incidence of rising sea levels and likewise suffered deterioration of habitability: Stricken by drought, their aquifers drained, their rivers dried up and/or poisoned, they ceased being able to sustain human habitation or food production.

It became apparent to the Managers of CUINTE[95] that action had to be taken to avert absolute catastrophe to the world's economy. Through a series of studies, Consortium scientists determined that free-standing and unadulterated, untreated water contained high levels of the chemical DHO, otherwise known as

---

[95] CUINTE - Consortium of Unified Inter-National Trade Enterprises. An international corporate cooperative established to maintain peaceful relations between corporations and adjudicate fair trading relations, manufacturing practices, and gowp-exploitation.

dyhydrogen monoxide, a dangerous contaminant which formed a significant portion of acid rain and contributed greatly to the heating of the planet known as the greenhouse effect, and was therefore a foremost cause of the planet's heating and subsequent desertification.

Further, the substance, the Consortium's scientists discovered, far from being the benign chemical compound it was believed to be in less enlightened eras, was actually the prime source or major contributor to erosion of the natural landscape, corrosion of metals, the failure of electrical systems, and as its presence directly correlated with cancerous tumor growth, a significant endangerment to human life span. In addition, immersion in this substance was found to be the third leading cause year after year of unintentional human injury and death in the world.

After studying and researching the global devastation wreaked by this chemical, it was determined that all the problems listed above (and many more – this being just a summary) had one common cause: naturally occurring water, which was thereafter dubbed NOCSUS.[96] It was therefore decided after long consideration and adjudication that NOCSUS be declared a dangerous, life-threatening pollutant, and that, first, every effort should be expended to eradicate all deposits of this dangerous element, and that, second, all human needs be fulfilled by the mining and processing of gowp, which existed in abundant, which is to say, nearly inexhaustible supplies in underground deposits, and which could be modified to satisfy any number of human and economic needs – including direct (and indirect) consumption, fuel for industry and transportation, raw material for manufacturing, and fertilizer for agriculture.

And as gowp was organic at its base and origination, the result of the death, decomposition, and fossilization of life forms previously in existence, the centering of the world's economy and society on it, rather than on water, was actually in a way life-affirming. in a way that DHO-based civilizations of the past were not.

In light of these findings, the tender was made by the Monstrato Corps to supply the needs of the world's population for this valuable, all-purpose commodity at the cost of extraction (plus a minor, reasonable mark-up for operating and administrative expenses).

Thus were the economy of the world and, as a side benefit, life on the planet saved.

---

[96] NOCSUS -- Naturally Occurring Contaminating Substance -- Underground or Surface.

mìcheal dubh

All glory to the Profit!

Cuilean, Son of the Tiger

(Before the Reaping)

Nam biodh am faodalach reamhar no caol, 's mairg an duine nach beathaicheadh e.
>Whether the foundling is fat or thin, pitiful is the man who won't feed him.
>Proverb from *Leabhar an Leaghaidh Mhòir* — The Book of the Great Melting

The fable of the children of the Wayp was that Cuilean had been left as a changeling in the woods by *na sìthichean* -- the fairies – who often left their own misshapen offspring in exchange for a healthy human baby, but in this instance, they'd mistakenly dropped Cuilean into the litter of a sword-tooth tigress – *an cat claidheamh-fhiaclach* in the FT -- trading a worthless, shaking, quivering, fear-ridden, skinny, multi-colored, fairy runt for a healthy, fearless tiger cub to take back to the other world.

Whether the transaction was purposeful or not was difficult to say and impossible to ascertain. Perhaps, for some reason, they'd conceived of a need for a healthy cub, or, alternatively, the changeling's leaving was the result of fairy ineptitude by an elfin bumbler who had been relegated the simplest task imaginable: "Here, you just have one job to do, Marigold" -- *Lus an Oir* in the FT. "Take this sickly fairy child and swap it for a healthy baby. That's not hard, is it? You think you can handle this?" Nevertheless, poor, simpleton, cross-eyed *Lus an Oir* had managed to bumble her task and left the infant to be reared by the mother sword-tooth, or to die.

However fanciful, the story wasn't far from the truth.

During the last snowfall of a winter, when in a final gasp of the cold months, before the rapidly approaching spring, the winds howled like an invading horde of banshees down the frigid sides of the mountain passes and the peaks pointed stiff and white like frost-erected nipples of *Cìochan na Màthar* -- the Mother's Teats. While he was out searching for a lost mammoth calf, Ròna's father

Dòmhnall Chamshroin – Donald Cameron in Simspeek -- came upon
the little valley where a cottage was nestled in the lap of the
mountain of the mother, a peaceful glade, blanketed with a soft
covering of snow. As late as it was in the afternoon, the winter sun
had already set. The moonlight sparkled across the icy ground like
a sprinkling of jewels. Dark shadows were cast across the ground in
large swaths, and when the moonlight broke through the gloom
unimpeded, it lighted surfaces with a pure white gleam. The stars
in the sky sparkled like so many embers of a dying fire on a bed of
black ash.

Wholly night.

Silent night.

Silent now except for the sound of Dòmhnall's tramping
through field and forest as he searched for a stray mammoth calf,
but not so quiet just a little earlier when shouts could have been
heard coming from the interior of a ramshackle hut: a woman's
hysterical screaming and a man's furious hollering, their voices
muffled by the thick-packed snow.

The man bellowing something like, "No manchild of mine is
going to cry like a baby!"

And the woman shrieking, "You're going to kill him!"

And the wailing of a terrified infant.

Inside the hovel, William the Carpenter – *Liam Saoir*, as he was
known, or or less favorably, and more pejoratively (but never to his
face), *Liam Garbh*, or Savage William in Simspeek -- was holding the
baby up by his feet and was beating him with alternately an open
hand and a closed fist.

The boy's mother cried out inarticulately and jumped on
Liam's back, and with a shrug of his shoulders, he threw her to the
side.

She ricocheted off the kitchen cabinet. Clattering down beside
her was a *sgian mhòr* – a large kitchen knife. Picking it up, and in
what was probably an instinctual action, that is, not premeditated,
in her desperation to protect her *pàiste* – her babe -- she lunged at
the man, the father of her child, the would-be infanticide.

She stuck the knife into his chest, so it protruded from between
his ribcage, but not so deeply that he couldn't grip her about the
throat and strangle her.

He drove her backwards, in his fury his hands clamping about
her neck, his legs entangling with her thrashing legs, and his blood
pouring out on the floor. His feet slipped on the wet mess, and
unable to gain traction, he bore down on her, and they tumbled
together, he on top, landing on the handle and driving the blade
that had been but partially embedded deeper into his chest,
puncturing his heart.

She let out a gagged gurgle and thrashed fiercely in desperation as she died.

His last word was a fluid-muffled "*galla* – bitch" as he coughed up his life blood.

Soon, all movements of the couple ceased.

In the process of the struggle, Liam had dropped the baby – more like forgotten about it and discarded it in his hatred of the woman.

Righting himself from where he had tumbled, barefoot, shit-sagging-poop-laden diapered, out into the cold and the snow, screaming in terror, or as much as he could scream between desperate gasps like a person drowning, frantically clutchings at air that caught in his chest before he could complete the breaths, the infant toddled as quickly as he could from the house.

The tot, with his wild disordered mane of hair, oddly tri-colored – *ruadh, bàn, donn* – chestnut red, blond, and brown -- ran as far as he could (which, objectively speaking, wasn't that far) before his legs sank thigh-deep into the powdered snow that blanketed the ground. His heart snagged in his throat, his choking sobs impeded his breathing, but the farther he sloughed through the deepening slurry, the more the echoes of his raging parents' yelling faded behind him in the muffling white drifts.

He ran and tottered – such as toddlers are able to run -- until he could run no more and fell into the snow, sobbing, gasping, and gradually as the heat from his exertion dissipated, shivering.

It was cold, so cold, his cries of terror turned to a baby's crying and faded to animal whimpers. Blubbering faintly, he crawled onward, his compulsion to continue to flee dominated by the residue of his panic.

The wind whipping over the snow cut into him with freezing cold. A scent came to him, wafting on the frigid breeze -- an oddly warm drift of air and a rank, putrid odor that smelled disgustingly of blood, shit, and placenta, but also of sweet milk, and above all else, of warm, sweaty bodies.

The child crawled towards the source of the stench until he was hoisted by the diaper, though it is questionable how conscious the toddler was of being lifted, except that one moment he was dragging himself forward with nearly inaudible whines, and the next he found himself in a snow-covered bower.

There was a pungent stench, and a low, gruff grunt, but most importantly, warmth.

He was nuzzled by a huge wet snout, and by that same snout, he was pushed into the midst of others about his own size. He was engulfed in a warm, rank smell of blood and milk and animal sweat, and pushed and nudged by a half-dozen other little bodies, whose fur not only insulated themselves from the bitter chill, but him, too.

And again the soft, muzzling grip, this time around the nape of the neck, that pushed him towards a steaming, soft, giving, forgiving surface, and nuzzled him towards a fleshy protuberance, and a nipple found his mouth, whereupon he began to suckle, and he tasted the pleasing, warm, buttery milk of the mother sword-tooth tigress course down his throat and warm him from the inside out, and eventually, his tummy filled, nestled snugly amidst his brethren tiger cubs, soothed by the rumbling purring of the great mother *cat claidheamh-fhiaclach*, he fell asleep.

Having gone out into the storm to find the mammoth calf that had strayed away from its mother, Dòmhnall found the babe upon his heading home. The mother had been rooted in the middle of the field bellowing for her calf and wouldn't move -- neither back to the shelter of the three-sided barn that Dòmhnall had built for his animals, nor to venture out to find the babe. She stood in the middle of the frozen meadow, trunk raised high, bawling long and plaintively calling.

Dòmhnall had had a suspicion where the young mammoth might have wandered, and at long last, searching in the rocky hillocks, he found it lodged in the boggy muck of a crevice. *Stupid animals, they knew how to go about searching for lichens and grasses to eat, but often forgot how to get out of where they'd gotten themselves into!*

At first, he couldn't see the calf, but he could hear its staccato series of demanding trumpet calls for its mother, comingled with its wailing complaints that she didn't respond.

Dòmhnall clambered down the embankment, carefully securing handholds and footholds on the slick, muddy hillside. At the bottom, the bawling animal crowded close to him, almost crushing him against the sides of the gulley. Dòmnhnall pushed the creature back, batting it soundly on the forehead to settle it down.

He was able to maneuver himself behind the tiny mammoth (well, tiny as far as mammoths go), and putting his shoulder to the animal's butt, he pushed and heaved and shoved. Clumsily, with this assistance, the calf made its way up the steep sides of the trench, slippery foothold by shifting, uncertain foothold.

At the top of the ravine, when its front feet fell on level, relatively stable ground, the calf, apparently forgetting its recent distress, trumpeted happily and bounded blithely back to its mother.

After Dòmhnall recovered, and his legs had stopped shaking from the exertion, he made his way back home through a grove of trees. He saw a dark lump in a snow bank in a thicket. Because of the drifting snow and the gathering fog, he couldn't make out what it was, but it didn't appear to be mere vegetation, something like a fallen clump of leaves. He first thought it might be a newborn from his herd but then suspected it to be a crouching bear-wolf, or even more dangerous, a sword-tooth tiger.

He heard mewing and meowing and the whining cries of infant animals. Curious, he barked loudly, "*Hoigh*! -- Hey!" to rouse a response that would help him determine just what it was, at the same time expecting whatever it was to start away, or at least to alert in readiness to defend or flee. The figure didn't move. He took a heavy step, sinking up to his knee in the snow and almost fell face first into the frozen powder.

Still the mewing.

His curiousity overruling his caution, Dòmhnall stalked closer and shifted the branch covering, and he saw the circling of small creatures under the snow-hung branches.

He recognized the litter of tiger cubs. He hastily withdrew his hands and glanced quickly around, the thought darting across his mind how lucky he was that the mother sword-tooth was not there. She would have leapt out in attack by now if she had been. Then his thoughts raced to fearing how close she might be.

But just as he was about to hastily retreat, his eye caught something else that drew him closer. At first, he couldn't make out what it was, so thick had the fog become. He had only vaguely registered a tossled mane of what he had first taken to be that of another cub. Encompassed by the tiger whelps, the creature had evidently burrowed itself into the middle of the litter to poach their body warmth.

Dòmhnall muttered to himself, "*A Mhàthair an t-saoghail!* – Mother of the world!" *It was a baby! A human child!* And one strangely cowled with a tigerish tri-colored mane that ran in streaks through its hair: *ruadh, donn, bàn* – chestnut red, brown, and blond.

The sword-tooth tigress hove into view. It was half-dragging, half-carrying a deer in its jaws. Dòmhnall had no more than *priobadh na sùla* – the blink of an eye -- to register the predator's sudden appearance before the tigress dropped its prey, and with a screech and a roar, she charged at the man.

He shouted loudly and deeply, made himself as big as he could, and waved his arms wildly, which gave the beast a moment's pause – which was only momentary, but just long enough as his heartbeats surged with a pounding insistency -- for his hands to fly with trembling urgency and lift the child out of the thicket.

Dòmhnall backpedaled clumsily in the thick snow, the tigress still screeching and roaring. As he gave ground, the mother advanced hurriedly, still continuing her threats. She circled the litter, growling all the while he retreated with the baby. She nuzzled the half-dozen cubs, seeming to count them, once, and to be sure, once again. Apparently satisfied they were all there, she covered them with her body, and gaping her jaws wide, she shrieked at Dòmhnall.

Dòmhnall backed away as swiftly as he could, not daring to turn his back on the sword-tooth, for doing so might well have triggered an instinctual attack on a fleeing prey. Once safely away, out of sight, but not out of hearing of the frightful screeching and roaring of the mother tiger, Dòmhnall fashioned a pouch from the plaid draped over his shoulder and stuffed the cold, little find inside his makeshift hammock.

He turned back and plowed through the knee-deep snow drifts *dhachaigh* – homeward.

When he walked into the family's cottage, his wife Siùsaidh reminded him sternly, "Shoes, off!" without even looking to see what he was carrying. *Men and dogs! Just when you think you have them trained!* Before she could add to her scolding – about how she'd just cleaned the floor -- she caught sight of the bulge under his plaid. "What do you have there?" she demanded suspiciously.

"*Fhuair mi e ann an cuain de chuileanan na bana-thìgeir.* – I found it in a litter of tiger cubs."

Their daughter, Ròna, happened to be in the kitchen at that moment. Her little ears picked up on what her father had said. "*Cuilean? Càite?* – A cub? Where?"

Barely waist high to her parents, Ròna asserted herself between her mother and father and peered intently at the surprise her *dadaidh* had brought home.

Her eager, tiny hands pried the plaid further open and revealed the baby boy.

Ròna gulped. *Is this where babies came from? Left in snow banks out in the forest!?!* she wondered. "*An deach fhàgail leis na sìthichean?*" she inquired. "Was he left by the fairies?"

"*Obh obhan!* -- Oh! Oh, dear!" Siùsaidh exclaimed, gathering the child up. In alarm, she called out, "*Tha e cho fuar!* – He's so cold! --

'*S geàrr bhuaithe am bàs!* -- And sharply close is death to him!" she exclaimed, glaring at Dòmhnall as if this were somehow his fault.

With sure fingers, she unwrapped the bairn from Dòmhnall's plaid. "*Cait' às an deach e?* -- Where did he come from?"

Dòmhnall told her what he knew, which was actually very little, and none of which mattered in the urgency of succoring the baby, and in spite of her having asked the question, she didn't wait for the explanation, for certain what to do, forgetting about his boots which were tracking mud and snow and muck all over her kitchen floor, Siùsaidh turned on the tea kettle and opened the oven.

"You aren't going to cook it!" Ròna yelped in fright.

"*Na bi gòrach*," Siùsaidh snapped. "Don't be foolish." *(Little ones! The strangest ideas come into their heads.)* "We're going to warm him up." And so saying, she handed the *leanabh* – the baby – back to Dòmhnall and directed him to seat himself in front of the oven.

She left the room and quickly returned with a blanket that she wrapped around the limp, cold-numbed body.

By this time, Seumas, Ròna's big brother, attracted to the commotion in the kitchen, had come in, followed by his bear-wolf cub, *Sgàth* – or Shadow. "What's that!"

"Your father found it in the woods," Siùsaidh explained, as she bustled around the kitchen, looking for a bottle and something she could use as a nipple.

Seumas edged closer to inspect the foundling. "Look at his hair! It's striped like a tiger! He looks funny!"

"You smell funny!" Ròna snapped.

"*Bi modhail* – Be nice," Siùsaidh admonished.

Sgàth sniffed the baby and issued a low-throated growl.

"What's wrong with him?" Ròna asked.

"He probably smells the cat on it," Dòmhnall explained.

"Get him out of here," Siùsaidh directed Seumas, stepping protectively between the bear-wolf and the infant and pushing the animal's head away.

"*Trobhad, a bhalaich* – Come on, boy," Seumas said to the bear-wolf. "It's no fun in here anyway." The boy huffed out the door, his bear-wolf Shadow trotting behind him, its claws clipping and clattering on the hard wood floor.

"*Dùin an doras!* – Close the door!" Siùsaidh called after her son. To no avail. The lad was already out of her hearing, or far enough away that he could claim that he was.

Ròna pulled a rocking chair up next to her father and climbed up on it. She held out her arms. "Let me hold it!" she commanded, even though she was barely bigger than it was, but so insistently did she tug on it, Dòmhnall pleaded with his wife, "What do I do?"

"I don't think it'll do any harm. *Ach bi faiceallach, a ghràidh* – Just be careful, love," she said to her daughter.

The infant, awoken by the commotion, started to cry.

Flummoxed, the little girl appealed to her mother, "Now, what do I do?"

"*Seinn dha* -- Sing to him," Siùsaidh said, and with that, Ròna launched into a lullaby her mother used to sing to her not that long before:

> *Bà, bà, mo leanabh beag.*
> *Ged 's tha thu beag, bi thu mòr.*

> Sleep, sleep, my little baby.
> Although you are small, you will be big.

In a few minutes, Siùsaidh returned with an old glove she had quickly fabricated into a simulation of a mother tigress's teat by cutting off the tip of one of the fingers. She attached it around the top of a bottle half-full with warm mammoth milk. "See if you can get him to eat a little," she told Ròna.

And so Ròna rocked the baby, breaking into childish hymns, songs, and lullabies, as best as she could remember them, the repetition bothering neither her nor the toddler. The little boy's shivering having ceased, he alternated between dozing fitfully and suckling on the old glove that Siùsaidh had prepared. Eventually, lulled by the gentle movement of the rocking chair, both Ròna and the *leanabh* went to sleep.

Siùsaidh nodded off at the rough-hewn kitchen table, her head resting on her crossed arms.

Dòmhnall draped a blanket across her shoulders before he left the kitchen and went to bed himself.

Periodically during the night, Siùsaidh woke up to check on the two children huddled together in front of the fire in the oven.

When morning came, Siùsaidh groggily checked the refugee from the storm. Satisfied that the babe was warm and well, she started water boiling for tea and porridge, set some sausage on the grill, and cracked a few eggs next to the slices of meat. She slipped a few scones – enough for all of them -- into the oven for warming.

Dòmhnall came in, and seeing that Siùsaidh had already started their morning meal, he told her "*Suidhe sìos, a ghràidh* – Sit down, love. I'll finish everything," and took over. Or tried to. Siùsaidh wasn't eager to relinquish her place, and so shoulder to shoulder, sometimes crowding each other, reaching over each other, they prepared the morning meal.

Seumas trundled in, rubbing the sleep out of his eyes. "*Suidhe sìos, a bhalaich.* – Sit down, lad," Siùsaidh directed the boy. "*Rinn d' athair bracaist.* -- Your father's made some breakfast."

"*We* made breakfast," Dòmhnall corrected.

Siùsaidh turned to Ròna. "*A ghràidh* -- Darling – let me have the baby. I'll take care of him. Come and have something to eat."

"No!" the girl protested. "He's mine!" As if the thought had just occurred to her, she asked, "What's his name?"

Dòmhnall spoke without looking up from the stove. "I found him near Liam Garbh's house. This might be his son – Colin, I think his name is."

Mishearing what her father had said, mistaking the name "Colin" for the word for "cub" – *Cuilean* -- and thinking nothing could be more appropriate, Ròna answered, "*Uill, ma thà, 's e seo an cuilean agamsa!* -- Well, then, this one is my cub! My Cuilean."

The adults, both tickled by the child's misapprehension, and cowed by the dauntlessness of her certainty, gave in. And so, that became his name, the lost cub, *Cuilean Mac an Tìgeir* – Cuilean, Son of the Tiger -- that at first Ròna's parents thought would be a cute nickname for the foundling – as good as any other *far-ainm* -- until they learned the kid's real name for certain, but as no one came to claim the child, and the bodies of his parents were not found until the following springtime when heather blossoms blanketed the pasture and the songs of robins filled the air morning and evening in the little glen where their cottage lay, that name stuck.

~~

Fraidy Cat!

(Before the reaping)

Tha e glic air a tha eagal ron uilebheist, 's tha e treun a bhios a' strì ris fhathast.
He is wise who fears the monster, and brave who still fights against it.
Proverb from *Leabhar an Leaghaidh Mhòir* — The Book of the Great Melting

Throughout her childhood, a constant thorn in Ròna's *bròg*[97] -- her shoe -- had long been her big brother Seumas.

He had always been a mean kid -- *borb 's cruaidh* – wild and cruel, as the words had it in the FT, though careful not to overstate the case, he never intentionally inflicted pain – in that pain itself was not the objective. It was just that his idea of fun very often involved seeing other people – or animals – squirm in discomfort, much like some people's idea of comedy involves watching others fall down, slip on a slick patch of mud, or get hit in the balls.

As a little boy, he'd throw rocks at small creatures and laugh at their fright – how ridiculous they looked as they scrambled to escape, even more hilarious because he really wasn't trying to hurt them at all, but because they were too stupid to know that. He thought it funny to see them fall all over themselves, and perhaps even run into something like a tree stump or a large rock, as they attempted to flee.

Sgàth – "shadow" in the FT -- his pet bear-wolf, was always eager to join the fun, though Seumas had to be careful not to set him on too dangerous a chase because while Seumas had the sense to run away, the resolute Sgàth didn't, like the time that he set off

---

[97] *Bròg* – "shoe" – a wrapped leather foot covering strapped around the foot: protective for traversing across rough ground, yet porous so as not to hold water in the wet climate and the often boggy landscape of the Wayp, the idea being not to resist the water, but to accede to the environment of water, letting the water in and out.

after a sword-tooth tiger, not thinking, *What if he caught the monster cat?*

The question always was: *Which animal should the boys choose to goad?* Or, more precisely, *Which victim would give the most satisfactory – which is to say, amusing – reaction (without incurring an incumbent risk)?*

As they grew, the boys graduated from beast to beast – those with an inborn tendency to charge being the most entertaining (for instance, a house cat would run away, a possum would lie down and pretend to be dead, a bear-wolf would stand and fight, dangerously so).

Pàistean – the wee children -- started off, if they were so inclined, with lambs, which would bound playfully around the field, tucking their heads down to harmlessly bump anything.

As the boys grew older and/or more proficient, they graduated to goats, which were notorious for head butting.

As older boys, they'd seek out the *bruic mòra* -- great badgers. These were about knee-high to a man and seemed to the bigger boys to occupy that space between small enough to not be *too* dangerous but large enough to provide a bit of what Seumas considered "fun."

Badgers were fierce, indomitable animals that even the sword-tooth tigers avoided. They were known to charge an enemy no matter how large (well, except for mammoths, but those placid behemoths gave no one any trouble). Seamus would lead his little band of brothers into the bracken – the tall fern-like growths that covered the hillsides – beating the bushes for a victim. They'd surround the animal as it charged first one boy and then another one of its tormentors. Stubby-legged, waddling creatures, the badgers were surprisingly quick but incapable of climbing, so the boy being chased would dart up a tree, leaving another boy to distract the harried animal from the rear, and so the game continued, until either the boys grew tired of the sport or the animal became fed up having to deal with such fools as these human youngsters.

There came a time in every boy's development – or at least and certainly in Seumas's and that of his comrades – that it wasn't only small things he would tease. Growing bored of the lack of adventure in prodding smaller creatures, he would take to poking and rousing the wild *mìneotarbhs* -- the huge ox-like creatures with wide-spread horns and ornery dispositions, who'd been known to face down, and even chase down, a sword-tooth tiger who had been foolish enough to encroach on their blissful grazing, or to threaten the cows or the calves of their herd.

Depending how competent, brave, or foolhardy one boy or another felt, he would tackle a *mìneotarbh* calf, or at most, a yearling (never a full-grown bull) of a size he thought he could handle, or better yet, wrestle to the ground. The boy would grapple the beast by the not-quite-yet-developed horns and attempt to twist its head and neck and wrestle it to the turf. More frequently than not, the calf would shake its head and send the youngster flying, to the great amusement of the other kids.

There was, of course, the danger that any one of these unwilling playmates might turn on its tormentor to gore or trample – the unfortunate fact being that these animals did not always understand the sporting nature of the proceedings, sometimes either taking the challenge to charge as a threat, or at best, an annoying distraction from their peaceful browsing.

When an angry, put-upon bull would turn on Seumas and his buddies, and the boys scattered for their lives before its galloping onslaught, Seumas thought he'd never had such great sport. He'd be laughing all the time that the horns of the bull were within inches of his butt. Once even when a goring propelled him to the mid-level branches of an oak tree, all the way back to the village, carried by his friends, all his cries and protests were interspaced with his own laughter, that in turn were punctuated with cries of agony: "*Obh! Obh! Tha sin gam ghoirteachadh! Gabh air ur socair e!* – Oh! Ahh! That hurts! Take it easy!" A laugh. "*Aobh!* – Ouch!" Another laugh, and "Did you see the expression on his face when he turned! Like, *Huh!? What the ...*" Punctuated with another cry of agony. "*Socair!* -- Easy! -- *Aob, ob, obag!* -- Ouch! Ou! Youiee!" (not that the screams and exclamations really need translation).

Mammoths, because of their sheer magnitude, were suitable for only the truly accomplished young adults.

And, for obvious reasons, carnivores – bear-wolves and sword-tooth tigers, for example -- were avoided because even though they might fulfill the requirement of charging when provoked, they very well were just as likely to catch and eat the nuisance rather than to return peacefully to the sunny rock or the shady bower from whence they came and resume their nap.

However, whatever their size, the one thing all these creatures shared that made them ideal playmates for this game was an inborn instinct to confront rather than flee.

Which was part of the fun.

This day was going something like that.

Sgàth – Seumas's bear-wolf – was dashing around the outskirts of the herd, barking and snapping at the heels of the younger *mìneotarbhs*. Whenever he got within reach of the older, bigger adults, they'd give an annoyed swipe with their horns or take a few steps toward him, or advance at half-speed just to be done with the pest.

Maggie – *Magaidh* in the FT -- and Ròna were lounging on a plaid blanket at the verge between forest and meadow, watching the several boys in the field -- Seumas, Cuilean's foster brother and Ròna's brother among them -- who were trying their hand variously at *mìneotarbh* wrestling and leaping.

Ròna had casually dropped their blanket, leaving it to Maggie to brush off the loose blades of grass and heather that had drifted onto it and to neatly arrange it on the ground.

Maggie was what was known as *bàn* -- sandy-blond -- with a slender nose and light blue eyes. Her hair hung in bangs down over the crest of her forehead almost to where her eyebrows curved softly. She was a sweet, mild-mannered girl, as placid as a stream of clear water. She was conventionally attractive, though shy of putting herself forward, so much so that often others did not notice just how pretty she was. In the presence of people she didn't know well, or even of those she did, she would lower her head, allowing her hair to fall over her face (or rather, not just *allowing* but purposely veiling), which oddly enough, only attracted more attention to her than she desired, as people – the boys, especially – were drawn to peek through the curtain, as it were. She was often seen walking with her arms crossed over her chest and her gaze directed downwards as if intensely interested in what her feet were doing.

At *cèilidhs* – the gatherings – she played sweet melodies on the fiddle, her face devoid of expression except for a quiet, intense concentration as if she were listening to an unheard tune. In her interactions with others, her manner was pleasant and light, giving the impression (often false) that she agreed with whatever the other person was saying.

Maggie had always tickled Ròna. Even as a small girl, she'd had *feadan eadar a cluasan*, as they said in the FT -- a whistling wind between her ears. When they were kids and they'd walk to lessons with the Sisters, Maggie would pile her books and papers so high in her little wood-wheeled, red wagon that the tower of her schoolwork and reading material would waggle back and forth as she pulled the cart along the dirt trail to school. Then invariably she'd misstep or the wagon wheel would catch in a rut or a ditch, and her load would tumble over, and her books and her papers would scatter in the wind. Rather than chase after them and pick them up, she'd stand helplessly wondering what to do, until somebody else brought them back to her (usually Ròna, because the other girls just laughed at her).

Far from being a shining, golden ornament of feminine beauty, Ròna was rather more of what was called a *nighean ruadh* in the Forbidden Tongue -- a strawberry-maned girl with a sprinkling of freckles across her face and torso as if she'd been besplattered by a swirl of paint the same color as her hair.

She'd propped herself up on her elbows and was leaning back on the blanket, bare from her midriff up – her pale breasts bared and soaking in the sun.

She was a slight young woman. Neither was her form especially what somebody might call "shapely." Nobody had ever referred to her as *brèagha*, the word the folk of the Wayp used to indicate "beautiful." Truth be told, objectively, she was of middling attractiveness. She had a borderline plainness about her, with a face that was framed with rounded cheeks, giving her the deceptive appearance of being chubby in direct contradiction to the thinness of her body. Neither did her pert breasts strike anyone as being particularly pulchritudinous. (She was known to joke that they had erupted volcanically into a short-lived voluptuosity on the day she had hit puberty and hadn't grown since.)

When she smiled, she smiled broadly and without hesitation or reserve, although unevenly, a crooked, beaming grin -- the lips pulled back more on one side than on the other. In spite of her plainness, many were tricked into seeing her as brilliantly captivating because of the vehemence of the emotion that flashed upon whomever she was speaking with and assured them that she took more delight in their presence than most people had any suspicion they deserved. It was because of this that many came away from encountering her with a conviction that she was, indeed, beautiful, so interesting a personality -- not because she was such in herself, but that rather she seemed to find others so captivating, apparently so desirable to be with and to listen to, particularly marked by her typical response to someone asking how she was – a non-committal "*Tha mi air mo dhòigh …*" in the FT, with a kind of verbal shrug – "I'm getting along" -- followed quickly by an enthusiastic, "But I want to hear about *you*!" -- her go-to response that she exclaimed with such verve that she gave the impression that she'd been holding her breath all day to do just that.

However, she was a specimen of contrariety. When angered, she flashed an expression of such devastating effect, that it alone often was enough to quell any opposition.

"Ròna!" a boy called out from the field, "I like what I'm seeing."

"Get an eyeful," the red-head responded, "because that's all you're going to get!"

"How can you do that!?!" Maggie rebuked her in a tone that was more shockingly admiring than scandalized, and tugged the collar of her blouse even more tightly shut, as if she herself were exposed just sitting next to her friend.

Ròna grinned in her tilted way. "What?"

"Just show ..." Maggie was at a loss for words. "...*a h-uile rud* – everything."

"Well, I'm not quite showing everything," Ròna grinned, amused at her friend's dismay – which is maybe why she did what she did: She got a charge from provoking reactions, seeing how close to the edge she could get. Going even further, she lifted the edge of her kilt at her friend.

From her angle, Maggie saw what no one else could: It was far-out enough that Ròna insisted on dressing herself in a kilt, which usually only the men and boys wore, but even more shockingly, she had on nothing underneath!

"No ... no ... NO!" Maggie shrieked with a laugh and turned away, holding up her hands as if to shield her eyes from the sight. "*Fòghnaidh na dh'fhòghnas!* – Enough's enough!"

Ròna followed up with a snort of a laugh. "Sure enough, there! They'd be swarming like bulls around a cow in heat if only they knew."

"*A Bhàn-dìa!*" Maggie called out to the Mother Goddess. "You're so bad!"

Ròna didn't deny the accusation – in fact, she might have rather relished the reputation. In a way, perhaps, her brashness was a defense.

Sitting on a stump just a couple blanket lengths from the girls, Cuilean tried hard not to look, although from time to time, his eyes darted furtively to Ròna's blanket on the grass and scuttled guiltily back when she seemed about to turn her head towards him, none of which was lost on her, her eyes wrinkling in amusement at him as if to say, *I caught you looking.*

Out in the field, stepping towards the *mìneotarbh* yearling, Seumas whipped off his shirt with a dramatic flourish. He was larger than the others his age, and broad of shoulder and muscularly thick of waist. His boyishly muscled chest and shoulders drew appreciative calls from the onlookers, half in mocking appreciation.

"Who-a! who-a!"

"*A shoaghail!* – Wow!"

"*A bhalaich ort!* -- You're the guy!"

He pushed his way to the front of the pack of boys. "Let me show you how to do it!" he exclaimed. He sized up a bull yearling that was about as tall as he was, and that was, like him, half-way between calf and full-grown bull.

Maggie, alone, did not gaze upon the young man openly but averted her sight and dipped her head, darting nervous, furtive glances of admiration at him, a gesture not lost on Ròna. With a change in tone, one tinged with curiosity, as innocently as she could manage, Ròna asked, "So, which one of these bulls might you fancy?"

When Maggie said nothing but rather inspected even more intently the pattern in the plaid upon which they were sitting, Ròna tilted her face to peek through her friend's veil, and with a sideways smile, she pressed, "Well?"

Maggie bent her head down even further, as if that were possible – her flaxen hair flopping over her face, hopefully covering her blazing, wistful, wishful blush.

Ròna made a high-pitched "Huh?" as if coaxing a kitten.

"You won't laugh?"

"*A ghràidhean* – Lovey, Of course not."

Maggie flitted a peek around as if to make sure no one else was within hearing range. "Well ..." She caught herself on the verge of saying something perhaps a little too revealing. "*Uill, 's caran smodaig a tha aonar* -- Well, one's kind of cute ." Reluctant to give up the name.

"*Cò* – Who?"

The urge to share what it was she felt so strongly overwhelmed Maggie's shy discretion. *After all, she had to tell somebody. Who better than her dear, trusted friend, Ròna?* She ducked her head and spoke – hardly audibly -- into the sandy-blond hair that fell across her face. "*Do bhràthair* – Your brother."

"Seumas!" Ròna shrieked, unable, despite what she had promised, to contain herself. Even more loudly: "Seumas!" She rocked backwards, her feet up in the air. It was so ridiculous. *Her brother! Her friend. Her best friend. Liked her brother! Her big lump of a lunkhead brother!*

Maggie was on her, frantically attempting to cover her mouth. "*Ist! Dùin do bheul!* -- Quiet! Shut up!"

Ròna forced herself upright and called out across the field, "*A Sheumais!* – Seumas!"

Maggie gathered up the end of the blanket and wrapped the plaid around Ròna's head. The two girls wrestled frantically under the blanket, Ròna screaming a mixture of her brother's name and shrieking in laughter, Maggie frantically seeking to hush her friend.

Ròna squealed in glee: "You like my brother! You like Seumas!"

In the field, Seumas, having become vaguely aware of his name being called, looked over and saw the two girls flailing around on and in the tangled plaid. He arched his brows in a superior, disgusted manner. "Girls!" he snorted in derision and turned back to the more important matter at hand: Wrestling the *mìneotarbh* bull-calf.

He pointed at the young bull and locked his gaze. The yearling lifted its head, its mouth full of grass, and looked placidly at the boy standing defiantly before him.

The creature dipped its attention back to its grazing. It plucked up a mouth-full of luscious greenery, lifted its head again, and gazed ruminatingly at Seumas.

The boy was gesticulating wildly. When that didn't arouse the bull-calf, Seumas strode forward and grappled the animal's horns, attempting to twist its neck and force it down to the ground.

With what seemed like an annoyed shake of its head, the animal tossed Seumas a few feet away where he fell into a pile of manure.

A chorus of laughter rose up from the onlookers – Ròna and Maggie, and a few more girls gathered at the edge of the meadow. Even Cuilean hid a smirk.

Seumas rose red faced, angry. "*Cò nì nas fheàrr!?!*" he shouted out as a challenge tinged with threat. "Who's going to do better!?!"

A general ducking of heads amongst the other boys and a looking away, as if they all had suddenly found much of interest in the sky, or the edge of the woods, or even their *brògan* – their shoes. Their shamefaced countenances betrayed their unwillingness to take up the challenge.

Seumas shifted his gaze from the girls to Cuilean, who was sitting next to them. The problem was that the *truaghan* – the puny weakling -- had been looking over at Ròna and was slow to smother the grin that her exuberant laughter had inspired.

Furious with embarrassment, Seumas yelled a dare at him. "You think you can do better, cat boy?[98] You think it's so funny. Come on. You give it a try."

Cuilean shook his head and spread his hands as if to say, *I didn't say that*, not saying what his smile told, *Just always thought you were full of bullshit. Didn't think you were covered in it, too.*

"Leave him alone," Ròna yelled.

"Shut up!" Seumas barked at his sister.

Seumas was furious with embarrassment, and as the others were his own age and near his own size and not so susceptible to

---

[98] "cat-boy" -- The nickname that had been given to Cuilean not only because of his having been found in a litter of sword-tooth cats but also because – perhaps mainly because -- of the odd three-colored striping of his hair – *dubh, bàn, ruadh* -- black, blond, and red – like the striped fur of the giant sword-toothed cat itself a likeness that reminded them and reinforced the *far-ainm* – the nickname.

threatening, Seumas had resorted to taking it out on the one boy he could bully. "You think it's so funny. You show us what you can do."

His grin dissipating quickly, Cuilean shook his head.

Ròna shouted, "'S e toll tòine a th' annad, a Sheumais -- You're such a shithole, Seumas!"

Which insult only brought a smirk to Seumas's face. Well he knew it, and well he was proud of it. The reminder of it seemed to invigorate him. Seemed to inspire him to double-down on his shithole-ness. He turned back to Cuilean, raised his fist, and shouted a threatening demand: "Get over here!"

"You don't have to do it," Ròna called after him.

Reluctantly, Cuilean stood and stepped into the field. He was quite a bit smaller than Seumas, and thin, with arms no thicker than the drones on a bagpipe.

Seumas grabbed Cuilean's pipe-thin arms and gave the much smaller boy a shove in the direction of the mìneotarbh, who was by this time growing more and more irritated at having been interfered with by these foolish human calves.

From behind Cuilean and over his shoulder, Seumas picked up a clod of hard-packed dirt and threw it full into the animal's face.

With a snort and a bellow, mistaking the source of the assault, the mìneotarbh trotted right at Cuilean.

The animal's approach was so sudden that Cuilean was taken by surprise. He managed to dodge out of the way, fumble-footed.

"A Chuilein! -- Cuilean!" Ròna called out in fear for her friend.

Just missing impaling the boy, the mìneotarbh grazed the Cuilean with his horn and brushed him aside with a side-swipe of his head.

Cuilean was thrown into the boggy mud of the field – much to the delight of the other boys – and only with difficulty did he manage to disentangle himself from the clinging muck and rise to his feet.

The mìneotarbh yearling swiveled and came snorting back at a gallop to finish the job he had begun.

Cuilean shifted his feet, feinted to one side, and dodged totally out of the way by diving in the complete other direction into the mud on the soggy, cow-paddy covered field.

The boys flanking Seumas burst into uproarious laughter at the spectacle of Cuilean standing shin-deep in the boggy muck, dripping with mud and cowshit, looking like some each-uisge – a mythical spirit from the swamp.

The bull, evidently and disappointedly tired of the game so soon, turned his back on Cuilean and returned to browsing in the tall grass.

A change seemed to come over Cuilean. Those close to him could have seen him set his jaw, his eyes narrow, the hair on his head bristle, and one shoulder rise unevenly above the other.

The lad grabbed a handful of mud and pebbles, stepped forward, circled around the animal's front, and threw the soggy mass directly into the bull's face.

The beast gave a deep-throated, angry bellow and hooved the ground.

Cuilean turned and ran away a few steps.

The boy stopped and looked back to make sure that the provocation had been enough to galvanize the bull into launching a full-speed attack.

Ròna shouted a warning from the *cochall a cridhe* – the very heart of her heart. "*A Chuilean! Thoir aire!* -- Cuilean! Watch out!"

With a quick glance at Ròna – too quick to tell whether it was a *watch-this!* invitation, or an *oh-shit!* look -- Cuilean took off at full speed for the trees at the edge of the clearing, the bull hot on his rear-end.

No sound came to the girls from across the field; everything happened before them as if in a pantomime. Ròna's hand floated up, and she held it over her mouth like a stopper as if it were actually, literally, holding her breath in because she did not dare to exhale as even the slightest breath from her would disturb the fragile tenuousness of the moment.

The lad made for the shelter of the trees, which offered the promise of safety as they were too tightly packed to allow the massive bull entry.

If only Cuilean could reach the palisade of the wood!

The mocking of the boys darted after him: "*Ruith air falbh*! –
Run away!" one shouted after the feeling Cuilean.

"*Teich, a ghealtaire!* – Take off, you coward!" another one
taunted.

"*Lag-chùis*! – Chickenheart!" another one derided.

"*Gog gog*! – cluck, cluck!" another one hooted out as a derisive
parting shot.

With a different intent and in a totally different spirit, Ròna
urged, her two hands funneling her voice like a megaphone,
"*Cabhag ort, a Chuilein*! – Hurry, Cuilean!"

But the distance was too great to the trees, and the mìneotarbh
too fast – despite its massive size – and it gained rapidly on the boy.

It didn't look like Cuilean would make the tree line before he
would be trampled from behind – certainly severely, possibly to
death.

This was too much for Ròna. She jumped up with an expletive,
"*Pit air iteig!* -- Flying vagina!"

Suddenly, surprisingly, the slender boy pivoted to face the
onslaught.

He did something really unanticipated.

He charged the bull.

The two – bull and boy -- sped towards each other, their
impending collision set to double the impact.

Just as the bull dipped its head to gore Cuilean, the boy gripped
its horns with both hands.

There was a general stunned silence amongst the onlookers as
the bull ripped upwards with its horns to eviscerate the skinny kid,
but contrary to expectations, the steel-hard horns did not meet
soft, yielding flesh, but rather just air.

Cuilean was flung upwards.

He somersaulted elegantly over the bull's back and planted a
two-point landing on firm ground.

Ròna pumped the air with her fist. "'*S thusa an duine, a
bhalaich!* – You're the man, lad!" she hollered out to him.

Confused by the sudden disappearance of his pursuit, the bull
pulled up short, looked around with angry snorts and grunts. If it
were possible for the beast to look confused, *that* was the
expression on its mug.

Cuilean took the moment's respite from the chase and the
opportunity of the bull's discombobulation to dart into the dark
shadows of the forest.

Searching still for Cuilean, the mìneotarbh swiveled itself
around.

There it saw, directly in front of its beady, near-sighted eyes,
Seumas and his troop of striplings, waving and jeering and hooting.

"You'd better run, *a ghealtaire* – Coward!" Seumas yelled after him, and adding – as he thought, wittily referring to his foundling -- "*A chait sgeunach!* -- Fraidy Cat!"

This witticism called up a new wave of mocking and inventive plays on name calling. "*A chait eagalach-feagalach!* – Scaredy cat!" another boy cried out.

Cuilean was thus figuratively pelted with derision and taunts as he fled.

But paying more attention to mocking Cuilean than to the furious, frustrated beast in front of them, the band of boys only drew attention to themselves.

Having turned around, its attention focused on them, the bull glared at Seumas and his buddies with mayhem in its pee-wee eyes.

It only took the animal a moment to gather its admittedly scant wits.

It hooved the soft turf and planted its feet.

The shift from stock still to a full-on charge took less than an instant.

"*A mhic na seana-galla!* – Sonofabitch!"[99] Seumas shouted as he and the other boys scattered helter-skelter.

The *mìneotarbh* blitzing close behind, Seumas made it to a tree and clawed and clambered his way up into the lower branches, and then into the higher.

The other boys did likewise.

The *mìneotarbh* paced angrily below the treed kids, grunting, hoofing the earth, and tossing its head angrily.

Then with a snort, it settled onto its haunches into what appeared to be a long, patient wait for the boys to climb down.

From the edge of the field, Ròna shouted out to her brother up in the tree. "*Cò an cat eagalach-feagalach an-dràsta!?!* – Who's the fraidy cat, now!?!"

~~

---

[99] *A mhic na seana-galla* – a fun little footnote: Actually more emphatic than merely "sonofabitch" – literally, "son of an **old** bitch!"

My poor little pussy (cat)

(Before the reaping)

Trì rudan a thig gun iarraidh -- Eagal, Eud, 's Gaol.
Three things that come without wanting them – fear,
jealousy, and love.
Proverb from *Leabhar an Leaghaidh Mhòir* —
The Book of the Great Melting

The girl with the red hair – *an nighean ruadh* in the FT -- was
crying over her dead kitten. (Literally *over* it, that is, above it, but
also, *over* it -- that is, on account of it.) And over the overturned
beehive (though not *over* in the literal sense, for that might have
been a bit chancy, the bees being agitated at the moment). And over
her ruined flowerbed. But mostly over her brother Seumas's
mocking laugh and wide grin, which set her teeth on edge and
made her hate him even more than she already did for what he had
done — or had allowed his damned bear-wolf to do.

That's when Cuilean stepped forward from behind her brother.
She hadn't even noticed the smaller, thinner boy through her tears.
Seumas was just her brother, but Cuilean ... well, he was her friend,
a stray cub her father had found in the woods and had brought
home. When he'd first come, he and Ròna had been close, but as
he'd gotten older, he'd grown apart from her and gravitated
towards the other boys until she became just another annoying girl
to him — not quite a mother figure always nagging him to be good,
to be mindful, to be careful (even though she wasn't any of those
things herself) — but a reminder to him not to be like *her*.

Not, ultimately, that it mattered much. After Cuilean had won, if
not the respect, at least the grudging acceptance of the other boys
on the *mìneotarbh* field, Seumas and Cuilean had gone their way,
and Ròna hers.

Cuilean knew Seumas shouldn't be mocking his sister's
distress, and he himself shouldn't be laughing at her, but he was
doing such a poor job of hiding his grin. He didn't mean to be cruel,
but it was just funny, so ridiculous. A bunch of dirt and a few holes.

And an overturned beehive. Nothing to cry about. (*You want something to cry about?* the man used to boozily yell at his mother before Cuilean had come to the home of Ròna's family. *I'll give you something to really cry about!* And a raised hand and a threat of more to come.)

He, Seumas, and a few other boys had been wrestling a half-grown calf – or rather, Seumas had – and no one had noticed that Sgàth, Seumas's bear-wolf, had wandered away. After calling for it repeatedly with no response, they suspected that it'd gotten itself into some mischief – or fun, as the case might be – and the youths had gone looking for it.

It was Cuilean who found the bear-wolf – along with evidence of the trouble it'd gotten himself into.

For her part, Ròna didn't know which was worse -- her overturned beehive, the ruination of her bed of daisies and bluebells and tulips that she'd carefully tended and brought to bloom, her dead kitten, or Cuilean's poorly concealed smirk.

"What's so funny!" Ròna demanded angrily, turning her wrath on him.

The word slipped out before Cuilean realized what he was saying. "You."

Which made her all the more furious. But that wasn't all. As if it weren't enough that this boy, who wasn't that much younger than she was, although he and her brother had precious little to do with her, which had long suited her just fine -- after all they were just *boys* -- but he was laughing at her in her fury and her pain, and on top of that, there was that stupid bear-wolf.

Big, hairy, and no doubt smelly on account of Seamus being notoriously negligent in washing it, or himself, for that matter (though she wasn't about to get close enough to either to find out). The stupid beast stood stupidly in front of her – everything about it was stupid, just as stupid as her stupid brother -- her poor kitten's body limply dangling in the mutt's stupid, smelly maw that reeked of its shit breath, and the stupid beast stupidly wagging its stupid stub of a tail at her as if she should congratulate it for killing the poor, dear thing.

And that Cuilean was standing there with a stupid grin on his face made her hate him even more. Her feelings toward him had been different when her father had first brought him home, having found the toddler out in the snow somewhere. She remembered very clearly, even though she'd been so small herself -- how wet, cold, and plaintively hungry he had been, and how she'd been overwhelmed with compassion and even love for the lost, stray, cold, soaked cub.

But now after all these years, now that she was nearly a woman herself and had little use for such ridiculous creatures as boys, these three had the nerve to come into her little garden and wreak such havoc. But what was most galling was that Cuilean, after all that she had done for him way back when, was just as bad as her stupid, stupid-head brother.

Ròna cried out, "*Mo phiseag!*" It was a *caoin* -- not really a word in Simspeek for it: a wail, a complaint, a sob, a cry of rage, all in one. "My kitten! My kitty! -- *Mo phiseag bhochd!*" The words unintendedly carried the same double meaning in the FT as in Simspeek – *my poor pussy*!

Cuilean's eyes went wide, which he was glad she did not notice (that would have made the situation only worse), but it was the incongruity, the unexpected *double-entendre* of the exclamation which brought home to him the seriousness of her plight.

She reached out and attempted to pull the dead kitten from the jaws of the bear-wolf. "*Thoir dhomh i!* -- Give her to me!" she ordered. But the beast clamped its teeth even more tightly on the cat's body, and baring its fangs around its limp carcass, it issued a low throated growl as a warning. Ròna hesitated and pulled her hand away.

Cuilean advanced to position himself protectively between Sgàth and Ròna. He demanded in a voice that was meant to be deep and intimidating, but broke in the middle as it started off squeaky before he brought it under control and deepened it, "*Tha mi ag iarraidh a piseag*! -- I want her pussy!" The lad was still enough of a boy (for all that that meant) that he couldn't say the word without a smirk, which he concealed by making a scrunched-up face in exaggerated concern and concentration. The subterfuge might not have been totally convincing, as out of the corner of his eye, Cuilean did catch her glaring at him. *Had she heard something in his voice?*

Dilating its nostrils, the bear-wolf smelled something which triggered its fury: the scent, perhaps, of its hereditary enemy, a whiff of *cat* on Cuilean, the same that had been on the kitten it now clenched between its jaws. In an instant, the huge predator dropped the kitten and lunged at the boy.

The attack was so sudden that Cuilean, a skinny youth, his mane of tri-colored hair flopping helter-skelter about his head, yelped in surprise as Sgàth leapt at him, and he stumbled backwards, his eyes closed, thrashing out with weak, chaotic, confused flailings that were more slaps than punches, more swats than blows, and which were ineffectual at best, and which at worst might have further angered the bear-wolf.

Cuilean felt his hand catch in the bear-wolf's maw. The animal clamped down on his wrist and forearm and shook its head as if it were whipping the kitten back and forth, or playing with a toy, or its dinner. Cuilean tried to pull his hand away, but the boy's arm was caught between the beast's jaws, so not being able to extricate his limb, Cuilean – not really thinking about it, but reflexively -- thrust forward as hard as he could deep into the animal's throat.

The bear-wolf ceased its roaring, and in the place of that terrible noise came a gurgling and a gagging.

Cuilean opened his eyes. The bear-wolf was choking on the lad's small hand and retching in its atttempt to disgorge it. As the animal backed away, it pulled the boy to his feet. Cuilean clenched his hand into a fist, and clamped his teeth as well, and the idea flashing upon him that if he couldn't go one way, he might be able to go the other, he propelled himself forward and jammed his fist and arm even farther down the beast's gullet.

Between the bear-wolf's desperate choking was emitted now a desperate yelping, much like that of a puppy being beaten.

Cuilean drove forward until the animal crumpled before him on the ground, and he placed his foot on the side of its head and yanked his now-bloody arm out of its loosened jaws.

The flesh was mangled, and blood streamed from the open wound, but Cuilean felt no pain. Standing over the stricken attacker, he panted exultantly.

Seumas, who hadn't done anything to mitigate the attack on the kitten, nor to respond to the corpse of the cat between his dog's jaws, nor to prevent his bear-wolf from attacking Cuilean, who now tottered, drained of blood before him, at the sight of his bear-wolf gasping for his very life on the ground (or so it seemed), exclaimed, "*Fhiadh-dhuine!* -- Wildling!" addressing Cuilean with one of the boys' usual taunts of the orphaned youngster. "*Dè an donas a tha thu a' dèanamh le mo mhadadh?*" he demanded. "What the hell're you doing with my dog?"

Cuilean faltered before him, blood streaming down his arm and dripping off his finger tips.

Ròna rushed forward, and arching up on her tiptoes, she shouted into Seumas's face (or, more like, up his nostrils, he being that much taller than she was), "What's your damned bear-wolf doing with *us*!?!"

As big as he was, especially in comparison to his little sister, if there was one person who could make Seumas give ground, it was Ròna.

"Get that critter out of here," she yelled at her brother.

"This is stupid!" Seumas declared, and with a kick, he summoned the prostrate bear-wolf in a tone that suggested he was bored with the whole stupid affair. "*Trobhad, a bhalaich.* -- Come on, lad." The animal staggered to its feet and followed Seumas.

"From now on, leave the poor animal alone," he threw over his shoulder at his sister as he left, meaning, of course, his bear-wolf, not the kitten.

It was as if their leaving – her brother and his stupid bear-wolf, or perhaps it was more like, her stupid brother and the bear-wolf (who was, after all, just being the beast that the Mother had intended him to be) -- lifted an oppressive fog from them, but Ròna was little mollified by the time Cuilean turned back to her, smiling awkwardly, placatingly, and extended to her the limp carcass of the dead kitten – soaked in the mixture of his blood and its -- that he cradled in his hands.

Though Cuilean in the adrenaline-charged excitement of the moment didn't realize the extent of his injury, Ròna did. She tore off a strip from her white hemp blouse. This she ripped in half and wiped the wound that ran up his arm from his wrist to the crook of his elbow that the bear-wolf had left. Once the laceration had been wiped clear of blood, it was evident that the damage was superficial. With the other half of the cloth, the girl wrapped Cuilean's forearm.

But if the boy was expecting that to be the end of the matter, or to be rewarded for his efforts and the wound he had suffered rescuing the body of the poor kitten from the jaws of the bear-wolf, he was to learn the painful lesson of the axiom that *cha téid an deagh-ghiomh ás gun pheanas* -- a good deed does not go without punishment.

"What am I supposed to do with that now?" Ròna snarled at him. "She's gone!"

He felt his heart go out of his chest for the poor little creature, a fellow cat, and for the girl to whom he was so strangely and so strongly bonded even though they had spent so much time apart, but he could offer only a blank expression and the simple words, "*Tha mi duilich* – I'm sorry. It's a bad thing that the beast did."

They stood in silence, the dead kitten balanced in Cuilean's hands between them.

"Where?" he asked.

"Where what?" she snapped in return though she was somewhat consoled by his tone.

"Where should we lay your ..." He couldn't say the word – not again. "Where should we lay *her*," he asked, taking a guess at the kitten's sex, "to rest?"

Although it had not been his intention, the question diverted her from her distress and towards the practical: the need to solve a problem. How to set things in order. Set things right.

She heaved a yawning sigh. She cast her glance about the little space of her father's yard that she had claimed for her garden. "*An* siud," she said. "Over there," pointing at a wide-spreading oak. "*Bu toil leatha a bhith a' streap na craoibhe* -- She liked to climb the tree." This was said in a sad, reflective voice, which took on a sharp edge when she added, reminding him that she would not forget so easily. "*Nuair a bha i beò.* -- When she was alive." This last was a reproach, and he felt its sting, though as she was no longer directing her wrath towards him, he felt it on her account, not his – for her, not for himself.

"Okay ..." he said, looking about. "Do you have a ..." In the stress of the moment, he was oddly stymied in his calling up the word. His tongue tangled, his head hiccupped, his mouth muddled, and his brain burped. In short, flummoxed by his desire not to upset this girl, combined with the guilt that he was somehow responsible for doing just that (in spite of it not even being his dog that had wreaked such havoc in her garden), and confounded by not knowing how to remedy her plight, he groped for the word that was embarrassingly common, as common as the dirt the thing would dig in, and so that was all he could manage in the naming of it: "Uh ... a digging thingy?"

If she hadn't been so angry, so bereaved, so ... alright, we'll say it, so mightily, royally pissed off ... she might have been mightily amused. "A digging thingy?" she taunted him, her ire returning to her voice. She needled him further: "*A bheil thu a ciallachadh* -- Do you mean ..." and here she listed off half a dozen possibilities in the FT: "A shovel? A spade? A scoop? A trowel? A spatula? An excavator?" each word being as emphatic as a slap across his face. (This last one was a stretch, as the word didn't really exist but was made up at the moment.)

"*Tha* -- Yes," he confessed, hoping his remorse at her distress was evident enough, and though it had not been *his* bear-wolf that had caused her pain, he was relieved that she was starting to emerge from her pit of despond, even if that meant stepping on him in her climb up and out of that abyss of anger and sorrow. Despite how she had so stingingly flung the words at him, he saw the humor in her tweaking him for his fumble-mouthed response. "All of those," he confirmed with a sheepish, embarassed grin.

"In this whole wide garden," she went on, "might there be a *digging thingy*?" She perversely enjoyed putting special emphasis on the phrase; perhaps, ridiculing him distracted her. "No, there might not be," although he wasn't sure whether she was saying there *might* not be one, but there might, or there definitely wasn't one, and he was about to quiz her on what she meant exactly by her phrasing, but a look into her eyes told him that considering the circumstances, that would probably not be the best question to put to her at the time.

She was glaring at him. Studying him. Scrutinizing him. *What are you going to do now, big boy?*

"That's alright," he offered. "I'll just …" and he made a vague gesture with his hand, the one that wasn't cradling the dead kitten.

She glared as if to say, *You just do that.* Even though he hadn't ventured what he would *just do.*

"*Fuireach an sin*," he said "Stay right there." And he disappeared around the other side of the tree.

Ròna glared so hard as if to bore a hole through the trunk, all the time mournfully cradling her dead kitten. Occasionally, a part of him would appear around the side of the tree, and he'd disappear again.

But there wasn't a moment that she didn't stare piercingly where she guessed he must be, and she, unknowing what he was doing, except for intermittent hints in the form of the sounds of scratching and hewing and once in a while a flight of sawdust or ribbon of wood carving.

Once, he retreated into the shadows of the forest, only to return with his hands full of something – just what, she couldn't make out.

After a quarter clocking of the sun across the sky, Cuilean reappeared to her in full. "*Tha e deiseil* – It's ready," he announced somberly, inviting her with a gentle sweep of his arm and an encouraging nod of his head.

Suspiciously, still cradling the limp body of her precious kitten, she edged around him. What emerged into sight as she rounded the tree came close to overwhelming her.

In the ground was dug a little grave – *leabaidh mu dheireadh*, as it was phrased in the FT, a last bed, a last resting place -- and beside that was a neat pile of stones in a *càrn-cuimhne* – a memorial cairn.

But what was above that was most astounding. For with his *sgian dubh*, Cuilean had etched a crude spiral on the trunk of the tree just above where the kitten would be laid to rest, an insignia that represented the Mother, the triple Goddess -- the maiden, the mother, and the grandmother, and the path through the realms of the labyrinth -- birth, life, and death.

He wasn't particularly religious, but he thought this symbol was appropriate. He had seen it engraved on a pillar in the House of the Sisters, and figured it must mean something – just what, he wasn't sure, since he hadn't paid much attention ... but *something*.

"*Obh, a Chuilean!* – Oh, Cuilean!" Ròna exclaimed in a hushed voice, her eyes watering. The tension in her frame, which had been as taut as a bow about to shoot an arrow, loosened. She became supple, pliant, as she glanced back and forth between Cuilean's handiwork and the boy himself. "*Tha e bòidheach!* – It's beautiful!" she finally was able to say.

He motioned towards the little grave, but Ròna stood transfixed, unmoving, so he stepped to her and gently, slowly lifted the body of the poor little kitten from her hands and carefully laid it in the hole.

With a soft nudging of his hand on her arm, he led Ròna close. He reached down, took her hand, turned it palm up, and poured a handful of earth into it.

It was only then that she came to herself and knew what she was to do. She released the soil to fall on the small body.

Cuilean kneeled in the dirt at the base of the tree, his kilt uncovering his bare knees. He scooped the grave full with the surrounding soil and rearranged the cairn over it.

Yet, Ròna waited expectantly, not quite satisfied, as if the thing they were doing had not been finished.

He stood attentively, with a puzzled, questioning expression while she pressed him with her stare. Cuilean couldn't guess what had been left undone.

Finally, the realization that *boys are so stupid, and apparently, they don't get any smarter when they get older* incited her to speak. "Are you going to *say* something?" she prompted finally.

"I'm sorry?" Half a statement. Half a question. He didn't quite know which would be more appropriate, so he had tried to split the difference.

But no, that didn't quite *do it*.

Composing himself in a respectful attitude, Cuilean tried again, this time summoning up the incantation he'd heard each moon at the *cèilidh* of the People: "From the labyrinth of the Goddess we emerge. Through the labyrinth of life, we grope. To the labyrinth of the Mother, we return. *Beannachd leat, a phiseag bheag.* -- Blessings upon you, little pussy." (He couldn't resist this last play on words, the little joke being, perhaps, the only thing that allowed him to retain his self-possession.)

The expression of gratitude on Ròna's face told him that he'd done the right thing, and he was glad that she hadn't caught his sly levity.

"Well, then," he said.

But still she wasn't done with him. She had other plans than to let him slip away. "What're you going to do about the rest of this mess?" A turn of her head indicated what she was referring to before she swiveled her relentless stare back to him. She was fierce, with a ferocity that matched the wild *ruadh* – red – of her hair, and now that fierceness was turned once again on Cuilean.

"I was just going to start cleaning up. Right now."

Her stone-faced expression told him he had better get to it, right then and there.

And so he did. Using his *sgian dubh* as a make-shift trowel, he first replanted the uprooted flowers where he could. He filled in the holes in their bed and trimmed back the broken branches.

Ròna caught him propping up one poor, fractured thistle that he tried to pass off as whole. She wasn't convinced, but with a pinched, steely frown, she let him get away with the subterfuge.

Finally, when he was done with that, his knees muddy and scuffed, the edges of his kilt soaked and dirty, Cuilean stood and slapped his hands together to shake the dirt off them but also to signify, *all done*!

But not quite.

Ròna glared pointedly in the direction of the fallen beehive around which bees still swarmed in agitation -- and who knew how many more lurked inside, ready to charge out and attack at another disturbance.

At this suggestion, he protested in alarm. "*Ach, cuiridh iad gathan orm!* -- They'll sting me!"

"'*Eil thu eagalach?* — You afraid?" There was a bite and a sting in her taunt, and it wasn't fair of her to put it like that, to present him with such a dilemma, but she knew this, which is why she had done it.

He forced a nonchalant shrug and a shake of the head.

With a quick survey of the site of the tumbled hive, he figured the best and safest way to restore the colony would be to do so quickly -- though not *too* quickly -- and to smoothly lift it in one even motion, and to set it back upon the tree stump where it had been placed before. With a deep breath, he stepped in and gripped the hive, lifting it and swiveling it upright in one motion, and put it back where it belonged.

No sooner did he step away to admire how neatly he had accomplished this restoration, that he was set upon by a host of bees, which now seemed to identify him as the perpetrator of their little world's ruin. Some landed on him, buzzing angrily. And most of these -- which Ròna saw from his starting and flinching -- stung.

With low, restrained groans and grunts and a couple imprecations: "*Tòn air teine!* – Butt on fire!" He slapped here and

288

there. On his shoulder. On his knee. On his hand. On his forehead. On his cheek. On his hand again. He hit himself in the face with the back of his hand to kill the two bees which were stinging him on his face and hand both.

Despite his efforts to swat the bees away – or maybe because of his flailings -- more and more of the angry yellow-and-black imps swarmed him.

Ròna waved her hand towards the loch in the near distance over the wall of her father's yard.

"*Dhan uisge!*" she directed. "Into the water!"

Without a heartbeat passing between her words and his response, Cuilean darted in the direction she'd pointed. Leaping the low wall of her garden in a bound, he dashed across the field, a black and at the same time flashing yellow cloud of angry buzzing pursuing him.

When he reached the shore, he pulled up at the water's edge as suddenly as if he had run into one of the stone walls that Ròna's father had built by piling rock on rock to separate areas of his fields.

The sentinels of the hive swarmed him, buzzing in materteral fury, laying on sting after sting.

Cuilean yelped in pain and swatted vainly in the air and at the spots on his body where he'd been stung – both actions equally futile.

"*A-steach anns an uisge!* – Into the water!" Ròna yelled, just now catching up with him, but stopping short of the swarming cloud.

Cuilean gawked at the water as if over an abyss but didn't move, rooted at the lake edge, swatting and yowling.

"*Amadain!* – Fool!" Ròna snarled under her breath. She hurriedly kicked off her brogs – the soft leather slippers of the people of the Wayp – and whipped off the plaid that wrapped around her waist and shoulders. With a few rapid steps, she charged him and hit him with a full tackle that drove both of them into the water with a sprawl and a flop and a plop, and just as he struggled in a panic to the surface, flailing and clawing wildly like a drowning cat, she drove him farther into deeper water and down beyond the reach of the hooked darts of the attacking sister bees.

When they'd moved enough laterally that she calculated they were removed from the multitude of attackers, she released him and swam to the surface, expecting him to follow.

She burst into the air with a laugh, exultant at their having escaped the furious avenging horde, which were scouring elsewhere in search of the toppler of their little tower of buzzing.

As she waited for Cuilean to come up, when the ripples on the face of the water smoothed to a placid, glassy sheen, and a single air bubble rose to pop softly as it breached the surface, and there was still no sign of him, her satisfaction turned to puzzlement, and then to surprise, and then to concern, and the fear swelled up in her chest, finally forcing a gush of exhalation from her lungs. "*A Chuilean, a charaid*!" came out like a little mouse squeak. Her breath caught in her throat, an involuntary sympathetic echoing of his own loss of breath. There was a hiatus in the beating of her heart, though not one she could discern – just as if the regular *lub-dub, lub-dub, lub-dub* had been replaced for an instant in its beating with *lub-dub ... dub*, before resuming, *lub-dub, lub-dub.*

Diving under the water, she didn't swim like the Children did – flailing their arms about over their heads – but rather she undulated like *an ròn* -- the seal -- after whom she had been named. As she glided through the water, and sought deeper strata, a nictitating membrane fluttered down over each eye to provide a translucent covering which allowed her to see clearly and far-sightedly into the deep void of the lake, and the gills on the inside of her mouth opened, allowing her to osmose oxygen from the water.

At the point where he had disappeared, she saw a faint trail of tiny bubbles rising, which she followed, like the girl in the old tale tracking where her brother was held captive by the evil *each-uisge* – the water-horse monster.

Finally, she saw a floating tuft of hair, *ruadh, 's bàn, 's dubh* -- red, blond, and black – and shot for it like an arrow from her bow. She reached for it but only managed to grasp a strand, which slipped farther away from her. She dove deeper, dart straight and quick.

With the second grab, she gripped a handful of Cuilean's mane, and with a twist of her wrist, she twined it around her hand.

His body was limp and lifeless, all the air having gone out of him.

There in the depth of the water, floating between heaven and the abyss, she pressed her lips to his and blew into his mouth and his lungs the oxygen she was drawing into through the fine gilled slits at the sides of her throat from the water around them.

The first breath, nothing happened.

She released their lips, drew in more, absorbed more oxygen, and again pressed her lips against his, and again blew into his mouth, deeper into his lungs.

Again, nothing.

Once more, she ingurgitated a lungful of oxygen from the depths, and again pressed her mouth on his, pressuring the seal of lips on lips *cho teann ri tòn an ròin* -- as tight as a seal's ass, as the saying went -- and exhaled air again into his mouth, and into the deepest portion of his lungs.

She felt his body quaver.

She secured her hand in the tangle of his long locks, and towing the boy behind her, she headed up.

As soon as she broke into the air, she ferried the limp body to the shore, and there, she lugged it to the beach, where he lay insensate, but breathing faintly.

His eyelids flickered and opened. *"Càit' a bheil mi?* – Where am I?" he asked weakly, sitting up.

"Fuireach an seo," she told him sharply – as if she were irritated that he was causing her so much trouble. She pointed at a tree stump that was caressed by the soft lapping of the toe-high lake waves. "Wait here."

He sat where he was directed. She walked away towards the garden. She returned shortly with a handful of honeycomb. From this she squeezed daubs of honey onto the bee stings.

"A little honey cures everything," Cuilean noted with a rueful smile.

Ròna was not amused. She shoved his arm away. *"Thalla! A-mach às an sin!"* she flared. "Get away from here!"

For a few weeks after that, as the last of the swollen wounds of the bee stings and the scar on his arm healed, he wondered in reflection of Ròna and her poor *piseag*, and his confused, jumbled feelings about her, just as she would occasionally pause by the wide-spread oak tree in her garden to reflect on the engraving of the sign of the Mother and on the kind words he had uttered over the grave of her dear pussycat.

That is, until the memory of his smirking stung her, and that bee-sting of a remembrance made her angry. And that anger prompted the recollection of the pain of her loss of her flowers, of the beehive, of her *piseag*, whose mewing she could sometimes hear calling out to her on the wind.

But more than all these -- there was a word in the FT that described it: *an darna shealladh* -- the second sight, not seeing with the eyes, but perceiving what the eyes cannot see.

She knew from that, from what she had seen and foreseen, that she was not done with Cuilean. She saw him in an entirely different light than she ever had before. It wasn't a feeling as foolish as love at first sight, but even worse, it was a *ro-fhaireachdainn* – a before-feeling -- of their fate and their lives together.

And that made her even angrier.

The reaping itself

Fear nach cuireadh cùl ri caraid no nàmhaid.
A man who wouldn't turn his back on friend or foe.
Proverb from *Leabhar an Leaghaidh Mhòir* —
The Book of the Great Melting

A season or two had passed after the incident in the garden of the murdered *piseag* and the toppled beehive when Ròna and Cuilean ran into each other again.

Ròna and her friends were in the city circle of Trayton, the Corps' trading town at the lip of the cliff and terminus of the road up from the DownBlow. They were raising a bit of a *hòro-gheallaidh*, as they called it between themselves -- to use the FT, a little teenage hullabaloo -- on the street, playing their music, having a bit of a romp. They had laid out an open fiddle case for people to throw money in, though money wasn't the point of it all.

The point was more the fun.

That night, Cuilean, Seumas, and a few of the other boys had meandered into town to see what excitement they could scare up for themselves on an evening off from herding mammoths. Attracted by the sounds of music, they'd drifted towards the town center and to the outskirts of the crowd.

At the center of which, Ròna was singing; Maggie was bowing the fiddle; Sheila was doing her bit on the elbow bagpipe – pumping air through the bag and into the chanter by means of elbow action on the bellows; and Seòras was enthusiastically banging a beat on the bodrum – the shallow, hand-held, tambourine-shaped, deep-thumping drum.

In short, the kids were having a grand, old, street *cèilidh*.

In the middle of the set, looking around the crowd and seeing nothing but friendly faces, Ròna thought the audience would appreciate a traditional song in the FT -- even though technically speaking it was forbidden within the domain of the Monstrato Corps (such as the city of Trayton). She made a signal to the others, and they struck up "*'S iomadh rud a chunna mi*" -- which could be translated as "Many things I have seen." It was a light, humorous, nonsense song, which told the story – if it could be called such – of somebody wandering out through the night and seeing strange sights: cats flying over the top of a neighbor's cottage, fairies dancing in the forest, and a mermaid moonbathing by the sea.

Ròna had just come to the line of the chorus, *"'S iomadh rud a chunna mi a-muigh air feadh na h-oidhche* – Many things have I seen wandering throughout the night"* when the aptrac rounded the corner and blocked the cul-de-sac the performers had taken over for their show.

The small band of musicians stopped playing, though not immediately, the music drifting off in the air, with Maggie leaving off stroking the fiddle and Sheila quitting in mid-pump on the pipes bellow, leaving Ròna to sing a couple notes acappella – what the children of the Mother called *port à beul*, or "mouth music" -- until she realized she had been left dangling in mid-air without any musical support or accompaniment, for when Ròna sang, she typically closed her eyes and lost track of what was in front of her, concentrating instead on what was inside of her, so it took her a moment or two of looking around to see what was going on. Seòras banged on a couple beats longer until Maggie poked him with her fiddle bow.

The aptrac's gangway ramp clanged down, and half-a-dozen PieceTaker Zziippps swarmed out of the armored vehicle. The beefy, hairy giants pushed their way through the onlookers and stood on the lip of the crowd opposite Ròna and her fellow street performers.

It was unclear whether the PieceTakers were on patrol or out on the town themselves and having a bit of the local *bainne na màthar* – milk of the mother, as they called it in the FT -- which was non-existent DownBlow in the Islands of the *Tìr na Smùid* -- the Land of Smoke.

Or, maybe the PieceTakers had been shooting straight Petrale, the concoction they made out of distilled black gowp sludge pumped out of the ground. Or, even more likely, the dim, preternaturally angry ogres were stuffed to the lowbrows with a cocktail of miscellaneous and various ingestible, injectable, and inhalable mind-gnarling substances.

Who knew? Ròna certainly didn't. She was still young and perhaps a little naïve as she'd been raised to be one of the Daughters of the Mother and didn't know anything about such things -- straight off the croft, she was. (Literally -- this being one of her rare excursions into the city from her parents' farm farther up the mountain near the village of Balnabane.)

At the time, she didn't know much about the PieceTaker Guardsmen or about the Corporation's claim to the water reserves

-- though she'd heard her father complain often enough about its charging the people of the mountain for what the Mother gave them for free. She just knew these huge, foreheadless man-trees served as enforcers of the Muluuh Corps, although they were a clueless sort of regulators, scarcely aware of what rules, laws, and codes they were supposed to be enforcing (though sometimes, it seemed, they understood only the *forcing* part of "enforcement").

Sort of like poor cousin Fergus who'd been kicked in the head by one of the hairy mammoth bulls -- and ever since had this look about him, like he was just about to say something really important, but couldn't quite remember what it was he'd wanted to tell, and would become angry with himself for not being able to recollect what just a moment before had seemed so vital to impart, as if he were at a loss to locate something that he'd wanted to share, for which stolen treasure he'd search with increasing suspicion of and anger at everyone he encountered, as if they might have absconded with his precious.

Duine bochd -- Poor man.

That's how the PieceTakers from the smoky lands below seemed to Ròna: to be always angry, ever ready to smash something or someone. To fight or kill. Tiny brained, bitsy-balled, hairy, angry giants. It was the first time she'd seen such a creature up close: a hulking monstrosity of a man-ape; tufts of fur protruding from under its uniform and body armor; a nose half as broad as its face and thick brow ridges that sheltered plate-sized, sunken eyes that glared out like those of the night predator whose name she knew only in the FT – *mathan mòr na coille* – the giant forest bear that the entire village would rush out to drive off when the snow and cold in the upper reaches of the mountains forced their usual prey down into the lower glens, and the fierce predators lumbered down in the shadows to hunt the people's herds during long winter nights, the enormous orbs of their eyes glowing brightly, terrifyingly in the dark.

The twin platters of the PieceTakers' eyes appeared even larger than they were as they seemed to float under the part of their breathing apparatuses that covered the middle of their faces. Her father had told her that the strange creatures needed the breathing masks to filter out the oxygen in the air, replacing it with the smoke and soot of their own Smokey Lands. After every snorting breath in, the creatures would let out a gush of particulate-laden smoke, so they resembled so many walking chimney stacks.

Ròna froze, not knowing what would come next, and one of the PieceTakers grunted, "Go" in its truncated vernacular, its voice squeaking high like an old screen door flapping on creaky hinges.

He flicked its hand at Ròna as if he were motioning a child to continue playing. "Uspela want hear."

She looked to her friends. They exchanged glances of mutual dilemma, *What'll we do?*

"Go," came the insistent squeaky urging again, but this time more of a command, with an undercurrent of a threat. "An' better no FT toktok. Is no-no law."

Ròna gave her friends a nod and signaled them to begin some insipid Simspeek number that was popular at the time about *stay happy ... dance all night ... la la la.*

One of the massive PieceTaker bully boys -- the largest one, with a fierce and scarred visage, the one they called Timo -- pranced into the middle of the tiny band in a comic, mincing dance. To Ròna it seemed as if a mammoth -- hairy, massive, slow, dim, plodding (although not anywhere near as gentle as the hairy pachyderm) -- were trying to trace a delicate pirouette, made all the more ridiculous by its staggering intoxication.

The other PieceTakers thought their friend's attempt to dance in time to the music was funny. The steps and claps were off, and the Zziippp would continually be stopping and bopping and bobble-heading to catch up to the rhythm and restart, only to lose the timing again and again.

But it all appeared to be good natured, so Ròna was relieved, thinking that the Guardsmen were in a good humor, and that aside from the unpleasantness of the palpable tension aroused by their unexpected appearance, everything would end well, but not having had much experience with the man-creatures, she was ignorant of the unspoken mantra of the Zziippp PieceTakers -- *no blood, no fun.*

The hulk danced with its arms curling up in the air and gyrated dervishly, making it a point to swing its hips against each one of the musicians as if it were bouncing off pylons in downhill parkour racing. The Guard-Zziippp was careening wildly and uncontrolledly back and forth, and after about two rounds, its hips smacked Maggie and sent her flying and thudding against the stone wall of the pub and crashing down on top of her fiddle. There was a sickening crunch as fiddle and skull cracked. Blood spewed. But the girl was able to think of only one thing. "My fiddle!" she wailed.

The dancing PieceTaker teetered to a stop like a top winding down.

Ròna had always been a bit *fiadhaich*, as they said in the FT – the words "fierce" or "wild" are as close as can be gotten in Simspeek – which probably came from having been born in the midst of a pack of wildling boys – she had had to learn to fight to survive. She planted herself right in front of the guard who'd knocked poor Sheila for a loop. Ròna arched up to look the Zziippp

PieceTaker in the eye. "What're you going to do about that!" she demanded, pointing at Maggie and the smashed fiddle. The fellow looked at Ròna as surprised as if it had been confronted by a shin-high dump rat.

He brushed Ròna aside -- literally *brushed* with the back of his hand. "Suck mepela ass," it grunted. Which seemed so much like splendid wit to the other PieceTakers that they all laughed, which prompted the Zziippp to follow up with, "Yupela fault."

Which made so little sense that Ròna just stared blankly at him. Which, in turn, he must have taken as her being stunned by his brilliant logic because he followed that piece of repartee with an invocation of PieceTaker authority: "Yupela no be on street!"

The other PieceTakers laughed again. And the one they called Timo turned with a smug nod back to the aptrac.

Being so contemptuously dismissed outraged Ròna, and being laughed at, even more so. She scurried to block the PieceTakers' retreat, which she had about as much a chance of effecting as she would have of impeding a stampede of woolly mammoths.

"You can't walk away from this!" she declared. "Don't you dare turn your back on me!"

The PieceTaker snorted in answer – whether in contempt, amusement, stupefaction, or confusion, it would have been difficult to say -- and no better response occurring to Timo, it swept Ròna up and flung her across its shoulder.

With her hanging like a sack of mushrooms across its back, the Zziipppaei lumbered towards the aptrac.

Recovering from the centrifugal force that had prevented her resistance before, she was now kicking, screaming, and beating it on its back and shoulders, reaching up and around to hit it in the face, but she was too awkwardly hanging upside down to land any effective blow.

The other Guardsmen were tittering in their high-pitched giggles, "Yupela funny!" as Timo strutted back into the midst of them. One after another crowded in to paw the girl.

"Okay, you've had your fun." Somebody shouted from the assemblage of onlookers. "Let the girl go!"

With a fierce chorus of growls, the PieceTaker soldiers turned their yellowed fangs to the crowd and circled their comrade and its captive.

Timo snarled, "Girl blong uspela!"

There were more shouts from the crowd, but no one ventured to block their way as the hairy, cyclopean PieceTakers, circling their fellow and its flailing, screaming catch, pushed as a phalanx back to their aptrac.

Ròna struggled all the harder as they neared the massive vehicle. She'd heard enough urban legends about girls who'd disappeared inside the vehicular fortresses to know that once she was dragged inside, it would be all over for her. But even as she twisted wildly and desperately, screamed, flailed her thin arms and tiny fists, and bent her head up to bite the thick ham of a hand that gripped her, all her struggles had as much effect as if she'd been a mouse in the claws of a sword-tooth tiger.

To Ròna, time seemed to slow. In her desperate casting about for help, she caught sight of her brother Seumas slouching against a wall. She called to him: "*A Sheumais!*" but he responded with just a drunken nod and a woozy wave of his hand as if to say, "*Sin thu –* There you are!" which, given his state, he could only inarticulately mumble.

For Cuilean, everything had happened so quickly, there hadn't been time at first to react, not enough time to process what was transpiring, but now fear erupted in his chest and rose to his gorge – only it was not a fear on his own behalf. There was nothing for him to be afraid of at the moment; rather, it was a fear for Ròna.

Suddenly -- or so it seemed to Ròna, though she couldn't tell, for time itself had seemed to stop as she was locked into this eternal, never-ending struggle -- but so surprising was it that Ròna ceased her fighting. Angling her neck and bending herself to see around the PieceTaker's massive back, she saw Cuilean standing in the way of the hairy brute, blocking the path to the Zziippp's colossal truck -- a monster truck for monster men.

The boy was quivering in terror – like a mouse facing off before a *mìneotarbh*. The dread was palpable and reflected in the distortion it forced upon his body. His shoulder was hunched, one of his eyes bulged strangely (or maybe the other was squinted, it all happened so quickly, she couldn't tell). His strangely tri-colored, tiger-striped hair stood up like a mane on his head.

"Out way, yupela ratshit!" the humongous PieceTaker growled.

But Cuilean was not to be chased off. He was preternaturally thin, as slender as one of the reeds that grew in the shallows of the *Loch na Màthar* – the Lake of the Mother -- and clearly no match for the much larger Zziippp. Besides which, the boy was shivering violently like a blade of grass in a stiff wind. Only clenching his teeth kept them from chattering out loud.

"Put the girl down," the youngster said, trying very hard (and almost succeeding) to keep his pitch in a lower register. The lad's fury was barely contained. As such, a kid trying to summon the tonality of a man, he could hardly control his voice, which quaked and squeaked. His body trembled with rage and stark terror alike.

But there was something in his eyes. A shaking, quivering determination. He planted his feet and refused to move.

All that Ròna could think of -- slung over the PieceTaker's wall-like shoulder like a rabbit dangling by its feet in a trap, mere lengths away from having the door to all future life shut on her -- was the line from an old song -- *gaisgeach las-shuilleach* -- "a fiery-eyed hero."

The massive Zziippp had been taken by surprise. Its face gaped wide for a moment, an instant which Cuilean had allowed to go on for too long to take advantage of any opportunity that might have come to him from an unexpected attack -- not that any strike by the puny boy, even the most unanticipated, would have had even the least effect on the huge Guard-Zziippp.

The Zziippp squinted his enormous eyes as if searching in the dark for an appropriate response. "Uh?" it finally said and stepped forward as if unconcerned by any chance of opposition. Cuilean flinched and half-leapt, half-fell backwards. With a grunt of a chuckle, the beastly Timo strode forward towards the gaping maw of the aptrac.

In his advance, almost as an afterthought, he swept Cuilean before him.

In a disorderly melee, the People of the Wayp who had gathered for the spontaneous street *cèilidh* shouted protests from a safe distance, but no others dared to oppose the monsters of the Monstrato Corps.

The PieceTakers scrambled inside their transport vehicle, and the gangplank swung up and clanged shut. Without regard for any of the people in the street, the giant vehicle lurched through the crowd.

The startling silence that was left in the wake of the music's stop and the aptrac's departure and the scattering of the crowd nudged Seumas awake. He stared about himself stupidly, wondering, *Where'd everyone go?*

In the maw of the monster

Sàthaidh bìd na cuileige sùil an leòmhainn.
A fly's bite will pierce the eye of a lion.
Proverb from Leabhar an Leaghaidh Mhòir —
The Book of the Great Melting

Slung over the PieceTaker's shoulder, straining, arching, and wriggling like a seal struggling to escape from a fishing net, Ròna bounced on the Zziippp's back as it made its way into the aptrac.

Cuilean, on the other hand, was dragged by the heels, his head banging against the metal plates that formed the floor of the vehicle. He arched up to protect his head and at the same time to reach for his *sgian dubh* -- his black knife -- but he couldn't get a grasp on it before the PieceTaker dragging him stopped abruptly and slung him into an open cage.

Before the iron gate slammed shut, the creature flung Ròna in after him, on top of him.

The inside of the aptrac was cavernous, much larger than it would seem from the outside. Heavy steps and loud voices echoed within the metal interior. The incessant noise of engine metal on metal and of grinding and whirling and chugging and pumping nearly drowned out all other sounds. Every step of the PieceTakers across the metal floor reverberated hollowly, but the noise of the interior was so constant and unrelenting -- nearly deafening -- that there was no discerning one step or one voice from another.

In the hold, the smells of the PieceTakers overwhelmed the pair as they slouched against the bars of the pen. The stench was unbearable – that of the unwashed PieceTakers mingled with a strange metallic, oily odor that was exhumed in an acrid, stinging smoke from the burning gowp that billowed up from the engine room. Together these combined in a gag-inducing, noxious atmosphere that was almost impossible to breathe as the air burned their nostrils and clogged their lungs.

Strangely, the Zziippp PieceTakers seemed to like the reek, for immediately upon entering the aptrac, they had whipped off their breathing masks, letting them dangle loosely below their chins.

The interior of the vehicle was as dark as a starless, moonless, midnight forest. The only lighting was from the occasional flicker through cracks in the exterior wall or glimmers from what might have been control panels along the sides.

The pair of captives squinted to make out the shadowy forms of the creatures peering into the cage, their huge eyes catching and reflecting what little light there was, so the softly luminous orbs floated above glowing leers that hung unsuspended below them. From these formless shadows occasionally emitted a chortling that made Ròna shrink back, though she couldn't identify exactly why, except that it made her feel as if she were lying on the forest floor and innumerable shadow spirits were peering at her out of the penumbra of darkness.

"*Dè tha iad ag iarraidh?* -- What do they want?" Ròna whispered to Cuilean in the FT – keeping her voice low though the PieceTakers wouldn't have understood her even if they had heard her clearly.

"*Chan eil fhios 'm,*" Cuilean said. "I don't know." Though he was full of apprehension - but not for himself, which was an unusual experience for him. Huddled in the unrelenting, steel cage, when he thought of his own prospects – what might happen to him, he felt nothing, even though normally, he was afraid of everything. He was afraid of the other boys, their taunting him, their laughing at him, their noticing him, and their ignoring him. He was afraid of the girls mocking him. He was afraid of the shadows in the forest, those that moved and those that didn't. He was afraid of the gentlest mammoths, and the fiercest *mìneotarbhs*. Everything made him start and quiver, but now nothing mattered to him. He felt no fear for his own sake, even for his own safety.

But for hers.

He breathed hard and quick, alert to every possibility of danger to her and hurt to her, though at his age, he didn't fully conceptualize what that harm might be. Nevertheless, though he felt it would be presumptuous to put his arm around her, he slid closer to her, and though he could not stand in the low confines of the cage in which they found themselves, he crouched protectively between her and the gate, his hand poised above his *sgian dubh*.

There was a sudden rumbling, and the massive vehicle lurched. Perched on his haunches, Cuilean steadied himself and, in the process, bumped against Ròna. "*Duilich,*" he apologized, hoping she would not think he had purposely touched her.

She shrugged away his apology. "*Na dragh ort* -- No worry on you."

It was her saying that which made him wish he hadn't pulled away so quickly. Touching her comforted him, perhaps even more than it heartened her.

They could feel the transport moving unevenly over the rough surface of the town -- over the cobblestone streets, probably up over curbs and benches, anything that would offer to impede it (but didn't, couldn't). The giant vehicle rolled on, the massive wheels grinding somewhere below them. There was a sound of something turning -- something besides the wheels and the treads which encased them.

What the two didn't realize was that below them in the engine room, alongside the furnace crew of PieceTakers shoveling gowp into the smoldering furnace was another crew laboring around a spoked wheel that the Zziippp engine squad pushed unceasingly, powering the circular gear that drove the aptrac.

As they became used to the rumbling, the noise, and the stench, and their eyes became accustomed to the dark, they noticed movements in the shadows around them, and a low moaning, a whimpering. In the darkness, Ròna made out a shadow of a small figure through the wire cage mesh.

"*Cuidich mi,*" a tiny voice mewled. "Help me." It was a little boy -- obviously one of the people of the Mother, for he spoke in the FT.

Cuilean was startled by the figure. "*Cò sin?*" he demanded. "Who's there!"

It wasn't just the one child. Ròna and Cuilean became aware of others. Others like them -- children of the Mother who were huddled in row after row of cages, like the one they were locked in, each cage containing small figures like penned-in chickens, each

cage like the one holding the small boy, or like the coop holding themselves.

The harshness of Cuilean's demand had silenced the child. He stifled his whimper with a sob.

"*Socair ort, a ghràidh,*" Ròna reassured the little one in the FT. "Easy, love. Don't be afraid." She asked into the shadows, "*Cò thusa?* -- Who're you?"

The child moved closer to press against the thick wire mesh separating them. A voice came back in a heart-touching, puppy whine. "'*S mise Gillebrìde* – I'm Gilbert." And the little boy, who couldn't have been more than four-years-old, moved towards her.

This exchange set off a cascade of pleas from other children -- from the sound of the voices, they were all children – although nothing could be seen clearly except for diminutive, shadowy forms. "*Cuidich. Cuidich. Cuidich sinn*! -- Help. Help. Help us!" came the pleading.

There was a rustling as row after row of children pressed forward against the wire meshes of their cages, as if, however far away they were held, they experienced some solace from being that much closer to Ròna and Cuilean -- who, although they were yet children themselves, were still older, closer to their parents' ages, and represented some safety and security, however illusionary that feeling was.

Speaking lowly in the FT so as not to be heard – though there was little chance of that, considering the ceaseless pounding and grinding of the engines below them and the stomping of boot-steps and clamor of voices echoing within the maw of the monster that had swallowed them -- Ròna and Cuilean quickly gleaned the gist of what had happened.

Like they had been, these others had been swept up in various raids. Gillebrìde next to them had been foraging for mushrooms with his older sister in the forest when suddenly a marauding party of PieceTakers had swept upon them. Being older and more agile, the sister had managed to escape, but he had gotten his feet caught in the web of undergrowth on the forest floor, and his little legs had tangled up beneath him, and he had fallen and so been snatched up by the child reapers.

The others had similar stories. They'd been separated from their older siblings or parents and hauled into the aptrac -- why or for what purpose, they had no idea.

The vehicle rumbled on, and the children lost track of time. They knew not whether it was day or night. It could have been one hour or ten hours. Some of the children sobbed in hushed puppy whines in their distress of not knowing what was to become of them, or in their fears of what they imagined. They might have cried even more loudly had they known. Some whimpered that they were hungry or cold or lonely or wanting their mommies.

They poked their fingers through the wire meshing for a comforting touch from the older kids. Ròna and Cuilean held their fingers, and Ròna sang a song -- a random assortment of words and ideas that came to her -- to soothe the little ones:

> Bi sèimh, a luaidh, a ghràidh.
> Fuireach ciùin 's sàmhach.
> 'S bidh sinn gu luath an àite sàbhailte.

Be calm, my darling, my love.
Stay calm and quiet.
We'll soon be in a safe place.

It wasn't the words or their meaning, *per se*, that calmed the children, but rather Ròna's soft, lilting voice, which for a moment, at least, soothed them of the terror of their situation.

But all that was put to a halt when suddenly the rumbling over the rough ground stopped, the noise from the engines dampened, and the deafening silence caused the children to stifle their crying in their throats in rabbity panic.

A reverberation of clattering and thumping and stomping of boots shook the steel plates of the floor. The children saw a flurry of action around the outside of the cages in which they were imprisoned, and the cage doors were flung open so roughly and suddenly that they banged harshly with a succession of loud clatters.

A shadow darkened the opening to Ròna and Cuilean's cage and emitted a squeak -- as often as Ròna heard it, she could never get used to the incongruity, it being as if one of her father's mammoths squawked like an angry chicken.

"Youpela out!"

The children in the other cages were similarly being driven.

Ròna, staying close to Cuilean, pressed herself against the gate-jam to stay as far away from the Zziippp as possible.

Immediately upon being released, a little boy who'd been in the next cage rushed to her and clutched her desperately, clinging to her like a small monkey onto a tree branch in a flood.

Again, the squeaking command: "Youpela go!"

Ròna, Cuilean, the child clinging to her, and the others made their way in a huddle to the now-opening gangplank.

They were apparently being herded like so many sheep towards a pen that was enclosed with a high, razor-wire fence.

Through the mouth out of the cavernous interior, Cuilean glimpsed an open field and beyond that, trees.

The creature tugged Ròna's arm. "No, youpela stay." There was a chortling behind the Zziippp as it peeled tiny Gillebrìde away from her and heaved the child towards the corral like an unwanted piece of trash.

Ròna raised her voice in protest. "*Chan urrainn dhut ...* You can't ..." It was not even certain what she said or was beginning to say before the PieceTaker clobbered her across the face and sent her sprawling.

"No tok!" The beast-man grabbed Ròna by the hair and yanked

her up. "All go!" it squeaked to everyone else.

While the children slunk towards the gangplank, Cuilean stood rooted in his place. The Zziippp yipped. "Youpela go!"

Cuilean took a step backwards, and the guard advanced.

This time Cuilean knew what to expect, for when the Monstrato monster stepped forward again and reached out to strike Cuilean, the boy wasn't there. The outstretched arm of the PieceTaker was the lad's signal and his advantage. Perhaps, it was because the Guard was distracted by Ròna's struggling against his ham-hand tangled in her hair, or by her scratching and biting his fingers, or perhaps it was the smoothness and alacrity with which Cuilean executed the *mìneotarbh*-bull leap -- so often practiced by the boys of the Mother -- but whichever it was, bracing upon the outstretched arm, Cuilean leaped high, and parkouring off the Guardsman's shoulder, he flipped in mid-air and dove straight down the Zziippp's back.

Half-way down, Cuilean gripped tightly around the Guard's waist. The sudden weight placed so awkwardly and unexpectedly unbalanced the Zziippp and toppled it onto its butt.

Rolling into the landing, Cuilean spun to his feet.

Bewildered -- with much the same expression as that of a mammoth bull when an accomplished bull-leaper executed a ball-tap -- the PieceTaker looked up at Cuilean looming above him.

The boy's fingers slipped the *sgian dubh* from its sheath just below his knee. With a deft stab, Cuilean plunged the dagger into the Zziippp's throat.

As if realizing only then what had happened, the creature fell to gasping hard and coughing desperately as it tried to splutter breaths of air through the greenish-blue blood that was spurting from the wound and gurgling out its mouth.

It squealed as best it could -- really more of a burble -- a shrill wail of distress.

"*Ruith!*" Cuilean commanded Ròna and the others. "*Ruithibh! --* Run!"

The entire skirmish had taken place so quickly that none of the other Monstrato Guards knew what had happened until Ròna, Cuilean, and the children burst out of the aptrac and were dashing down the gangplank and heading towards the trees.

A few of the Zziippps stepped forward to stop the rush of escapees, but they moved so clumsily that the children dodged out of their way.

Cuilean cut down one of the Guards with his green-blue blood-dripping dagger.

Several of the PieceTakers swarmed to their stricken fellow, and as it shrieked in panic, holding its throat, its comrades joined in with their own shrill cries of fear and outrage. In their growing alarm, they set up whooping in rapid, short bursts, sounding very much like a troop of the gigantic apes - - *na h-apaichean mòra* in the FT -- that lived in the thick mountain forests above the village of Balnabane, beyond the farms in the far reaches of the Wayp that had not been colonized or hardly even explored in the ages since the land had first been colonized.

The stricken Guard, cupping its gashed throat, gasping for breath in between shrieks of outrage, and spitting out bloody blue-green sputum, screeched angry commands to stop the captives from escaping. "Get 'em-pela! Get 'em-pela!"

But the children had already disappeared into the trees past the reaping corral of the Monstrato PieceTakers.

Into the woods and across the water

Bheir eu-dòchas air luch ionnsaigh a thoirt air leòmhann.
Desperation will make a mouse attack a lion.
Proverb from *Leabhar an Leaghaidh Mhòir* —
The Book of the Great Melting

The children fled through the forest. Above them hung the
deep span of sky, which arched over the tree tops. A cloud floated
across the opening far above and passed before the moon, though
they felt no breeze where they were, where the leaves on the trees
hung perfectly still, a quietude in startling contrast to the desperate
panic here far below.

Behind them, the children could hear crashing in the forest and
the wild yelps and howls and hoots of the hairy man-beasts. It was
as if the creatures were as excited by the prospect of the chase as
by their anger at having lost their captives.

Of all the cries of rage that the children might ever have heard
or might ever have imagined in their most horrifying nightmares,
none were so terrible as now emanated from the throng of
pursuing PieceTakers – outraged that one of their number had
been slain and even more so that their prize reapings were
escaping from them. They shouted at each other to catch the
children who fled, arguing amongst themselves what to do with
them once they were snared.

In this running debate, one cried to kill them all. Another
shouted to kill the murderer who had slain their friend and to just
whip the other children. Another shouted that whipping and killing
were too easy; they should all be tortured to death.

The PieceTakers – heavy, plodding creatures that they were
even in the best of conditions, such as in the hard-packed barren
lands of the DownBlow – could not move stealthily. The Zziippp-
heads sloshed through water, were confronted and confounded by
trees, ran straight into branches, got snagged in brambles, fought
their way through bushes, and got their feet tangled in underbrush
that tripped them up and slowed them down. They screamed in
rage as they were caught in shrubs and undergrowth they did not

know how to navigate as if they were completely mystified by the concept of following trails.

One Zziippp PieceTaker ran into a shrub, fought his way through it, only to hit another bush. The trail was on his flank, but he seemed to be totally ignorant of its use or purpose. They shouted curses at the forest, at the branches that impeded them, at the undergrowth that tripped them, at the whole damned, damnable Wayp and its profusion of life that seemed designed and intended to thwart and torment them (so unlike the tamed and civilized natural world they'd left behind, whose surface was entirely paved and gowp-topped).

The children felt the terror of hunted prey, of gracile red deer fleeing a pack of howling bear-wolves, perhaps even more terrified by the shouts and the threats and the voicing of hatred than the actual prospect of being harmed.

Cuilean, especially, felt the resurgence of the long-ago, gasping terror. That primal panic that had strangled him when he had run out into the snow bank. Only this time there was no suckling mother tiger to protect him, to succor him until he was to be scooped up by friendly arms.

So burning was the white-hot fear that enflamed him, that he had to restrain himself from overtaking the little ones, trampling them, and outpacing even Ròna: all to go where, he didn't know – just away from here, as fast as he could run.

Ròna led the way, clear-sighted in the shadows of the night forest, and it was all that Cuilean could do to keep himself from overtaking her. At the back of the children, he pressed them forward while he hung behind. Whispering loudly in the FT, he urged them, "*Cabhag oirbh!* -- Hurry up!"

A little one fell in front of him, and Cuilean scooped her up and grabbed the hand of another child and so carried one and towed the other. Up ahead, Cuilean saw that Ròna, too, had picked up a child -- it might have been the one she was singing to in the cage, or maybe not, he wasn't able to tell who or which one.

They ran on, in a seemingly never-ending flight in an interminable nightmare.

Ròna directed them into denser and denser parts of the woods, figuring that the PieceTakers, much larger than any of the children, would be slowed, squeezing through the closely-pressed trees.

The spaces between the thickly-growing trunks grew narrower and narrower. The smaller children were able to dash right through, but Cuilean, even with his preternatural thinness had to turn sideways and snake through the maze like a winding eel.

The Zziippps were still behind them -- though at a greater distance now. The children heard the man-beasts fighting with the trees, attempting to knock them over, and shouts of dismay as the forest seemed to wall off their great bulk.

As quickly as the kids ran, or tried to run, they advanced slowly – all too slowly, it seemed to Cuilean.

Ròna came to a pause in a clearing to allow them all to regroup and the stragglers to catch up.

Peeking through the opening in the forest canopy above them, in the otherwise black night sky, the moon hung like a flaming torch.

Ròna cocked her head and listened. Partly because of the children's greater speed (as slow as it had seemed), and perhaps even more because the Zziippp pursuers had lost the track of their prey in the darkness and had veered off in the wrong direction, the volume of their whoops and howls and hoots were growing gradually fainter and fainter, more and more remote, and their shouts and curses and thrashings and crashings and breakings and wreckings were subsiding in the distance.

"*Tha mi sgìth*," Ròna said -- not so much a complaint as noting a fact. "I'm tired. And the little ones must be even more so. *Sguireamaid*. -- Let's stop."

There was a bower – an overarching of low-hanging branches that formed a sheltering cove. "We can rest here," Cuilean said. "*Bidh sinn sàbhailte airson greis* – We'll be safe for a little while."

Truth be told the boy was tired, too, more tired than he had realized. They'd been going for a long time. When they'd started, the moon had been almost directly overhead, and now it was sinking behind the trees on the far hill, and even besides the length of time that had passed, the stress and the strain of their captivity in the aptrac and the pursuit of the beast-men were enough to totally exhaust him.

The children threw themselves on the ground, clustering around Ròna and Cuilean. He did a count: there were six children. A couple he recognized: little Murdo Macdonald and Alex Cummings; three girls he might have seen around -- maybe they were sisters of his own friends, but he wasn't sure. And of course, there was Gillebrìde, the little one they'd encountered in the holding cage.

Cuilean sat down against a log, but when one of the little girls whined, "*Tha mi fuar* -- I'm cold," the older boy scooted over, and they huddled close for warmth. He wrapped the end of his shoulder plaid around her. She burrowed into his side, and they curled together like puppies.

Ròna was both frightened and confused herself. Frightened naturally enough by the circumstances they found themselves in. And confused by both those circumstances -- she could only vaguely figure out what exactly was happening; though actually, well she knew the *what*, it was just the *why* or *how* or *in what world* such a thing could happen that human beings could be put in cages when they – the Children of the Mother -- hardly ever put even animals in cages (and then, only for their own good).

And confused by Cuilean himself. He seemed totally different from the person she had long known. Did people change so completely, so quickly? Or was he the same boy, but she was just seeing another side of him?

Truth be told, she didn't know what to think. This was Seumas' friend who had been there when her brother's bear-dog had so brutally murdered her *piseag* and over-toppled her beehive. For this, she'd held a stone in her heart for him, partly blaming him for what her brother and his stupid bear-dog had done.

Though it was true that afterwards, he'd helped her.

But after *that*, he'd run away like a *gealtaire* – a coward – from a bunch of harmless honey bees!

But now he'd put himself in danger for her. And what danger, too! When her own brother... She would have been at a loss for words to explain it. Except, maybe, there was that expression in the FT that fit: *Cha toireadh e cas an déidh na té eile air a son* -- her own brother, when she was being dragged away by those monster-men, wouldn't put one foot in front of another for her.

But this one could have died trying to help her ... and still might.

Was this the same boy whom all the other kids called *cat eagalach-feagalach* – "Fraidy cat"?

What was she supposed to make of all this?

Whatever it was, she concluded, at least for now, she and the little ones gathered around her depended on him, as he depended on her. They depended on each other.

They had run into the night as long and as hard as they could, so hard and so fast that their pursuers had failed to overtake them, although weariness had. And even if Ròna and Cuilean might well have been able to continue by themselves, the children could not.

They were all so overwhelmed by the adrenaline rush and the sudden letdown at the withdrawal in its aftermath that they crashed into a deep sleep.

The next thing Cuilean knew, he was awakened by filtered light striking his face and by the loud cawing of a raven on a branch above him. The large black fowl flapped its wings angrily. Cuilean felt it was as if the bird were scolding him for falling into a slumber, and by his negligence, putting not only himself but also the girl and the children in danger, despite knowing how perilous – how deadly – sleep might be.

In a panicky moment, Cuilean looked around frantically, anticipating the PieceTaker beast-men to come breaking through the dense thicket. But there was no movement. He listened carefully, and there was no sound besides the rustle of wind through the leaves of the trees, the chattering of an irritated squirrel, and above him the cheeting and pipping of a black-capped sparrow.

On the branches of a nearby tree, an irritated bluejay (at least it sounded irritated – but they always did, that was just their nature) squawked at the intruders.

But then, he heard the faint sound filtering through this peaceful respite: that of their pursuers in the distance coming closer. They must have circled back, following now the road not taken before, or perhaps somehow had picked up the children's trail.

What's more, overhead floated a spy dirigible – floating black and big bellied above the tree tops, its blades whirling, and its rear end farting smoke. He felt a stab of apprehension that it might already have caught sight of them.

After his fright subsided, he realized that Ròna was curled up next to him, that his arm was wrapped around her and hers around him. He gently extracted his numb limb, which had fallen asleep from the pressure of her head on it.

Aroused from her lethargy, Ròna was not unaware of his moving away as she stepped through the process of awakening. First forgetting where she was, she drowsily followed him with her eyes, trying in her half-sleep to decipher from his posture, the movement of his body, his manner of walking, what to think of him -- just before the memory of the terror of the chase flashed upon her.

She started upright with a gasping "What!" Probably exclaiming too loudly.

"*Ist* – Shh," he said as he took a few steps in the direction of the sounds made by their chasers, as if those steps would put him closer, and being closer, he'd be better able to hear. He concentrated.

"We have to hurry," he said, turning back.

"Where're we going?"

He made an *I-don't-know* gesture. "Get the little ones up. I'll check ahead."

And just like that, he was away. He wasn't sure where he was going, but he jogged in the same direction they had been fleeing a short time before.

Having forged through the forest a short distance from where they had paused their flight, Cuilean came to a sudden, horrified stop. With the cacophony of their hunters coming up ever more closely behind them, he faced the worst thing he could have imagined.

Well, if not the worst – that being the PieceTakers themselves – then, the next worst: an impassable obstacle, an arm of the Lake of the Mother.

The wood had opened up upon a small patch of sand and opposite that the shallow beach of a river swollen with rushing water, it being the time of the spring floods caused by the snow melting up the mountain.

Their chasers were nearing. For the children – including Ròna and Cuilean, who, afterall, were still essentially *kids themselves* -- there were only three ways to go: across the water, laterally along the shore, or back. The first one, for Cuilean, seemed impossible, and the other two would be disasterous as they would be cut off and retaken.

Having woken the others and rejecting the suggestion that she wait helplessly for Cuilean's return, Ròna gathered the youngsters to follow where he had gone. Children are quick to trust, quick to make friends, quick to love, and so was it with the sudden faith that they had imbued in the older girl – who to them was such a grown-up, such an adult, and as such, a protector. She successively touched them awake, saying, "*Bith sàmhach* – Be quite. *Tiugainnibh.* --* All of you, come on."

And they did what she bid.

Coming upon the beach, with the children huddled close around her, Ròna found Cuilean standing flummoxed on the shore. "*Dè tha ceàrr?* – What's wrong?" she asked.

He held out his hand, not putting his sense of helplessness into words but communicating it clearly, nevertheless, as if to say, *We can't go any farther. We're trapped.*

Ròna argued: "When we get across, we'll be safe. *Cha bhi na fuamhairean molach a' snàmh* -- The hairy giants," he said, referring to the PieceTakers, "don't swim."

If you had asked her, she wouldn't have been able to tell you how she knew that. It was just common knowledge, she would have guessed: *Everybody knew it.* Not only did the PieceTakers not swim, they feared water -- probably because the seas surrounding the desert islands of the Archipelagos were so acidic that they scalded the skin and burned the eyes.

"But how do we get across?" Cuilean asked. He was like a drowning man grasping at floating sticks and twigs to keep himself afloat. In reality, he was grasping at some excuse not to have to enter the river, for like the Zziippps, he himself was averse to water although for a different reason. Afterall, he was *Cuilean mac Tìgeir* – Cuilean, son of the tiger, *Cuilean nan cat* -- Cuilean of the cats. And like all cats, he hated water on principle.

"The water's too fierce for the little ones," he equivocated. "Maybe we could find a bridge."

Ròna surveyed the rushing torrent in befuddlement. It could easily be seen there was no such structure.

"A ford, then." Cuilean suggested, hoping for a shallower, calmer place to wade across. He wouldn't have minded so much if the water were only ankle deep.

"*Seo againn,*" she said, with growing exasperation. "This is what we've got."

"Or, we could get something to float on." he ventured.

Ròna's impatience had risen to a level that she was about to burst with it.

On the wind, the sound of PieceTaker chattering came to them, growing closer and closer. Soon the Monstrato guards would be upon them.

To her nonplussed expression, he mansplained. "A raft or something."

"What're you talking about?"

He was starting to think she was dense. Why didn't she *get* it?

"*Càit' an ifrinn an geibheamaid bàta?* – Where in the hell would we get a boat?" she exclaimed. "It's not that far. We'll swim across."

"We can't swim all that way," he protested.

Finally, Ròna understood what he wouldn't say. The remembrance came to her. "*Nach urrainn dhut snàmh?*" she asked. "Can't you swim?"

"Of course, I can," he responded defensively, "but ..."

There was something about the ellipsis, the pause that made her examine him closely.

"*Ach chan eil mi math air* – But I'm just not good at it."

"That's it!" In spite of their straits, the thought brought a smile to her face. "You're like a cat ... you can't swim!" The eye-roll: *Why didn't he say so? Boys! Why couldn't they just fess up? It would make things so much easier.* She followed this with a rough guffaw. She didn't mean to be *mocking*, it was just that the absurdity of his prideful face saving -- now, of all possible times -- made her laugh in spite of the circumstances.

Before he could say anything else, she had already plopped herself down onto the rough sand and was taking off her leather *brògan* – the soft-soled, wrap-around slippers that the people of the mountains wore.

When he saw she was having trouble untying the laces – in her hurry and her fear, her fingers were trembling -- he bent down and dug his fingernails into the tight loops and pulled them apart. He partially unlaced the slipper and pulled it off and finishing the job, pulled her sock off after it. She was already untying the other shoe, when she caught him staring at her foot.

"What're you looking at?"

"Tha do chas mar phliùt ròin!" he blurted out. "Your foot's like a seal flipper!" Though he would have been less blunt if he had spent more time with people and less with the mammoths he herded for her father, and this wasn't really the time to be launching into this topic of conversation.

"They've always been like that!" she said too loudly, too defensively, although actually, her response didn't make much sense. Self-consciously, she jerked her foot out of his grasp and tucked her feet under her haunches.

"Well, I've never seen them."

"There's a lot of stuff you've never seen," she snapped back. And pushing herself upright, she added, "And never going to." She unfastened her hemp blouse, tossing it onto the ground next to her, and unwrapped the kilt from around her waist and dropped it around her feet.

"What're you doing!" Cuilean exclaimed with a startled glance at her nakedness and an embarrassed look-away.

"Maybe you don't know about swimming," she snapped, "but I can't swim in *those*. They'll just weigh me down, especially if I'm hauling the kids."

"Come on," she told the children.

"An fhaod sinn ar rùsgadh fhèin cuideachd?" Murdo asked, so excited by the prospect of going skinny-dipping that he forgot the peril they were in. "Do we have to get naked too!"

"Just take off your shoes." Cuilean told him. "That'll be enough." *Won't it?* he asked Ròna wordlessly with questioningly lifted brows.

"That'll be fine," she said, talking past him to the children. "Just your shoes," adding a jibe for Cuilean's benefit, "unless the sight of their toes is going to freak you out."

"Bidh sin ceart gu leòr," he said with a wincing smile. "That'll be alright."

315

Without a further word, she scooped up two of the littlest ones. "*Greim teann,*" she told them. "Hold tight." She dove into the water – relieved at finding a path to their escape, of course, but also to get away from Cuilean's astonished expression, which had lingered too long for her comfort.

With undulating, seal-like movements, she cut through the turbulent water and made for the far shore, sometimes diving under and sometimes coming up to the surface, the children riding on her back.

Ròna made the opposite bank, dropped the children off, and gave them a quick push towards the trees. "*Falaichibh an sin,*" she told them -- "Hide there," and swiveled immediately back into the water.

Cuilean lost sight of her as she vanished under the surface of the lake, but as he was searching the distant shore, she popped up in front of him.

She gathered up two more children who were whimpering in the sand, quivering in fear.

As soon as Ròna had disappeared into the waves again, Cuilean heard the tracking drroaens[100] overhead, their helicopter blades *whoop, whoop, whooping* towards them over the tree tops. It seemed an interminable length of time for Ròna to make it across the water. Perhaps, he thought, he should have attempted the

---

[100] drroaen -- Dirigible Remote Reconnaisance, Observation, (and) Annihilation Engine: A dirigible, usually designed with a distinctive red under-belly and with a jet-black back, wings, and propellers.

swim. He tried to wipe that idea from his mind. Logically, he knew he wouldn't have been able to manage the rough current, yet he still felt guilty that he had come up short.

But by now, she was heading back. Cuilean gathered the two remaining children and scanned the tossing waves for a sign of her. She was nowhere to be seen.

Cuilean shifted the girl to a seat astride his slender shoulders, which thrilled the child out of her worry. *She was so high up!* He held the boy under one arm, but the kid wasn't happy about that, what with the water hitting him in the face. His yelps of complaint and protest were intermittently drowned out by surging waves, but with one arm freed, Cuilean was able to half-wade, half-dog paddle through the rushing flood.

By the time he'd made it to the hip-high shallows, Ròna had popped up in front of him. Cuilean passed the boy to her and was slinging the girl off his shoulder to hand her off, when they heard the crashing of brush and the yips of the Zziippps at the tree line.

As Ròna grabbed the child, she nodded towards a large piece of driftwood, a fallen tree trunk that was planted in the sand at the water's edge. "*Falaich an sin* – Hide there," she said. Her final words were drowned in the water as she dove away with her precious cargo. "*Tillidh mi 's gheibh mi thu!* -- I'll come back and get you!"

Coming up on the other side of the water, and dropping the two last children in the sand, she told them with urgency, "*Ruithibh a-steach anns a' choille!* – Run into the woods!"

No sooner had she done that, but she turned and dove into the water and swam hurriedly towards the opposite shore.

The Zziippp PieceTakers streamed out of the woods and across the beach. Apparently, they hadn't seen Cuilean yet, perhaps because their attention was diverted by the sight of Ròna slipping through the water towards them and the children retreating into the cover of the forest.

One pointed, and several others gesticulated, and they all set about with peeping and squeaking in Toktok. The Zziippps made for the shoreline, and apparently, unknown to themselves, straight for the tree trunk Cuilean was crouching behind.

With her undulating swimming -- breaking the surface and diving down again – Ròna breached the turbulent waves and saw this. She murmured to herself, beseeching him, "Do what you know how to do, *a Chuilein*," and dove under the water, doubling her effort.

But the next time she came up, he hadn't moved, and driven by her anxiousness and her fear for him, she cried out, "*Ruith air falbh!* – Run away!" before she went under again.

Alerted by her call, the Zziippp chasers saw the movement in the water. Pointing excitedly at Ròna coursing through the waves, they shouted to one another and pressed to the bank.

Crouching low and hiding within the branches of the fallen tree, peeking out at the Zziippp chasers, Cuilean was startled to see his pursuers moving in a direction away from him and was alarmed to see them now hovering at the water's edge, and at the same time, loading their kabloeys and firing into the lake at Ròna.

Cuilean jumped up with a yowl and rushed to attack the attackers. He roared terribly, like an infuriated sword-tooth cat.

Startled, the PieceTakers pulled up in their tracks.

Cuilean charged at the head of the gang. His *sgian dubh* flashed in the sun, steel bright, and as he withdrew it, it dripped green with PieceTaker blood, and he immediately pivoted and fled across the beach towards the dense covering of trees.

It took the drool of Zziipps a moment to process what had happened. They gathered about their fellow PieceTaker who'd been stabbed and had fallen into the sand. "Himpela make Bibblebop die!" one of them screeched.

"Himpela make die notherpela us!" another Zziippp wailed.

With a cacophony of shrieks, the pack of Zziippps took off after the boy.

That was the last Ròna had seen of Cuilean until he returned.

7. The best of times

B' e linn an aoigh nuair a cheileireadh na h-eòin an teanga na Màthar.

It was the age of joy when the birds sang in the tongue of the Mother

Leabhar an Leaghaidh Mhòir —
The Book of the Great Melting

Wiktionary: The settling of the Wayp

Professor Harold Harischandra Higginsbottom (editor)

Many of the details of the actual settling of the Wayp have been lost over the thousands of years or so since the time of the Great Melt. What is remembered or has been passed down through legend and oral history (before being recorded in the annals of this Wiktionary) is as follows.

The ancient societies in existence at the time of the Great Melt[101] did nothing to mitigate the environmental disaster that was unfolding on several fronts. Indeed, some governing bodies – as near as we can tell from the fragmented records still in existence from those ancient times – passed laws making it illegal to even mention any of the environmental challenges facing the planet.

The false profits of the previous religion, people who called themselves "scientists," were shouted down by adherents of and believers in the one true faith of the Profits of GAWD.[102] So-called "scientific" conferences that were held to discuss the impending climate disaster were either shut down by military powers or overwhelmed by mobs incited by the fears that their freedoms were about to be stolen by unelected technocrats out to deprive them of their livelihoods and/or their pleasures.

In the face of this mass movement, it became increasingly dangerous to be an "academic." Universities were raided by gangs of "Gowp Shirts" – self-appointed militias wearing uniforms smeared in the distinctive coloring of brownish-brackish gowp, and determined to install the unspoken, ineffable, unknowable, traditional faith of the Invisible Hand of the Profit.

---

[101] The Great Melt – as mentioned before in these pages, an environmental crisis that included (amongst other things) the desertification of the lands, the rising seas, the disappearance of bodies of fresh water – both surface and underground -- the pollution of what water resources remained, and the toxification of the atmosphere.

[102] Gawd -- Global Access to Wealth Directorate

It was a time of turmoil, when the encroaching deserts and the rising seas were blamed on those who called attention to the environmental circumstances of the age. Chanting "It is what it is! Ain't nothing else!" murderous mobs descended upon schools of every form. Libraries were ransacked, whole collections of "books" (an ancient form of knowledge recording and retrieval) were doused with gowp and burned, as were educators of all kinds – college professors, high school instructors, and elementary school teachers.

It was the worst of times to belong to a profession that required – or even might be thought to require – an education beyond the most rudimentary lessons in how to tie one's shoes or how to put one's pants on. In orgies of righteous fervor, anyone with an education or training could be "gowped and tethered" and thrown onto the bonfires.

Scattered amongst the annals of the cosmic neuronal net are anecdotal accounts of college professors, doctors, lawyers, and accountants (to name just a few examples) who bribed friends, chance acquaintances, or even complete strangers for jobs as taxicab drivers or janitors – just to escape the lynch mobs of the gowp-shirts. Legends abound of the "killing times" and the desperate measures some members of the educated class took to save their lives: College professors who pretended to be uneducated and bribed corrupt municipal officials to let them scour toxic-waste dumps for trash; Medical doctors who hawked household cleaning products as medicines to ingest internally that they claimed would "cleanse" the body of infectious diseases – the number of dead patients providing proof of how truly, safely, ignorant of the "science" of medicine those practitioners actually were; Authors who claimed to be totally illiterate so they could teach children how not to write.

New "Profit Driven Schools" supplanted former institutions of education, and the only criteria for being employed as a teacher were a devotion to the Invisible Hand of the Profit, an adherence to the Wuarardd of Gawd,[103] and a complete lack of previous "indoctrination" in the subject taught.

In those troublous times, a small group of people who for ideological reasons or because they had come to the attention of the Monstrato authorities as dissidents and so feared their imminent arrest (and gowping-and-tethering), under the guise of taking a sight-seeing cruise to enjoy the sight of the spectacular

---

[103] Wuarardd of Gawd -- Worldwide, Universally Accepted Reality Authorized by the Regulation of Dogma Division of Gawd (see Gawd)

northern lights,[104] chartered the Shenannoah's Monarch, a tour boat that had been relocated from a formerly, but now dessicated, great river of the Merican Pelago and repurposed for ocean travel.

With the passenger manifest and sailing plan approved -- none of the named travelers being on no-sail lists (though there were, the oral histories tell us, a few people voyaging under assumed names) -- the ship sailed into the North Debris towards the Arctic Circle, but once out of view of land and satellite tracking, it veered dramatically from its putative course and set out on a 40-year, zig-zagging quest for refuge from the rising tides of violent ignorance, polluted waters, and dying land.

Historians have since pieced together an approximation of the composition of this band of refugees – which was apparently made up of people either associated with each other previously or connected by a social network. Mostly comprised of women, but with a considerable number of accompanying children and some men – the group of wayfarers included "intellectuals" or "thought-leaders" (academics, writers, environmentalists, scientists, medical professionals, and researchers), a scattering of artisans and tradespeople (such as metal workers, plumbers, carpenters, electricians, engineers, and even a couple of janitors), and artists in various media – wood, metal, stone, paint, film, and digital -- as well a small number of people whose skills or occupations have not been accounted for.

At first, these ancient boat people had no clear idea where they were headed, or if they would be allowed to land once they got there. Various regional authorities refused them the right to disembark either out of concern of establishing a precedent and thereafter being swamped by invading hordes of escapees from other, more devastated parts of the planet, or out of fear of retaliation by the Monstrato Corps, which was growing ever more powerful and influential in world affairs.

In its hegira through international waters, the Shenannoah's Monarch finally came to rest (in fact, to its last rest) on the southern shore of the terminus of the Great Sulphurific Garbage Patch, at the foot of the towering cliffs of the polar continent[105] at the opposite cap of the globe where they had started their odyssey.

This, however, was not the end of their wanderings through the wastelands of the DownBlow. Nor was it even the beginning of

---

[104] Northern Lights -- the burning of the methane deposits in the Siberian desert, the flames of which could be seen rising into the sky from the North Atlantic. Came to be known in the FT as *na fir chlis*, or the "dancing men."

[105] The land, which after being freed from under the unimaginable weight of the continent-sized icecap, in a series of tremendous shiftings of tectonic plates, rose up into the mountain range that we now know as the Wayp.

the end. It was, however, perhaps, the end of the beginning, for upon landing, they faced a seemingly impossible climb up the face of the cliff, an ascent they managed by navigating a narrow, mountain goat trail from the sea to the heights of the Wayp.

We can only imagine the surprise and jubilation this small band experienced upon discovering that as they ascended the thousands of lengths to the upland plateau, the toxic fumes of the DownBlow dissipated and that they could breathe without the apparatuses that were so necessary in the low-lying lands they had just left.

As pioneers in a strange, new, barren land, the pilgrims set about enlivening the environment with a number of living species that had survived the long voyage from *an Seann Tir* – the Old Land; by nurturing the embryos and seeds of existing species that they'd incubated over the course of their wanderings; and through the reclamation of the DNA of ancient lifeforms that they'd recovered from the melting ice.

It did not escape the attention of the refugees that in addition to seeding the new land with non-human life, they would have to

populate it with humanity. Humorists then and in the millennia since have had fun speculating on what it was like for the relatively few men in the band of intrepid voyagers – most jokes revolving around a wearisome litany of the conflict between sensual excess and tiresome duty.

But alongside of that, for the new land to survive and even prosper, and in order not to replicate the disastrous decisions that had led humanity to create the conditions that led to the Great Melt, the settlers decided they would have to formulate a new way of being. A lesson they learned during their 40 long years plowing through the Great Sulphurific Garbage Patch with the threat of destruction hanging over them, their lives hanging by a quickly unraveling thread, was that they had to hang together, or else they could hang it up as they would be hung separately -- either by the Monstrato PieceTakers or by all the forces of environmental disaster then wreaking havoc upon the planet.

The few men in this tribe of refugees were tasked with guarding the trail up the cliff-rampart to their new home, lest Monstrato PieceTakers track them and attempt in one way or another to interfere with the founding of this new world order.

The others were tasked with the building of a new world order, one built upon a network of relationships totally different from the one that had destroyed the old world.

As part of their re-imagining of the relationships, first, between humanity and nature, and second, between people, they came to see themselves not as owners of the Wayp, not as dominators of the new land, but rather as the "children" of the mother of all life, and so they referred to themselves as *Clann na Màthar* -- Children of the Mother.

Their number being small and the environment of the Wayp harsh, they organized themselves into a single enclave centered around what they called in the FT, *taigh nam peathraichean* -- the house of the sisters. Although they were not all related (and thus, not *sisters*, per se), they saw themselves -- if not literally, then figuratively – as a single family, and – though not all women -- the foremothers of the new land.

Though the structure of the Wayp society became more complicated in the millennia since its inception, at the beginning, there was one maxim that to this day remains at the core of its ethical functioning:

Honor the Mother who gave you life.

A violation of which law could be punishable by being set upon by the collective body of "sisters" and being summarily returned *an dòigh chas*, as they put it in the FT – the quick way[106] – to the DownBlow; that is, by being thrown headlong over the edge of the cliff to plummet several thousand lengths through the gowpy, smudge-cloud covering that floated between the Wayp and the sea of fire that surrounded the risen continent.

---

[106] *An dòigh chas* – as with other words, phrases, and expressions in the FT, this phrase is difficult to translate succinctly, as the word *dòigh* can signify either a path or a manner in which something is done, and *cas* embodies meanings as varied as rapid, precipitous, headlong, sudden, or steep.

Rose from a pile of shit

An ròs dearg a dh'fhàsas san òtraich, 's e nas àirde a thogas a cheann.

The red rose that grows in the shitpile raises his head the highest.

Proverb from *Leabhar an Leaghaidh Mhòir —* The Book of the Great Melting

It was hot and stuffy, and a pungent ammoniac stench permeated the close air. A weight crushed his chest when he moved, which he could do only with difficulty -- partially because of that weight and partially on account of the pain constricting his torso.

He lay still and listened. There were voices some distance away. Many voices. Angry voices. A cacophony of commanding voices which drifted to him, and were rendered indistinct through the muffling of his fever dream and the fetid walls of his enclosure.

"Where is he!?!"

"Where himpela!?!"

"Càit' a bheil e!?!"

Which all might as well have been tongues from other worlds, but nevertheless made his head hurt just to hear them.

And a trampling of furious feet back and forth.

Then he drifted into a deep tunnel in which massive bodies moved -- aptracs? Great lumbering beasts plodding across a verdured meadow? Giant subaquatic creatures gliding with glacial deliberateness?

Exactly what, he did not know.

All was dark, and he felt himself sinking. One moment he (or at any rate, the *he* who wafted in this fugue) was running across a boggy moor, where the muddy soil was covered with a tall, deep-green grass, and the next instant, the ground became soft and wet and of the solidity and consistency of pudding, into which he found himself sinking, first to his ankles, then to his knees, then up to his neck. The slime covered his head, and he was submerged in sodden, soggy, stygian darkness.

A hand reached down and griped him by the hair and wrenched him up out of the mire that was sucking him down, his mouth and eyes and nose plugged with the stinking muck.

Everything changed, and there was no hand pulling him up, and he floated powerless, unable to move or rise, in the black, softly constraining sludge.

As he was drifting submerged in the nightshade, bright visions came to him in his dark fever dream: the riot on the heights, the tumbling over the edge of the cliff, the fall towards the DownBlow, and then some vague hallucinogenic, foggy dream of being lifted and carried away.

There was light, and a lifting of the weight, and the air suffocated less, singed his nostrils and scalded his throat less, though the atmosphere still reeked with that nostril-piercing caustic. They -- for there was no name at this point to attach to the slender hands, though he would come to realize that it had been Ròna and the others -- changed the bandages around his midriff and his head with sure, deft touches in the blackness. The tarp (for he'd figured out the nature of his womblike envelope by then) was placed again upon him.

Pairs of hands – more than one pair – fluttered around him. They rolled him slowly, though excruciatingly, to unwrap the swathing, causing him to groan in his stupor, which was less a human sound than more that of a wounded animal. He felt a loosening of the binding around his middle, a burning heat where they applied the ointment, and a sharp rising odor stinging his nostrils.

A pressing to his lips softly wedged them apart, and a heated draught seeped into his mouth. A warmth rose to his brain and engulfed it. Oddly enough, even though flat on his back, he had the sensation that his skullcap was elevating straight up like a hat.

After which the dreams became more numerous, more vivid, with indistinct images of being trampled, and dragged, and thrown, and beaten -- tempest tumulted, lifted, wrenched, and twisted. Whipped like a loose branch in a gale-force storm rushing down a mountain pass. All very confused – his mind as tumbled as his body.

In the mental murk, appearing as a wraith, hardly more substantial than the miasma which enwraped him, she came again.

There were voices in a language he did not understand and which pained him to hear, inflicting stinging stabs as if he were being attacked by a swarm of bees.

"*Feumaidh sinn* -- we have to," said the one whom he would come to understand was Ròna.

"*Carson?* – Why?"

"*Airson fhaighinn a-mach cò e* – to find out who he is. -- *A bhith cinnteach.* – To be sure."

It was at that point that Ròna stood over him, scooted behind him and under his shoulders, and cradled him in her lap. She crouched to lift the top part of his body and wrapped her arms around his head and twisted and wrenched and pulled and tugged at the living, tentacled cowl that covered the top part of his face and skull.

The creature-cowl came alive, its tentacles whipped about in resistance, and it released its fang grip from the base of the man's neck and arched its head towards Ròna in threat, as if to say, *This is for you if you don't stop.*

The man howled blindly like a wild boar impaled on a spear and lashed out, flailing his arms about, punching wildly, blindly, without precision and without landing a blow on either the women who had gathered around him nor on the specters that now arose in his nightmare.

He heard voices coming to him out of the darkness again.

"*Dè tha thu a' dèanamh?* – What're you doing?" one of the voices demanded.

"*Feumaidh sinn an rud a chur dheth* – We have to get that thing off him," another voice responded.

Continuing in the FT, the other one protested. "You're hurting him!"

"Nothing like what they're going to do to him. I have to find out."

"Leave him alone!"

It was less because of the other woman's objections than because of the apparent impossibility of wrenching the cowl off Cuilean's head that Ròna reluctantly gave up.

The voices moved away but continued outside the hearing of  the panting man, his head still swirling from the agony of having had his head pulled apart, sweating and reeling in pain as if he had just been dragged the length of the glen behind a rampaging mammoth.

Ròna protested. "'*S e esan a th'ann* – It's *him*," she said. "*Tha fios 'm e* -- I know it. *Tha mi cinnteach!* – I'm certain!"

"We'll find out soon enough."

"I don't know what they'll do to him. They might not even bother finding out."

Later, not right then but in a few days – though he had no conceptualization of days or nights or the passage of time -- he was able to move a little more, in what small space had been afforded him, and he would drift more and more out of the inky darkness into which he had sunk and float up into a liminal, dozing lucidity. He came to realize he was encased in a narrow tent-like structure -- much like that which he would build when he was a child with other children – another boy and a girl, especially – the tarp stretched over low-hanging tree limbs, but unlike then, when the make-shift *bothan* afforded the children the comfort and security of a make-believe castle, now the weight of the sagging tarpaulin nearly smothered him.

As he rose out of the mental shadows, the stink became more oppressive. He gagged in reflex.

He sank into sleep again, and he dreamed, if a dream it was. The images came to him accompanied by a dull insistent hum, a muffled roar like that of an aptrac rumbling along a mountain trail, or the tumbling roar of a waterfall.

As I lie here in the dark, a stone upon my chest.

He was a stag on the mountain; a salmon leaping in the crested river waves; an *aon-adharc* charging across the field; a holy maiden birthing a babe; an old grandmother guiding a child; a warrior wielding a sword against the enemies of the Children of the Mother, the head of the enemy of the Children upon a pike.

As I lie here in the dark, this stone upon my chest.

Neither male nor female, neither of the two-legged nor the four-legged races, nor of the finned nor scaled nor feathered, but all things -- those that ate and those who were eaten.

He opened his eyes and the images faded away in the gloom of the tomb.

These were the things he saw as he lay in the dark, enveloped in the womb of this *bothan* -- this tiny cottage -- whose walls looked out like windows upon the entire world that was, that is, that will be.

As he lay in the dark, this stone upon his chest, the cool fingers of the *ceò* -- the mist -- wrapping around him like the fingers of the Mother, he dreamt this, but he visioned it, too, the images and sounds and sensations coming to him unbidden, without his asking.

A vision enwrapped in a dream, a dream enfolded in an apparition, which is happening, which did happen, which will happen, which has always happened.

He is two-sighted, and this is his *darna shealladh* -- his second sight – one of this world, and one of the other.

One of what is, and one of what is to come to be.

No matter what he had done in his lifetime before, no matter how many drugs he had taken, no matter how much PetrAle he had drunk, no matter how many times he'd been zapped by the thought-detecting cowl, he had never been able to shake the ghost images that came to him – neither when he had been awake, nor when he had been asleep. They had always been images of an age of joy, which however pleasant they might have been, the cowl headpiece he wore would shock him awake with white-hot pain, and he had learned to fear those visions and to fend them off.

The dreams had not all been identical although they were alike in that they were of the same tenor or seemed to be located in the same impossible place – a place that was, for one thing, impossibly green and alive: Impossible because outside the algae-farms in the domed nurseries of the agro-units of the Pelagoes, green as a naturally-occurring color did not exist. But in the febrific nocturnal emissions of these apparitions, the world was alive with greens and browns and reds and yellows and pinks and violets. The sky was impossibly, implausibly blue rather than its natural shade of brown and smudge (except in particularly vibrant sunrises or sunsets in the DownBlow when the fire geysers inflamed the low hanging methane atmosphere, and the entire skyline glowed a bright orange).

But as odd and fantastical as these dreams had been, there had been one that repeated and that was his favorite. Sometimes, he was in it, that is, he actually existed in the dream -- it was he who acted and felt -- and other times he was an observer watching an avatar of himself from a distance as if on a screoin show.

In either case, he was on a beach somewhere -- it must have been a lake because he could see across the water to another shore -- and there were rows upon rows of green things that poked up high in to the sky -- he hardly had a name for them in Simspeek: They were brown poles with green fringes or sometimes dappled with multi-colored tufts. They stood in rows, skirting the sand that was improbably white at the edge of the water that was itself impossibly clear, rather than the natural color of sand -- gowpy brownish-grey -- or the usual shade of bodies of water -- mucky, brackish brown.

He was not just sitting in the sand or standing or walking, but he was playing a game -- maybe a child's game of Insurge Heroes with a red-haired, freckled girl, who threw herself into the trench they had just dug, and with a passionate pretend voice that was imbued with the heart-deep conviction only children can muster, she whispered fiercely.

In his dreams, he had never fully understood what it was she said because she spoke neither in Simspeek nor TokTok but rather in some other language, an *impossible* tongue that did not, could not exist: *ha ee-ad chee-in,* it sounded like she said, which didn't make sense because they weren't really words, and as many times as he dreamt this particular dream, the words still did not change -- if they were *words,* though what she'd said seemed to make sense to the dream-*him,* for he – or the boy who seemed to be *him* – readied himself on the lookout for *them* whoever *they* were, and together, he and the scrawny, red-haired, freckle-faced girl, who was so brave and so alert and so concentrated, as sharp as the prick of an arrowhead, raised the sticks they imagined to be swords against the advance of whatever enemy it was that was coming.

Sometimes the intensity of the waiting came to be too much, and she would scream *"Tha iad a' tighinn!"* again; only this time, he somehow understood what it was she was saying – "They're coming!"

And they would jump up out of the sand trench, and screaming and swinging their stick-swords, they'd charge at the invisible enemy.

And they would fall in a heap, sometimes play-victorious, sometimes play-gasping their last play-breaths in the sand, and play-dying.

There was a giggling, childish glory about it until he would awake with a sharp pain that radiated from the top of his skull and spread throughout his mind like a lava flow, and the vision would disappear in a flash of blinding, white, fiery pain as the cowl-leash stabbed him in punishment for his wayward, forbidden thoughts.

Then she came. Again, it seemed to him, as if she had come before. Though he couldn't tell whether this was the dream or if it were really happening, nor could he have told what *really* was, and what was a chimera.

But in any event, she came again: She, his ministering angel, his salvific goddess, his incubus, his Lilith, his friend, his sister -- the one who came in the dark and raised him up.

Perhaps, there was more than just her, for there seemed to be other voices, a laying on of many hands which smeared on his body pungent ointments and unwrapped and wrapped the bandages which bound him.

He first heard the scraping and plopping of mass after mass landing on hard ground and felt the lifting of the weight suspended above him, and as her hands cut the bandages from him and washed his chest where his broken ribs were healing and lightly sponged the length of his body, he asked, "Who are you?"

There was a long pause before the answer came, not so much

an answer but a response: "So it's possible for you to be speaking."
Her voice was low, soft, gentle, but firm and observational.

"Where am I?"

"Here." Though it was unclear whether this was supposed to be
informative – or not – or a delay for the gathering of thoughts for
what might be an appropriately informative answer, or an outright
refusal to answer directly: None of which possibilities the man
consciously calculated.

"But why?" he insisted.

So, then she spoke to him, recovering from the surprise of his
awakening, and relieved that the man she had cared for would not
die -- or at least that there was a chance he would live, though he
was possibly still in danger from his injuries, and more probably
from the PieceTakers, who even now and again swept across her
father's croft, searching for what she had buried beneath the pile of
manure outside the stables, and most likely from the searching
parties of her own people, who scoured the Wayp to cleanse it of
the danger he represented to them.

"Where am I?" he repeated.

"In my father's barn," she said.

He stretched his hand out and poked the soft, warm mass that
pressed down on the top and sides of the tarp. "What's this?"

Without thinking, she responded in the FT. "*Cnoc de chac.*"
Then she posed the answer in Simspeek: "A pile of shit," she said.

"What?"

Though he couldn't see her any more clearly than a dimly-
viewed figuration through a gowp-smudged window, and he didn't
comprehend what it was she was saying, he could hear the satisfied
smirk of amusement in her voice at the irony. "*Mar ròs dearg tha
thu air fàs nas slàine 's nas làidire ann an cnoc de chac* – Like a red
rose you've grown healthier and stronger in a pile of shit."

More seriously, she expanded with an explanation. "*B' fheudar
dhomh do chur am fàlach aitegin* -- I had to hide you someplace.
Àiteigin far nach sireadh iad -- Someplace they wouldn't look. *Shaoil
gum b' e an t-àite seo na b' fheàrr* -- I thought this was the best
place."

He hardly grasped the meaning of the words as they swarmed
around him like midges – wee, biting, tiny, flying creatures that
swirled in his skull and tore out even tinier bits of brain flesh.
Every word was a mind-stab, a poke with a sharp barb, that he
could not understand, yet strangely did.

~~

Sometimes you choose the mountain, sometimes the mountain chooses you

'S ise a tha nas fhaide air an t-saoghal seo, nas motha a chì i.
She who is the longest in this world sees the most.
Proverb from *Leabhar an Leaghaidh Mhòir* —
The Book of the Great Melting

But the real question was not *why?* Why did she give a monkey's shit about this stranger with the even stranger hood locked on his head and face?

The real question was, *Who? Who was he? Who was this masked man she'd lugged back? Was he who she thought he was?*

And more importantly, perhaps, *How could she go about finding out?*

It was in the midst of unraveling this knot that Ròna found herself meandering past the little cottage at the end of the village where the Big Sister lived. There the old woman was sitting in a shade of a yew tree that stood next to the house – in fact, that formed part of the structure – in its hollowed-out section.

Ròna held back until the *cailleach* – the old woman – finished her morning devotions.

The Sister's prayer was short. With her eyes half-shut, she held her hands up to the sky as if receiving a boon and voiced an invocation:

> *Tha sinn làn bhuidheachais.*
> *Thàinig sinn uile às a' bhrù a' bhan-dè*
> *'s tillidh sinn thuice*
> *mar bhoinne an uisge*
> *a dh'èiricheas far a' mhuir*
> *'s air ais a thuiteas.*

> We are full of gratitude.
> We all came from the womb of the goddess
> and to her we shall return,
> like a drop of rain
> that rose from the ocean

and will fall back again.

Upon finishing, Mairead, tall and straight for all her many years, opened her eyes and seeing Ròna hanging back, nodded and beckoned. "*Thig, a ghràidh* – Come, love."

Ròna approached, only to stand uneasily as the Sister gestured for her to wait. Mairead cupped her hands over her mouth, forming an improvised megaphone. She pursed her lips and blew from her diaphragm, creating a series of sounds in a decrescendo - *aack, aack, aack, aacck.*

A waddle of ducks and ducklings appeared around her feet.

"Walk with me," she told Ròna. "The girls want to eat, and we can talk."

The aged woman moved slowly, stepping carefully so as to not tread on any of the ducks and not to trip herself. They moved into the vineyard that stretched out towards the forest from her cottage. There, the ducks went to work, snapping up snails, slugs, aphids, beetles, weevils, and mealy bugs. Every now and then, Mairead would shift her position, guiding her pest patrol a few steps father.

At the edge of the vineyard lay a felled tree. This is where she sat. "*Suidhe sìos, a ghràidh* – sit down, love." The Sister patted the place on the trunk next to her.

They sat quietly, watching the bustle amongst the waddle, as the ducks, quacking and chortling, went about their business of clearing the vineyard of pests and feeding themselves at the same time.

"You had a question," the *cailleach* noted. Not a question itself, but a statement of fact.

Which made things easier for Ròna because indeed, she did have a question, though she had not completely voiced it yet, not even to herself. Though she had long known the aged Sister, it was marvelous to the younger woman that the elder always knew what to say, always posed the right question to ask, always had the appropriate answer, which quality, many of the younger people of the village attributed to her having *an darna sealladh* -- the second sight -- being mysteriously and magically endowed with the ability to see what could not be seen, but which actually came from little more than having lived as long and from having seen as much of the world as she had. Having paid attention over her long years, for the Sister, everything fell into a pattern and had less to do with the second sight than the old aphorism: *'S ise a tha nas fhaide air an t-saoghal seo, nas motha a chì i.* – She who is the longest in this world sees the most.

Just as the fact that Ròna had a question failed to surprise the older woman, neither did the nature of the question itself. In fact, Mairead anticipated it: "You're wondering what you should do about him. That man you brought back and you're now hiding." Again, a statement, not a question.

Without waiting for a response, much less a confirmation from Ròna, the Sister went on. "Perhaps you should ask yourself, is this who you think it is?"

She let that question sink in before going on, "Even if it is who you think it is."

Having dropped that koan, the older woman scrutinized the younger intensely.

"And then, and only then, can you ask, what should you do?"

"Yeah, but, why me? Why do I have to be the one?"

"Because you brought him here. You claimed him like a lost cub that followed you home. You've always done this, *a ghràidh.* You should know this about yourself by now. You take responsibility for things that other people pretend aren't there, and either ignore or push away. You can't say, 'It just followed me, I didn't have anything to do with it.' When something happens out in the world ..." Mairead spread her hands in an enveloping gesture that swept in their surroundings ... "that connects with something inside your heart ..." here the Sister touched Ròna's chest ... "*chan e tuiteamas dall a th' ann* -- That's not blind accident. "*'S e co-thachartas a th' ann* – It's a happening together. *Tha an saoghal a-muigh 's an saoghal a-staigh co-cheangailte ri chèile.* -- The outer world and the inner world are linked."

This might have been more of a riddle than Ròna had the patience to puzzle out. She didn't want insight. She didn't want wisdom. She wanted a practical answer to her problem: "But what do I do with him?"

"*Chan fheum thu a' bheinn a leum a dh'aon bheum, ach sreap e ceum air cheum,*" a rhyming proverb that could be translated as, "You don't have to leap the whole mountain at once, just climb it one step at a time."

Ròna mulled over this one. "So, what's the first step? What do I do? How do I find out?"

"*Chan e ach aon dòigh ann,*" Mairead said. "There's but one way."

Sometimes, the Sister's coaxing people to think things out for themselves could be irritating, if not – as in this instance – bordering on infuriating.

"What is it!" Ròna demanded desperately, as if she were seeking to keep from slipping through her grasp the one, last, slender thread suspending over the abyss the man *she just knew* was the man she thought he was, to save him from plunging to his death. "Tell me! I'll do it."

"I've seen it done before," said the Big Sister. "It'll wound you terribly. Cost you great pain."

"Whatever it is, I'll do it."

The Sister leaned in, and placing her mouth close to Ròna's ear, she murmured.

Ròna blanched, set her teeth, and nodded tightly.

~~

micheal dubh

Together

Clanna na màthair, ri guaillibh a chèile.
Children of the mother, shoulder to shoulder.
Proverb from *Leabhar an Leaghaidh Mhòir* —
The Book of the Great Melting

Meanwhile, away from the cottages of the village, and out in the forest where the presence of *a' Bhan-Dia* – the Goddess -- was palpable, under the wide-spread branches of the oldest oak tree in the Wayp, sat the *Àrd-Phiuthar* – the Big Sister – alone in the center of the convocation, around whom all the life of the council flowed and ebbed.

She seemed as ancient as the great oak itself. Indeed, so old that stories about her had passed into legend: that she had come over on the ark that had brought the first *inn-imrichean* – the first incomers, the first immigrants; or if not actually one of those, she was so aged that she had known some of those first pilgrims; or she had known those who had known them. (If this seems a bit vague, the people of the Wayp had more important things to do than go about their lives counting days. After all, there were the mammoth herds to watch over; calves to help birth; game to hunt; mammoth wool to weave; mushrooms, nuts, and berries to forage; and while one was about those tasks, songs to be sung, stories to tell and hear, babes to birth, children to nurture, birds to watch, flowers to smell, loves to bind, and other countless much more interesting and more important things to do.)

From where she was seated on the ground – so to be in contact with the Mother herself – the Big Sister placed her hands on the earth and pressed her fingers into the soil, and thus touched the filaments of the universal consciousness – the mycelia and the hyphae of which they were comprised – the roots, the tendrils of the trees, the plants, and the fungi which permeated and interfused all being.

The Sister had summoned the people of the Mother together to consider what to do with the stranger that Ròna had retrieved from the cliff side and brought back with her. And in this, the arguments

336

went back and forth, coming and going fast, heavy, and loud, with no consensus being reached or formed.

"We don't know who he is."

"He came up with the PieceTakers!"

"It's dangerous to keep him."

"Monstrato will come and get him."

"And get us too!"

"Kill him and hide his body in the forest."

"Let the bear-wolfs and the sword-tooths eat him!"

"Throw him over the edge. Back to the DownBlow!"

Finally, Ròna found a space to protest: "He's one of us!"

"How do you know that?"

"I recognize the scar."

"That's not your cat-boy. Just because somebody has a scar on his arm ..." Seumas, ever doubtful, was resentful of anybody else's truth but his own. "How do we really know that he is who you say he is?"

"He got that scar when your damned bear-wolf killed my *piseag* -- my kitten."

"You don't know that."

"I was there!"

"You're just making that *cac* up," Seumas scoffed. He explained dismissively to the assembled crowd. "My sister thinks she has to take care of every stray, simpleton, abandoned chick, and changeling fairy. One day, she adopted this cat-boy ..."

"So, you admit it!" Ròna exulted. "I'm right!"

"No, no, no! Just a slip of the tongue. But you have to admit you did adopt that stray wildling that *ar n-athair* – our father -- found in the woods." This last phrase was directed to the entire assemblage: The indignity was too much for him to hold his long simmering resentment. "That she adopted as our brother! Like she didn't already have a brother! Like I wasn't good enough!"

"You still aren't!"

Seumas seethed, but he trailed off and didn't follow up with any further response, the awareness striking him that perhaps he'd already revealed too much – and you could tell that this part of their history together had really hurt, how deeply he'd been wounded, for of all grievances, none are so bitter as those which are most primal.

For Seumas, this is what the assembly was actually all about, whether he realized it or not: He'd been supplanted once and was determined not to let it happen again. He was the rightful brother, the true son of their father, not some changeling that the fairies had left in the woods in exchange for a healthy *cat-claidheimh* – a sword-toothed cat.

"Our *bothan* – cottage -- was more like a wildlife refuge all the time I was growing up," he complained to one and all.

He turned to their father, Dòmhnall, who was sitting at the outer rim of the circle. "Isn't that right, *a dhadaidh* – Dad?"

Dòmhnall shifted uncomfortably. He'd never liked being drawn into the disputes between his children. He'd much rather be in the field with his mammoths and his mìneotarbhs than arguing about things that would never change, no matter who said what. "Well," he temporized, seeking the words least likely to offend anyone on either side of the argument (which more often than not was guaranteed to offend *everyone*), "She's always had a soft heart ..." He trailed off, hoping his having said something – even something so lacking in substance that it did not really address any question, nor hardly even qualify as an answer to anything – would allow him to waft even farther back into the recesses of the crowd.

Even though Dòmhnall had attempted to keep out of the cranny that trapped him *eadar dà chloich chruaidhe* – between two hard rocks, as they said in the FT -- Seumas leapt upon his words: "Soft heart!" Accompanied by a snort. "More like a soft head! She'd bring home a broken-winged bird that couldn't fly straight and would flutter around bumping into the walls and bombing the entire house with shit. There was the time she brought home the blind bear cub that kept on trying to eat the baby squirrel that'd

fallen out of its nest, and the squirrel would get away by climbing up on her, and she'd walk around with a squirrel on top of her head, and everybody'd make fun of *me.* I could hardly learn my lessons."

This accumulation of childhood grievances rushed out, to which Ròna snapped back, "The reason you didn't learn your lessons is that you were stupid and didn't pay attention."

Angrily pointing her finger at her numbskull brother, Ròna accused him of what she imagined was his greatest crime: "He couldn't learn them himself. I had to recite them over and over, and even then, he couldn't remember them! He made me stand behind that tree," she revealed to the Sister, indicating the scene of the crime, "and whisper the stories to him when you had him recite the catechism of the Mother."

The old woman made a *fiamh-ghàire* – a hint of a smile. With a faint nod, as if to say, *I know. You think I didn't see you? Couldn't hear you?* As if exposing for the first time a long-held secret, she confided, "You don't whisper that quietly, *a ghràidh.*"

Ròna shot a last gibe at Seumas. "*A bhuamastair!* -- Blockhead!"

This touched too painfully on a sore spot. There being some truth to Ròna's description of him as a *blockhead*, he wasn't able to come up with a cogent repartee, so instead he exploded with an invective: "*Ris an tìr-ìosal leat!* -- Go to hell!" or even worse, "To the DownBlow!"

The crowd erupted in shouts, arguments, invectives, angry denunciations, and threats. Ròna's hand went to her bow but was stayed by the Big Sister's standing up. Just that simple act by itself quieted the hubbub.

"Children!" she chastened, not loudly, but clearly. "This is the most discord we've experienced in a long time. Perhaps since that troublemaker Robert Morunx came into our community and claimed kinship with us." This reference was underlined by a significant, stern, though subtle glance in Morunx's direction.

Morunx, who'd been silent this whole time, spoke up in broken FT to defend himself. "*E tha fìor* – Is true it. *Mo màthair* – Mine mother ..." Stopping short, having explained nothing, he gathered his thoughts, righted his tongue, and launched again into an attempt to clarify: "*Càirdeas agam* – Friendship at me." But in the blathering, running smack into a wall of discombobulation, he confused the words for kinship and friendship and came to a flummoxed stop.

From somewhere in the midst of the assemblage was heard, "Yeah, but you've refused to learn the Tongue!"

"*Mi tha beagan* – Is little I," Morunx countered brokenly. Exasperated, he switched to Simspeek, "If it wasn't such a damned confusing language."

"*'S e an cuspair agamsa gu dearbh!* -- That's my point exactly! Confusing for *you!* Not for anyone else!" Of course, being in the FT, what had been said was totally missed by Morunx.

During this tumult, unnoticed by most in the congregation, the eyes of the *Àrd-Phiuthar* – the Big Sister – glassed over as she entered the realm of the other world to consult with the spirits of the ancestors.

Gradually, the other sisters noticed, and they raised their hands over their heads, and with their thumbs and fingers, they formed the sign of the trinity of the goddess – *a' mhaighdeann, a' mhàthair, 's a' chailleach* – the girl, the mother, and the grandmother.

The others in the convocation took notice as well and likewise raised their hands in the triangle of the Mother, and soon all were quiet.

The Big Sister spoke, though it was not with her own voice, but with one that arose from the other world.

"If you remember the old stories – as some of us might and some of us might never have learned ..."

Although the reverie which the Sister had fallen into precluded personal digs or sarcasms, as her mind had left this domain, and the voice that came from her emanated from the other realm, whether intended or not, the reference to Seumas' cheating at his lessons was inescapable. Wry glances were thrown his way, and he ducked his head with a sour look and a wry grimace as if one of the *balaich* – the boys, his buddies -- had just given him a viciously fierce titty twister.

"From the very earliest times, when the Children of the Mother first came to the Wayp, and we were travelling across the land," the Sister continued, "the only way we could cross the furious streams and rivers that were pouring down from the melting ice caps was *ri guaillibh a chèile* – shoulder to shoulder, arm in arm. Together we strived, we lived, we survived, we thrived."

The import of her words sank in. Gradually the enveloping spell lifted, and blinking her eyes like someone awakening from a deep sleep, the *Àrd-Phiuthar* returned from the land of the ancestors. Her face focused in an expression of purposefulness, she posed the question: "*Dè dhèanamaid leis an duine cèin?* – What should we do with the stranger?" The query settled in amongst the convocation and swelled until it filled the entirety of their attention.

The Sister said simply, softly, but with an authority that had to be heeded: "*Rachaibh 's thoiribh dhuinn an seo e.* – Go and bring him here to us." Significantly, she said to Ròna, "*Bi sinn ga fheuchainn.* -- We will see if he is who you say he is."[107]

And though the *àithne* – the commandment – was not the immediate *fuar-bhuille* – the "killing stroke," or the "cold blow" – that Seumas was wanting, it was all that he needed to propel him to his feet in that it gave him reason to hope that this intruder would

---

[107] *Feuch (ga fheuchainn)* – the translation in the text gives the sense of the word in Simspeek, although like many words and expressions in the FT, it is more complex in the multiplicity of its meanings, for it touches on "trying" and "testing," but "trying" not in a legal or judicial sense, but in the sense of somebody "trying on" a piece of clothing (to see if it fits, for instance), or "trying" something to see what it actually is or can actually do, or "testing" in the sense of "trying it out" to achieve a true sense of its qualities (though none of these explanations really gets at the word's deep feeling of meaning).

be exposed for the imposter that he was and dealt with appropriately.

He snarled at Ròna through clenched lips, "Tell us where he is. I'll go get him!"

~~

Return of the Indiginoe

*Am fear as fhaide a chaidh on taigh, 's e an ceòl bu bhinne a chual e
riamh: "Tiugainn dhachaidh."*
To him who's gone farthest away from his birthplace,
the sweetest music he ever heard was, "Come home."
Proverb from *Leabhar an Leaghaidh Mhòir* —
The Book of the Great Melting

Cuilean was lying in his narrow, stinky cell when they came for
him. The tarp was thrown back, the bricks of peat and the piles of
manure quickly cleared aside. Two men, one of them who was
vaguely familiar — a thought stabbed him and made him wince --
was it a memory? He questioned: *Seumas*? He was a big fellow, who
was hazily familiar, with a shock of wild, unkempt, curly hair that
swept from the top of his head and tangled with his furry beard,
presenting him with the appearance of a dark, shaggy bush with a
face peeking out

The red-haired girl stood behind the man, and they spoke back
and forth angrily and rapidly in the FT – in a way that gave Cuilean
a headache. A stream of words like the *rat-a-tat-tat-tat*-ing of a
couple of red-cowled woodpeckers, one at the outside of his skull
trying to burrow its way in, and the other on the inside, tunneling
out. Cuilean's face screwed up in incomprehension. He didn't grasp
what these strange people meant with their weird mouthings,
although the words did sound vaguely familiar — the haunting
echo of something he had heard a long time ago – *cluinnte mu
thràth* -- but he did understand the girl's drawn and anxious
expression, and that recognition did not give him comfort.

The man — *Seumas*, Cuilean decided, though how he was so
certain of this, he wasn't quite sure (he might have been naming
him anew for all that) – motioned to Cuilean with a commanding
gesture. "*Tiugainn*," he said gruffly. "Come with us."

Cuilean scooted back as far as he could go until he was pressing
against the wall of shit-pies and peat.

"*Na bi nad shalachair*," the man said with a tone of impatience
discernible even if the exact meaning of the words were not. "Don't

be a shithead."

"Simspeek!" Cuilean demanded, his voice all the shriller because of the pain the words from the big fellow caused him.

"*Dè tha e ag ràdh?*" asked one of the men. "What's he saying?"

From the back, Ròna called out, "He says he doesn't understand."

The big guy — the one Cuilean had named Seumas -- turned away from Cuilean to respond to the girl in the FT: "Or he doesn't want to."

Against his inclination, Seumas found himself dragged into a revival of their dispute. With a gotcha smirk, he added, "But if he doesn't understand, that means he's not who you think he is."

"Or maybe he does understand," Ròna countered, "but doesn't want to admit it because he remembers what a bastard you are."

The ramifications and extensions of this labyrinthian maze of speculation were too complex for Seumas to follow in their intricate windings. "*Pit air iteig!*" he cursed with a shout – "Flying vagina!" and he rushed at Cuilean and grappled him.

Seumas was followed quickly by the man, a tall, lanky fellow with a sallow complexion and a vacant expression.

Cuilean struggled against their grip, but they'd come on him so suddenly, tying up his arms and pinning him against the wall of the stable, that he couldn't fight effectively, having so little room to maneuver, and besides that, he was weakened already, the torsion of his mid-section paining him, so he wasn't able to bring his full strength to bear; nor did bracing his feet against the posts of the pen nor straddling the doorway keep him from being dragged out into the wider barn, and from there out of the stone building altogether.

All this time, Ròna was screaming something unintelligible. She launched herself onto Seumas's back, but he was so much larger than she was that he tossed her aside as if she were nothing more than a kitten. She gathered herself to her feet, but another woman wrapped her arms around her from behind – not so much actually holding her back, but by moral suasion, restraining her.

The struggle took Cuilean and Seumas and the others into the middle of the courtyard, roughly paved with rounded river stones, and it was here in the open that Cuilean could maneuver. He twisted one way and another, first against a grip, and then into it, and then jerking free from it. Released finally from the hands that held him, Cuilean bolted across the paddock.

There was a gap in the courtyard enclosure, but it was blocked by yet other men. Instead, he ran towards a door in the two-story structure.

Behind him, the men called out indistinctly as they chased after him.

Inside, Cuilean found himself at the foot of a staircase. Unsure where to go, he clambered up the stairs. At the top, a short hallway led to a room, closed all around except for the door he'd just bolted through and opposite him, a window overlooking a field and facing some woods in the distance.

That's when time slowed down. Cuilean felt a strange calmness come over him. Just previously, it had been all frenetic action and movement -- motivated by his expectation to die in a frantic sweat, and even more than that, by his not knowing what to do; but for some strange reason, as he now saw a clear path before him, a calm settled over him.

He gazed upon the woods in the middle distance and heard the sound of the clomping footsteps of the men who were chasing him up the wooden stairs.

When they burst into the room – there were four of them now – they came to a halt. He turned from the window and faced them. He smiled distantly at them, as if they were guests expected to tea.

The man they called *Aillean Caol* – Thin Allen – slipped around the edge of the room to flank Cuilean. Aillean was followed by two others. Seumas, thick and muscular, stepped forward and cooed, "*Bi ciùin, a bhalaich* – Calm down, buddy," but even though Seumas had spoken in what he intended was a soothing manner, the FT words were bee stings in Cuilean's ears, to which he responded with a paroxysm of action: He charged Aillean, and catching him in the armpits, he lifted the thin man just enough to take the weight off his feet and drive him towards the open window.

They toppled out the breach in the wall, and when they landed, Cuilean's fall was cushioned by Aillean's body. Furthermore, anticipating the impact, Cuilean rolled to diffuse the shock and bowled to his feet.

Leaving the groaning Aillean behind him, Cuilean broke for the woods across the flat meadow. He was buffeted by knee-high heather and thigh-high brush, and as he entered the trees, he was hit about the head and chest by low hanging branches, as if the forest itself was stretching out its arms to stop his getaway.

He heard the stomping of pursuing feet and the shouts of the men chasing him.

And behind those, more distant but coming up fast, he heard heavy clomping.

He saw a break in the trees ahead and made for it.

He broke out of the forest into a small clearing and pulled himself up in mid-stride as he found himself teetering on the brink of a cliff that fell down to a wide body of water – *Loch na Màthar* – the Lake of the Mother.

He caught his balance only with a wild waving of his arms.

The surface of the water shimmered, presenting itself as variegated shades of blue, azure, green, turquoise, and in some places as clear as a cloudless sky -- totally devoid of the gowpy sheen, the muck coloring, and the covering of polymer and plastic beads and bobbing turds that covered the surface of the seas where people in the DownBlow went to vacation.

Far across the water, hills rose, one row behind another, peaks descending out of shrouds of faint mist, and into an area that looked like the brownish molting of an animal shedding its fur. The tree covering passed from a splotchy uncertainty into a solid, deep green. The hills themselves lay under the patch-work sky where clouds of pristine white, silvery grey, shimmering grey-blue, and pitch black slowly floated.

Cuilean gathered himself. Though he was not confident of surviving the jump, nor even of his ability to swim, in a quick calculation, he figured his chances were better in the water than to the not-so-tender mercies of the men coming after him.

He balked when he saw something under the surface of the lake: a huge, dark shadow moving between this shore and the opposite bank.

That lapse was enough to allow his pursuers to come upon him.

But instead of arms grabbing him, a rope lassoed him and went taut. The jerk of an irresistible force dragged him away from the ledge.

Cuilean looked up, and there she was: the red-haired girl again.

His head hurt when she said, "*Chan e an dòigh dhut, a bhalaich* -- That's not the way for you, lad. -- *Ach na dragh ort. Bidh a h-uile rud ceart gu-leòr* – But don't worry, everything'll be alright. -- *Tiugainn dhachaigh còmhla rium* – Come home with me."

"*Thoir e dhuinn!* – Give him to us!" the big man shouted angrily.

The red-haired girl circled her unihorn to block the pursuing mob from getting at their escaped captive. "*Thoireamaid e air-ais!* – Let's take him back!" she called out. "*Mar a dh'iarr a' Phiuthar oirnn!* – As the Sister wanted us to do."

Although Cuilean didn't understand what she'd said, and he blinked in uncomprehending pain at her as she said it, he felt unaccountably relieved with the feeling that he was in safe hands.

And so he was trussed back to the *Comhairle nam Peathraichean* – the Council of Sisters – but his return, rather than being the culmination of anything, only sparked further dispute. As he stood before them, his arms pinioned to his side like the wings of a bound, captive angel, the arguments as to what to do with him started all over again.

The red-haired girl was arguing with whomever she thought she had to persuade. *"Chan e duine coigrich a th' ann. 'S e Cuilean nan cat-fiadhaich.* -- He's not a stranger. He's Cuilean of the wild-cats."

Cuilean looked on as if in a trance – everything was hazy. The Sea-wyrm whose fangs were imbedded in the base of his skull leaked its brain-numbing toxin. Each shout in the FT was like the blow of a hammer

The big man – *Seumas Mòr*, whom Cuilean somehow knew, though how he knew, he could not have said – vehemently argued in the FT. *"Chan eil dòigh ann sin a dhearbhadh.* -- There isn't any way to prove that. He doesn't belong here. He's an illegal. He came with the PieceTakers. He deserves to be sent back."

Though Cuilean had no idea what was being said, that the man was in fact arguing that they return Cuilean the "fast way" over the cliff to the DownBlow, he had a very strong impression that the big guy meant him no good.

This went on for some time. Finally, the *Àrd-Phiuthar* – the Big Sister – held up her hand. Quickly, the quarreling subsided, with one last faint protest from Ròna -- *"Ach* – But ..." which died with a stern glance from the Sister.

Seumas wasn't deterred. *"Cus amaideas!* – Too much nonsense!" he called out in exasperation, and reaching to tug the cord around Cuilean's neck, he declared, "Let's settle this!" But as he touched it, the cable twitched – it was alive! -- and the head of the wyrm came loose from the base of Cuilean's skull. The creature bared its teeth at Seumas in threat. *"Cac!* – Shit!" he yelped, stepping back, nearly tripping over his own feet.

The wyrm quickly reattached its fangs to Cuilean's neck and tightened its tentacled-grip around his throat.

Angered at being thwarted – and even more so than by being (as he imagined it) made a fool of (perhaps even doubling down on that feeling, this would not have been the first time this damned cat-boy was at the root of that!) -- with a violent movement, Seumas whipped out his *sgian-dubh* – the "black" (or secret) knife tucked into the top of his stocking just below his knee length kilt -- and made a move as if to cut the creature free from Cuilean.

When Seumas edged the knife close to the wyrm, it released its grip on Cuilean's neck and bared its fangs at Seumas, making the man step back again, and then it tightened its coil around Cuilean's neck and returned to digging its fangs into the base of the young man's skull.

Ròna cried out, "No!"

"Why not!" Seumas snapped back, even more infuriated than before, now that he had Ròna to blame for his own hesitancy. "You want to find out who this is? We'll just cut the damned thing off! Then we'll know one way or another."

Laying a hand on Seumas's arm, the Sister spoke in a calm voice: "If you harm it while it's still attached, it'll pump poison into his brain and kill him."

"*Chan e an trioblaid dhomh!* -- Not my problem!" Seumas exclaimed, and to the Sister's disapproving glare, he deflatedly asked, "Okay ... How then?"

The Sister turned to the others near her. "Bring the barrel *airson teatha na màthar.* -- The barrel for the Mother's tea," meaning they should fetch the barrel in which the sacred brew was distilled.

"What do we do with the *tea?*" Seumas whined, all of a sudden, his concern shifting. It was, after all, one thing to get rid of this *Gall* – this foreigner – but quite another thing entirely to offer up the sacred distillation as a sacrificial dram.

"Pour it out," the Sister said with a sideways tilt of her head and a clenching of her lips, as if to say, *regrettable but necessary*.

"Nooo!" A little boy's cry of distress colored Seumas's wail.

The Sister gave him one of those looks, and he slumped, responding meekly, sulkily, "I'll help."

As they filed out, Seumas nudged several of his friends. "*Tiugainn, a bhalaich* – Come on boys," he said, resignedly. "We'll see what we can save."

So, Seumas and the "boys" hurried ahead to the distillery shed where the sacred tea of the Mother was brewed, and before the Sisters got there, they'd scooped out as much as they could of the tea – into buckets, glasses, bonnets, sporrans, purses, any container, no matter how porous.

One of the "boys" came running with a chum bucket from the coop where their hunting eagles were kept. The container was bloody and coated with the residue of the raw meat which they fed to the fowls, and once they'd scooped a portion of tea into it, the liquid swirled with streaks of red and floated with bits and pieces of meat, but this contamination of the sacred brew was of no concern to them in their desperate quest to save what they could of the precious *teatha*.

In fact, such niceties were of so little concern, that regarding the bits of raw flesh floating in the salvaged tea, and weighing drinking the beverage with a little added protein or not drinking it at all, with a deep breath, Seumas ordered, "Get more of those chum buckets!"

They'd filled aside several such containers by the time the sisters arrived. One – Agnes – a stern, thin, tall, handsome Sister of middle age, snapped, "*Fòghnaidh na dh'fhòghnas!* – Enough's enough! Tip the barrel!" and so with deep and reluctant breaths, Seumas and his three friends spilled the rest of the tea.

They dragged and carried the *teatha* distilling barrel, which was large enough to fit two people facing each other.

At the Sister's direction, several others were bringing in buckets of heated mammoth milk and pouring them into the vat.

Drugged by the repeated bites of the agitated wyrm, Cuilean stood as if a man half asleep. He looked on everything around him as if through a gauzy haze.

They stripped the clothes from him and lifted him into the cask, now half filled with the warm milk.

At a nod from the Big Sister, Ròna stripped and got into the tub, too, facing the young man.

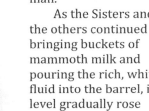

As the Sisters and the others continued bringing buckets of mammoth milk and pouring the rich, white fluid into the barrel, its level gradually rose and buoyed Ròna's breasts on the surface.

Ròna reached out her hand to Seumas. "*Do sgian-dubh,*" she said. "Your black knife."

The Big Sister touched the head of the sea-wyrm. The creature released its grip, and looking around, sighted Ròna directly in front of it. It hissed a threat and reattached, tightening its coils around Cuilean's neck.

Again, the Sister touched it, this time between the eyes.

The serpent again detached itself, extending towards Ròna in snaky curiosity. It slithered across the surface of the milk, its forked tongue shooting out to smell, before it retreated to its sinuation around Cuilean's neck, constricting its coil even more tightly than before, so tautly that Cuilean gagged.

The third time, the Sister touched its nose.

The hydra released its bite, unwound its length, and slowly approached Ròna at the level of the milk's surface. With a lightning strike, it shot at her and clamped its fangs onto her breast.

The girl was ready. Just as quickly as the wyrm's strike, her hand and arm erupted up from the milky bath, the *sgian dubh* flashing in the air, and with a banshee howl and a ferocious slash, she hacked at her own breast, slicing off the tip just above the teeth-grip of the sea-wyrm. At the same time, with her other hand, she clamped the snake's body, and as it writhed viciously in her grip, she hacked off its head.

The white milk swirled with her red blood and the green ooze that flowed from the now lifeless basilisk.

Ròna wobbled woozily, took a half step, collapsed, and sank into the red, white, and green bath.

What Cuilean experienced was more astounding to him than any severing of the monster's head was to the witnesses amongst the people. The wyrm cowl went limp and fell off Cuilean's skull and face. Unleashed from the creature's coils, and freed from its brain-numbing, thought-killing, memory blackening venom, Cuilean awoke as if released from a coma. He was inundated by a full flood of images, memories, sounds, feelings, and emotions of a former life. All the strange dreams he'd had in the DownBlow crashed upon him like a tsunami as they transformed into memories.

His vision clouded over with tears. He gasped for breath. He gulped for air. He panted like a dog after a long run. He heaved with desperate gasps as if he'd been punched in the solar plexus. He could hardly believe the sight around him: Having been so cruelly taken such a long time ago, like a sailor long presumed ship-wrecked and lost at sea, and washed up as if dead on the beach, he looked around and saw what had for so long been no more than a faded dream.

One sight hit him like the full blow of a mìneotarbh charge -- to his horror: that of Ròna sinking in the bloody milk. He lunged forward, wrapped his arms around her, and lifted her to the surface. The words he'd long forgotten coming back to him, he shouted, "*Cuidich mi!* -- Help me," and suddenly, shaken out of the shock at what they had just seen, several hands reached forward to help him out of the tub.

"Where can I take her," Cuilean asked desperately.

The Big Sister made a motion for him to follow her. Wordlessly the old woman waved her arms at the assemblage that had clustered around them as if to part troubled water.

With faltering and limping steps, the Big Sister led Cuilean and his bloody burden to a *bothan beag* – a cozy cottage -- made of stacked stones: two parallel walls about a foot apart with peat and grass insulation between them. Outside the doorway was a trellis of honeysuckle resplendent with butterflies, and a short distance from the cottage were wooden stands festooned with grapevines, and still farther away spread a walnut tree, and across from that, an apple tree blossomed.

Inside the cottage, Cuilean lay Ròna down on a heather-cushioned daybed. She was immediately surrounded by the Sisters, who pushed him out of the way, though it wasn't a *pushing* per se – more like the movement of a stream current that carried him from Ròna's side to the outer fringes of the group that was crowding into the small room.

The Big Sister called for water, bandages, and *bainne na màthar* – the restorative, soporific Mother's milk. Tipping a cup at her lips, Mairead was able to dose her with enough of the tea to carry her away from the immediacy of her pain.

They quickly staunched the oozing bleeding. They washed the wound and bandaged her. The girl lapsed in and out of consciousness, though to be more exact, more like various stages of semi-consciousness.

When they were done, the Sisters filed out silently and quickly. "You stay here with her," Mairead told Cuilean before leaving, "as long as she needs you."

~~

Everything depends on the doodlebug

Millidh sìlean nimheil cuain de bhainne.
Nì aon bhoinne de bhainne mamot mòr.
One poisonous drop can spoil a whole sea of milk.
One little drop of milk can make a giant mammoth.
Proverb from *Leabhar an Leaghaidh Mhòir* —
The Book of the Great Melting

Several times a day, a Sister or two would bring supplies –
food, drink, and whatever else Cuilean had said was needed. At
first, they offered to change the dressings on Ròna's wounds,
removing them, applying the herbs they'd gathered in the fields
and forests and the ointments of oils they'd distilled, but after the
first couple times, Cuilean told them he could do that. So, they
stood back and observed as he unwrapped her blood-crusted chest,
carefully cleaned the wound, applied the ointment, and re-bound
her with fresh bandages.

For the first few days, Ròna was barely cognizant of her
surroundings, much less of him. She floated in and out of a healing,
dream-filled sleep, partly induced by the trauma of the excision,
and partly by the potent *bainne na Màthar* – the sticky-sweet
mushroom tea that was heavily fortified with mammoth milk.

Even after Ròna started to grow aware of her surroundings,
nodding in and out of a drowsy consciousness, able to stay awake
for short periods of time, the Sisters still came to bring supplies and
to check on her, but perhaps more, to check on Cuilean and his care
of her.

While she was still too weak to care for herself, he would bathe
her. The first day, he sponged down her legs, feet and arms, and
avoiding intruding upon her, he wiped under her gown only as far
as his fingers could reach. But seeing that procedure did little more
than soak the edges of her garment, on the following days, at the
same time he changed her bandage, he removed her frock and
washed her entire body, gently sponging the oozing gash that ran

351

across her right chest, and before carefully dressing her again, giving a salvific kiss to the wound.

On the seventh day, she woke with a start just after he'd finished drying her and was applying the ointment to her healing wound. *"Dè tha thu a' dèanamh? –* What are you doing?"

"Tha e ceart gu leòr – It's okay," he said softly in the FT, for the language was starting to come back to him, albeit in fits and starts. But here he stumbled, for he didn't quite know what to call her, what she was to him, nor he to her. *"A ... a bhalaich,"* is what he finally settled on. "Buddy, pal, friend, dude." And then to cover his stutter-step, he repeated himself as if that is what he had intended to do all along. *"Tha e ceart gu leòr.* -- It's okay. You've been hurt. I'm taking care of you."

In her fog of awareness, she was comforted by the familiar words and the vision of the Sisters floating, chaperoning watchfully behind him. She nodded wanly before easing back into a sleep.

Ròna's wound was healing nicely – partly due to time, her youth, and her underlying health, and partly due to Cuilean's care under the direction of the Sisters. Each day and night, he would wash the wound, being as careful as he could not to press too hard or rub too vigorously.

Gradually, the periods of Ròna's waking grew longer, and she grew more aware of her surroundings and in a sense more sensitive of what he was doing. Occasionally, she would flinch – *"Obh! A bhalaich! Tha thu ro chruaidh* -- Oh, lad! You're too rough."

Wincing as if he shared the pain he had inflicted, he would apologize, and when he resumed, he would attempt to minister barely touching, hovering his hand over the gash.

He would salve the cut with an ointment concocted by the Sisters, one made of various plants, roots, herbs, and other remedies: golden flower, mandrake root, moon herb, and mountain aloe, and shavings from a unihorn's horn, all mixed in a salve of *bainne na Màthar* and butter.

Then came the time -- either late in the afternoon or early in the evening, when given the latitude at the bottom pole of the planet, no matter how long after the morning it was, the sky glimmered with an indirect light, and the day ghosted imperceptibly into night, a span of hours which the people of the Wayp called *feasgar* -- when Ròna announced that she was feeling well enough to venture out from the confines of the cottage.

After shampooing her hair with a lotion that smelled of the lavender that climbed the outer walls of the cottage, he helped her outside. It was slow going as she was still unsteady on her feet. In a sunny clearing, not far from the tiny building, they made a soft couch out of a bed of low-growing heather, and propping up her shoulders against him, he brushed her hair smooth.

On another day, not long after that, they rode on Dìleas's back, Ròna in front and Cuilean behind.

Along the way, they crossed paths with a parade of mammoths ambling across a clearing.

A small pack of *madadh-allaidh na coille* – forest wolves -- slinked through the shadows.

The great huntress, a sword-toothed tiger, sleepily sunned herself on a high, over-arching tree branch.

They passed a meadow where a small *beannachd* – a "blessing" or a herd -- of unihorns was pasturing. One particular female there piqued Dìleas's attention. Picking up his snout and sniffing the air that was wafting from the clearing, he gave a snort of interest. Ròna chuckled, and noting, "*Chan ise air do shon-sa, a bhalaich* – She's not for you, lad" -- she squeezed his sides gently with her legs to prompt him forward.

Skittering in and amongst the foliage they saw also the little creatures that the Mother loved just as well as the great ones: the badger and the hare and the vole and the deer squirrel and the red-crested woodpecker, and many others unnoticed, such as the crawling fire ants, and the beetles burrowing into the bark of the great oaks, and the brown spider weaving a web so thin it could hardly be seen.

They came to a spot where a colony of beavers – *bìobhair* in the FT -- had built a dam across a stream. The water spilled over the ramparts, and the mist from the splash of the cascade filled the air like rain that not only fell from above but rose from below. A patina of dew hung on the blades of grass that sprouted around the bottom of the falls and on the leaves and blossoms of the trees that rose above. Around this spot sprang a stand of cedar saplings, which had grown chest high, straight, and strong in the enveloping and continual brume that rose from the spray thrown up by the cataract.

Although the beavers themselves were massive -- about the length of a grown person -- they were peaceful, unless meddled with, of course, and went about their business with an industriousness and diligence that had inspired the idiom – *cho dìcheallach ris na bìobhairean* – "as diligent as the beavers." They toiled in the pool at the top of the falls -- shoring up the weir, which needed constant maintenance lest it be swept away by the strong current; diving down to gather soft water grass that grew at the bottom of the stream; swimming out to gather water lilies, clover, ragweed, cattails, and watercress from the banks where they and other succulents sheltered from the rushing water torrent; and scooting in and out of the lodges they had built there, bringing home to their just born kits the wealth of their gleanings.

Sharing this constructed pond, although undisturbed by the comings and goings of the beavers, a solitary duck-billed platypus slid under the water out of sight at the approach of the three intruders.

A tulip tree arched above to the height of ten men, its bell-shaped blossoms attracting a buzz of hummingbirds – red-throated, blue-wing-tipped, black-hooded -- which severally darted towards and away from the flowers, strafing and dive-bombing each other as they maneuvered for the right to a particular nectar-filled bloom, each one staking out a territory in the air. As one suckled a blossom, another would buzz in and strafe it, which would send both off in flight and pursuit, leaving the way for a yet another floweret sipper to swoop in and guzzle the precious nectar.

Under the sheltering arms of this tree, after they dismounted, Cuilean spread a plaid and laid out their meal of meat pies, cheese, and bannocks -- a pancake-type bread, humped in a mound. They ate their picnic, washed down with a flask of *bainne na Màthar*, and Dìleas turned to browse the surrounding vegetation.

It was still too soon after Ròna's wounding for her to be feeling totally recovered. Even though they'd ridden the distance, Ròna was tired after the trek. She lay back and soaked up the sun. Her gaze shifted to a large grey squirrel that was chittering on a stump, the remnants of a tree that had been felled in a storm some time before. Ròna shifted her sight away from the remains of the trunk as it reminded her of her own scarred stump of a breast.

Dìleas, the reins loosed from their tethering, moved away softly. (For all their bulk, unihorns could move discretely, delicately.)

Ròna noted with a tolerant smile, "*Tha i deiseil dhutsa, nach eil, a bhalaich?* – She's ready for you, isn't she, lad?"

Dìleas snorted an affirmative.

"*Uill, ma dh'fheumas tu, feumaidh tu.* – Well, if you must, you must," Ròna said with a permissive cock of the head.

With a happy puff, the unihorn turned with the alacrity of a youngster and trotted across the field towards the she-nihorn.

Pretty soon, Dìleas and the mare were cavorting in the heather. He nuzzled her, and she skipped away and turned and waited for him to catch up. They sidled close to each other, nose to tail. Again, she scampered away, and stopped suddenly and spun to face him. He trotted in front of her, pivoted in a near-pirouette, and shook his broad shoulders in display. He galloped in a wide circle around the filly, kicking high and bucking.

"Now, he's showing off," Ròna chuckled.

Together, the two unihorns raced across the field and into a stand of trees.

"We won't see them for a while," Ròna said, clucking her cheeks.

Again, Ròna dozed off, either because of her full stomach, the fortified *bainne*, the warmth of the sun, or the comfort she felt in Cuilean's lap.

He was careful not to move lest he disturb her.

Cuilean's eye was caught by a movement on the blanket beside him. There, a beetle no bigger than his fingernail was pushing a dark, fibrous ball across the cross-hatched patterning of the blanket directly towards Ròna. Cuilean started in alarm at the ugly little creature and its strange doings.

He cocked his hand defensively to swat it away. The sudden jerk jolted Ròna awake. She immediately took in the sight of Cuilean about to strike the beetle struggling with its Sisyphean boulder on the plaid.

She held out her hand to stop his blow, which, if he had dealt, would not have been impeded by her light finger brush any more than a prowling sword-tooth would have been obstacled by a blade of grass.

But it was more her words that caused him to pause: a sharp "*Dè tha thusa a' dèanamh?* -- What're you doing?"

"That thing ..."

"I know, the *daol-chac*[108] – the doodlebug -- what about him?"

"It's ... it's ..." He was at a loss as to just what about it troubled him: probably, that in the DownBlow, where he'd spent so many years of his young life, there were no such creatures, the environment having been successfully sterilized of nearly all non-human life forms over the millennia.

"*Na dragh ort* – Don't worry about it. He's not bothering anything."

"It was gonna ..." He pulled up short. He found himself groping for what exactly it was that he feared the little creature was *gonna*. And once he tried putting his concern into words, he realized that saying it out loud would make him sound even sillier than he already felt.

Ròna caught him out: "You thought he was going to attack me? With his shitball?"

---

[108] *Daol-chac* – literally, shit beetle

That piece of added information was even more confounding. "What?"

"Yeah, that's a little piece of mammoth shit he's hauling. Unless it's mìneotarbh shit, or unihorn, or sword-tooth, or ... *Cò aig a tha fios?* -- Who knows?"

He started back in revulsion with an exclamation: "Ugh! That's disgusting. Let me get rid of it."

She held her hand up again. "No."

"Why not? It's just a useless shit-eater."

"And you think you're better?"

"Well, I sure don't eat shit."

His assertion was met with a sly smile, as if to say, *you don't know the half of it, buddy*. But instead, she took a less sarcastic route: "Aside from that, he's not useless. We need him."

His brain was (figuratively) spinning. He gave his head a quick shake as if to clear the dizziness (which, if it had really been spinning, would have only increased the gyration and subsequently, the associated disorientation).

Ròna went on: "Everything depends on the doodlebug."

If the phrase, *That don't make no sense* had existed in Simspeek, or if he had known the FT expression *Chan eil bun no bàrr aige* – it has neither bottom nor top – he might have blurted out those words.

Ròna was amused by his perplexity, but never having been one to torment helpless creatures, she was moved to relieve his quandary: "It's the last stage of returning nourishment to the soil and beginning the cycle all over. This little, useless, disgusting creature – as you put it ..."

"I didn't say that," Cuilean protested. "You're putting words in my mouth."

Ròna grinned broadly at him. He really was too easy to tweak. "I wouldn't want to do that. Instead, let me try putting an idea into your head. This little shit-beetle replenishes the spiral of life. He spreads the seeds that the animals have eaten, so new plants can sprout again. Those feed the animals ... and us." She made a circular movement with her finger that spiraled forward and upward in the air. "'*S cacaidh sinn* – And we poop, and so the cycle of the Mother goes on."

With that, she turned her attention to the little black bug. "*An seo, a charaid,*" she said. "Here, friend," and scooping up the beetle and his burden in her hand, she lifted him to the edge of the plaid and set him down on a bare patch of ground, the dung ball in front so he might continue in the same direction it had been going in before it'd been so inconsiderately interrupted. "*Thalla* -- Go on," she said softly.

Cuilean, for his part, flipped his palm upwards as if asking for more.

Ròna held out her finger in the flight path of a butterfly. She lighted there. "We wouldn't have any of this," she said, making a motion with a tilt of her head towards the forest and the surrounding meadow, "without our little shit collector there and this lady here, the *dealan na bàn-dè* – the lightning of the Goddess. Without them, none of this would exist. This little one," she said with a nod gentle enough not to startle away the flutter-by, "spreads the seed of the Mother from one flower to another, and that's the beginning of it all."

"And the doodlebug is the end?"

"*Sin agad e!* – There you have it! Which leads us back to the beginning. Everything small and great *o bhonn gu bàrr* – from bottom to top -- depends upon the butterfly and the doodlebug. It's all connected."

Ròna gently stirred her hand and sent the butterfly on its way.

"Let's go down to the *loch,*" she said abruptly, and without waiting for a response, she called out, "*A Dhìlis! A bhalaich! –* Dìleas! Lad!" which summoning she followed up with a long, piercing whistle, but there was no response. No answering clippity-clop of her mount's returning.

"*Tha e a' ruith an nighean bheag sin* -- He must be chasing after that little girl," she surmised with a knowing lift of the eyebrows. Embarrassed by what she was alluding to, Cuilean shifted his gaze away.

His shyness had always tickled her.

"It's not that far. Let's walk," she said.

He gathered their stuff, and once on the shore of the *loch,* he could tell she was close to being herself again when upon seeing a pod of seals cavorting in the water, popping their heads up and then rolling under the waves and roiling back to the surface, she dropped her plaid and waded into the water. Still clutching her right arm close to her body, she dove into the *loch,* and swam and swirled with the seals.

When she returned to the shore, she evidenced a grimace of discomfort, but also a smile of satisfaction.

She stripped off her now-wet undergarment and threw it over a driftwood log to dry.

"*Dè air an t-saoghal mhòr!*[109] – What in the world!" Cuilean yelped, startled at her sudden and unexpected undressing. "What're you doing!"

"It's wet. I want to dry it off. I guess, I should've thought of this before I went in the water." Big grin.

"But ..." Cuilean stammered.

"Don't look if it bothers you," she said with a teasing laugh. "Turn around. Go over there. Make yourself useful and set up some targets for me."

Of two minds, that is, wanting to look, and embarrassed at the same time to be desiring to – a dilemma which did not escape Ròna's amusement -- Cuilean turned his back on her and jogged a short distance off and set up some small pieces of flotsam on a smooth tree trunk that had washed up onto the shore.

She waved him away, nocked the bow, and took aim, but when she drew it, attempting the pull tore at her wound and painfully stretched the skin and strained the muscles around her chest. "*Pit air teine*! -- Flaming cunt!" she cried out. Disgusted with her weak condition, she tossed the bow and the arrows down with the complaint, "*Feumaidh mi bogha pàiste a ghabhail* – I'll have to get a baby's bow."

"It'll come back," Cuilean consoled her from a distance, starting back.

She bent to pick up the bow where she had thrown it down. She was brushing the sand off it, when with hardly any warning except an angry squawk a moment before he was struck, Cuilean was knocked down from behind. He landed flat on his face in the sand. Looking back, he had only an instant before

---

[109] If anyone had been paying attention, they would have noted that the FT was coming back to Cuilean, as the first elements of language to be learned or restored are swear-words and curses.

a giant predator *iolaire mhòr* – a great eagle twice the size of a man – having risen a couple dozen feet off the ground, swooped down on him again.

He jumped up with a cry of surprise and stumbled into a run towards Ròna. They retreated towards the cover of the forest.

"We must've gotten close to her nest!" Ròna shouted breathlessly as they dashed.

"How can you tell it's a 'she'?" Cuilean called out as the bird banked in a turn and dived towards them again.

"Protecting her young! But does it matter!?!" Ròna shouted as they ran.

The eagle swooped at them again. Stranded in the open, they were still some distance from the protection of the trees.

"I guess not!" Cuilean shouted back.

Ròna attempted to draw the bow but couldn't do more than release the arrow to flop ineffectually just a body length away.

Cuilean picked up a piece of driftwood -- a length of a branch half as long as a man and as thick as a forearm -- and swung it to swat at the bird, knowing full well he wouldn't injure the fowl but hoping that he could at least scare her away. Instead, the flying beast grabbed the wood between her talons, rose rapidly, and then swooped towards him again. In flight, she released the branch, in effect flinging it at Cuilean. The stick clattered against his head and arms, but even though he'd been able to deflect most of its force, his feet caught in the sand, and knocked off balance, he toppled over.

Taking advantage of Cuilean's vulnerable position, the eagle plunged and hooked him, her claws digging into his flesh, and turning upwards, she flapped her wings to take flight, lifting the both of them aloft.

It happened faster than she could think that Ròna swung up into a handstand, her back arched. Clenching the bow between the toes of one foot, and the bowstring caught between the toes of the other, she drew and released the arrow. The dart's flight caught the eagle in the wing, and the ferocious bird gave a squeal – not the angry attacking squawk it had voiced before, but in an odd transition from cruel killer to wounded weakling, rather a shriek of distress like that of a hurt chick. Bird and Cuilean tumbled to the ground.

With a groan, Ròna collapsed into a heap, clutching her right chest.

Cuilean had seen what Ròna had done only in his peripheral vision, so it was not totally clear to him how she had brought the eagle down; besides that, it had all happened too quickly. All he knew for certain is that one moment he had been suspended in air and rising higher and higher, and the next, he'd found himself lying under the inert predator.

He struggled to extricate himself from the body of the giant bird, and after some contortions, he did manage to free himself, pushing the body off him, noticing only then the arrow through its wing.

As if shaken awake from a shock, the eagle gave a distressed, shrill screech, flapped her unwounded wing, half-beat the air with the other, and fluttered off, lopsided and cockadoodle, like a drunk correcting and over-correcting her careening from one side to the other.

Cuilean rushed to Ròna.

Blood was oozing from where the wound had torn open. She was gasping in pain, gripping her chest.

Stripping himself of his own shirt, Cuilean applied it as a compress on the open laceration to staunch the flow of blood.

He held the material against her and gathered her to him, rocking her gently to soothe her, muttering, "*Tha e ceart gu leòr, a bhalaich* – It's okay, pal."

When her panting subsided and she recovered herself, still cradling her, but relaxing his embrace, he remarked, with a little surprise in his voice, "I didn't know you could do that."

"Neither did I!" she replied with a snort of shared astonishment.

So strangely exhilarated after their narrow escape were they (well, Cuilean's escape, and her rescue of him), that this struck them as wonderfully witty and funny. Mutually, they let go of a long burst of laughter.

Their laughter slowed to a stop, drifting into a series of deep breaths and reflective chuckles.

Whereupon, they looked at each other and burst out laughing again.

This went on for a few more rounds, each gust of laughter being less jubilant and of a lower tone than the previous.

Until finally, Cuilean gave a last chuckle.

To which Ròna responded with a nod of her head. She cocked her ear, listening, and sighed, "*Feumaidh sinn dhachaigh* -- We'd better get back home. It's going to rain."

"How do you know?"

"A little birdie told me."

"Yeah, right."

"No, I mean it. *Ist. –* Quiet." She placed her forefinger across his lips. "*Èist. --* Listen."

From a nearby birch tree, with its white, black-streaked bark, and its multiple trunks branching up from the ground, came a loud staccato warble of the *breacan-beithe* – the gray-hooded, russet and black speckled finch (named after the tree, the *beithe*, which it inhabited). The chirps were distinct and spaced: *Run run run run.*

She tried calling Dìleas but quickly gave up. "*Tha e air falbh –* He's gone. *'S cha till e.* – And he's not coming back!" In a tone that allowed little dissent, she added, "*Rachamaid. Sa mhionaid.* -- Let's go. Right this minute!"

Cuilean got to his feet and gathered up their stuff – which wasn't much: the bag in which they'd brought their lunch, the thick plaid they'd lain on, her bow and quiver of arrows. He helped Ròna to her feet. They headed back, but while they were still a field away from the cabin, the rain started, softly at first, and within moments as if the cloud overhead had burst open, they were deluged with a downpour that fell so hard, it seemed that the flood was threatening to beat them to the ground.

"Hurry!" Cuilean shouted.

Ròna tried a few steps of a run and then stopped, grasping her side. "I can't."

Dropping the load he was carrying, he swooped her up in his arms and broke into a trot.

She cried out sporadically as spasms of ache stabbed her not yet totally-healed and now partially re-opened wound, these cries interspaced with squeals of giddy laughter, joined by Cuilean's wild howl as he raced towards the cottage.

Finally, they reached the door and burst into the shelter. As carefully as he could (there was a little dropping involved), he placed her on the cushioned daybed, collapsing breathlessly beside her.

Suddenly modest, she fumbled with the bed cover and pulled it to half-cover her body.

They lay side-by-side and panted together, in synchrony. Gradually, another spasm of laughter swept over them.

Finally, noting the heavy drumbeat of raindrops on the roof of the cabin, Cuilean looked at her quizzically. "How'd you know it was going to rain?" quickly adding, "and don't say a little birdie told you.'"

In accordance with his instruction, she said nothing except, "*Ceart gu leòr* -- Okay," her brows lifting and the corners of her lips micro-millimetering up into an enigmatic Mona-Lisa smile.

Which first tinged him with irritation, before they joined each other in laughter at her mischievous compliance.

Back to the Garden

Thug a' Mhàthair pàrras air uachdar na Talmhainn dhiubh. Tha e
an urra ribh fhèin nan cumadh sibh e no nan caitheadh sibh e.
The Mother gave you paradise on earth. It's up to you
whether you keep it or waste it.
Proverb from *Leabhar an Leaghaidh Mhòir* —
The Book of the Great Melting

Shortly after the time of *Imbolg* – which the Children of the
Mother called the first days of spring – when life sprouted in the
womb of the earth,[110] when the lambs were born, and the first
springtime flowers were blooming, and the heat was returning to
the lowland farmlands of the Wayp, the people of Balnabane
transmigrated from the meadows of the lower lands through the
forests of the gently sloping trails to the cooler highland pastures
that they called *Gàrradh Èite*,[111] taking with them their blessings of
the *aon-adharcachs* – their unihorn herds -- and parades of
mammoths, and bevies of the great *fèidh* – or deer, whose antlers
spread out on either side the length of a person -- as well as their
flocks of sheep and llamas, and herds of cattle and *mìneotarbhs*.

It was a time of celebration, play, and toil, all mingled together,
with little distinction between them. A time of pleasure and delight.
No one worked except to provide themselves with food and drink,
intermixing labor and fun to such a degree that no distinction could
be made between industry and pastime.

No effort was extended except to fish or swim in the mountain
loch, or dance, or by the men to wrestle with each other, or to race
their one-horned steeds, or to engage in the sport-of-all-sports –
mìneotarbh leaping -- or by the boys to tussle with *mìneotarbh*
calves.

---

[110] Some authorities posit that the word *imbolg* is derived from the FT phrase *ann*
am bolg, or "in the womb," that is when the "seed" of spring has been imbedded
in the "womb" of nature.

[111] Or to transliterate phonetically, the Garden of Ay-cha. The derivation of the word
is ambiguous but is thought by some to signify a holy location in the sense of
"nucleus," or "core," or "kernel," that is, the place where "it" all began ("it"
being the revived and risen world of the Wayp).

It was a time of the telling of stories and singing of songs, of the creation of music and of the dancing to lively melodies, both new compositions and old favorites.

It was a time when the unihorns, the mammoths, the mìneotarbhs, and the much smaller hairy red cattle would calve, and the sheep and the llamas would lamb, and the children of the people would take delight in playing with the newly born young of every type. It was a time when the people would shear the mammoths, a practice that served the dual purpose of harvesting the wool that was so important to the Children of the Mother and of relieving the huge beasts of their winter coats so as to make the hot months more bearable.

Likewise, the preparing of the mammoth wool was a time of communal activity as the fur was spun into thread, and at the climax of the preparation – of singing, joking, storytelling as the (mostly) women engaged in its *luadhadh* – the waulking -- its final transformation into usable woolen cloth.

There was much drinking of the *teatha na màthar* – the tea of the Mother -- the magic elixir distilled from the water that flowed from the snowy-white paps of the mountain peaks, and the *balgan-buachair* -- the mushrooms that grew wild in the pastures all around them.

At this time of year, the days grew so long that the sun didn't set until past the middle of the night, and the dew that settled on the ground during the evenings provided a gratifying relief from the heat of the summer. During the short period of dark, in the distant sky at the edge of the horizon, the *fir-chlis* – the dancing men -- the aurora that glimmered and glowed in the high night sky, blue and red and yellow, and all the other rainbow colors, emblazoned the imaginations of young lovers, delighted the children sleepy from playing all the day, and lighted the stories, reminiscences, and music of the troop laid out on the grass, in the heather, and beneath the swinging canopy of the forest.[112]

But to get there – the upland shielings -- the people had to caravan up the mountain slopes, and for this, much preparation was necessary.

Early on the morning of departure, the village of Balnabane stirred with activity. Seumas was packing his fishing equipment – long poles and short poles, his nets and hooks and baits, while

---

[112] It should be noted that this mass gathering also served as protection from the foraging direwolf packs, the hunting threats of sword-toothed tigers, and the predation of lone bears – *na mathain mòra* in the FT – who stood twice the height of a grown man and who were just then awakening from their winter-long hibernation.

Maggie gathered the food they'd need for the migration. Seumas strapped himself with a carrying pack for *Seumas Beag* – little Seumas -- a tow-headed, eager little boy, who as their friend *Iain Caol* – Thin John -- put it, didn't just go somewhere – he *made for it*; the little boy would take off in a sprint for whatever he wanted to get and in whichever direction he wanted to go.

Iain himself who always traveled light, simply strapped a knapsack onto his back and strung his fiddle by his side in a sling, and, the bow protruding from the top of the pack, was ready before anyone.

Cuilean sat in the grass at the edge of the village, quizzically looking on the hurried proceedings– trying to figure out the full import of what was happening.

When Ròna walked by in the busyness of her preparation, he held out his hand to pause her. "*Dè tha dol?*" he asked. "What's going on?"

She hardly had time to explain. "Wait right there." She hurriedly explained, "We're going to the shieling."

"Where?"

"It'll be clear soon enough." Just wanting him to stay put and not wander off and get lost, perhaps in all the bustling and hustling confusing him with her unihorn mount. She was feeling better now, more her old self (if that meant being firm to the point of "bossy"). "Wait here. Don't go anywhere."

Several youngsters hurried excitedly by, their animated voices speaking to the urgency of the preparations in that peculiar half-child / half-adult way that they had of placing the utmost importance on things of the most trivial significance.

Here was Sìleas shrieking at Iseabail, her mother: "I can't wear the red ribbon! Seonag has the red."

"Well, wear the yellow one then."

"BUT I LIKE RED!"

"Then wear red."

"DON'T YOU UNDERSTAND ANYTHING!?!" the girl screamed. She threw herself down on the pile of bedding that her mother had staged for loading onto the cart yoked behind their mammoth matriarch, whom they called *Sìleas Bheag* – Little Sìleas (an ironic name because Sìleas, Iseabail's daughter, was of course, much smaller than their mammoth companion and family member, but the girl was known as *Sìleas Mhòr* – Big Sìleas, so *sin agad e* – there you have it).

"*A ghràidh* – Love, everything will be alright. Here, you can wear mine," and Iseabail returned to their cottage and came out with a splendid plaid ribbon that sported a soft green background and was streaked with a blue that was almost concealed as it was nearly the same shade as the green, just a little darker, all offset against swatches of brilliant red.

"You see, you wear them together – the red and the yellow – and everybody'll see how beautiful they are, and it really shows off your eyes," for indeed, Sìleas had beautiful blue-green eyes.

With a squeal of glee, the girl ran off to the stream to see herself in the reflection as she tied the ribbon pair in her hair. *Perhaps, it would look best interwoven and dangling down, or maybe, it would be better tying her hair back, or conceivably, she should loop it around her neck and throat as a provocative choker.*

Each cottage in the village was abustle with activity like this, each with its own special and unique but all the same, common concerns.

Finally, the trek to the summer pasturage started. The stream of human and animal life was one full of noise and celebration of the long summer months of relaxation and pleasure ahead of them. The procession was full of anticipatory joy, intermixed with the "singing" of bagpipes – both the great ones with their drones sprouting out the top that provided a sonorous under-current accompanying the high-pitched melodies, and the smaller, sweeter, elbow-bellowed pipes; and the pumping of harmoniums, the blowing of harmonicas, the fiddling of fiddles, and the blowing, stringing, plucking, or banging of any other musical instrument devised or imagined or created by the Children of the Wayp, blending together with the excited barking of dogs, and bellowing of deer, and the trumpeting of mammoths, all together sending up a cacophonous symphony of music (or, a symphonic cacophony, depending upon your point of view).

Conversation was lively, full of ribaldry, joking, and excitement. Teenagers danced, and children scampered about in, amongst, and between the feet of the adults and the tree-trunk legs of the beasts of burden -- the giant mìneotarbhs, mammoths, the massive bear dogs that stood guard at the flanks of the procession, and Ròna's own unihorn, Dìleas.[113]

---

[113] It should be noted that not only did the custom constitute a kind of summer vacation, but the tradition was, as well, a conscious re-enactment of the exodus from the DownBlow into the area of the Wayp that was initially settled by the first pioneers. As such, if the editor might be allowed a little wordplay here, it integrated both *recreation* from the mundane affairs and day-to-day needs of getting a living and a *re-creation* of the origin myth. But as tied the yearly event was to the creation of the Wayp and the Children's observance of the Mother, it would be incorrect to say they came to worship the goddess because that word would imply something else besides what they did although what they did constitute in a way a kind of worship – if what was meant by that word includes singing and dancing and revelry; or the young people going off into the woods in pairs

On the way, the caravan passed a lek – a field or arena – where a couple dozen male capercaillies – *capall choille* in the FT, or "horse of the forest" – had gathered. These were mostly-flightless birds (though they were capable of fluttering or wobbling short distances in the air), about half as tall as a person, and while the males faced each other in a rough circle, an assortment of females stood by, shifting their feet, spectating from the sidelines. The males, red wattles displayed like caps atop their heads, and their tail feathers fanned vertically in a threat display, flapped their wings and rushed at each other, hitting each other with their wings or pecking at their rivals' heads. After this competition had gone on for a bit and during a lull, a hen would walk into the midst, and each male would tilt towards her, turn in half circles around her as she walked, a display that was a kind of a fowl runway strut, a noiseless calling out, P*ick me! Pick me!* After some consideration, the female would stop before her favorite contestant. She had chosen.

For the journey, Cuilean was seated behind Ròna on Dìleas' back. The couple were quiet as they rode, the awkwardness of their seating, the still strange newness of their being together – especially out in the open in plain view of everybody else in the village -- and the novelty – for Cuilean -- of the surroundings, being unconducive to conversation.

Ahead of the pair, Ròna's father, Dòmhnall, guided the horse that pulled the little cart in which the girl's mother, Siùsaidh, rode. He was a large, quiet man, gentle in manner and speech, quick to smile – indeed, often giving a smile and a shrug and a dip of his head in lieu of the words that eluded him. He was amused by the antics and the play of the children, though always careful and restrained among them, as if he were afraid that he might, in his clumsiness, break one. As he admitted himself, he was not quite so knowledgeable of those he called *na h-ainmhidhean dà-chasach* -- the two-legged animals.

Mostly, he was perceptive of the moods and inclinations of the animals he tended. Animals often flocked to him, demonstrating their affection by simply assenting to being in his presence, manifesting a feeling of security near him. With a chuckle, he'd often jest, "*Tha mi glè eòlach air bèistean, ach chan eil mi cho*

---

and small clusters on the long sun-lit evenings of this southern high-flung continent; or sitting long evenings together spinning mammoth-wool plaids and stories, alike; or playing tunes and songs on their fiddles and -- as they put it in the FT -- singing the pipes. So in this sense, their time in the summer shielings did constitute a kind of "worship" in that it was a combined a celebration of life with a remembering and recognition of the source of all life.

cinnteach air daoine – I'm very familiar with beasts, but I'm not so sure with people."

Ròna's gaze was drawn farther ahead to a bustle of small children laughing and bounding around a figure. Because of the distance and the flurry of obscuring little bodies, she couldn't quite place where from or when she knew the man at the eye of the storm of giggling children, who were capering uninhibitedly around their grown playmate. Occasionally, one of the bolder ones would fling himself at the man in such a way that if he hadn't caught the kid, the child would have come crashing down painfully, but the youngster, being so certain of the dexterity of the older playmate, and his care, would climb up onto a wagon or a cart or even the back of a nearby pack animal and launch himself into the air towards the man, who invariably caught the flying squirrel of a child and brought him safely to earth, though not before shaking him, turning him upside down, or tickling a stream of giggles out of the little one.

Little Catrìona came up to what for her was his huge presence – she all of 5 years old, small, and normally timid – and looking up at his towering eminence, she beckoned to him. He bent down to hear what she had to say, and with a leap up and a quick swipe of her hand, she filched the bonnet – a flat, tartan-patterned tam-o-shanter -- from his head and ran off with a squeal.

The man pretended to give chase, and "pretended" is an appropriate word because he somehow never quite caught her, despite her being so young and little and he being capable of long-legged strides that somehow never matched hers.

The little girl ran mindlessly, heedless of the tromping legs and hooves of the assortment of massive creatures in whose midst she was bolting. Although the play seemed helter-skelter and totally out of control, Ròna was impressed by the pains the man took to ensure the little girl wasn't hurt in her heedlessness. At one point, he reached out and tapped her out of the way of a carriage wheel, and he gave a shout of warning of "*Thoir aire!* -- Watch out!" at some teenagers who were dancing their way along the path, and he shoulder-checked a mìneotarbh hard enough to give the animal pause in its step, so it didn't trample the child.

The grown playmate did not catch up with little Catrìona until her legs buckled under her, and she collapsed in a gasping heap, and he administered such a vigorous tickling that her squealing giggles attracted the attention of the other children, who promptly rushed over to rescue their friend by jumping upon their large comrade's bent back, whereupon he himself was borne down to the grass and the heather under a mob of gleeful attackers.

As Dìleas plodded closer, Ròna made out who was at the center of the children's romping: Robert Morunx, *mac a' choin* – the son of a dog – whom she had arrested for desecrating the temple of the Mother – it must have been about a year ago – and whom the Sister had saved from being tossed over the cliff back to the DownBlow from where he'd come. *And here he was, enjoying himself!?!* Playing with the children as if he weren't the criminal that she knew him to be!?!

Tumbling about in the trodden heather of the trail, Robert Morunx looked up into Ròna's face. He froze as the two locked stares. With an apology, *"Duilich … uh, duilich,"* he stood up, gently disentangling himself from the children, stumbling with his attempts at the FT in the process of explaining and excusing himself, *"Duilich, ach gu leòr* -- Sorry, uh, sorry, but enough!" To the protests of the children who wanted to play just a little longer, he responded, *"Mar am facal, fheàrr aig àird an spòrs fàgail* – Like the word, best the height of the fun leaving," he explained, mangling the old saying.

The children, despite their disappointment at having their play disrupted, burst into titters at their friend's funny way of talking.

Morunx picked himself up, shaking off a couple hangers-on -- in this case, literal "hangers-on" – like four-year old Hector MacEachern, who clung tenaciously to Morunx's coat sleeve even after the man stood straight up. Robert pried the child off as he might have picked off a nettlesome burr, and setting the boy on his feet, gave him a gentle tap on the bottom in the direction of his mother. *"Thalla, a bhalaich … uh, uh … ath-uair.* -- Go on, lad … uh, uh … next hour."

Morunx composed himself, and looking up at Ròna, stood stock still like a man before a judge.

Ròna ran her tongue around the inside of her mouth as she

thought of what to say. Finally, "The sister tells me it'll soon be time for you to leave *Taigh nam Peathraichean* – the House of the Sisters."

The information seemed to strike Morunx as a surprise, and not just a surprise, but an unwelcome one. "That can't be right," he protested. The progression of time was something he'd tracked when he was first sent to the House, notching the door post to his room, counting the days towards the time when he would be released to return to his all-important business affairs, but as he had become immersed in the cycling of the days and weeks and months of the Sisters' routines of caring and nurturing and working and making, he'd quite forgotten about looking forward to that ill-defined future hour or how the accumulation of gowp-creds would somehow make that day to come so much better than this day.

But calculating quickly, he realized that what Ròna had said was right. His time was close to being up.

A protest went up from the little ones clinging to his hand and the fringe of his kilt. *"Chan eil! Chan eil thu gar fàgail, nach eil, a Raibeirt!?!* -- No! You aren't leaving us, are you, Robert!?!"

Robert looked around at the little faces and back to Ròna. He asked with a bit of a plea in his voice. "You think I might stay a *little* longer?"

"What about your business?" Realizing she didn't quite know just what his "business" was, she balked. "Your money making ... stuff?"

He made a wry face and a shrug. "I promised the little ones I'd go to the loch with them," he explained. Here he stumbled over the phrase in fractured FT. *"Sinn dol dhan loch airson ionnsaich a-mach* -- Us going into the lake for learn outside."

Ròna smiled at his lame attempt, but noted approvingly the effort, however hobbling it was. As the old saying went, *nas fheàrr an teanga na cloinn bhriste nan cànan cèin cliste* – Better the tongue of the Children broken than fluent Simspeek.

Morunx went on, wrestling with his fractured FT, but giving it a brave go: "Sisters teaching everything depend on doodlebug ..."

"Please! Please! Ròna! Please!" several of the little ones exclaimed, totally unashamed or uninhibited to flash their hearts' desires in the open.

In the face of such earnest pleadings, Ròna had to give in. "I'll talk to her," she conceded.

"Hò-rò! Hu-rè!" shouted the children in hope as they commenced to dance around Morunx. One intrepid boy jumped up on his back and weighted him forward so that the man stumbled and fell.

"*Mo chreach!* – My ruin![114]" Robert exclaimed as he was going down. Immediately, three other children leaped onto the dog pile.

As he struggled to free himself from the entanglement, he scolded, "*A Chamshroin!* – Cameron! -- *Nach dèanamh sin, laochain!*[115] – Not doing that, buddy!"

"I see your language learning is coming along," Ròna remarked with an uneven smile, remembering his expression of contempt for the tongue of the Wayp when she'd last seen him.

He made his way to his feet. "*Agam tha mi* – Me has to." He thought hard to summon the words: "*Iad ùpraidichean smachd cumail* -- Them hooligans control keeping." But he used the word with such affection and love that the children beamed proudly to be called "hooligans," even as they laughed at the funny way their friend had said it.

"Enjoy learning about doodlebugs," Ròna said as she turned away.

Robert reached down and tickled a little girl who was close to him. "*Seo mo 's fheàrr daol-chac* – This my best shit-beetle."

The tiny one giggled in delight.

~~

---

[114] *Mo chreach* – translates literally as "my ruin" but is actually a mild exclamation, that might be uttered if somebody trips or spills milk; somewhat akin to the Simspeek / DownBlow expression, "Cockroaches on my toes!"

[115] *Laochain* – a language footnote might be of some interest here: the word means literally, something like "little hero" or "little champion" and is used as a term of affection for a little boy, much like in Simspeek, a young male might be addressed as "little corporate manager" or "young focwaod."

Waulking the mammoth

Nuair a sheinneas na mnathan nan òrain, cluinnidh na h-eòin air na meuran-craoibhe.
When the women sing their songs,
the birds listen in the tree branches.
Proverb from *Leabhar an Leaghaidh Mhòir* —
The Book of the Great Melting

In preparation for the dog days of summer that were coming, the wooly mammoths had to be sheared and their wool processed into usable fabric. In spite of the work involved, the whole complex of activities around this process – the shearing, the cleaning of the raw fur, its transmutation into spun wool, and eventually into clothing and other materials -- was a time of great festivity.

For the shearing, anticipating the bliss that was coming, the giant mammoths would plop themselves down on the grass, rolling over on their backs like giant puppies waiting for their tummies to be rubbed. As the herders went to work trimming and shaving them, the combination of combing, brushing, and clipping aroused a happy trumpeting and a concordant purring that signaled the beasts' pleasure.

Then, the sheered wool had to be cleaned by washing it in the piss that had been collected in knee-high barrels spread around the shieling for just for this purpose. Boys – and sometimes even girls (though for obvious reasons, it was easier for the boys) – typically thought it great fun to add their contributory drops to the collection of the ammonia-rich liquid.

There was a joke told – exactly by whom, we have been unable to ascertain -- about a visitor from the DownBlow sneering at one of the Children of the Mother, "You smell like pee!" The native of the Wayp smiled in appreciation. "Thank you," he said, beaming proudly. "New suit!" Although the jest was no doubt apocryphal as mammoth wool was washed thoroughly before being woven into any finished product.

Many of the women – those who weren't shearing and gathering with the men or lounging by the streams, or swimming in the lake that watered the luxuriant highland valleys – were engaged in processing the lush wool into swaths of cloth. There were those who loomed, those who wove, and those who formed the material into finished products: blankets, sweaters, kilts, dresses, trousers, shirts, skirts, and bonnets, not to omit carpeting, furniture upholstery, window drapes, cushion stuffing, building insulation, and whatever other use the mind could devise for a soft and sumptuous substance, one that both protected against the cold and conditioned against the heat. There wasn't an explicit competition, but those engaged in this work strove to create the most inventive patterns, the most luxurious material, and the most attractive garments.

Although anyone was free to participate to the best of their ability in this process, it was mostly women who did so because (although it was never quite said out loud) there was the general belief that men were – for the most part – too clumsy, too thick-fingered, too impatient, too (in a word) simple to concentrate with the intensity required by the importance of such work.

Besides, although men were welcome, most chose not to take

part, many of them being more interested in leaping the mìneotarbh bulls, or wrestling with each other, racing their unihorns, or "singing" their musical instruments.[116] It wasn't that the people had to do this work together, for the tasks were such that many of the different processes in the creating of the finished product could have been done separately, with each worker finishing a task and then passing their piece of the whole on to another, with no one ever talking to anybody, no one needing to speak to anyone else. But the Children of the Mother *liked* to work

---

[116] "singing" the instruments -- borrowing from the phraseology employed by the FT, in which one could "sing" the fiddle, or "play" it

collectively. After all, wasn't it better to be together than to be apart? Wasn't it better to work together where they could talk, sing, share stories, laugh, and sometimes cry together rather than be boxed up in cramped, confining cubbyholes?

In a clearing, separated from the strand near the loch by a stand of trees, as part of the final process of the preparation of the wool, the women and the few men who did take part sat opposite each other across crude tables – actually just boards set up on sawhorse trestles.

This makeshift work space provided the stage for the final step in the fabrication of the finished product, a process that consisted of pushing, pulling, and pounding on the fabric after it had been sheared and spun into thread and woven into swaths of multi-colored woolen plaid. The people so engaged stretched the material and compacted it, making the weave of the mammoth wool swaths tight, resilient, water resistant, and wind proof. This was known as waulking the mammoth wool – or *luadhadh*, in the FT.

The method was comprised of a rhythmic, syncopated stretching and compressing of the textile, accompanied by coordinated thumping of the table, which provided a beat to which the waulkers timed their songs and coordinated the preparation of the fabric. This work, if work it was,[117] was accompanied by raucous conversations, gossip, and songs, both traditional and improvised.

At one table, presided an older woman who was known as Grandmother – *Seanmhair*[118] in the FT -- an appellation that was more one of respect and deference than direct relationship, although she was so ancient that she had long been as a "grandmother" to everyone in the village, even to some of the grandparents themselves. "Tell us," the *Seanmhair* said, turning to Agnes, a flaxen-haired woman, big-boned, and beefy, with a broad, pancake-shaped face, who, the older woman had noted as she was

---

[117] "if work it was" -- a question because though what the effort produced was valuable and much needed by the community in that it could be used and shaped into clothing and blankets for humans and animals to shield against the cold of the Wayp winters; it furnished insulation for homes, upholstery for furniture, and carpets for buildings; and as well, it was a commodity that could be traded or sold to other communities, including sometimes, to those in the DownBlow, it was not "work" in the sense of being drudgery, for the activity was accompanied by the buzz of *craic* – chatter and lively conversation – as well as song and music. As such, the people had so much fun in the course of this activity and took so much joy in the process that very few would characterize it as something they *had* to do rather than something they *wanted* to do, something that they *looked forward* to doing, and that being the case, how could it be called "work"?

[118] *Seanmhair* -- *Seann Mhàthair*, if the word is broken down to its etymological roots, or "Old Mother"

speaking and at the same time scanning the expressions of those around her, was leaning in with an impatience borne of a desire to say something.

Agnes was taken aback at having been picked first (even though that was what she had desired), but she was impelled by the expectant gazes of the other women. "I ... hmmm ..." she began in the tone of somebody confessing. "I was always getting irritated at *Seann Phàdraig nan Gobhar* – Old Patrick of the Goats -- for letting his animals wander out. They were always getting into my vegetable garden and eating my carrots. I'd have to be chasing them out, and it made me angry. And I'd yell at him." She paused with a guilty grimace. "Then Pàdraig died, and I realized he was old and just needed help. And I wasn't there for him."

The women flanking Agnes reached over and laid their hands on the big woman to comfort her.

The Grandmother nodded. "Sometimes we don't see things that are right in front of us. But then we learn."

And with that, she started a song:

> *Leig Seann Phàdraig*
> Old Patrick let

Thump as they stretched the wool out.

> *Na gobhair aig' a-mach*
> His goats out

Thump as they pushed the material tight together.

> *Leig Seann Phàdraig*
> Old Patrick let

Thump!

> *Na gobhair aig' a-mach*
> His goats out

Thump!

> *'S dh'ith iad a h-uile càl agam.*
> And they ate all my cabbage!

And *thumpity-thump-thump!*

Other people added lines about what damage the goats did –

how they ate all the clothing on the wash lines, how they chewed through the fencing of the chicken coup, how they scared the mammoths, and how finally they were chased out of the village and returned to old Pàdraig.

After the laughter subsided at the end of the ditty, Grandmother looked around and caught the eye of Dolag, who had been looking at her in her anxiety of being called on next. "You have something to tell us, Dolag," the Old Mother said with a tilt of her head.

Dolag took a deep breath. She was a compact woman with stubby-fingered hands that were much stronger than they looked, what from the years of wrangling the one-horned herd on her little croft. She was renowned for rearing the fastest, strongest, best behaved unihorn steeds in the Wayp. When asked how she accomplished this -- how her "children," as she called them, were always winning races at the summer games – she typically responded with a sly wink that it was the special fodder she fed them, though the more observant noted her firm and motherly attentiveness to each of the calves, sometimes extending to sleeping with the newborns as if she were indeed their mother herself. She was in her late 30s and had been with her man for nearly 20 years, though they'd had no children together. "I have children enough," she'd say with a chuckle, and sometimes with a following sigh.

She'd been holding her secret in for so long, it spurted out of her. "I don't know if I love Niall anymore. Maybe I just stay with him because I don't want to be alone. Or I'm afraid of losing the children." The way she said the word, to someone who didn't know her, it might well have sounded like she meant human children, children of the Mother. "Maybe, I just love the habits I've laid down over the years," she shrugged, with a glance around the work table.

Fionnghal, a young woman with coal-black ringleted hair, confirmed the feeling. "Been there, girl."

Dolag was surprised that a woman who was so much younger than she was shared her experience.

The *Seanmhair* interjected with a knowing affirmation: "Sometimes it happens in 20 years, sometimes it takes only a year." She looked around the assemblage. There were a few nods in agreement.

"Sometimes it passes," the Old Mother continued, "and sometimes it stays."

"With me," Nansaidh said with a sly, shy twinkle as she spoke, "sometimes Peadar makes me so mad, I can't stand to even look at him. And I want to kick him out right then. But then ..." she drew a deep breath. "Let's just say, he knows how to scratch me where it itches. No way I'm going to go without!"

Which prompted another roundelay (with the accompanying beats on the table top) regarding Nansaidh's predicament:

> *Tha bod mòr aig duine Nansaidh*
> *Tha gràin mhòr aice air*
> *Ach chan eil dòigh ann air talamh*
> *A bhios i a' dol às aonais!*

> Nancy's man has a big dick
> She can't stand him
> But no way on earth
> Is she going to go without it!

The women laughed, and several nodded appreciatively in sympathy with Nansaidh's dilemma.

Another woman, Agatha, sang a snatch of a song in the FT.

> *Seann duine cha taobh mi idir*
> *Bhiodh e mall ag èirigh*
> *B' annsa leam air mo thaobh nam leabaidh*
> *Òigear làidir tapaidh.*

> No old man beside me lying --
> He'd be too slow rising.
> I'd rather in my bed
> Be a young, strong, heroic lad.

Peigi, a young woman, heavy in her last month of pregnancy, moaned softly and shifted her weight.

"*Dè tha ceàrr, a ghràidh?* – What's wrong, love?"

Peigi winced, holding her swollen belly. "It's sore ..."

"Not as sore as it will be when the baby comes out."

"Don't let her worry you, *a ghràidheana* – love. It won't hurt that much."

"My first one -- she was the hardest," another offered. "After that, they just fell out. I could be walking down a trail, and one would plop out, and I wouldn't even notice it."

"Unless somebody behind you shouted, 'Hey! You dropped something!'"

"I'm not going to have any more," Peigi asserted.

"Your husband doesn't look like a man who'll stop at just one."

"She has something to say about it, too."

"All's I'm saying is, *s' e duine tapaidh a th' ann* – it's a big, strong, strapping fellow, he is!"

There was an appreciative collective guffaw.

"I was talking to someone who's spent time in the Smokey Lands – *Tìr na Smùid*," another woman put in, in a stream-of-consciousness kind of way somewhat shifting the track of the discussion. "They don't ..." she stopped and thought of what she wanted to say. "I'm just saying, I heard they do weird things there." She lowered her voice. "They don't love like we do. They use *machines* ... what do they call them? *Chan eil fhios 'm* – I don't know. *Seòrsa de robatair-feise* -- a kind of sex robot."[119]

A universal expression of mingled disgust and noncomprehension went around.

Except for Ciorstaidh, who blurted out, "Sometimes, I could use one of those *robatair-feise,* myself! *Mo dhuine* -- my man -- is always complaining I wear him out!" This was punctuated with a guffaw.

But the topic offered too rich an opportunity for exploration. "What's with those people in the Smokey Lands? It's like they don't want babies."

"Well, you know, sometimes, I feel like that too," Baraball chipped in, "with the little ones keeping me up half the night long, and then as soon as they go to sleep, *tha Tormod ann a' gnogadh aig mo dhoras* – There's Tormod, knocking at my door." Though this took on the form of a complaint, she spoke with a touch of resignation, mingled with a hint of bragging.

"I think it's more like they can't."

"All Alasdair has to do is touch me," Ceiteag Bhàn – Fair-haired Caitie -- offered, "and I'm pregnant ..." She sung, lifting her voice in an ironic cadence:

> "*Claidheamh brìoghmhor fada aig mo dhuinne*
> *deiseil gu bràth air mo dhuille ...*
>
> A long energetic sword has my man
> always ready for my sheath ...

The women laughed and picked up the verse and improvised upon it, with, of course, the accompanying *thumps* of their work.

"I don't get it!" a sprightly girl exclaimed, loudly calling attention to herself hiding in amongst the legs of the adults, who had thought all the little ones were safely out of hearing. But Evangelaidh, ever inquisitive, had snuck in, and had hidden her

---

[119] Referring to the practice that had evolved with the spread of the ZZyzx-virus in the overheated Smokey Lands and had infected the majority of the Goill, the people who lived in the desert Pelagoes, and twisted their DNA into misshapen Quasimodo tangles and given rise to the race of Zziippps, those ramp-browed, reputedly tiny-brained giants.

growing amazement at what the grown-ups had been talking about until she was no longer able to contain herself. She demanded, "Why's that funny?"

"I'll tell you later, *a ghràidheana* – dear."

"Or, she'll find out soon enough on her own!"

The women laughed knowingly, as they launched into bragging about their husbands or their lovers – or the men they wanted to be their husbands or their lovers -- or conversely, complaining about or making fun of the men. One older woman had just finished singing a ditty advising the younger women to keep a lover on the side, "just in case."

To the thumping rhythm of the work, one woman sang:

> *Bod brìoghmhor aig m' Iain*
> *Fada fèitheach reamhar dìreach*
> *Cruaidhe slìogach rèidh*
> *Deiseil mo chur reachd-feise*

> Powerful is my Iain's dick
> Long, sinewy, straight and thick
> Steel-hard and smooth as beeswax
> Ready to make me climax

Somebody else threw in, prior to elevating her own man, a comical disparagement of this mythical Iain's prowess:

> *Chunnaic mi a shlat aig àm*
> *crìon 's slìomach 's lag*
> *cho beag ri lann an fheòir*
> *nach lìonadh tòn dreathain-dhuinn*

> I saw his rod one time
> Weak and withered and slimy
> As small as a blade of grass
> That wouldn't fill a sparrow's ass.

And after the raucous laughter died down, Ealasaid, a *cailleach* -- an older woman -- who had been sitting quietly in the group until now, growing ever more reflective, finally spoke. "I remember ... don't give me that expression. You girls look at me, and all you see is my skin like a dried mammoth hide and my tits hanging down to my knees ... but there was the time ..."

"We *know*," someone groaned in a tone of a resigned -- though deferential -- *not this story again.*

The *cailleach* was not to be dissuaded by the lack of

enthusiasm for her tale. She was tall and wore a long flowing skirt. White hair haloed her head. Even though her skin was translucent with broad veins showing through, her fingers were sure, strong, and supple; her hands could still weave the most beautiful plaid, or castrate a bull mammoth, or tend a baby's coming. "I could tell you stories about some of the *bodaich* – the old men – around here. About the time when they weren't so old." Her speech came out broken in segments as the memories came back in bits and pieces. "Which of them came after me. Some of them almost broke their necks in the mammoth field trying to impress me!"

The memory lit up her face. "Yes, in my day in the shieling ... one lad after another ... I could tell you stories."

"I'm sure you could, Ealasaid."

"There was a time ... I won't say who ... but I could tell you." She bit her lip gently in the recalling. But the temptation to overshare overruled her reluctance to tell ancient secrets. "*Daibhidh Mòr* – Big David! To see him run! He'd run down the hill and take a flying leap over the wall of my father's mammoth pasture ..." She chuckled at the memory. She was less talking to the others, less telling a story, than remembering out loud.

"*Old* Davie?"

The elderly woman nodded knowingly, revealingly.

"He can hardly walk!"

"*Sin e* – That's the one."

Ealasaid stood and danced a few steps, recapturing for a moment a younger, wilder time. Surprisingly nimble for her age, she leapt high and in midair spread her legs wide and upon landing, came down on the balls of her feet, as she used to back in the day when she'd been the most celebrated dancer in the Wayp. "It's been a long time since I've done that!" she exclaimed in the FT.

One brown-haired woman, nursing a baby at the end of the table, scrunched her brow and pulled the conversation back to something Ealasaid had said, and which needed to be resolved: "I never thought of this before, but Davie's just a wee fellow. Why do they call him ..." She broke off, hesitating to venture *there*, but an inquiring mind has to know. "Why do they call him *big* Davie?"

With a glance at diminutive Evangelaidh standing wide-eyed in their midst, the *Seanmhair* forestalled Ealasaid going into further detail by raising her hand. She winked and gave a sly nod with her brows arched as if to say, *figure it out for yourself.*

The eyes of the younger women grew wide. Mouths gaped open. A few giggles erupted.

"What? Why? What's she talking about?" Evangelaidh demanded. By this time, the little girl had had enough and wasn't about to tolerate any more nonsense. "Grown-ups are so silly! You don't make sense at all!" Deciding that the big people were too stupid to put up with, she wrinkled her face, got up, and went outside to do something sensible, like play *falach-faigh* – hide and hunt[120] -- with her friends.

The women went on as they worked, blending stories and conversation with songs, both remembered and improvised. One might start a well-known *oldie*, and one after another, they would add verses – sometimes competing with each other to see who could raise the loudest laugh or deliver the most scandalous line.

The topics weren't always frivolous, rowdy, raunchy. Sometimes the flow of the conversation was weightier, more serious, or even somber, venting about troubles or *caoineadh* – lamenting – woes; sometimes, seeking advice, or sharing perspectives. Not uncommon were complaints about the impositions and inroads by the Monstrato Corps and strategizing about how best to deal with them.

So, it went on with them: sharing their trials -- their most vexing tribulations, as well as their niggling irritations – and their joys and their hopes, until each had spoken, and the making of the woolen fabric had been completed.

~~

---

[120] Archeo-Anthropologists have been unable to trace the origins of this childhood game but speculate that it might constitute a form of unrecorded folk culture that dates back as much as several hundred years.

Tapping the mìneotarbh's balls

Chan ann le tuiteamas gur e gaisgeach gaisgeach a th' ann.
It is not by accident that a hero is a hero.
Proverb from *Leabhar an Leaghaidh Mhòir* —
The Book of the Great Melting

It was a long, lazy afternoon on the shieling, though the sun was still high in the sky and would not set for a long time, and then only briefly, leaving a glimmering twilight of a nightfall before rising again in the new day.

On a broad, flat area near the loch, where half-a-dozen mìneotarbhs browsed, Seumas and several other of the young men were preparing for bull leaping. This was part of the observance to honor the Mother in the months that she again gave birth to the world and nourished it in its thriving: to leap the mìneotarbh bull without hurting the creature (not that the bull felt the same compunction about not hurting the boys and men).

Seumas whistled sharply to Sgàth, his bear-wolf, who was crouched in the grass under the shade of a spreading oak tree. The beast crept forward on its belly -- mimicking the predator behavior that was encoded in its genes -- and the mìneotarbhs edged away from it towards the flat area near the loch. On a double whistle from Seumas, the bear-wolf flanked the herd. In response, the fanged, ox-like creatures crowded together, not so much intimidated by the bear-wolf's presence than circling to face the attacker before charging out at it themselves.

Seumas signaled Sgàth with a rising whistle. "*A chulaidh*! -- Puppy!" he commanded in a sharp tone (even though the bear-wolf was far from being a "puppy" in any sense of the word). "*An seo! --* Here!"

The bear-wolf relaxed, rose to full height (about the height of a man's shoulder) and trotted over to lay down at Seumas's feet.

At Seumas's direction, the other young men and boys separated out a particularly agitated bull mìneotarbh from the herd. With more glee than he probably should have felt, Seumas found it incredibly funny to prod the animal in its ass: first a poke, at which the bull pivoted and made an irritated grunt; then a jab, which provoked an angry, warning growl.

The bull's growing ire elicited a broad grin from Seumas.

Ròna's brother then turned his attention to Cuilean, with the same mischievous expression as he had just poked the unoffending bull in the balls. "You!" Seumas called out. "If you are who they say you are, you remember this."

Cuilean nodded.

"Come here, then. Show us what you can do."

Cuilean hesitated.

Seumas jabbed his finger in Cuilean's face: "Or *not* able to do. You were never able to do this before. Let's see if you learned anything in all the time you spent in the DownBlow."

Reluctantly, Cuilean rose and walked slowly out into the field, knee high in furze and heather, grass and fern. It'd been several years since Cuilean had been taken -- as they said in the FT, *air falbh thar thairis* -- away across the sea to the islands of the Merican Pelago.

From behind the giant beast, Seumas delivered a full-on blow to the bull's hanging testicles with a tree branch he'd picked up, gripping and swinging the stick if it were a *claidheamh-mòr* – a claymore, a man-length, two-handed sword.

The bull raised its snout and let out a titanic *raoic* – a sound somewhere between a bellow and a roar, so loud and fierce that a flock of *ealachan-bàna* – giant white swans -- rose up off the surface of the loch a quarter of a farsaing away, and a murder of *feannagan* – black crows – fled the branches of the fir trees at the edge of the clearing.

Which signaled to Seumas that it was time for the fun to begin. He ran towards Cuilean and swiveled to position himself behind him. The bull squinted near-sightedly at Seumas's movement – as the young man bounced up and down behind Cuilean, waving his arms.

The mìneotarbh bull focused on the dim, moving shadow in front of it and rushed forward in a galumphing charge.

At the last moment, attempting to gore Cuilean, it dipped its horns and swept them up viciously.

Caught flatfooted, it was all that Cuilean could do to awkwardly grapple a horn with his outstretched arms.

The mìneotarbh flicked him to the side with little effort, and with a satisfied grunt – as in, *that pest is taken care of* -- it returned to browsing in the tall heather.

As Cuilean picked himself up from the mud and muck, Seumas laughed loudly and hard. "I don't know if you are who you say you are," he mocked, "but if you are, you haven't changed much. *Leig e seachad* – Let it go. Go wrestle the lambs with the other little boys. Leave this one for the men."

Suddenly overcome with a strong thirst, Seumas turned his back on the field, and with a very clear gesture of contempt – a wide wave of both arms – he shouted out a directive, "Somebody take over for this one!" as he strode off the field. "*Chan eil ann ach luspardan gun fheum* -- He's just a useless puny runt!"

The shouts and cheers coming from the bull-leaping men jarred Ròna upright from her seat at the edge of the waulking group. As much fun as the activity was – or rather, the conversation that accompanied it – the stillness and the droning sameness of the palaver had bored her into a drowsy doze.

Her attention was drawn to the raucous shouting coming from the other side of the stand of trees. The cheers of encouragement and the sympathetic groans were so intriguing and enticing that she longed to go out and find out what was happening. As if peeking through an opening in a curtain, she craned her neck to see through a break in the forest.

It might be too much to say that she was drawn to the field like ... well, if her brother Seumas were making the analogy, he'd say, like a cow mammoth in heat allured to a bull, though perhaps Ròna might opt more for the simile of bees attracted to pollinating flowers, for after all, many times, she'd seen bees swarm *lus na meala* – a honey bush -- or the *dearc-mheala* -- blue-berried honeysuckle – while one bee would wander by itself to a bud on another, nearby bush to gather the sweetness unguessed at there, unsuspected by all the others, the secret sugar of that one flower.

For her, she was that singular bee, and Cuilean that lone blossom.

But that would probably be too long and complicated a simile for her simple-minded brother to grasp.

In the middle of a recitation by one of the women, she shifted her seat, and she made as if to step over to the array of food laid out on the grass: there was *taigeis* – haggis -- of the meat and mushroom variety; pies heavy with potatoes, meat, turnips, and yams, all cooked in a savory sauce and stuffed into a crust; and *ceann-cropaig* -- a delicacy consisting of a boiled fish head stuffed with oats and fatty meats; and there were incredibly sweet treats – so sweet they'd make you pucker; and fresh fruit and berries from the fields nearby. She picked up a plump strawberry, which filled the palm of her hand and that oozed sweet juice when she bit into it.

From the field, another shout went up.

Ròna edged through a gap in the trees just as Seumas was leaving the bull-leaping pasture.

Though Ròna was familiar with the sport, as she cast her view over the spectacle, there seemed something different about the bull-leaping this time. The young men seemed more excited, their shouts more animated, louder, their encouragements and their calling out of advice more urgent.

Just as Seumas was striding from the field, Ròna moved closer to the outer periphery of the spectators and stood by a barrel of lemony *teatha na màthar* – the tea of the Mother – a potent beverage brewed and distilled from the mammoth mushrooms that filled the Wayp.

Across the pasture, a man faced off against the mìneotarbh bull. Another man stepped forward – to take a turn, Ròna guessed – but the first man vigorously shoved the air with his arm, gesturing him and all the other men away as if pushing them with a force field of will. At this distance, it was difficult to see exactly what happened next, but it looked as if in a flurry of arm movements, the bull leaper was stripping off his shirt.

With a shout over his shoulder – "I'll tell you a good one just as soon as I get myself another drink!" -- Seumas appeared next to Ròna at the tub. Unceremoniously, he jogged her out of the way – not a purposeful shove, per se, just a relatively mindless, bullish, I'm-in-this-space-now, you're-not-even-here type of nudge.

The distraction lasted but a moment before her attention was jerked back to the field by a collective shout. The man – so small in the distance she couldn't make out who it was, and besides, because he was partially obscured by the men surrounding the bull-leaping field -- had just been thrown into the water.

Again, the men shouted.

And he – whoever *he* was -- came sloshing out of the loch and again took a stance in the middle of the field, naked to the waist, kilt belted tightly around his middle, his figure long and slim, with lean and muscular lines. This fellow confronted the bull in a sugarfoot stance, feet spread shoulder width, one foot cocked back and the other planted forward, posed like a runner about to shoot forward, or a wrestler poised to take on his opponent.

Seumas squinted into the distance. Her brother was a big man – a kind of bull himself, whose eyesight, coincidentally, was no better than that of the mìneotarbhs in the herd. "*Cò sin?* -- Who's that?" he asked, in mild curiosity of a not-really-interested variety.

Ròna moved closer and made out the leaper's distinctive three-stripe mane. She gave a long shrug, as if to emphasize her point, and at the same time murmured, "*Chan eil fhios 'm* – I dunno," but in a mumble so ambiguous, it could not be said whether Seumas could have heard her. "Maybe somebody from one of the other villages," she added.

Seumas was not convinced, but even less interested to follow the issue further.

In the distance, the man strode towards the mìneotarbh across the short span of knee-high furze and heather, grass and fern, which lay between him and the monstrous animal.

Seumas turned his attention to other, more important matters: At this moment, those concerns constituted his complaining to his circle of listeners (it might be discussed whether Seumas truly had any friends rather than a collection of hangers-on who flocked around him as the dominant bull of his own little herd). The issue currently the topic of his discourse was the Monstrato Corps' pressing him for fees for water that belonged to no one, except the Mother herself (even though the few times that he invoked *her* name was when he thought doing so would get him out of having to pay a tax or a fee or a charge, even from the Council of Sisters itself).

Seumas moved away with his attendant audience, and Ròna focused on the action in the field, watching – if not breathlessly, at least with short, constrained, shallow breathing and intense scrutiny – as time after time the man engaged the bull mìneotarbh.

The fellow in the field would charge forward, right up to the nostrils of the monster bull, and smack its snout and retreat. For all the size of the mìneotarbh, its nose was a tender organ, and each it was swatted, the bull would shake its head angrily, bellow, and take a few steps forward, only to stop when the man had fallen back out of reach.

As the bull made a tentative, annoyed charge, the 3-striped bull wrestler grappled one of the animal's horns and attempted a back-flyover leap, but on this particular try, the momentum provided by the mìneotarbh was not sufficient to propel the leaper, and the beast again tossed him aside.

Again and again, the man picked himself up out of the muddy field and ran forward to incite the mìneotarbh. He would retreat before the responding charge before stopping and attempting a slippery grip on the animal's horn. Each attempt ended in the same result: a toss upon the grass, onto the cushiony heather, into the water, or a splat in the mud.

Seumas returned for another mug of the mushroom brew. He peered through his mole-eyes at the mìneotarbh-leaper in the field. The vaulter who controlled the arena – and had for a while -- made a run and a jump, but he was swatted aside in midair by a sweep of the giant mìneotarbh's head. The man flew through the air and landed in the mud by the side of the lake. "*Cò sin an-dràsta?* – Who's that now?" Seumas asked.

"*An aon fhear* – the same one," Ròna replied simply.

Seumas shook his head in derision. "*Amadan* – fool," he said. "*Feumaidh e a bhith claoidhte mu tràth* – He has to be worn out by now. He's just going to get himself killed."

"*Chì sinn* – We'll see," Ròna said. "I have a feeling about this one. He's going to keep on -- *gus an dèan e no am bris e* -- until he makes it or breaks it."

"What he's going to do is break his neck," Seumas snorted knowingly and turned back to tell his friends about the twin mammoth calves that had been born to his herd.

Ròna edged closer as the struggle continued between the mìneotarbh and the impertinent mouse of a man who was by now covered in dark, peaty sludge that bristled with various flora – blades of grass, twigs of heather, mats of lake moss.

For its part, the animal seemed to be now concentrating seriously as if it too were invested in this contest, a competition that was not as harmless as it might seem (if man against monster could be deemed a "hurtless" sport), for despite the boggy softness of the ground, people had broken limbs, necks, and backs being tossed by a bull; either that, or by being trampled and stomped in the immediate aftermath of contact as the beast made sure its lazy grazing wouldn't be interrupted further by an impertinent ant.

The half-naked one faced the bull again. He paced backwards, seemingly in retreat. The mìneotarbh trod forward, intensifying its threat.

Then with a roar -- one so sudden and fierce that it startled even the giant mìneotarbh -- the *man* charged forward.

It was time for the giant creature to be caught unawares, unprepared. The beast recovered itself, and as if aggravated past all patience by the nagging, mosquito-like bites of this stupid little prick, in a quick regrouping of itself, the great beast let out a *raoic* – a roar – of its own. It reared up on its hind legs and crashed down on its forefeet with such force that the impact shook the ground. Its momentum drove it forward as it dipped its head to gore the intended victim.

The unexpected sound and the sudden movement caught Seumas's attention, or maybe it was the sound of Ròna's gasping and the riveted expression on her face that directed her brother's gaze to the mìneotarbh-leaper who'd just at that moment scooted low to feint the mìneotarbh into lowering its head even further before he suddenly leapt up to meet the hulk's charge and gripped its near horn with both hands.

Reflexively, the mìneotarbh jerked its head up and hard, throwing the leaper high into the air over its back where the player performed a perfect *tòirleum* – a leap over the animal's shoulders into a handstand, and a flip into a somersault across the bull's back, followed by a plunge that cleared the behemoth's rear, as the man was propelled by his momentum and gravity over and down the mìneotarbh's backside to give a final victorious tap on the bull's testicle sack – a rap that elicited the confirmation of his '*clach-bhuaidh*' -- his stone-touch -- in the form of the distinctive squawk of surprise from the mìneotarbh bull.

"*Sin agad e!* -- There you go!" Seumas exclaimed, crowding closer. "Now that's how it's supposed to be done!" He squinched his eyes. "*Cò sin?* – Who is that?"

"*Cuilean nan Cat,*" Ròna said flatly, casually, over her shoulder. No inflection in her voice, though the barb and the rebuke were there, nonetheless. "Cuilean of the Cats."

The age of joy

Cha robh aighear mòr riamh, gun dubh-bhròn às a dheigh.
There never was a burst of joy, that deep grief did not follow.

Proverb from *Leabhar an Leaghaidh Mhòir* — The Book of the Great Melting

There was hardly anything better to do the night at the end of summer than celebrate *Oidhche Shamhna*, the holy night of Samhain, when day and night were of equal length and thus in synchronicity, when the two branes, that of this world and that of the other, slid so close to each other so as to touch, and beings from the other realm passed into this one.

This time marked the end of the People's stay in the upland pasture, and as such, the day gave cause for festivities when

> Spread was the banquet,
> Pipers and fiddlers arrayed,
> The dancing stage set,
> The banners displayed.
>
> The festival prepared,
> Torches and lanterns effulgent,
> Voices lifted in the air,
> And celebrations' commencement.

This was the time when the *Clann na Màthar* – the Children of the Mother -- observed the completion of the harvest season, the fertility of the Goddess, and her walking the earth among them. They donned costumes that memorialized the life that she had spawned, which included all creatures great, big, and teeny-weeny. There was a deer, a one-horned, a *mìneotarbh*, a bear-wolf, and even a mammoth, which was of course, much smaller than the actual thing, being composed of a costume that fit three people -- one the rear legs, one the front, and one riding on the shoulders of the forelegs to work the head and trunk.

There was even an *iolair* – the fearsome eagle with talons like curved scythes and a wing span twice the height of a man. Somebody was outfitted like an owl – *cailleach oidhche,* an old woman of the night in the FT – who was amused to wander around the gathering uttering the call of that bird – *siu-hù, siu-hù* – with what looked like a mouse in its beak (though really just a woven puppet in the shape of a rodent).

Many of the children were dressed in costumes of small animals. There were little squirrels, rabbits, a hedgehog, a badger, and a fox. There were several birds, and the children dressed in these guises ran about helter-skelter in pretend flight, flapping costume wings and calling out *peep-peep* and *caw-caw*.

Cuilean – at Ròna's prompting – was made up like a sword-tooth tiger, as was only appropriate considering his foundling, but which made him feel ridiculous and unnecessarily triggered. He'd deferred to her but had resolved to shed the costume as soon as he could so he wouldn't have to politely endure people mimicking tigers by roaring and growling in his face. These displays had uncomfortably reminded him of the bullying taunts he'd received as a boy, whereas for Ròna, his disguise had recalled the fond memory of how he'd first come to her: *Cuilean nan Cat, fhàgadh leis na sìthichean* – Cuilean of the Cats, left by the fairies.

Even Ròna was dressed in a costume, made out to look like a *ròn* – a seal in the FT – carrying a child's stuffed-seal toy and her face seal-freckled.

Anticipations rose as the sun fell slowly behind the mountain peaks. At the limen of day and night, light and dark, the High Sister called for the togethering, which constituted the official nascency of this final night's gala (if anything amongst the Children of the Mother could ever considered "official," there being in their culture an aversion to hard lines of demarcation). However, everybody understood the implication of what the High Sister had announced: the *togethering*.

Accordingly, the people divided themselves into groups of nine (more or less, but *who's counting?*) and waited as the *Àrd-Phiuthar* signaled for the chalices filled with the *bainne na màthar* – the mother's milk, much more potent than the more common *teatha* of the mother – were brought in and distributed.

When the mugs were circulated, one to every coven, following the signal from the Sister – which was simply her taking a drink from the grail and passing the vessel to the woman next to her with the words, "*Thugam 's bhuam-sa* – to me and from me -- *gun astar eadarainn* -- and no space between us," the rest of the congregants did likewise.

It wasn't long after that the togethering started small enough, in signs almost indistinguishable.

Maggie noticed the mouse-shaped mole on Seumas's cheek and gave a chuckle at that small reminder of his human frailty, his vulnerability, the flaw that marked his beauty, his human loveliness.

Ròna filled her lungs with the fresh breeze blowing down from the snow-tipped twin heights of *Cìochan na Màthar* – the Mother's Teats -- and growing fascinated with the shape of a blade of grass, she stretched out on the forest floor under the spreading oak tree to watch it grow, waving away those who would disturb her. She rolled onto her back, and as she gazed up, she was filled with a sense of the glory of the forest and the unending expanse of the sky.

Dòmhnall gazed upon Siùsaidh, consumed to tears by a feeling of tenderness for her, and she wrapped herself in that love and felt warm and safe.

Even Morunx was moved to the togethering. He engaged a couple standing near him in a lengthy (probably too much so) and comical story about the children he was caring for during his time on probation, but because his tale was half in broken FT and half in Simspeek, it was totally unintelligible, but his listeners laughed anyway because ... well, because they were *together*.

A joy rippled through the congregation like a soft breeze through the leaves of the forest ... rustling gently, touching, stirring, but not disturbing ... a warm feeling of happiness, for was this not the purpose of life? The Mother's wish for them? That they be happy, and love one another like family? That they be united in their togethering?

Differences melted, as their individualities flowed united in a stream like the waters from *Beinn na Màthar* – the Mountain of the Mother -- mingling in the great lake.

"*Cuimhnich i on tàinig thu*," the Big Sister reminded them of the ancient proverb. "Remember Her from whom you came." The first *àithne* – the first teaching of the original founding mothers -- the first injunction, the first knowledge, the first principle, from which all else flowed.

This was the summoning that arose from amongst them, and from their *togethering* arose the visioning of the ancestors, which swirled as a luminous mist, accompanied with a murmuring from the leaves in the trees, the fragrance from the blossoms, the sproutings of the blades of the grasses on the forest floor -- all as voices emanating from the Mother herself, heard even though not quite understood. They heard it in the *hoo-hoo-ee* call of the hoo-hoo bird – a black fowl with yellow tufted wings that graced the upper branches of the forest canopy and sang its call to come together ... *hoo-hoo-ee*.

Then came the songs, popping up like stories told between long-time friends re-united and recalling, "Do you remember when?" or "Do you remember the time?" The ballads that made their hearts sing, the stories that made their hearts weep. Somebody would begin with the lyrics and many more would join in. Somebody would tell a story, and those around would listen until another would pick up where she had left off. And in the songs and the stories came their remembrance of who they were and where they had come from.

Finally a mist came filtering down, settling upon their collective consciousness like a soft, cool dew -- memories infused with the lives of the ancestors: the exodus across the rising seas at the time of the Great Melt; the struggle when so many of them were lost in their striving up the cliffs of the Wayp; their toiling to settle the barren landscape of the risen land and create the living garden made possible by the melting milk of the Mother; and the beneficent, loving warmth bestowed upon them, because even though the air was cold, the volcanic thermo vents provided them warmth and energy; the application of their knowledge of the various technological and life-sciences, in which many of their number were proficient, allowed them to retrieve the ancient seeds of life which they'd both brought with them and those which they had found in the fossil memory of the newly risen continent; and their contending against the PieceTakers of the DownBlow, who were ever seeking to take and despoil their sacred waters.

These and more: Some stood and danced when *Fionnlagh na fidhle* – Finlay of the fiddle – picked up a tune on his instrument. He was a thin, quiet man whose hands would inevitably stray to the strings and the bow. Whether herding the sheep which he tended, or standing in a pasture watching the mammoths, or sitting with friends around a hearth fire, he would make the fiddle sing in communion with those in whose company he found himself -- human, or beast, or bird -- inspiring smiles on the faces of his friends, luring sheep to herd closely, lulling cows to low softly in response, and inspiring the birds in the trees to accompany his melody with their own.

There was a double reason for celebration this night – not just the Samhain, but as well, the betrothal of the seal and the tiger. They called this the *rèiteach* – the arrangement, the agreement, the announcement -- of their intention *cheangal ri chèile* – to join together, which triggered a great celebration, even larger, even more joyous than usual at this time of the height and culmination of the Mother's fertility.

The poet *Donnchadh Bàn nan Òran* – Fair-haired Duncan of the Songs -- composed a poem about the occasion:

> 'S ann bun os cionn an cruinne-cè,
> 's tha ciall tro-chèile.
> 'S iad a bha air an sgaradh --
> An ròn 's cat nam fiaclan-sgèine --
> Nis nar h-aon air an ceangal ri chèile.

> The world is upside down.
> Reason and sense confounded.
> Those who were torn apart –
> The seal and the knife-tooth cat --
> are now as one compounded.

The officiant, the *Àrd-Phiuthar* – the Big Sister -- intoned a *beannachd* – a blessing:

> Mathas mòr na mara dhiubh
> Mathas mòr na talmhainn dhiubh
> Bidh ur beatha sìolmhor slàn
> Mathas mòr na Màthar dhiubh

The great bounty of the sea be yours
The great bounty of the earth be yours,
Your life be healthy and fruitful,
The great bounty of the Mother be yours.

The Sister took the tartan ribbon that was draped around Ròna's shoulders. She bid the two to hold hands. When they did, she lightly wrapped the ribbon around their hands with the words, "Let not be torn asunder what the Goddess has joined together."

Dòmhnall's heart was spilling over with joy. He could feel his chest swelling as if it were a ballon about to burst. The cups of his eyes ran over with tears. The entire widespread community of the Wayp had gathered: Not only had his beloved foster son, Cuilean, returned, but his daughter, his beloved daughter – his *blàthan beag na beinne* --his little mountain blossom, the fabled flower from the ancient legends that bloomed only once every hundred years – was being betrothed.

Dòmhnall pushed to the center of the gathering and positioned himself to address the couple and the assembled. "*A Chuilein* – Cuilean. As you are truly now a member of our family, just as much my child as any other ..."

Here, Seumas grimaced as if he'd been pricked by an irritating memory – the intrusion of Cuilean into their home. The wince grew into a frown and then a scowl as Dòmhnall went on.

"I have something to give to you." At this, Dòmhnall drew out from under his plaid a man-length sword – which the people of the Wayp called *claidheamh mòr an t-solais* in the FT – the great sword of light. It had long hung in the central room of their home, and it had long been Seumas' expectation that it would pass to him.

But remembering what Blind Bridget had foreseen, Dòmhnall presented the claymore to Cuilean: "This sword represents the protection of our people and our way of life. It was carried against our enemies at *Blàr Chùil Lodair* – the battle a thousand years before the Great Melt, when the Children of the Mother lost all that we had -- and at the Battle of Mammoth Gap where we won back our freedom. It symbolizes the protection of our people and the continuation of our world."

The older man paused portentously, and taking the gap in his speech as a signal that he was done, the assembled people broke out in tentative applause.

"I'm not done," Dòmhnall growled (which put an immediate stop to any signal of appreciation from the *hoi-polloi*). He handed the man-length sword to Cuilean. "Now you have a long tooth like the cat you came from. You know *them*, those you came from, but

394

you stand with *us -- eadar na creagan 's na gàir-thuinn* – between the rocks and the roaring waves."

A shout went up as more than a couple in the crowd took the opportunity of Dòmhnall's pause for breath to interrupt his disquisition and break off his speech before it grew lugubrious beyond enduring and he completely embarrassed himself and totally killed the mood of the evening.

Under the brilliant, crystalline sky, there was a sudden upsurge up of the *cuirm-ciùil* – the concert, the "picnic of music," literally, in the FT. The musicians let forth a torrent of melody like a flood of water that had been restrained behind a dam: the fiddler playing on a stool alternating with the piper promenading in a tight circuit, along with a guitarist and a melodica player, who had all been kept well lubricated with goblets brimming with the mother's milk, until their heads and those of the other celebrants swam with the intoxication of joy, music, and beverage; with the heady emotion of the Samhain celebration; with the spinning in a gyre of movement; with the skipping and tripping in a dizzying reeling of motion and emotion; with the rapid, fleeting, flying forming of circles, figure eights, and box sets; with the linking of arms and joining together and breaking apart; and with the switching of partners and the re-meeting of chosen dance mates, and possibly, night mates, and occasionally, life mates.

Turning aside from his chagrin at having been overlooked, Seumas danced with his son *Seumas Beag* in his arms, named Little Seumas after his father. The child seemed to take delight in everything. "He was born with a smile on his face," his mother, Maggie, had once said in Ròna's presence, and then concerned her friend might take offense as she quickly remembered how Dòmhnall used to joke that when Ròna was born, he'd thought the baby was smiling at him but then realized he was holding her upside down, she hurriedly added, "Not that there's anything wrong with not smiling."

"In other words," Seumas taunted, "nothing wrong with having an ill-tempered, scowling, bitch face!"

For which Ròna had punched him in the arm, a blow she followed with an exaggerated scowl.

Dòmhnall himself stood at the side of the dancing set with Siùsaidh, who was unable to move with the alacrity required of the frolic, and as much as he ached to join the general hubbub, he stayed near her and danced circles around her, switching arms one side after another (which was probably just as well, as his old knees would not have long endured any attempt to keep up with the younger folks). She kept on telling him to join the general dance but was pleased that he did not. She laughed at the silliness of his capering but loved that he included her.

Brìde Dhall and *Fearchar Crom* – Blind Bridgit and Hunched Fergus -- sat on the edge of the melee. Glancing over, Dòmhnall noted a look of concern across her face, but then he passed her by and thought no more about what the implication of her expression might be. Fergus, as usual, sat just behind his mother, dutifully waiting upon her need.

Raibeart, having reconciled with the Sisters, was charming *Beathag Mhòr* – Big Bertha -- a rich widow who was in possession of a herd of 100 llamas and another of several mammoths. She was a pudgy, middle-aged woman with shy, downcast eyes, a subdued smile, and the face of a Jack o' Lantern that had been left out too long and had smooshed in on itself. Not that her appearance mattered to him – for as he said, once in her presence even, "All kittens are black in the dark" (which might not be an exact translation), to which she bowed her head, cast her eyes even further down, dropping her hair over a wide, toothy grin. This night she had pressed herself against a tree at the edge of the clearing, as if attempting to fade away from sight into the woods. But Raibeart had sought her out and was regaling her with his charm.

The members of the Council of Sisters danced in their own circle, the Big Sister the same as the others, though they kept to themselves, laughing at their private jokes, sometimes pausing in the middle of a set to talk and gossip about or comment on those in the more general crowd, but always keeping their conversation low, confidential, and inaudible to others.

Cuilean the tiger and Ròna the seal scampered in the midst of all this – he, breathless and high-leaping, she silly and waddling, her arms held straight down and her hands flapping at her hips to mimic flippers. Each time the ring of dancers parted in the mad, joyous carousing, as required by the form of the reel itself, he felt a tug of the heart at their separation, and each time they came together and joined arms once again, he felt as if it were a joyous reunion.

As the night went on, the celebration of the *cèilidh* became even more ecstatic, and the people grew more and more excited in their celebration of the fructifying of the world via the body of the Mother. The dancing became even more wild and frenzied. The sounds of the fiddles and the pipes rose up in the night sky and strove against each other, the songs and tunes of one village mingling with those of another in a mixture of color and movement and sound, all of which, although not synchronized, was not discordant.

Later, hand in hand, some short distance away from the festivities, Ròna and Cuilean walked as if children, not caring nor knowing where they went, but mystified by the magical quality of the colors and sounds that danced and swirled in their minds: the music and the stream of voices and the laughter from the *cèilidh* in the near distance; the chirping of crickets; the repetitive rising *whip-poor-will* whistle of the *sgreuchag-oidhche* – the screecher of the night; the *sìu-hù* of the owl; the yowl of the forest fox that sounded like a woman's shriek out of the darkness; the plaintive howling at the moon of the white snow wolf; the croaking symphony of frogs from the lake nearby. Everything – even in the darkness of the forest – seemed to sparkle with a preternatural light.

In the DownBlow, where the sky was not visible above a gowp-smudgy cloud cover a few hundred feet above the ground, the people there admired the fires burning the exhalations of gas from the methane geysers that gushed from the earth like the wheezings of a dying mammoth.

On the other hand, in the Wayp, where a clear view of the sky was not obscured, the People of the Mother enjoyed the full panorama of *na dannsairean nèamhail* -- the heavenly dancers – a display in the night sky that was varicolored, polychromatic, multi-prismatic, kaleidoscopic, *all the colors of the rainbow* (though even in this, language deceives, for it is too reductive as there were more colors in the display than in a rainbow, more than any language named or even any human eye could see). As the heavenly dancers

pirouetted above the tree tops, fireflies swarmed like a cloud of glittering fairies around the couple. It was a dizzy moment.

At one end of the shieling, there was an array of large stones – each roughly rectangular, though uncut and unformed – that had been set upright in the ground in a pattern that approximated a cross with a circle at its heart where the two arms crossed. Nobody remembered when the display had been erected – for obviously, it had been built, it hadn't just appeared out of nowhere; its erection could have been around the time of the first settlers in the Wayp, or later. There was even some uncertainty as to what exactly it was or might represent. Some said it was just a random cluster, some conjectured that the individual stones represented the ancestors who guarded them, while others argued it had been configured to symbolize the Mother herself.

Ròna and Cuilean walked a little farther to where they were within sight of the lake and found themselves beside a low shrub splashed by the moonlight. Cuilean's attention was drawn to a movement on one of the branches. There a spider was performing a strange series of contortions. It repeatedly lifted what could be best referred to as a multi-colored "tail," predominantly streaked with red, white, blue, and black, which the bug repeatedly lifted and lowered, flapped and waved, in the direction of a larger spider – not anywhere near as colorful, but dappled brown and a dull grey. This larger insect stood stock still, seemingly intent on studying the flag-waving arachnid.

"What's that?" Cuilean asked.

"'S e damhan-peucag a th' ann – It's a peacock spider."

"What's it doing?"

"He's trying to attract the girl spider."

"What's going to happen?"

"She's either going to mate with him ..." And here, a portentous, wry pause: "Or eat him." Ròna's expression was deadpan, without any leaking of a hint whether she was joking or serious. Her eyes narrowed in cold, sober slits, but ... *was that a slight upward flicker at the side of her lips?*

In the glare of her steely stare, Cuilean gave a noncommittal cough of a laugh, which could have been taken to mean he understood what she was saying, without giving away, in case he was wrong, what he thought was signified by the substance underlying her apparent meaning.

Ròna's attention shifted. She slipped her hand sideways and gingerly reached into the bush. She took his hand and placed in his palm something that was cool, soft, and damp. When he looked, he saw it glistening in the moonlight. "*Feuch e,*" she said with a gesture toward her lips. "Try it."

Tentatively, he did, and a sugary taste bubble exploded in his mouth with such a delicious moistness as he'd never tasted.

"*Tha e blasta, nach eil?*" she said. "It's delicious, isn't it?"

He peered intently at the bush, searching for another dark cluster hiding in the shadows and plucked one for himself and ate it.

He offered one to her.

"I know what it tastes like," she demurred.

"Sure, but I can't eat alone."

She acceded and took it, her lips lingering for a moment on the tips of his fingers, her eyes cradling his for a *priobadh na sùla* ... a blink of time.

Then she offered him another one.

He took it, and he plucked one for her, and thus they fed one another: a gentle offering turning into a playful push into the lips, and then a frisky smear from nose to chin, until the blue stain of the crushed fruit covered cheeks and faces.

And as they eat more, the ecstasy of the Goddess envelopes them. They live in an eternal *now*. Nothing else exists or has been or will ever abide again as they thrust their hands greedily through the tangle of prickly briars of the *dearc-choille* – the forest berry -- and greedily devour the fruits, offering their gleanings to each other as if in an ecstatic sacrament of sharing.

In the frenzy, Ròna grabs a handful of berries, smushes them in her fist, thrusts her hand down the front of Cuilean's shirt, and smears the pulp on his broad chest. He retaliates by reaching under her blouse with a glob and rubbing it up her stomach towards her peaked breasts.

While he is turning back to the bramble bush, she thrusts a mass of crushed berries on his back under his shirt, and as he swivels to return the attack, she pushes her berry-smeared hands under the top of his pants.

He reaches deep into the bush, ignoring the spikey pinpricks of the nettles, grabs a handful of fruit and reaches up the front of her kilt, smearing her thighs.

A mass of berry goo is now stuck to and dripping from their clothing. Cuilean rips off his shirt, revealing his blue chest.

She does likewise. Her torso is splattered and glistening with blue.

Cuilean thrusts himself at her, rubbing his naked chest against hers, slopping and co-mingling the pulp in their playful grappling.

Her remaining clothes clotted with the residue of the pulpy mass, she unfastens her kilt and tosses it aside, and in the same motion, she flings herself at him, leaping up to straddle him, forcing him backwards. He tumbles into the briar. There is no distinction between the tiny needle thorns, the soft lusciousness of the berries, and the intoxicating scent of her.

Sweet pricklings!

In the branches above them, a white-breasted goldfinch -- *lasair-choille* in the FT, a "flame of the forest" -- chitters. The bird's harlequin face displays black eye patches surrounded by a circle of pumpkin-orange, which is itself haloed by a ring of white, and capped by a final black crest atop her head. Her back is swathed in a soft brown down that cascades to a pitch-black tail that is itself fringed by a brilliant yellow. *Tha i a' ceilearadh a h-òran binn* – She warbles her sweet song.

Ròna's lanugo - a coat of delicate, reddish brown, downy fuzz like that on a peach -- stands upright on the goose pimples that arise to her thrill and forms a soft coating, barely visible, from her chest to her bare mound and down her legs to the crest of her feet.

The two mix their juices as sweet as the berries they have just picked, mouths parting, panting deeply, vision dimming, star-seeing, chests heaving, sweat dripping like dew, pale, fragrant, soft, yielding, hard, penetrating, engorged, opened-mouthed, tongues intermingling, their bodies entwining together in a knot that has no beginning and no end.

If only time would stop now! For this moment is complete – is all they might have wished for, fulfilling if only for an instant their deepest yearnings. Perfect except for its impermanence, beautiful like Ròna's breast in its imperfection – hacked and scarred, but all the more beauteous because of its flaws.

He kisses the gash in awe of it, in worship of it, and of what it signifies.

She, for her part, also knows this night is transient, will not last long, and that this time having come, will go, and therefore is all the more to be treasured because of that ephemerality. The short span will die away like the last notes of the beautiful song trilled by the feathered "flame of the forest" above them and endure only in their memories.

This is their moment, now when the moon is low over *Cìoch na Màthar* -- the Breast of the Mother, as the People call the mountain peak that rises over lake: a heartbeat of time that will have to last a lifespan; a night when the sand gleams with a phosphorescent glow that proceeds from the moon-broach – a large bright halo circling the moon, which has emerged now that the holy sky dancers have passed over the horizon.

This is their time – when the waters on the surface of the lake glimmer, and patches of light and dark flicker under the glow of the full moon, and everything seems to pulse and breathe with the inbreath and outbreath of the Mother.

Cuilean remembers everything about his life before the reaping. It is as if before he was floating in a sea of forgetfulness but is now rising to the surface. It all comes back to him. Most of all, he recollects the red-haired girl who took him, who taught him, who rescued him, and whom he rescued, and to whom he is bound as if by fibers of steel-strong spiderweb silk.

Later, they awoke entwined upon her plaid, which protected them against the chill of the pre-dawn – half on it, half under it. The fog rising from the lake nearby wreathed them with gossamer garlands of mist. A thin line of light appeared on the ridge of the mountains.

She gazed upon his face, wondering, *Cò seo?* – Who is this? His lids flickered open, and like two people simultaneously opening windows facing each other across a gap, they were mutually startled to be looking directly, intimately into each other's souls.

She rubbed her face and wiped her seal face-paint-smeared

hand on the blanket. At a loss for anything to say, she noted flatly, observationally, "*Tha beul na madainn a' liathadh* -- The mouth of morning is blue-greying," that is, dawn was shifting the pitch black of night to a lighter, paler shade of grey-blue.

He nodded in agreement, though there wasn't much to agree or disagree with. "I didn't expect this," he said, and although it was a non-sequitur, she caught what he was referring to.

"Nor I," she said, "*fhir a' bhàta*," alluding to the sailor of the song – the one who had gone away over the water, leaving no sign of when, if ever, he would return. "We didn't expect to ever see you again." She added the particular emphasis they had in the FT -- "*Idir, idir, idir.* -- Not at all, at all, at all. We thought you were gone forever."

He wasn't quite sure who the *we* was that she was referring to. It could have meant the wider community of the Wayp, or only *her*; she just didn't want to admit as much by using an *I*. But for all that, he couldn't imagine the likes of Seumas having given him, his going, or his returning much thought.

The light from the stars and the moon sparkled upon the water. Everything -- what he saw, what he felt, Ròna's presence beside him -- seemed more radiant, more alive. "I forgot how beautiful these things are," Cuilean said. "It's been so long."

"They're not things," Ròna corrected, intoning the catechism: "They're the breath of the Goddess. They are one with the Mother. We are one with the Mother. And with them."

With those few words, Cuilean experienced a shift. Although it had seemed to him before when he had lived in the *Tìr na Smùid* -- the Land of Smoke -- that there were differentiae between objects, creatures, and ideas, suddenly he saw that these distinctions had been but an illusion of a gulf because in reality, linked were they all, all part of one. All were part of the web which interconnected one to another, and any vibration of those filaments shuddered through to affect every other strand.

The doodle-bug in the soil, the flutter-by hovering over the blossom, and the mammoth in the field, however different they might appear on the surface, were linked by an unbreakable chain of relationships. The leavings of the *daol-chac* – the shit-beetle -- fed the grass and the trees that the deer and the mammoth ate, which in turn were eaten by the wolf and the sword-toothed tiger, and the excreta of all of these were in turn consumed by the shit-beetle to return the cycle to the worm, and thence to the flowers, whose pollen was scattered by the *dealan na bàn-dè* – the fluttering lightning of the Goddess; and so it went on, each linked to every other, either directly or through strands of the web, none lower nor higher than any other, none more important nor exulted than any other, but each equally necessary to the life cycle of the whole.

All parts were of the whole and necessary to the whole, as knuckles could not exist apart from the hand, nor a hand apart from the arm, nor the brain separate from the heart. So, indeed, the world was not composed of isolated things like rocks on a shore but commingled indissolubly as if of water, it being impossible to say that this drop was disassociated from and independent of that, for all flowed together, dissolving and merging one into the other. There was no division between things. There was no longer lake and mountain and sky and tree, neither badger in the underbrush nor sword-toothed tiger in the tall grass nor mammoth upon the field nor the *daolag-chac* – the doodle-bug in the mammoth's shit -- nor man nor woman as separate, distinct entities, nor he apart from she. All were but manifestations of the wholeness of the Mother.

On the shore of the lake, he looked out upon the thin ribbon of sand that gleamed like a silver necklace around the dark waters at the base of the moon-streaked woods that ran up the slope of the mountain. The breeze caressed their skins. Everything vibrated with aliveness.

She sat up and tugged the plaid out from under him. She stood, gathered it, belted it around her, and transmuting it from blanket to garment, formed her kilt again.

Without discussion, but by a common thought and intent, they walked towards the shore.

Time hovered like a *seabhag* -- a hawk – circling the tips of the tall pines that overhung the loch. She looked away to where just above the hill opposite them, the moon hung haloed.

"*Seall an seo!*" he said excitedly, jocularly, his voice changing tone suddenly, shaking the heartbreaking solemnity of the moment. "Look at this!" He had stopped beside a thin log stretched out in the sand. It was about twice the length of a man and had been washed clean and white by the ebbing and flowing of the water. "It's been a long time, but let's see if I can toss it."

So as to be in complete competitive spirit and to free his hands, he fit the tiger's head back on and lifted the thick butt of the tapered tree trunk, and bracing it in the sand, ran the timber up till it stood on its narrow end, a good man-length over his head. He grinned. "Little did you know that the First International *Farpais Cabar Loch na Màthar* -- Lake of the Mother Caber Championship -- would be held tonight."

"Where are all the other competitors?" Ròna asked, looking around sardonically.

"They must not have gotten the invitations. Nevertheless, the game must go on!" Cuilean crouched and slid his hands under the end of the caber, steadied himself, and in a swift, remembered motion, he hoisted it. He cupped the tip of the log, bracing the long trunk against his shoulder, so it stood straight up.

He took a few steps forward, and quickening his pace for a step or two, with a dip in his knees and an explosive spring, he threw his arms up. The log arched upwards, now free from his grip, landed on the top end, and teetered. It tipped forward, away from him.

"The crowd goes wild!" Cuilean intoned in an announcer's voice. He imitated the cheer of the imaginary audience of sports fans. "A new champion!"

"*A bheil pòg agad airson a' ghaisgich ùir?*" he asked, beaming, lost in the moment. "Do you have a kiss for the new champion?"

"*Tha* – Yes," she said, and kissed him fully.

Memories swirled about in Cuilean's mind. Words long forgotten surged towards him in a wave and then receded. One set perched on his lips, and he repeated them as if they were being whispered to him from behind a curtain. "'*S mise an daolag-chac a bhios a' fuireach ann am buachar a' mhammoit* -- I am the doodle-bug that lives in the mammoth shit." He grinned.

Ròna looked at him as if her unihorn Dìleas had recited a poem. "You remembered that!"

Cuilean was no less surprised than she was. "It just came to me."

But she had cause to remember, too. This was the boy, a man now, of course, who several years before had stood on the shore and watched her as she swam to safety, and in giving her time, space, and opportunity to escape while leaving himself in danger, he had done the greatest kindness anyone had ever done for her. It was true that he had run from the man-monsters, but in fleeing in the other direction, he had drawn away from her those who would have done her irreparable evil.

And at what a cost to himself! Which, until now, she had had no opportunity to requite.

As her thoughts returned to their long-ago peril, the memory of which because they had survived it, along with the events of the evening, should have filled her with joy, she felt suddenly overwhelmed with an unexpected foreboding. She turned away and gazed over the water. "You've come back at a *droch uair* – at a bad time, in a bad hour," she said.

At first, he thought she was referring to him. "*Duilich* – Sorry," he mumbled.

She hurried to add, "*A bhalaich* – Buddy," which was the way they'd taken to referring to each other. They were friends *ri guaillibh a chèile* – shoulder to shoulder, comrades arm-in-arm -- united by their shared experience, their shared pain, that was somehow deeper, stronger, and more profound than any expression of hearts and roses, which just seemed too weak, too casual for the bond they shared. "It's not your coming that's bad. That's perfect, no matter when. It's just everything else that's happening now." She finished her thought. "They're sucking it dry."

"The *loch*?"

She nodded. *Yes.*

He had suspected as much. The lake didn't seem to be as full as it had been when he was last here – in the time before that fateful reaping. Since then, the water had fallen, edging away from the beach as if at perpetual low tide.

The rushes that years ago as children they would plow their skiff into, using the tall grasses to anchor while they played undisturbed on the shore, had once been soft, moist, and yielding, but now as the couple walked through them, instead of bending and wafting in the wind, they stood stiff and brittle. The reeds snapped at odd angles and crackled under foot as the couple tramped through the brush.

She stopped. She cocked her head. "Listen," she said.

He frowned. "I don't hear anything."

"That's because you're using your ears."

"What am I supposed to hear with?"

"*Ist* – Hush." She placed her fingers on his forehead and slipped them down over his eyes, as if she were lowering window blinds. "Can't you hear it?"

He shook his head. Nothing. "Just the water. The wind."

Not satisfied with his answer, Ròna looked away and to the side in concentration. "Up here," she said, and as if obeying a summoning, she walked ahead, her hand gripping his, as if pulling him on a leash.

They meandered farther up the slope to the trail that lined the crest of the hill. Guided by an unthinking intention, united by an unspoken agreement, they returned to the place where they had first been joined together, or rather where they had been rejoined, where they had been re-united. They came to the edge of the world where the air whistled up the steep sides of the cliff overlooking the DownBlow.

Ròna listened as if that wind were telling her something. She heard the leaves rustling. The birds crying. The kits mewing. The bear-wolves howling. The frogs croaking. The *langanaich* – the bellowing – of the bull stag on the mountain slope. The water gurgling in the pond, the splash of the salmon on the surface of the lake, the rush of the stream into *Loch na Màthar* – the Lake of the Mother.

All that she heard was laden with a portentous intonation.

And more: She heard that which should not be heard: Voices rising up from the synapses of the tuberous, rooty soil. The whispering of a hundred million stars in the black sky. The crying out of the stones on the lake shore they'd just left.

She stepped away from Cuilean to the edge of the precipice that overlooked the gowpy clouds blanketing the smoky lands of the DownBlow, out of which arose the black spiral tower of the Monstrato Corps.

Cuilean looked after her quizzically, for her mood and demeanor had altered so dramatically from one moment to the next, but there was something about her that precluded his asking what had happened to bring about such a change. Something about her that demanded that he wait in silence, something that had to be respected, something that would be revealed when it was ready to be birthed into words.

Her toes hanging over the edge of the cliff, below her the gowpy clouds swirling and tumbling in uneasy roiling, she listened. She smelled. She felt the downy peach-fuzz hair bristle on her arms and shoulders and the nape of her neck. She peered into the deep reaches of the sky, farther than any girl had ever seen before.

Then it came to her. Without seeing or hearing or feeling. As if on the wings of the various trees spreading around her on the heights over the DownBlow susurrated a voice as gentle as a zephyr: She gave a tight nod as if in acknowledgement of what she had been told.

Her silence, her separation from him, had gone on so long that Cuilean had felt his patience stretching so thin that he felt compelled to break the stillness. "*Dè tha dol, a bhalaich?*" he asked. "What's going on, pal?"

She turned her head to Cuilean so when she spoke – low, calmly, and with certainty -- he would be sure to hear her.

"*Tha iad a' tighinn,*" she said. "They're coming."

~~

Glossary

AAIRE – Artificial Atmospheric Inhalable Respiratory Environment

Anboarnh - Assembled Nucleic-acid Based Organic Artificially Replicated (and) Nurtured Humanoid; a DNA selected and modified, test-tube engendered and petri-dish gestated, and ecto-incubated humanoid. Because of the infestation of the Z-virus and the pandemic of unmitigable mutations which resulted in the swelling of the population of the natborn Zziipppaeis (Zziips, Zziipheads, etc.), the elites of the DownBlow resorted to non-sexual reproduction, which consisted of in-vitro fertilization and body-external gestation and incubation.

Angil – Agent of Notification of GOWD's Instructions and Leadership

APTRAC (aptrac) -- Armored Personnel TRAnsport Conveyance

Arl - average rat length. As this was determined from the height of the "average" rat, which stood about as tall as the knee of a Zziipppaei, for consistency, the "official," "standard" arl was established as 3.1415926535 8979323846 2643383279 5028841971 6939937510 5820974944 5923078164 0628620899 8628034825 3421170679 times the "average," "standard," "official" height of the rat.

atmopuro or atmopuro mask – atmosphere purifying mask, filters out harmful gasses and impurities from the ambient atmosphere, including toxin amounts of oxygen, and creates individualized mini-atmospheres suitable for breathing.

BABLE Act: Binding Articulatory Basis for Language Expression; law that established Simspeek as the sole legal form of language expression within the domains of the Monstrato Corps.

Balnabane – transliteration of the name of the "village of the mountain" – *Baile na Beinne*.

BilWee - formally known as GXDNUDJBILWEE, which was the randomly generated 10-place designator engraved on the chest of the short-lived and disposable Zziipppaei

Darchives -- the Dark archives, illegal repository of ancient, forbidden knowledge

BM — designating the period Before the Melting

CACA – See CacaHed (below)

CACAAAAAAHED, also known as CacaHed, or CACA – acronym for Chief Administrator - Capital Acquisitions, Annexing, Abducting, and Appropriating, Antipodean Archipelago: Head of External Development.

CAGAAAA - slogan of the Pelago - Creating Archipelago Greatness, Affluence, and Abundance Again!

CUINTE - Consortium of Unified Inter-National Trade Enterprises. An international corporate cooperative established to maintain peaceful relations between corporations and adjudicate fair trading relations, manufacturing practices, and gowp-exploitation.

Darchives -- the dark archives – contained within the neuralnet; the "memory" of the cosmic mind, which is itself the source of all being and the repository of all knowledge.

drroaen -- Dirigible Remote Reconnaissance, Observation, (and) Annihilation Engine: A dirigible, usually designed with a distinctive red under-belly and with a jet-black back, wings, and propellers.

drool -- Simspeek retained special terms for certain groups of things, such as a *mischief* of rats, a *slime* of slugs, a *creeping* of cockroaches, and a *drool* of Zziippps.

Focwaod = official title / acronym of middle-level Monstrato Corporation manager: Facilitator of Corporate Work and Other Doings

Frotch - "fire crotch" - slang term for native inhabitants of *An Tìr os cionn na Smùide* -- the Land above the Smoke -- a large percentage of whom are red- or "ginger" haired

FT - a polysemic acronym: Forbidden Tongue / Forbidden Thought. It was held that language and thought were intertwined: that either language preceded the thought – that is, the word for something made the thought possible, and more than that, not only made it possible, but in a sense, required it; or that the thought of something demanded the construction of a word to express it.

GAWD - Global Agency for Wealth Development

Gowpaleen – plastic, easily shapeable material fabricated from gowp

GOWPCRED -

Gowp-cred – gowp credit, unit of exchange in the Pelago, and all territories of the Monstrato Corps. Another term (general) for money

GOWPS – (also, referred to as GOWP, or gowp): General-purpose organically-derived waste, propellant (and) substance

Half-formed – an epithet, pejoratively and dehumanizingly referring to an Anboarnh-Zziippp crossbreed, with implications of suspicious, illegitimate, or uncertain origination.

HOOMAN (as in Hooman life) – Humanoid Organically Originated (or) Manufactured (and) Artificially Nurtured

Hooman-itais – the study of Humanoid Organically Originated (or) Manufactured (and) Artificially Nurtured -- Intercommunication Tween Anboarnhs and Infected Sentiences

HUOMH -- Habitation for Unhoused Orphaned Minor Hoomans (see Hooman)

Indigenoe (plural, Indigenoes) = indigenous resident of the Wayp; the *Sluagh*

InterNews – broadcasts of information and propaganda

Leabhar an Leaghaidh Mhòir — The Book of the Great Melting, a compendium of stories, histories, poetry, songs, moral lessons, and proverbs collected from *Tìr fo na Tuinn* - the land under waves — circa the time of the Great Melting. The original version is now lost.

leash -- Livestock Evasion Avoidance Shackling Harness that monitored the movements and whereabouts of SLAIVs.

Length = a unit of measurement, reputed to be the average height of the female passengers aboard the ship The Queen of the Night, fleeing the flooded homeland at the time of the Great Melt.

Listmus – annual wholly day of the Profit, for which Anboarnh and Zziipppaei pupae make lists of all their "must-haves," which they hope to receive as gifts.

MMMMM - Mixed Maximum Martial Melee Match, also known simply as Melee Match, or Melee, or mmmmm.

Monstrato Corps -- (shortened from MMMMONSTRATO) -- Multi-Pelago Manufacturing, Marketing, and Merchandising Undertaking, Un-Limited Amalgamated Hegemonic Corps. The ruling corporate body over the Pelagoes and any other area, resource, asset, or property to which it lays claim.

Muncaidh – Metamorphosed Untypically Neuronal -physiological Contagion Affected In-utero Devolved Humanoid (though some experts favor *Mutant Ungendered (by) N- Contagion Anomaly Initiating Deviant Humanoid):* Mutated humanoid sub-species, thought to have been reverted to ancient ancestral hominid form through exposure to Z-virus during gestation in utero of human mother. Sometimes, muncaidh-man or muncaidh-woman, etc. See: Zziipppaei, Ziip, Ziiphead, or Natborn.

NAIM -- case-sensitive Numero-Alphic Indentifying Mark, which is coded in a microchip inserted into the folds of a ZZiipppaei's pericardium when their generation has been registered, and tattooed across their forehead when come to full growth at the age of six

Natborn - a person manufactured through the primitive method of "natural" conception and birth. In the DownBlow, most often Zziipppaei, Ziiphead, Zipp, or Muncaidh.

NSSA - Network SpiderWeb Surveillance Agency

OUG – One Universal Grammar.

PieceTaker — corporate asset of the lowest rank, a blunt enforcer of Corporate Policy.

screoin (Screoin or SCREOIN) -- SCanning Remote Environs Optic INstrument

Simspeek – see SIMSPPIWEEEEC

SIMSPPIWEEEEC – Simplified Interpersonal Messaging Speech Parlance (for) Phonic (and) Inscribed/Written Expression (and) Exchange (of) Efficient Effective Communication. The only authorized and official language in the Monstrato corporate domains (notwithstanding the existence of such non-standard varieties such as TokTok -- the patois of the Zziips -- the outlawed FT of the Wayp, into which the corporation had intruded the most tenuous tentacles of control, and other such extra-territorial languages). Pronounced "Simspeek," and often spelled thusly, as well.

SLAIV – Situation: Lifelong Assignment, Involuntary or Voluntary

snorter – slang term for Zziipppaei, called that because the microcephalic squashing of their brain pans compressed the nasal cavities, producing a snorting sound when they breathed and/or spoke

TACS - Toll of Aqua-pura Cost Appraisal -

vaycay - vacation/vacationing -- ironic slang used by PieceTakers for serving a tour in hostile environment, as in "I was vaycay in the 3rd Battle of Quonlong."

Weaedaarr = Waste Excrement and Excreta Derived Aqua Alternative Reprocessed Replacement

Wuarardd (WUARARDD) of Gawd -- Worldwide, Universally Accepted Reality Authorized by the Regulation of Dogma Division of Gawd (see Gawd, sometimes known as the Wuarardd of the Profit)

Wayp - The mountainous territory at the Southern Pole of the planet that rose in elevation when the massive ice-sheets that had been weighing the continent down melted. *Etymology*, TokTok, derived from Simspeek "Way Up"

Wholly Seize of the Profit -- the inalienable right of the Monstrato
    Corporation and affiliated and subsidiary bodies to seize
    any and all profit-making opportunities as its own, wholly
    and without regard to any other claims, within or without
    its domains and jurisdictions.

Zziipppaei – Zzyzx Zymotic In-uterine Infected Partial Person
    Presenting Abnormalities Externally and Intellectually.
    That is, a person (though this designation is subject to
    disputation), "naturally" born and because of that, infected
    with the ZZyzx virus, which caused almost universal
    congenital abnormalities and defects. Often shortened
    (pejoratively, as an epithet) to Zziippp or Zziipheads. It is a
    matter of linguistic controversy whether the plural adds an
    "s" as in standard Simspeek, or whether the plural form is
    unmodified from the singular. (See Muncaidh, Natborn)

Zzyzx virus (pronounced *zeez*): contagion thought to have been
    released from the melting permafrost during the Great
    Melt and spread by mosquito vector. Contagion caused
    widespread (which is to say, universal) birth abnormalities
    and defects, which were congenital and transmissible
    across generations. See Zziipppaei.

~~

End book 1

The end of The Girl who Rode the Unihorn, but just the beginning of the saga, for the future history of our Mother Earth is not completed.

What will happen? Will the Monstrato Corps succeed in its scheme to exploit the resources of the Wayp? Will Ròna and Cuilean be safe? Will their happiness last? Or will they be destroyed along with the peaceful paradise of the Wayp?

Find out in

Book 2

of

Chronicles of the Future Foretold

The Girl who Fell from the Rainbow

Afterword

By mìcheal dubh

Dear Reader, Patron, and Guardian of the Mother,

I hope this chronicle has struck a chord, for the end was not in the writing of the story, which again, I hope you liked. My writing, and even your reading, was just the beginning.

Before we leave each other, please allow me to say that I do hope you enjoyed reading this story. That is, I hope that it entertained you on a sheer, visceral story level; that you got a *kick* out of it; that it was fun.

But here, we're going to get serious for a moment (although, whether you know it or not, we've been deadly serious for the entirety of this book), because more than being entertained (as if there is anything more important than enjoying a story!), I hope the issue at the heart of this story -- that is, of the destruction of the natural environment that we are facing today -- strikes a chord with you.

And if it didn't before, that it does now.

Having been privileged to receive this history of our planet's future out of the Darchives,[121] where the knowledge of all possibilities is retained after it is first dreamed in the black hole out of which our universe is birthed, I feel emboldened to add a few short words of my own.

We stand on the brink of a literary revolution: whereas most stories we encounter in our media recount events that have already happened, thanks to the intrepid spelunkers into the Darchives of the neuralnet, in this book, we have been able to glimpse the prehistory of times yet to come in the form of an adventure that not only ignites the imagination but kindles a fire for change.

As you've just experienced, *The Girl who Rode the Unihorn* is an soul-shaking journey into a world devastated by global warming, where the fight for survival intertwines with the majesty of nature. It is not *just* a novel, but an immersive experience in the reality of our planet's future.

---

[121] Darchives -- the dark archives – contained within the neuralnet; the "memory" of the cosmic mind, the source of all being and the repository of all knowledge.

As such, this prehistory of times to come is a call to action. In the face of climate change, *The Girl who Rode the Unihorn* provides a disquieting reminder of the consequences of inaction, as it aims not only to entertain but also to inspire change.

How can a story bring about change? you might ask.

In our times, we are faced with an unprecedented environmental catastrophe. Scientists from many different disciplines continue to add to our knowledge about this subject, but unfortunately, many times human beings are not motivated by facts. We hear and read every day about new scientific studies that predict the end of the natural world, but sometimes, perhaps, those studies, as valid as they are, fail to resonate, fail to make an impact: they're so dry, so technical, so abstracted and so distant from our daily lives, which is one of the reasons I chose to write this book – to make the absolute disaster facing our planet -- facing the human race, and all other species on earth – real, visceral, and personal.

Felt, not merely *thought* about.

Which intention, I hope – at least in some small way – I was able to achieve in the passing on to you of this history of our planet's future.

Daily we see in the print and video media scientific forecasts of the devastation being wreaked upon the natural world: droughts, glaciers' melting, wildlife going extinct, air and water being poisoned, and all combined with and compounded by a rapidly heating planet.

We have the information, yet we do nothing. The forces of greed and the apathy of a future that is too distant, too abstract unite to encourage our inaction.

It's our conviction that not only do we require information to save the planet, but we require a paradigm shift in our thinking, such as envisioned in this prehistory of times to come.

The world that Ròna and Cuilean inhabit is one that we will be living in if we continue down our current path of inaction on the trends towards environmental destruction. The devastating consequences of what is often called "global warming" are already being felt around the world, and the time is coming when we must take action to prevent further harm, or that harm will not be averted.

The devastating consequences of global warming are already being felt around the world, and the sands in the doomsday hourglass are trickling out. Soon, it will be too late to take action and stave off catastrophe.

The time is drawing near when the course our world is on hits the environmental tipping point, the point at which the world of the DownBlow and the Wayp become inevitable. A "tipping point" is when a situation suddenly changes. It's the last-straw that-broke-the-camel's-back phenomenon. Everything is going just fine with loading the camel with straw, and the camel master decides that one more straw won't hurt, but the result of adding the weight of that tiny straw to the camel's load is the point at which the result to the camel (and its back) is totally out of proportion to the weight of the straw: The camel collapses with a broken back under the weight not of the single straw, but of all the straws.

Climate scientists tell us we are nearing our environmental tipping point. Everything seems to be going along hunky-dory, but the time is coming rapidly when the "camel's back" of our environment is going to break, the signs of which include:

- Massive, one-in-a-thousand-year storms – year after year.
- Sudden experience of drainage of the aquifers – as for example, areas in the Southwestern United States are experiencing right now, resulting in communities not being able to provide water for desert cities such as Phoenix, and conflicts over increasingly scarce water resources. It should be added that the shrinkage of water supplies is a world-wide phenomenon, not isolated to a single region in the Americas.
- Poisoning of the oceans, lakes, rivers, as evidenced by the Great Sulphurific Garbage Patch, a continent-large collection of waste and refuge floating in the middle of the Pacific Ocean.
- Destabilizing mass-movements of populations who are fleeing suddenly uninhabitable territories.
- A die-off of species at a rate not seen in thousands, if not millions of years.
- The disappearance of fishing stocks – previously natural sources of wild fish have been shrinking to the point of being practically non-existent.
- Toxification of farm land from overuse of chemical fertilizers and profit-driven dumping of hazardous wastes.

- Acceleration of species extinction, brought about by the squeezing out of non-human life forms from their natural habitats – either by human crowding or by the transmigration of non-native species because of climate change.
- The intrusion of heretofore unknown diseases as pathogens are enabled by changing climate and human crowding of isolated areas to invade human population zones.
- The mass destruction of forests, wild areas, wet zones, coral banks, which heretofore have served as the "lungs" of the planet – but which are rapidly being killed off so that our mother earth will no longer have resources to breathe at all.

Those of us now alive may not live to see the utter devastation our choices today wreak upon the world tomorrow. But the morality of my actions does not depend totally on whether those actions hurt me.

I could leave the glass from my broken beer bottle on the beach, and not care that it cuts the foot of a child I don't know and will not see.

I could dump oil into a stream and as long as I don't drink the water downstream, not care who it poisons.

These same kinds of choices face us today. Only the "later" is far later, and the "downstream" is downstream in time.

But just because we perhaps won't see the results of our actions – or our inaction – doesn't mean they are justified.

There are two considerations here: One is that it has been thought that the ultimate morality is to base one's actions upon considerations of how the results of those actions will reverberate in time; in the case of the situation now facing us, how one's decisions will affect generations unborn.

Will a toddler cut her foot on the glass that I litter on the beach?

In a sense, it's the planting a tree idea. Plant a tree today that you will not live to sit under because we are mindful of the benefit to future generations, to people who come after us.

We don't think just of our future, but the far future of the planet we live on that our descendants will live on.

The other idea is that we don't refrain from polluting or destroying the environment just because how other people will be affected, but because the natural, which is to say, the inhuman, non-human, world has a right to existence in and of itself.

The recognition of the rights of the natural world is alien to many modes of thought prevalent in our contemporary, industrialized, corporatized world, which is capable of conceiving of the world only in terms of human constructions. (As in, what good is the tree if I can't cut it down and make a wooden nickel out of it?)

- Recently after a poisonous algae bloom that left the water of Lake Erie unusable for days, the inhabitants of the city of Toledo sought to protect the water on which they depended from the pollution of agricultural run-off. They discovered that this was legally impossible as the lake itself had no rights. Their recourse was to pass a law that gave rights against harm to the lake. However, a United States federal court overturned the law, ruling in effect that nature had no rights or protection against damage, as did neither the human inhabitants whose lives were harmed by the destruction of the environment in which they lived.
- Likewise, when it was suggested that the Brown Thrasher be replaced as the state bird of Georgia, arguments in favor of the much more profitable chicken, around which a major industry in the state was centered, went something to the effect of, "What has the Brown Thrasher ever done for the state of Georgia?"

In this worldview, nature has no value unless and only to the extent that it can be monetized.

However, what if we shift that paradigm? What if we come to see that a tree does not validate its existence because somebody comes along, cuts it down, and makes a table or a baseball bat out of its wood?

What if we come to see that the tree's existence is validation enough, in and of itself. That the tree doesn't exist just for *us*, and that the crime of environmental murder is not just that humans are affected, but that all living things are affected.

What if we imagine a world where nature is taken seriously – as in the culture of the Wayp in this history of the future? Such considerations are not so distant from our time of the 21st century.

When indigenous people of non-European traditions seek to protect the land on which they live, they often refer to terminology which seems – to many Westerners – as quaint, backwards, primitive, superstitious, the native peoples often make reference to the *spirit* of a mountain, say, or the *soul* of a forest, or even the *rights* of nature or a part of nature, as a way of expressing the idea that contrary to the long tradition in the West of the dominion of humans over and ownership of natural resources – to *laissez faire* – to do with as they (we humans) please, nature itself is endowed with -- as stated in the Declaration of Independence of the United States in regards to "all men" – "certain unalienable rights." Which usually means, in contemporary context, the right to strip mine, to burn the forest, to dump toxic run-off into waterways that people drink from and bathe themselves and their babies in.

When indigenous people of non-European traditions seek to protect the land on which they live, and the nature within which they live, they often employ terminology which seems – to many Westerners – as quaint, backwards, primitive, and superstitious, making reference, for instance, to the *spirit* of a mountain, say, or to the *soul* of a forest, or even to the *rights* of nature or of a part of the natural world, as a way of expressing the idea that contrary to the long tradition in the West of the dominion of humans over and ownership of natural resources – to *laissez faire,* to do with as they (we humans) please, nature itself is endowed with, as stated in the Declaration of Independence of the United States, "certain unalienable rights." Which is usually taken to mean in the contemporary West, the right to strip mine, to burn the forest, to dump toxic run-off into waterways that people drink from and bathe in.

In contrast, in Africa, a tribal tribunal punished an entire clan when one of its members was found guilty of killing a mother hyena that was still suckling pups.

The nation of Ecuador has incorporated into its constitution recognition of the rights of nature both to exist and to be unharmed by human action.

In a similar vein, the Swiss Constitution recognizes both the rights of dignity to individual plants, the right of life to a species, and the right of an ecological system to biodiversity.

In the history of the future within these pages, we see two possibilities – one in which nature and humans thrive, and another in which the forces of greed and exploitation win out, and the world dies. This multiverse reality plays out in time as different potentialities manifest in parallel. The world described in these pages does exist, these events have happened, are happening, will happen.

However, a prophesy is not deterministic. There is still time. It is, like the fate of the cat in Schrodinger's box, only probabilistic, only a possibility.

If you're not familiar with this thought experiment by the theoretical physicist Erwin Schrodinger, to explain uncertainty around particle physics: namely, that we cannot know with certainty the location – or state – of a particle until we observe it, not only that, but that the particle actually exists in two states, which he illustrated with the thought experiment known as "Schrodinger's cat."

A cat is placed in a sealed box with a mechanism that contains a poisonous nuclear element. The mechanism might or might not release the poison that would kill the cat. Not only do we not know whether the cat is alive or dead, but more than that, the cat is actually **both** alive **and** dead. It's only when we open the box and observe the cat does the reality (not just our knowledge of it) of the cat occur.

Of course, Schrodinger's Cat is a thought experiment, intended to show a difficult-to-understand aspect of the weird world of infinitesimal particle physics, that we think doesn't play out in our macro world, but actually does, for all these events, and the possibilities of many more in the future, already exist.

The good news is that the fate of the planet that is foretold in this history of the future is not pre-determined. What if we imagine a living world of the Wayp rather than a dead one of the DownBlow? Through our imaginations and our will, we have the power to create a human society that reveres the living world gifted to us by the Mother of all life. It is up to the readers of this history of the future to determine which cat they find in the *box* of the world to come – the live one, or the dead.

Before you go further, I have a request.

It is important to bring home the experience of climatic devastation that our Mother Earth is now facing. Which is also why I have made this book free or as low a cost on as many platforms as is possible, for it is my goal to get this book in the hands of as many people as I can.

What we need to do to avert this foretold history is more than what we are doing. We need to change the entire paradigm by which we operate on this planet, and how we interact with the planet, because the old ways are killing us and killing our Mother earth.

And you can participate in that change by sharing this story forward, for this is our future history.

The paradigm shift starts now.

The shift starts with you.

Believe it.

Share it.

Tell it.

Change it.

Be it.

Okay, but I'm just one person, what can I do?

Remember the proverb of the Wayp --

Clann na Màthar ri guaillibh a chèile –
Children of the Mother, shoulder to shoulder, arm in arm.
Together we strive,
together we live,
together we survive,
together we thrive.

Become a Guardian of the Forest alongside Ròna in her fight to protect the Mother. Changing the course of our future history is not accomplished individually. No one can effect it alone, separately. We must Link arms with others as a Guardians of the Forest of the Mother. You'll not just be supporting the continuing telling of this story; you'll be advocating for environmental awareness, action, and change. Together, we can kindle a spark that ripples beyond the pages of the book, fostering a collective consciousness for the preservation of our natural environment.

First – and this suggestion will seem strange in a world of competitive commerce, where every impulse is towards the realization of *glory to the profit!* I'm going to ask you **not** to make a profit; in fact, I'm going to suggest that you …

Share this book forward.

In other words, give it away.

If you have a hard-copy book, when you have finished reading it, give it to a friend, and ask them to read it, and then to share it forward themselves.

Or, donate it to a library.

Or to a thrift store.

If you have a digital copy, point your friend to an Internet site where they can buy an inexpensive copy. (I will attempt to keep the price low, but the online retailers need to be compensated for their expenses of hosting the book.)

Even this is not the end-all and be-all, but hopefully it is the beginning. Let's intensify the conversation about what we can do to turn aside from the course we are on and to avert the history of the future that has been recorded in these pages.

How Else You Can Link Arms with Other Heroes:

Leave a review on Amazon, or on another book-retailer's website, or a social media site such as Goodreads or Facebook will encourage other people whom you don't even know yet to learn this history of our future.

Subscribe to our newsletter. Join with a community of like-minded individuals committed to the cause of preserving the Garden of the Mother.

- Receive updates on the recording of this prehistory of times yet to come.
- View vlog reports on the fate of the Mother.
- Get sneak peeks to yet more chapters and early releases of the continuing history of Ròna and the people of the Wayp.
- Listen to advance releases of the audiobook.
- Contribute part of the prehistory yourself with our fanfiction blog.

You will not just be supporting a story; you'll become part of a changing the destiny of our Mother Earth. Your participation will shape the destiny of people yet to come, influence their stories, and impact the world. With your support, we'll not only tell an unforgettable story but also contribute to the urgent cause of safeguarding our planet.

Thank you for being a part of this change. Together, let's undertake the writing of a story that transcends fiction, the creation of the epic adventure to save our world, one story at a time.

https://michealdubh.substack.com/

mìcheal dubh

Acknowledgment

by mìcheal dubh

Ultimately, this is the one for whom this book was written: a longtime friend of mine – I'll call him "Rod" (which may or may not be his real name). Rod and I essentially grew up together, went to school together, ran the streets together, got into trouble together. And then parted and went our separate ways into adulthood.

A short time ago, I happened to bump into Rod. So many tears had gone over the bridge of the nose, so to speak, that we couldn't let the unexpected meet go by with just a "Hi, how're ya doin'? Give me a call sometime. We'll have lunch," but we had to stop, and so, shortly afterwards, we found ourselves in a local bar catching up over a couple pitchers of beer – you know, like old friends do (at least, where we came from) – picking up where we'd left off the last conversation, and eventually, we came around to, "So, what're you doing now?"

He told me about serving a couple stints in prison (one of which involved a year-long sentence for trafficking guns, it being his firm conviction that there aren't enough guns in the world, and it being his Jesus-bestowed duty to correct the deficiency of the ways and means of killing other people).

When it came my turn, I told him about this book – *The Girl who Rode the Unihorn* – and my concern about the looming catastrophe of environmental collapse facing the planet.

"Ahh," he brushed off the issue with a gesture like someone would make swatting away an annoying fly. "Just a bunch of bullshit."

Curious how he could so cavalierly dismiss such a massive body of evidence, I asked him, "Have you read any of the scientific literature?" And then realizing it was presumptuous of me to expect him to have read the actual literature (and a trifle insulting to call attention to the fact that he had not), I corrected myself: "Or read about it, like in the news? You know, somewhere in the vicinity of 99 percent of all climate scientists agree with the idea of human-caused global warming."

"Naa, I don't have to," Rod said with a puff of air that was somewhere between the hawking out of a loogie and a sneer of contempt. "They're just making it all up."

So, this one goes out to my old friend -- poor, benighted Rod -- the one left behind, and all those of a similar mind.

About the author

Mìcheal Dubh lives a hermit's life in a small cabin near the mountain village of Balnabane with his son and a blue-eyed wolf-dog. His idea of fun is to sit with his dog in quiet solitude, listening to birdsong, remembering, reflecting on, sometimes smiling about, and sometimes regretting his wild and misspent youth. He feels deeply and passionately about the fate of the natural world in the face of environmental degradation, and he enjoys all forms of stories -- which tell the truth of who we have been, who we are, and who we will be.

Printed in Great Britain
by Amazon

38978226R00249